D1414763

THE STONE ANGELS

THE STONE ANGELS

STUART ARCHER COHEN

ORION

First published in Great Britain in 2003 by Orion Books
an imprint of The Orion Publishing Group
Orion House, 5 Upper St Martin's Lane
London WC2H 9EA

A CIP catalogue record for this book is available
from the British Library

ISBN (hardback) 0 75285 989 7
ISBN (trade paperback) 0 75285 990 0

Typeset at The Spartan Press Ltd,
Lymington, Hants

Printed and bound in Great Britain by
Clays Ltd, St Ives plc

I couldn't have written this book without the help of the following people:

Titi, Cristina, Marcos, Anabel, Karina and the *muchachos del barrio*: Chispa, Pépe, Gabriel, Enrique, Cuervo and Fabian.
Ricardo Rajendorfer and Luis Ernesto Vicat, who shared their knowledge of the Buenos Aires Provincial police.
Fellow writer Comisario Mayor Eugenio Zappietro of the Federal Police of Buenos Aires, who was generous with his time and explained so much without explaining.

The following people provided help and personal support along the way: Brad Curé, Jonathan Wolfson, Bruce Kimball, Jed Cohen, Dr Ken Brown, Lt Kevin Siska, Eliot Cohen, Bess Reed, Luisa Hairabedyan, Sheila Ferreira, Raul Schnabel, Mariana Ponce de León of Amnesty International, Hebe de Bonafini and Sergio Schocklander of the *Madres de la Plaza de Mayo*. A particular thanks to Dra. Maria del Carmen Verdú and Paola of the CORREPI.

I must acknowledge the inspiration and information provided by the courageous work of Argentine investigative journalists Miguel Bonasso, Ricardo Rajendorfer and Carlos Dutil, Andrés Openheimer and others. Foremost among them Rodolfo Walsh, author of *Operación Massacre*, and Jose Luis Cabezas, whose murders are still awaiting solution.

Thanks to Joe Regal, loyal and tireless agent and friend, who encouraged me to keep running. Body of a rock!

And I thank especially my prized friends Martin Vilches and Claudio Vilarino, *que me bancaron cuando yo hacia mi ultima jugada.*

For my three treasures:
the Queen, the Messenger and the Hunter in the Stars.

En el mundo del Destino, no hay estadistica.

(In the world of Destiny, there are no statistics.)
Martin Alberto Vilches, *Voces*

PART ONE

17 STONE ANGELS

CHAPTER 1

Robert Waterbury's body had been discovered last October in a smoking Ford Falcon on the outskirts of Buenos Aires with six chalks of Chlorhydrate of Cocaine and his skull perforated by a nine-millimeter bullet. Thus these stories often began, and thus they usually ended, except that Waterbury was a Northamerican, so that final tableau kept coming up as a topic of conversation between the United States embassy and the Argentine Ministry of Justice. The politicians had kicked it back and forth through the violent January heat and the fierce cancer of summer. Now the gringos were sending their own person down to investigate and he, Comisario Fortunato of the Buenos Aires Brigada de Investigaciónes, was being assigned to assist and support on behalf of the Buenos Aires police.

Fortunato turned loose a long exhausted breath and finished lighting his wife's votive candle, then placed it gently on the windowsill. He glanced at his watch. The feeling of decay that had clung to him since Marcela's death three weeks ago sloughed down on him again, merging with the monotonous autumn overcast that hung over the city like a sentence of perpetual chains. He brushed a cigarette ash off his sportscoat and reached for his car keys.

The assignment depressed him. He knew that the Waterbury investigation would be a sham, that it was political, and that the Chief was in on it. He knew that the reason he'd been appointed to head up the investigation was for the express purpose of *not* finding the killer. He knew that clearly, because he was the one who had put the bullet in the side of Waterbury's head.

The face of Comisario Miguel Fortunato was that of a weary beaten angel that had had too many losing days at the track and told too many lies. It was a face that seemed to comprehend all human pain. Wide and soft, it was anchored by a thick drooping mustache that presided over stubbly jowls. His large dark eyes radiated a profound melancholy, matched by a voice so low and gentle and courteous that his gaze and a few simple words could console even the most distraught or unreasonable of souls. For that reason he had often been called on to lend his saintly visage to certain tasks within the police department: he greeted the families of victims when they came to identify a body, and got a ten percent commission on the funeral arrangements they entrusted to him; he explained the necessities of enrollment in the police private security program to neighborhood businessmen. As he'd climbed through the ranks, Fortunato's face had brought him the role of the 'good' cop in the 'good cop, bad cop' game, and that had become his image of himself: the good cop. Over the decades his wavy chestnut hair had gone the color of iron, and his features had softened into a mesmerizing vision of nearly religious intensity. It inspired confessions, like the mournful face of the Virgin.

As Fortunato opened the garage door he glanced reflexively up and down the street. His neighbor was talking to his two teenage sons and the three of them fell silent under his gaze. He eased his car onto the pavement, then closed the sheet-metal doors behind him. He drove a late-model Fiat Uno that he'd gotten through police channels, with falsified papers and a phony bill of sale. He put it into gear and watched the cramped houses of Villa Luzuriaga squeeze past him in a tight continuous line, their windows barred and their walls topped with broken glass.

Fortunato would have preferred to stay home. He didn't like to think about the Waterbury murder, and though it wasn't his style to complain, he knew someone had given him the hide to eat on that one. The day after he'd killed Waterbury, Marcela had received the diagnosis of cancer and a few months later she was dead. Fortunato couldn't help but link those two events in his mind. He wasn't superstitious, but beyond all ideas of Karma or Destiny he was a cop, an investigator, and given the evidence available he could only feel that they related to the same case: the case of Miguel Fortunato.

La Gloria had been built longer ago than anyone remembered and lingered on next to a raw-brick building which housed a clandestine mechanic's shop. Lost in the shabby exurbs of San Justo, the bar had survived through the decades nearly unchanged, absorbing the years and the black residue of a million cigarettes into its dark wainscoting. A wooden refrigerator clunked away beneath a picture of the Argentine soccer selection of 1978. The green plaster walls rose twenty feet towards a dim distant ceiling. There was a smell of dust and floor cleaner. Oozing from the loudspeakers came the vaguely insidious chords of the string introduction to the tango 'Tabaco.' Chief Bianco liked this bar because they played an all-tango radio station, and the Chief was a semi-professional singer of tangos. They called him *El Tanguero.*

Four old men were playing cards at the entrance, their table heaped with small piles of kidney beans and half-empty bottles of beer. They looked up at Fortunato as he came in. 'Miguelito!' one of them said.

'How's it going, Blacky?' Fortunato leaned down and kissed him on the cheek, then sprinkled a few greetings around the table and moved on toward the back. The Chief was waiting for him in the rear alcove with a big smile. 'Miguel!'

As Fortunato got closer he made out the two men sitting with the Chief and felt his throat tighten. He swallowed and continued on, exchanging a distracted slap on the shoulder with a couple of Inspectors sitting near the pool table.

The Chief was wearing a clean navy suit and beige silk tie and he stood up to exchange kisses with Fortunato. The other two stayed seated. Fortunato heard the clicking of the Chief's lips in his ear as they kissed, smelled his cologne and the aldehyde overtones of his hair pomade. The familiar sensations and the crisply trimmed white hair and blue eyes reassured him a bit, like the presence of an elder brother. Seven years older than Fortunato, Bianco had taken him on as an *Ayudante* fresh from the Academy in 1968 and had brought him from comisaria to comisaria as he'd climbed the ranks. Now Bianco was said to be a possible successor to the chief of the entire *Bonaerense*, and Fortunato had become his man in Investigaciónes in San Justo. The Chief scraped a rickety chair over to the table for him and motioned toward it with his hand. Fortunato noted the over-friendly air of someone selling faulty merchandise.

Bianco indicated his companions without offering an introduction. 'These are two friends. They came to explain to you the problem with the American so everything is clear.'

Fortunato looked at them. They had that leaden unsmiling quality of people accustomed to making unilateral decisions about other people's lives. One was tall, about forty-five, with close-clipped blond hair, wearing a blue suit over a polo shirt. He had unsettling hazel eyes. The other was younger, *morrocho*, black-haired and dark-skinned in a navy jogging suit. Fortunato spotted the slight hump of a shoulder holster under his left arm. Both looked fit and self-contained, the kind of operatives who lifted weights and went to the shooting range. Heavy men. Ex-military. He knew the type from the days of the dictatorship.

He smiled at them. '*Bien, muchachos*. What's up with the North-american? We put that case to sleep two months ago.'

The two men looked at each other and the Chief started in with a warm serious tone, like that of a concerned relative. 'Unfortunately, Miguel, as I told you over the telephone, the case seems to have aroused some interest in the exterior. We've been feeling some pressure from the Northamericans to open it up again, shuffle some papers, that sort of thing.'

Fortunato steadied his voice to keep out any hint of complaint. 'You told me he was nobody.'

'He was nobody. But Mr Nobody had a wife and child. It seems his woman has been crying to some senator about her poor dead husband, and finally the senator started making noises, too. It's cheap publicity for him.' He took a sip of his beer, then added ironically: 'You know, Miguelito, "human rights" are very much in fashion these days.'

Fortunato took in the information without commenting. He'd gotten lost in the first part of the explanation, that Waterbury had a wife and child. It was one of the few facts he knew about the man because Waterbury had told him that himself, in the early part of the kidnapping when he'd been trying to impose some fiction of normalcy on the situation. Fortunato felt Waterbury's dead weight come down on him again, then focused in on what Bianco was saying. 'The gringos are negotiating some new privatizations and the Minister of Economy has to show that he's cooperating.'

'I understand. Why do you choose me to deal with the gringos?'

'For that face!' the Chief said. 'Who wouldn't believe that face!' No one laughed at the joke so the Chief went on. 'Well, Miguel. It happened in your district. You're a high-ranking investigator of homicides with more than three decades of service in the Institution. You have complete credibility.'

The blond one interrupted. 'You're the one who fucked up, Fortunato! You were supposed to squeeze him, not kill him.'

The Chief winced and tried to calm things down. '*Ché!*' he told the blond. 'The Northamerican acted badly. Everone knows that. It was his own fault. Comisario Fortunato is one of the best officers in the Force. I trust him completely.' He turned back to Fortunato. 'It's a formality. All you need to do is air out the files, tour the crime scene and buy her a steak before she goes home.'

'Her? Who are they sending?'

The Chief glanced at the blond man and they both smiled. Even the dark man seemed to lighten his expression a little. The blond one answered the question. 'La Doctora Fowler, from Georgetown University. Activist in human rights issues and an expert on the history and culture of Peru.'

'Peru?'

The other three looked at each other and broke into laughter. 'So you can see,' the Chief continued, 'it's not such a big deal. The gringos don't want to touch it but they've got this senator swelling their balls.'

A number by Pugliese came on the radio and the Chief raised his hand to the opening bars. 'That's how I like it! Dry tango, without adornment!'

The heavy men stood, and Fortunato inclined his head to look up at them. He felt weak as the blond one stared silently down at him, then the two left without a handshake. Fortunato watched them file past the card players into the brilliant doorway.

'Who sent the monkeys?' he asked.

The Chief sighed. 'It's a bit complicated, Miguel.'

'Who do they belong to? Carlo Pelegrini?'

The name startled Bianco. 'Why do you say that?'

Fortunato looked at him sharply. 'You sent me into the shit with that operation. Are they Pelegrini's or not?'

Bianco looked away across the dark interior, shook his head. 'It's complicated.'

The assignment had been to pick up a man named Robert Waterbury outside his hotel on the Calle Paraguay and give him a scare. He hadn't known who Waterbury was or who they were squeezing him for, only that it involved some notebooks that Waterbury was using to blackmail someone. Waterbury didn't carry a gun and wasn't violent, so it looked like an easy job: they would grab him, cuff him, put a gun to his head and drive him out to a field. Maybe give him a few stiff ones to get his attention. Then they would empty his pockets, dump him in the mud, and leave him to find his own way home. All without explanation; part of the psychology was to let him use his imagination.

Fortunato shook his head. 'I only took that job because of you. And you stuck me with Domingo and his nose-stuffer. How was I supposed to work with a car full of retards with their noses full of *merca*? How?'

The Chief opened up for a moment. 'I didn't want Domingo. They suggested him.'

He thought of Domingo, with his boyish black hair and his phony servility. Behind that fleshy smile was the ever-present desire to put a bullet in someone's back.

'Who suggested him?'

The Chief looked past him toward the old men playing cards. 'Look, Miguelito: don't ask me more because I can't tell you.' Then, commandingly, 'But don't go throwing around the name of Pelegrini.' He seemed to regret his sudden harshness, tossed his head dismissively. 'It's not for so much, Miguelito. The judge is Duarte. If we have to arrange something we can count on him. You should look over the *expediente* again and familiarize yourself with the case.'

The irony of Fortunato familiarizing himself with a crime that he had committed seemed to escape the Chief, but maybe he was right. There was the crime, which was the reality, and there was The Case, which was all the fossilizations of that reality. Two very different things, especially in Buenos Aires.

'What about the Northamerican? This Waterbury. What else do I need to know about him?'

'Not much. It seems he was some sort of journalist, but not very successful. He had money problems, and that's why he came down here. He must have had some kind of scheme.' The Chief's eyes shifted sideways, then back to Fortunato. 'You can ask the rest from the gringa when she gets here. It will make you look more sincere.' The Chief took another peanut from the little dish in front of them. 'It's not such a big deal, Miguel. Put on your idiot face for a week and it will all solve itself.' He brightened. 'Look, Soriano's singing at El Viejo Almacen next weekend. Take her to hear some authentic Buenos Aires tango, show her a few steps. She'll forget all about this idiocy.'

8

'She's coming next week?'

'Sí, Señor. And be nice to her,' the Chief said. 'It's her first time to Argentina.'

CHAPTER 2

Fortunato went to meet her at the *Aeropuerto Ezeiza* with a little placard that said 'Dra. Fowler,' and a driver in an impeccable blue uniform. At the last minute he'd brought along Inspector Fabian Diaz to bulk up the delegation.

Fortunato had explained to Fabian that this new investigation was political and would be pursued at a pace he described as '*tranquilo.*' In reality, Fabian took all his investigations at that pace. Loosely attached to one of the five '*patotas*' – plainclothes investigative groups that Fortunato directed – Fabian worked gambling and vice and used that as license to dress in clothes Fortunato considered too flamboyant for a serious policeman. He spent most of his days on obscure '*operativos*' to the race track and the football stadiums, putting in only a few hours at the station and writing up scanty reports that always contained the words 'continuing investigation in process.' It didn't matter; he collected the appropriate tolls from the pimps and illegal lotteries, and in his remaining time he arrested enough criminals to keep his record presentable. About thirty, he had dark blond curls and a fashion-model face. At the station they called him Romeo. Fortunately, he'd dressed relatively sedately today in a black and white check sports jacket and a black polo shirt. They scanned the arrivals for the gringa.

Fortunato caught a woman's face out of the crowd and felt a mixture of hope and dread that she would be the one. Her wheat-blonde hair swept back from features that wavered between beauty and a disconcerting irregularity, with eyes perhaps too far apart or too penetrating and a mouth that could be construed as either delicate or cruelly thin. A sphinx face. A face like expensive perfume. When Fortunato saw her break from the throng and move toward him, he felt something come floating free in his chest.

She looked startlingly younger than he'd expected: perhaps in her twenties or early thirties, and slim, with sure, athletic steps made easy by flat shoes. She'd dressed in a tan skirt with a matching jacket, and a white blouse slightly rumpled from the flight. A gold chain gleamed at her neck and her fingers moved up to touch it nervously as she felt the three men watching her. She looked business-like and competent, but he noticed that she held her portfolio in a strange way, in front of her thigh, rather than to the side.

'Doctora Fowler.' He offered his hand, resisting the normal impulse to kiss her.

'Señor Fortunato? It's a great pleasure to meet you.'

'The pleasure is mine, Doctora,' he said softly. 'Welcome to Buenos Aires. This is Inspector Fabian Diaz.' Fabian nodded gravely, on his best behavior. 'And Officer Pilar.'

As she moved to shake hands with Fabian, Fortunato realized that she had been using her portfolio to cover a large red stain on her thigh. It looked like tomato juice. 'Doctora Fowler,' he said, 'they dirtied you on the flight!'

She peered down at the stain, then blushed. 'The passenger beside me spilled his drink.' She tossed her shoulders girlishly. 'With luck the hotel has a laundry service.'

An awkward moment passed as the three men stared at her, then Fortunato said, 'Of course they will. Let me help you with your luggage.' The driver seemed to get hold of himself and lunged for the bag before they headed across the cavernous lobby of the Arrivals terminal. The touts and taxi drivers recognized them as police and gave them a wide berth. Ezeiza was well-known for its taxi mafia, which gave arriving passengers the choice of being fleeced by the *taxistas* themselves or by the overpriced tickets sold in their phony kiosk. A fat business controlled by the *Federales*.

La Doctora was craning her head as if she'd never seen an airport before, gazing intently at the newsstands and the advertisements. Outside he could sense she was breathing in the rich and humid air of Buenos Aires, scented with exhaust fumes and subtropical foliage. Even among the vast pavements of Ezeiza, one could still smell the damp black earth of the pampas. He opened the car door for her, then slid in on the other side. Fabian sat in front. 'To the Sheraton, no?'

'Please.'

The driver flashed his badge at the man in the parking booth and was waved past.

'Is this your first time in Buenos Aires, Doctora Fowler?'

'Athena,' she said. 'Call me Athena.'

'The goddess of Wisdom, no?'

She smiled. 'And the goddess of War.'

A potent little silence passed through the car, and Fortunato settled into his seat as they picked up speed toward the center.

All around them the thirteen million inhabitants of Buenos Aires were furiously dreaming of a city that used to be. Eighty years ago Buenos Aires had been among the richest cities of the world, had made legends of its extravagant playboys and their Tango. A city of whorehouses and opera halls, of mansions built by cattle and wheat, duels fought with knives; of silk shirts, stockyards, carriages and silver. A city built to outshine and outspend the best of Europe. A Lost City now, bankrupted by fifty years of dictatorship and plunder, but still retaining, in its turbid streets, a tawdry and exhilarating magnificence.

It was a metropolis haunted by beautiful faces. The streets coursed with Berliners and Venetians, British, Basques and Poles, all the fair features of Europe made richer by the Argentine climate and the dark eyes of the Andes. Children of war criminals mingled with the children of their victims, Indians with descendants of their brutal conquerors while, invisible among them, floated 30,000 victims of the dictatorship whose features, like their bodies, had simply 'disappeared.'

La Doctora addressed the Comisario in her textbook Spanish, spoken with a slight Mexican accent. He was pleased by the note of youthful admiration in her voice. 'I'm eager to begin working on this with you, Señor Fortunato. The State Department spoke very highly of you. They said that you have an excellent reputation. A citation for excellence for capturing a serial killer of children. Another for breaking up a kidnapping.'

Fortunato shrugged. 'One tries,' he said vaguely.

'They said you've even investigated other policemen.'

Fortunato needed a few seconds to recognize that she was referring to the time they'd accidentally investigated another Comisario's stolen car operation. By the time they realized who it belonged to, one of the honest cops had turned the evidence over to a judge, and the judge's patrons had found it expedient to widen the net. He could see that Bianco had put together a rather heroic dossier for him. 'Sometimes duty is painful, but thus is life, Doctora.'

She nodded, watching him with her spotlight eyes. She seemed to want to begin the investigation immediately. 'Do you know much about Robert Waterbury?' she asked.

'Very little,' he answered. 'I just came into the investigation a few days ago. I was hoping you could tell me. He was a journalist, no?'

'No.' She reached into her portfolio and pulled out a book. Fortunato read the title in English: 'The Black Market.' *El Mercado Negro*. She turned it over and handed it to him. Between his fingers gleamed a soft-focus picture of a fair-haired author with a tranquil smile. Fortunato recognized him instantly.

'This is Robert Waterbury's first novel. It was published in twelve countries and won several prizes.'

Fortunato heard his own voice. 'What is it about?'

'It's about a banker who makes a trip to the Underworld to find his wife. Along the way he realizes that his life is a lie. It's very good.'

For some reason the book's theme irritated Fortunato. The Chief had said Waterbury was a journalist and tied him to some sort of blackmail scheme. 'So he wasn't a journalist?'

'No. Who told you that?'

'I'm not sure. I thought I saw it in the files.'

Her gaze seemed to linger a trifle too long after his answer, then she reached into the portfolio again. 'I brought this for you also.' Fortunato didn't want to take the snapshot she offered him, but he had no choice. 'You can keep it,' she said. 'I have another one.'

He slipped on his reading glasses and examined the glossy little square. In a sunny photograph the late Robert Waterbury sat on the beach holding close to him a little blond girl and a dark-haired woman who looked serene and pretty. The little girl was clutching her father's arm, grimacing joyfully towards his face. The wife was lifting a handful of sand that trickled through her fingers.

A feeling of deep anguish came over Fortunato as he looked silently at the photograph. He thought of his own father, whose death when he was eight had left a particular tang of sadness that still came back to him these fifty years later. He imagined the little girl. Even now, after four months, she would still be waiting for her father in that childish fantasy world in which hope persisted against all knowledge.

But thus was life. Waterbury had tried to reel in a fish too big for him and things had gone wrong. That's what happened when you blackmailed people.

Fabian broke into his reverie, turning round in his seat to face the gringa. 'You know,' he said to La Doctora, 'I'm a writer also.'

The absurd lie flopped out like a water balloon and Fortunato could see a grin crease the driver's profile. Fabian was famous for his verses, but Fortunato had assumed that he'd know when to keep his mouth shut.

'Really?' she said politely.

'Yes,' he said, as if he were sitting in a literary café on Calle Corrientes with the other *boludos*. 'I'm writing a book. It's a *policial*, set in Buenos Aires. I have a cousin in Los Angeles and he's going to be my representative to the film industry there. I'm developing the story and he's going to write the screenplay. And me, being a real policeman, who's better qualified?'

'That's a good point,' she answered.

'Yes. Perhaps someday I'll tell you what it is about. But meanwhile, we'll concentrate on finding Robert Waterbury's assassin.' He waved his hand as if she had heaved a sigh of admiration. 'It's the least I can do for a brother writer.'

Fortunato let the outburst run its course without reacting. They were zooming over the outer rings of the town on the elevated highway and the warm autumn air was fluttering through the windows, making Fortunato think of butterflies. He saw his visitor looking out at the balconies and Beaux Arts facades of the Palermo district. They formed a mineral froth of molded pilasters and lintels, the elegant architectural elements of a half-dozen civilizations jumbled together. Green copper domes and black slate roofs went tumbling through the sky, stitched with wrought iron and draped with masonry garlands, shields, nymphs and demigods.

'This is really fantastic,' Athena said. 'How old are these buildings?'

A pinhole of an opening. 'About ninety years. The golden age of Buenos Aires was in the first thirty years of the twentieth century, when Argentina was one of the richest countries in the world.'

'What happened? I mean . . .' she added quickly, as if afraid of offending them, 'I keep reading in the newspaper that things are very bad here.'

Fabian answered, playing the leftist. 'First there was the Dictatorship of the Seventies, which octupled the debt in only six years. Then came the IMF and their strategy of privatization and Free Trade. Now we have this . . .'

They had been stopped by a demonstration whose angry principals were banging drums and chanting down the Avenida Santa Fé. The driver swore softly under his breath.

'What's going on?' the gringa asked.

Fortunato peered through the windshield at the passing signs. 'This is Aerolíneas, no?' To the woman: 'It's the employees of the national airline. They were privatized ten years ago and now they're being closed down by the parent company.'

'The airline was making a profit when they privatized them,' Fabian explained. 'They sold it at a discount to the Spanish and the Spanish sold off all their routes and airplanes and put the loot in their pocket. Now they're firing everyone.' He rubbed his thumb and forefinger together, the symbol of money changing hands, wrinkling his nose as if something stank. 'The Spanish are the only people more *hijo de puta* than the Argentines.'

'It already *is!*' the driver burst out in annoyance at the passing marchers. 'The money's in Geneva and Miami. Why go swelling balls here?'

Fabian gave his dog smile to the woman. 'They privatized everything: the highways, the hydroelectric, the telephones. Now they want to privatize the post office. After that,' he shrugged, 'they'll privatize the air.'

CHAPTER 3

Miguel Fortunato's comisaria sat in a three-story building in Ramos Mejia. Though fifteen miles distant from Buenos Aires proper, Ramos enjoyed a relative degree of prosperity, supporting a bustling five-block commercial zone and spreading out into the small neat concentrations of houses of the middle class. Further out the houses got smaller and crouched behind walls topped with broken glass. Here transpired the modest lives of the working class, for the last decade focused on the continual belt-tightening as their wages sank and their factories closed. In the ten years since the ascension of the clown-thief President Menem, all except the wealthy were struggling to hold their places.

The Ramos Mejia Brigada de Investiciónes had a reputation for yielding a good haul. It was wealthy in stolen cars, drug distribution, clandestine lottery outlets and a rich network of protection rackets that took weekly payments from ambulant vendors, small businesses and the few remaining factories. These were the classics, but a good comisario could multiply his profits by making files disappear, freeing criminals, neglecting to arrest fugitives, or arresting those fugitives who could be squeezed for extra pesos. Fortunato kept a list of such unfortunates to be arrested and squeezed on a rotating basis. In a good month, the Brigada might bring in $100,000, and Fortunato parceled out the income according to a precise formula: a quarter for himself, a quarter for the *patotas* who made the collections, and half to be sent upstairs to the Chief.

Despite its robust income, the comisaria was innocent of the gleaming technology Fortunato saw on the Northamerican police shows. Its communications room held a simple radio and several maps with colored pins to mark various crimes – red for robbery, blue for theft, black for assault. Typewriters hammered out *denuncias* on violet carbon paper. There was no fingerprint lab or interview room, and the evidence locker consisted of an old strong-box at the sole disposal of the one man most certain to compromise it: the Comisario.

Nonetheless, in the week before the gringa's arrival Fortunato had tried to polish the fiction of crisp professionalism. The prisoners had been ordered to put a new coat of paint in the waiting room and to scrub the floor tiles with stiff brushes. Desks were neatened and the *calabozos* that housed the delinquents rinsed with antiseptic. They even dusted off the picture of the Virgin of Lujan that hung above the dispatch radio. He was telling a story now, a story of a hard-working detective eager to crack a case. A bit weary perhaps, a bit cynical, but nonetheless trustworthy and capable of wringing from the Buenos Aires underworld any justice that could be had.

The morning of La Doctora's first visit seemed blessed by good omens. The night before they had arrested a pair of delinquents suspected in a series of auto thefts that had been allocating many red pins to the crime map in the Sala de Situaciones. He'd instructed the Sub-Comisario to leave their filed-down knives and key blanks on display to show the gringa when she arrived. As a bonus, one of the *patotas* had called in after tracking down a load of hijacked merchandise to a grocery store.

'Five thousand,' Fortunato told the Inspector over his cell phone.

'I tried five thousand, Comiso, but he says for five thousand he'll take it up directly with the judge.'

'Tell him five thousand and if he doesn't pay put him in cuffs right there and bring him in for processing. Tell him you're seizing all the questionable merchandise and closing the store until the investigation is complete. When you get him in the car, tell him seven thousand, and that if you have to bring him here, it's ten thousand. If not, he can try his luck with the laws of the Republic.'

'Fine, Comiso.'

He turned off the cell phone and heard a low chanting at his open door: 'Bo-ca! Bo-ca! Bo-ca!'

It was Fabian, crowing about Boca's victory over River in last night's SuperClassic. River had lost it on a last-minute goal, enabled by a questionable hold by a Boca wing. Fortunato had bet on River.

'It was a foul, *hijo de puta*. The referee was in on it.'

Fabian strode in, one hand extended like an orator. 'Comi! The SuperClassic is sacred! Even that jackal Morelo has to try to be honest for an hour and a half! Though the effort costs him.' Fabian was dressed today in a lime green jacket and a flamboyant tie plastered with little gold roosters.

Fortunato looked at the handsome, ridiculous man, with his curly blond hair and his clownish garb. 'You would know,' he said, picking up his pen. 'You're the one who spends all his time at the stadium and the hippodrome.'

Fabian nodded at the Comisario's freshly tidied office. 'The place is looking good. Even the *calabozos* smell like a pine forest. La Doctora Fowler will be very impressed. What a piece of woman, no?'

His superior's annoyance at being stuck with the investigation returned all at once. 'She's here to investigate a homicide, Fabian, not to hear your verses. You made us look like idiots last night with your little story about being a writer.'

Fabian couldn't seem to lose his smile. 'But it's true, Comiso!'

He held up his hand. 'I know. You're going to fill yourself with silver at any moment, and now is the chance for a smart woman to hook you and ride you to Hollywood.'

'Comi,' he gave an intimate little shrug, 'I don't have a monopoly on verses here.'

Fortunato leveled a long dusty gaze at his subordinate that, over the course of five seconds, dried up Fabian's grin and sent his left hand fidgeting at the inside of his pocket. 'Listen, Romeo, while the Doctora is here I want you to stay busy with your own investigations. If she asks you something about the Waterbury case, direct her to me.'

'That was a strange case, no? Six chalks of *milonga* and a dead foreigner. Domingo was telling me about it. Somebody was settling accounts.'

Fortunato's stomach tightened at Domingo's name. He didn't welcome Fabian's interest in the case. 'Thus the theory.'

Fabian nodded. 'I looked over the *expediente* a few months ago. Nothing's going to come out of that mess.' Fortunato didn't answer and Fabian dropped it. 'Whatever, it should be interesting to work with a police from the United States,' he said.

'She's not a police. She's a professor. A specialist in Human Rights.'

Fabian raised his eyebrows and shook his head, laughing as he turned to leave the office. 'This is a thing of gringos!'

She arrived promptly at eleven o'clock, accompanied by a young weightless attaché from the United States embassy. The embassy man, a Mr Wilbert Small, introduced himself with an accent that tried hard to accommodate the Italianate cadences of Buenos Aires. Fortunato could tell he was a man of little rank. If the embassy was serious, they would have sent over someone from the FBI. Fortunato offered them a coffee and ceremoniously took a few coins from a wooden box. He handed them to a sub-inspector and asked for him to bring three *cortados*, the thick spicy coffee with a dollop of milk.

They sat down and the embassy man started in with his embassy verses: the United States was grateful that the *Bonaerense* had agreed to indulge the family in one last attempt to put the case to rest.

'It's a tragedy,' the Comisario said. 'I'll do everything possible.'

He and Wilbert Small chatted lightly about Argentina and the United States for a few minutes until the diplomat left them to attend an important reunion of the Anglo-Argentine Cultural Society. Fortunato shut the door after him and sat down alone with La Doctora. He wanted to find out what suspicions she entertained about the case.

'Doctora Fowler,' he began, 'something I want to say from the start. I know that your training is in human rights, and, while I know that those issues are extremely important, especially with our recent history here in Argentina, I don't feel that we're dealing here with a human rights violation. Our indications are that this is a simple criminal case. Is there something that makes you think otherwise?'

'I think it's always better to begin without preconceptions,' she said a little too crisply. She seemed to regret her brusqueness and flashed an apologetic smile, then opened a notebook and glanced quickly at a few pages of notes. 'I'd like to go over briefly some of the details of the case, Comisario Fortunato. When the family was contacted by the US consulate it was told that Waterbury's death was considered a suicide.'

'I think that was a confusion, perhaps because the cause of death was identified by the mortuary as a shot to the head. I remind you that it happened on a weekend, when I have my days off, and I think that the Sub-Comisario Gaitan, who was on duty at that time, unfortunately didn't communicate clearly.'

She pursued the theme. 'I was told the body had several other bullet wounds and was discovered in a burning car. It seems a little bit demanding of Sub-Comisario Alper to expect a man to shoot himself several times, get out of his car, set it on fire, then get back in, put on handcuffs and shoot himself in the head with a second gun.' She softened the implications with a little shrug. 'Wouldn't you say so?'

Her attack on the most obvious flaw in the investigation unsettled Fortunato a bit, but could not disturb his tranquil exterior. 'Doctora Fowler, of course the confusion of suicide was an error in communication either on the part of Sub-Comisario Gaitan or by the embassy staff, and I apologize for the anguish that must have added for the family.'

She reached absently for her gold necklace and twined it between her fingers for a moment. 'After that, at the family's request, the embassy made some inquiries and was told that it was a suspected drug-related homicide. Even though the family informed them that Robert Waterbury had no criminal record and no history of drug use.' Her voice became at once accusatory and tentative. 'Why did the investigation stop with that conclusion?'

Fortunato cleared his throat. He meant to say that it would be logical for a man to conceal drug use from his family, but the inquisition of La Doctora's silence sent him off track. He remembered Domingo sprinkling the chalks in the back seat and Vasquez, with his goatee and his earrings, cursing at Waterbury's twitching body. The victim's last silent plea for help. 'It seems . . .' A few seconds passed, but the room – usually so fertile with such answers – was still empty. 'Forgive me, Doctora Fowler. At the time of this investigation my wife was dying of cancer and perhaps I delegated more than I should have. I am to blame.' Fortunato hadn't expected to use that excuse; it had floated up by itself, out of character, but its effect wrote itself instantly on Athena Fowler's face. Her features softened and she seemed lost for a moment. 'I'm very sorry, Comisario Fortunato. When did she pass away?'

'Three weeks ago.' He looked away from her. So strange to confess it to her like this. He barely mentioned Marcela's death to anyone else. Her next words caught him off guard.

'I know how difficult it is. My father died six weeks ago of cancer.' She pulled the chain from beneath her blouse and showed him a gold wedding band. 'This was his.'

They sat in the altered silence for a moment. Fortunato felt off-balance, resisting the urge to talk with her about watching Marcela wither away before the ferocious onslaught of the cancer. The sub-inspector knocked on the door with the coffees and a few slender paper tubes filled with sugar. He distributed them and left, and they uttered a few nonsense phrases while they put sugar in the cups. Wilbert Small's abandoned *Cortado* sat cooling on the tray.

He cleared his throat, returning to the task at hand. 'As to the matter of drugs: you're aware that several chalks of chlorhydrate of cocaine were discovered in the automobile?'

He could tell the news surprised her. 'No.' She hesitated, embarrassed. 'What do you mean by a "chalk" of cocaine?'

Fortunato grimaced, reluctant at having to deliver such inauspicious details. 'A chalk is a little cylinder that the traffickers compress the cocaine into for smuggling. One of the traffickers' methods is to stuff the drug into a rubber balloon and have the accomplice swallow many of these balloons. When we find a chalk, it's almost always in a concentrated form and involves someone who is distributing the drug as a business.'

'That doesn't match anything I was told about Robert Waterbury.'

'This is how I hoped you could help me, Doctora Fowler. It's very difficult to investigate a case like this solely on the forensic evidence. To understand it better, I need to know more about the victim. Why did Señor Waterbury come to Buenos Aires? What was he doing here?'

'As I told you, Robert Waterbury was a writer, and he came here to research a book he hoped to write. His wife said it was supposed to be some kind of detective novel set here, a thriller.'

'And why Buenos Aires?'

'I believe he thought it would make an exotic setting for his book. He lived down here for several years about ten years ago. He was working for AmiBank.'

Fortunato smiled and indulged himself, guessing that his words would resonate with a woman involved with human rights. 'AmiBank!' he said brightly. 'The famous money launderers! If he worked for them ten years ago, he had a front row seat to the most predatory of the privatizations and debt re-financing.'

He'd hit it right on. The gringa couldn't suppress the trace of enthusiasm that broke through her gray professionalism. 'You know about AmiBank?'

'Señorita,' he cocked his eyebrows slyly, 'here I apprehend those miserable *chorros* that grab a *moto* or rob a house. Of the experts, I can only read in the newspaper!' He held up his finger. 'If I remember well, AmiBank was involved in the Aerolíneas privatization. Of the demonstration we saw yesterday?'

She was conspiratorial now. 'In the United States all you see are commercials with friendly employees helping young couples buy a house.'

'Thus the machine,' Fortunato said.

Fortunato knew that in a real investigation he would exhume Waterbury's former contacts at AmiBank, search through his address book, subpoena his hotel's telephone records and try to trace every movement he'd made since landing at Ezeiza. Instead, he crunched his brows together. 'But you were telling me about Robert Waterbury. You said he was a writer. Writers are famous for their problems with money. What was Señor Waterbury's economic situation before he came here?'

He could see La Doctora considering the possibility. 'It was a bit difficult, according to his wife.'

'Did he have many debts?' Fortunato asked gently.

'I think he did. Yes. His wife said he wanted to write something more commercial, that he could do quickly.'

'So,' Fortunato nodded, allowing just a trace of self-righteousness to enter his voice, 'he *did* have money problems. And so we could say that the Homicide investigators who worked on the case, Inspectors Velez and Braun, were not completely unjustified in thinking that the presence of the chlorhydrate of cocaine might indicate some sort of settling of accounts by colleagues within the drug business, or perhaps a deal that went bad. When people have large debts, Doctora, they are inclined to do things they wouldn't normally do.'

Her protest sounded hopelessly innocent. 'But it seems completely out of character!'

He put on his Good Cop face. 'Doctora Fowler, we live in a world of appearances. It's quite logical that Robert Waterbury might want to conceal some aspects of his character, or even that his wife might prefer not to cloud his memory. We all want others to believe in the image that we create for them, because it helps us to believe it ourselves. But me, after thirty-seven years as a policeman,' shaking his head gently, 'I have lost interest in appearances.' A strange shudder passed over him as he said it, a sensation of detachment from himself. He didn't know why things were going so far off-course. 'Perhaps this is a good time to examine the *expediente*,' he suggested, indicating the judicial archives of the case. 'In an investigation like this, one should always begin with the facts.'

He felt his cell phone chirping in his pocket and held up his hand toward Doctora Fowler as he answered it. His investigator had just taken the cuffs off the grocery store owner and turned him out of the car. They'd gotten six thousand from him.

The *expediente* of a crime in Buenos Aires is as baroque and ostentatious as the city itself. The investigation is directed by a lawyer working for the judicial system and called an On-Duty judge. The judge decides what steps to take and the police carry them out. As evidence and testimonies are gathered, the judge issues new directives and the police diligently respond. This vast inquiry unfolds across hundreds of pages contributed by the *Departmento* of this, the *Ministerio* of that, by police stations and laboratories and morgues. Judge's orders go out lathered with seals and signatures and are answered with the dignified medallions of the comisarios and their clerks. Dozens of *declaraciónes* unwind in a tone of cool detachment, and a parade of photographs bolsters these testaments with shots of bullet-riddled cars and sequestered evidence. At last come the portraits of the unfortunate dead, sheathed with blood, shirt-tails untucked, captured at the most inopportune moment of their lives. An aura of absolute fact prevails – the perfect setting for absolute fiction.

Fortunato drew the folder out of a scratched metal filing cabinet. The packet had the thickness of a small-town telephone book, cluttered with papers that shimmied out at the top and sides. He led Athena into a conference room with a scarred wooden table and motioned to a seat opposite himself.

'I can only show you the photocopies,' he said. 'The original is at the Judicial Deposit.'

The first declaration described the arrival on the scene. Fortunato could imagine the clerk's disinterested typing as the officer related his name, parents' names, rank, age and civil status. After a half page of such preamble, the story began:

At approximately 01:38 the declarant was directed by radio dispatch of Comisaria #35 of San Justo to report to the 1400 block of Avenida Santana, district of La Matanza, at the crossing of Calle Avellaneda.

A narrow lot between two abandoned factories, their long empty walls closing off the view. Broken glass and a few burnt-out cars left by dismantlers, lit only by the pink glow of the city lights against the thick mist. Fortunato had known the place because his brigada used to provide 'security' for the factories until Chinese imports had driven them out of business. He had chosen it with the same care with which he'd conducted the surveillance and planned the abduction.

He and Domingo had watched Waterbury for five days, noting his movements and his habitual places. Waterbury went around with a pretty woman who frequented the Bar Azul, some sort of tango dancer. He had a friend who worked at Grupo AmiBank in the financial district, someone high enough in the hierarchy to have a car waiting for him after work each day. Another day Waterbury was visited by a woman who arrived in a limousine and carried a cardboard portfolio, returning twenty minutes later without it. A curious assortment. With more time and more men he would have found out everything about the target and his associates, but this was only a squeeze, so they did the minimum and marked out the night.

Waterbury had gone to dinner at his habitual restaurant and Onda, the lookout, advised them on the radio when he paid the bill. He came strolling toward the entrance to his pensión seventeen minutes after midnight. The building on the corner was getting a new facade, and Fortunato approached him behind a large container full of construction debris.

'Señor Waterbury,' he'd said, addressing him like an acquaintance.

Waterbury stopped short. Maybe he'd already been jumpy, or perhaps he sensed Domingo and Vasquez approaching ten meters behind him. Maybe he realized that the scaffolding and debris concealed him from the street.

'I've heard a lot about you,' Fortunato had said, appealing to his ego. 'May I chat with you for a few minutes?'

'About what?'

He shrugged. 'Not about big things. Just to chat.'

'Who are you?'

By then Domingo and Vasquez had caught up with Waterbury, and as he heard their brisk footsteps among the crumpled papers he turned. Domingo had the stun gun out. 'Excuse me,' Domingo said in a friendly voice. 'Is there a problem here?' This confused

24

Waterbury for just the amount of time necessary for Domingo to close in and hit him with fifty thousand volts. Waterbury went down and in less than ten seconds they had him cuffed and in the car. Domingo pushed him to the floor. 'Tell Onda to follow us closely,' Fortunato told Vasquez. When they drove off Waterbury was still disoriented, indignantly demanding answers from below. Domingo said admiringly 'They're very good, these little machines, no? In the old days, you'd have to split their heads open to be sure they were down.' Only thirty, Domingo referred to the days of the Dictatorship like a golden era. That puffy dark smile in the rear-view mirror. Fortunato said nothing.

There the declarant found an auto Ford Falcon, sedan, color metallized gray, interior color light brown, serial #A287–56682–306–1986, with the front doors closed and the rear doors open. The auto was burning, with most of the damage being in the front section, around the motor. Both rear doors were open, and the deceased could be seen on the rear seat, stained with a substance that resembled human blood, apparently dead. The firemen of Cuartel de Bomberos de San Justo arrived at approximately 01:40 and rapidly controlled the fire.

Waterbury's voice came up from below the seat. 'What is this about?' Domingo had his foot on Waterbury's head so that he couldn't rise, and Fortunato saw Domingo shift positions as he shoved the gringo's face into the thin carpet. 'Don't be clever,' Domingo snarled at him. 'You know why you're here.'

'If you move I'll blow your balls off!' Vasquez added. His nose was running and his greasy auburn hair flopped across his forehead as he looked down at the gringo. The gold hoops glinted in his ear.

'Is this Carlo?' the writer had asked in a muffled voice. 'Did Carlo send you? Tell him he's made a mistake!'

None of them answered. Carlo who? They let the silence work on Waterbury as they crossed into the exurbs of La Matanza.

'Tell Don Carlo that he has nothing to worry about,' Waterbury said from the floor and then yelped, which told Fortunato that Domingo had kicked him in the head again.

'*Tranquilo*,' Fortunato said in his calmest voice.

Waterbury spoke again after a few minutes, sounding more frustrated than fearful. 'I didn't do anything! You understand? You have to tell him that. Or better, I'll tell him. Take me to him right now and I'll explain the whole thing myself.'

'Of course,' Domingo laughed. 'But no one needs your explanation.'

Fortunato sensed that even now Waterbury retained a certain amount of composure. Still banking on his passport. He probably thought that things like this didn't happen to people like him.

'Listen, tell Señor Pelegrini that all I want to do is go home to my wife and daughter and forget all about this. I know nothing and I care about nothing. Understand?'

Carlo Pelegrini. The vaguely familiar name made Fortunato uneasy, but then Domingo kicked another yelp out of the gringo. 'Shut up, faggot! Nobody wants to hear your lies!' Fortunato took a breath and reassured himself. Waterbury was a blackmailer and he had to learn the hard way. It was a necessary part of the operation.

They'd reached the poorer streets where the houses became scabbed with tar paper and corrugated tin. Weedy lawns languished beside vacant lots. Onda's headlights in the rearview mirror. The Northamerican couldn't see anything, but maybe he sensed that he had reached his ultimate destination. Fortunato could hear a new timbre in his voice. Now he was truly afraid. 'This is Renssaelaer, isn't it? Renssaelaer sent you.'

The sound of the gringo name puzzled the Comisario. Renssaelaer . . . and Pelegrini . . . What was this?

'Tell Señor Renssaelaer he has nothing to fear from me. I'm going home and I won't tell anyone. I'll go home tomorrow!'

The fire extinguished, the declarant examined the body and found it without signs of life. The cadaver was of masculine sex, in a fetal position with his dorsal side to the back of the car and his head towards the passenger side. The cadaver's hands were cuffed in front of him, with handcuffs of make Eagle Security.

Idiot Domingo! To leave the cuffs at the scene! Eagle Security was the police brand. Why didn't he just write down his badge number on the dashboard! The gringa was scribbling something in her notebook, something about the handcuffs, and he felt his stomach tighten.

The cadaver presented five wounds, presumably from firearms, one in the left hand through the palm, one in the left thorax, frontal zone, one in the frontal zone of the right thigh, one in the testicles and rectum, one in the right temple apparently exiting through the left socket.

'They tortured him!' La Doctora said, shuddering. Her sharp green eyes flickered into Fortunato's. 'How could they be so cruel?'

Fortunato didn't answer, hiding in the dispassionate typescript of the declaration. Finally he croaked, 'The one in the hand is a defensive wound.'

The night was going off again, like an alarm. Domingo and Vasquez in the back seat, Vasquez with his swastika tattoos and his *papelitos* of *merca* one after the other. Vasquez, an addled coil of blue-tinted muscles, a *guapo* of the new style, always ready for a fight, but preferring a few bullets pumped from behind to a head-on contest with knives. Bad news from the start, and now coked up so high that his eyes were blazing. They'd pulled Waterbury upright in the seat so they could hit him in the face more easily, Domingo shouting, 'You think yourself clever!' A blow. Water-bury's nose bleeding, his eye swelling up. 'You think yourself clever, eh?' Waterbury no longer protesting about Carlo Pelegrini. He kept looking at Fortunato because Fortunato was older, the orderly one with the comprehending face and the voice of a kind uncle. Fortunato tried to tell him with his eyes, *Bear up, hombre. Nothing's going to happen.*

'I have a wife and daughter,' the gringo said to him. 'You know that?'

Vasquez spitting at his victim, 'We'll fuck your wife in front of the daughter, and then we'll kill everybody.' Waterbury still looking at him over the seat as if they were in this together, because, after all, he was the Good Cop. And Domingo was supposed to scare him. He was the Bad Cop.

The following items were collected from the floor of the car. Rear seat section: one bullet, apparently 9mm. Five shell casings, four .32 caliber, make: Remington. One 9mm, make: Federal.

La Doctora scribbled another flurry of words in her notebook.

Three pieces of blue metallized paper, each containing traces of a white substance, similar to that known as chlorhydrate of cocaine . . .

Vasquez' ten-peso folders. Domingo, getting out to piss and making that long loud snuffing sound and turning to the car again with the white crust of *merca* hanging from his nose.

'Son of a bitch, what are you doing? You can't do that on a job!'

Domingo with shining eyes now: 'Don't fuck with me, Comi.' Even Waterbury sensing that things were getting out of control. 'Look –' the gringo began. Domingo grabbed his jaw and pulled his face close. 'No, you look, faggot! You think you're a clever gringo! More rapid than anyone else –'

Vasquez suddenly with his gun out, a little silver .32 automatic, putting it to Waterbury's temple. 'Is this clever, *hijo de puta*? Is this clever?'

Waterbury was starting to panic and Fortunato felt it spreading. 'Put the gun away!' Command words, trying to stifle the hysteria that had invaded Vasquez' burning eyes. But Vasquez didn't hear him. He was in it already, his little fantasy of power, owner of life and death. As Fortunato watched he took the gun and pointed it down again, grinding the barrel into the writer's thigh and then, with a twitch that came from the drugs, or maybe from the writer's involuntary flinch, the gun exploded.

The rest happened before Fortunato could move. Waterbury thrust his manacled hands towards the gun, wrestling it sideways, and it went off again.

Vasquez screamed. 'Aaaah! My foot! You son of a bitch!' and in the dirty light Fortunato saw the gun come up again. Domingo shouting, 'No, idiot, you'll hit me!' and grabbing at the little packet of dull silver, and for a moment four hands contested. It went off again, blasting through Waterbury's hand and into his chest, and at this Domingo managed to wrestle the pistol free. Vasquez was howling and swearing, Waterbury instinctively putting his hands up for protection.

'*Puta!*' Domingo screamed, and he lowered the gun and shot directly into Waterbury's groin. In five seconds, everything had gone out of control. Vasquez was cursing and Waterbury was screaming and twisting on the bloody vinyl. 'Give me that, Domingo.' Fortunato reached for the barrel of the gun and peeled it down and sideways out of Domingo's hand. Waterbury was still writhing.

Domingo was cursing at him. The gunshots had roused Onda from the second car and he was staring into the window with his mouth open. Onda, *Vibe*, only twenty-one, just a hippy thief hired to drive a car, not to witness a murder.

Fortunato ordered Domingo out of the car and then went around and pulled the wounded Vasquez out, throwing him into the mud. The dome light cast a dirty gray film over the seat and the bloody victim. Waterbury was rolling on the seat in torment. Fortunato knew the Northamerican was screaming, but as he looked at him he was conscious only of a deep sense of silence that seemed to engulf the car and the arid vacant lot. The wound in Waterbury's inner thigh was bleeding heavily and his groin was worse. He had another wound in his chest, and Fortunato could see blood bubbling in with his saliva. His eyes looked like those of a deep-sea fish pulled suddenly to the surface. Fortunato took out his Browning. He could feel Onda watching him.

People said that the first person you killed was always the worst. 'Look, *hombre*,' the Chief had told him at a barbecue the following week. 'There are unpleasant things to be done and one has to have the balls to do them. That's how it was during the war and that's how it is now. This Waterbury was mixed up in *something*.' He'd spotted Fortunato's discomfort. 'Besides, the truth is that it was the other two morons that killed him. You just put him out of his misery. Should you have let him suffer for a few more hours?'

La Doctora reached the end of the first declaration and hurried through photocopies of various receipts and credentials. The first photos of the crime scene stiffened her.

Even in black and white, they were horrific. The first was an exterior of the car with the back door hanging open. The front of the car was blackened from the fire, its hood flung open. The windshield was shattered by the heat. Through the dark opening in the door projected a shoe, and a leg in light-colored trousers.

The next photo was closer, through the open window. Waterbury lay on the seat with his mouth half-open, his skin laced by rivulets of black blood. The next photo was a closeup.

Athena gasped, turning away and closing her eyes.

Fortunato stared dumbly at the photo, remembering how it had looked the night of the *operativo*, the haze of gunsmoke in the auto, Waterbury's last twitches as he settled into the seat. Behind him

Domingo: 'You calmed the *hijo de puta*, Comi.' Yes, he'd calmed him. Everything was calm. Everything calm for the father. And then the next day, at the clinic, when the doctor told Marcela why she was losing so much weight, it had just kept getting calmer and calmer. She'd given up and dissolved away, leaving only that calm empty house that found him every evening. Perhaps like the house of Robert Waterbury.

A clerk knocked at the door and thrust his head in.

'Comisario, forgive the interruption. Something has happened outside.'

Fortunato came to his feet and hurried out, followed by the Doctora.

A dog lay bloody and yelping in the road beside an unmarked police car while the driver, Inspector Domingo Fausto, was fending off the furious attack of an eight-year-old boy. Fortunato recognized the dog and the little boy as residents of the house across the street. He always kept a few pieces of candy in his pocket to give him when he passed by.

'*Chico!*' He grasped the little boy's shoulders from behind and pulled him away from Domingo. The boy's face was flushed and shining with tears.

'It wasn't my fault, Comiso,' Domingo began, flustered. 'The dog jumped out from between the cars.' He turned to the boy. 'Why didn't you hold onto him, *retard*!'

The child's anger collapsed into a whimper and he bent down close to the dog and stroked his head. 'Tiger!' he cried. 'Tiger!' The dog's front legs waggled uselessly before its crushed body, and Fortunato could assess the hopelessness at a glance. He looked back at Domingo, who dismissed it all with a click of his tongue and a toss of his head. Beyond them, La Doctora was watching.

'Take care of it,' Fortunato told him under his breath, then he crouched down to the boy's level and turned on him the full sympathy of his weary face. '*Chico*, come with me over to the kiosk. Let's get a soda. I want to explain something to you.'

'But what about Tiger?'

'Tiger is badly off, but we're going to help him. Come on. What kind of soda do you like?' Fortunato put his arm around the boy's shoulders and began leading him across the street to the kiosk. The dog was still yelping, now with a gasping labored chortle in it.

The boy hesitated. 'But Tiger –'

'I'm going to get you a new dog.' Fortunato steered the skinny shoulderblades away from the street. The harsh report of Domingo's .25 automatic leapt off the pavement behind them, and the boy broke free and spun around. Domingo was standing over the shuddering animal in a little cloud of gunsmoke, and the boy put his hands on his ears and began screaming, his eyes wide open, screaming. He took a step towards Domingo and the dog, looked at it, then turned towards Fortunato with an expression of misery and disbelief. He shook free and ran off down the street with his hands waving above his head, slicing the leafy air with his high-pitched shrieks. Fortunato watched him disappear behind the parked cars of the shady lane.

He walked slowly back to Domingo. The officer's corpulent features reflected the satisfaction of a job well done, the trace of a grin humping up his oily cheeks. 'It wasn't my fault. He has to learn to take care of his pets.' He knelt down to put the small automatic back into his ankle holster, oblivious to the intensity of Fortunato's stare. 'What a mess,' Domingo said, as he glanced at the ruined corpse. He stood up and gave a tiny shrug. 'I did him a favor by killing him.'

CHAPTER 4

Athena sat back in the conference room and thought about the morning. It wasn't easy getting her bearings after a day like this: first the glad-handing introduction by Wilbert Small, then the graphic photos that had showed her up as an amateur. The bizarre incident with the dog had capped everything. Even the Comisario seemed shaken up by that one: after the little boy's screaming exit he'd left her to examine the *expediente* alone, under the sacred gazes of General San Martin and the Blessed Virgin of Lujan.

From the time she'd gotten off the plane she'd been trying to focus on the inquiry, but the buzz of arrival kept sweeping her away. It was cool to have a delegation of cops pick her up at the airport, to have the clerks at a big fancy American hotel call her Doctor Fowler and charge it all to Uncle Sam. Just to be in Buenos Aires investigating felt spy-like and thrilling. Despite the murder at the center of this inquiry and the vertigo of potential failure, some small dirty part of her kept patting herself on the back. Now, though, she had to produce some results. She began leafing through the stack of documents before her.

She had seen plenty of pompous Latin American documents before, but the *expediente* had the surreal feel of a story by Cortazar. The initial pages had to do with the crime scene and the evidence found there, but after that the paperwork began to multiply in number and complexity. Declarations were made by ambulance attendants and tow-truck drivers. Forensics tests were ordered and carried out. The police dragged the hapless owner of the stolen car in for questioning and, as a final irony, processed him for an unpaid traffic ticket. Several *declaraciónes* attested to the trajectory of the body's paper-strewn final tour, with receipts signed by the responding police officer, the ambulance driver, the clerk at the morgue, the forensic surgeon, the mortuary, and a bill of 198 pesos accepted by the United States Consulate for cremation. Despite the copious information, the scene yielded surprisingly few clues. Waterbury's body had been stripped of identification and had lain in the morgue for two weeks before the missing persons reports plucked him out. Somewhere beneath all the cold, objective description, the man who had been Robert Waterbury had endured his last brutal minutes of fear and pain.

One document emerged from the blur to claim her attention. The coroner had inventoried the victim's clothing, analyzing the blood stains and the entry and exit holes of the various bullets. There, in that long list, *One pair of pants, type Khaki, with a label that says 'Allesandro Bernini, Industria Italia, Pura Cotone' stained with a red-brown substance consistent with human blood, with a hole in the right thigh, front part.* Then, in a detail that seemed to have been over-looked by the responding officers, *In the watch pocket of the pants, a blue piece of paper inscribed 45861921 – Teresa.*

Teresa. What did it mean to find a woman's phone number in a dead man's pocket? Athena copied it into her notebook, resolving to keep it to herself for the time being. *Teresa.* Maybe nothing: the telephone of a woman who did clothing alterations, an employee at a photocopy shop. The real problem with the number was the fact that no one had yet bothered to call it.

The investigation up to that point had been almost willfully torpid, and Comisario Fortunato had as much as admitted it. Nothing shocking about that. The *Bonaerense* had a damning resume in the files of the various human rights organizations she had contacted, and she had known that their methods wouldn't conform to the strictures of the police handbooks she'd read as preparation for this assignment. What made things weirder was the knowledge that all policemen older than their early forties had been active during the time of the Dictatorship. Who were these middle-aged men that greeted her, these Sub-Comisarios and Sargentos that shook her hand with such formal courtesy in the hallways? Night-mare panoramas kept ghosting through her imagination: a Sub-Co standing above a hooded prisoner or hustling someone into an unmarked car. On the other hand, Comisario Fortunato seemed all the opposite. His exhausted dignity had something comforting about it. He'd admitted the mistakes of the previous investigation and taken responsibility for them. As the single person in the *Bonaerense* on whom her success depended, she had no choice but to get along with him, but it went deeper than that. At a level she hated to admit to herself, Fortunato's weary face and quiet manner reminded her of her father.

She put her pen down on the *expediente* and slumped into her chair. Her father had always been a man to play along, an Insurance Adjuster given to describing things in measured and reasonable terms even when a situation was patently obscene. It had infuriated her growing up; she'd preferred the fearless combative style of her mother, whom she had once seen slap a clerk for insulting a black woman. In the end, though, she had learned from her father. At dozens of State Department cocktail parties and conferences she had played the bright young technocrat, discussing American training of torturers or aid to fascist regimes with the cheerful detachment of one who *had no political bias*. She learned to discuss those horrors the way the remote language of the *expediente* described Robert Waterbury's murder, speaking of devastated Latin American economies as if they were simply imperfect markets, stressing that human rights had to be viewed 'in context.' She sent a hundred follow-up letters and placed a thousand business cards with all her father's insurance-man thoroughness. All in the hope that when it came time to send someone to El Salvador to observe an election, or to author a report on the effect of crop substitution in the Bolivian *Chapari*, they might remember her name and face, the authentic sound of the Spanish words dropped into conversation. At last her acting paid off in a phone call from Senator Braden's office. There was a matter in Argentina to investigate, a question about a human rights violation of an American citizen. Might she be available?

After that the interview with Waterbury's wife, still oppressed by the murder and its clumsy inquiry. Naomi Waterbury had met her at the door with a grievous, distrustful stare, her handsome features spoiled by the loose crescents under her eyes and the bitter turn of her mouth. She described her husband's life carefully, struggling to keep a distance from her grief. The State Department's sudden flourish of goodwill had not appeased her, and as they talked her manner seemed to churn slowly through resentment, nostalgia and a mutilated sort of hope.

Her husband, she said, was a writer. He had freelanced for various magazines and had written two novels. The first novel had gone well, and the second had gone badly. He'd gone to Buenos Aires to research a third, a detective thriller, which he'd hoped would resuscitate his career. 'He wanted to write something commercial,' she said. 'His first two books were literary, and after the second one failed, he thought he should just try to write whatever the market wanted. I hated to see him setting out to write something mediocre, just for the money.' She sighed. 'I supported him in it because he was desperate. We were all desperate.'

'Mrs Waterbury, did your husband give any indication that he was involved in anything dangerous? Did he show any sort of alarm?'

She hesitated as she braced herself against the memories. 'At first he talked about the people he'd met, how good it was to be back in Buenos Aires. He used to see one of his old banking friends, I think his name was Pablo. Then, he started to sound a little . . . evasive. He said he was on to something that would take care of us, but he wouldn't say what. He seemed a little ashamed of it. I think something *was* going on, but he didn't want me to worry about it, which of course worried me more. The last time he called he sounded tired and upset. He said he'd had enough, he was coming home.' Her face suddenly seemed to lose its internal structure and to twist into something child-like and hurt. 'That was the day before they found his body!'

It was devastating to watch, and it made Athena say something she never should have, an unkeepable promise uttered in a low voice as she reached out and touched the widow's shoulder: 'I'll find out what happened to your husband, Naomi. I'll find out.'

The fastidious details of the *expediente* had become impenetrable now. She sighed and picked up yesterday's newspaper from the Comisario's desk. A certain Carlo Pelegrini was decorating the headlines in a scandal which she'd arrived too late to make sense of. Something complicated about bribery and the Argentine postal service. She saw the name of the president and various Air Force officers. Someone knocked on the door. A cloud of green wavered in the frosted glass.

'Ah, Doctora Fowler! I see you're already on the march.'

Fabian was lighting up the gray confines of the police station with a parrot green sports jacket and a pink shirt, an outfit he could carry off by virtue of his handsome face and thick blond ringlets. Gold roosters crowed on his silk tie.

'Inspector Diaz!'

'Please,' he said in English, giving her one of those handsome-man smiles, full of laughter and warmth. 'I am Fabian!' He came into the room without an invitation, and she caught his eyes traveling quickly down her body to her waist with a brief, almost professional scrutiny. As he bent down to kiss her on the cheek she smelled his cologne: a pleasant, spicy aroma, slightly intoxicating.

'Fabian. I didn't realize you speak English.'

He stumbled on, his smile becoming slightly more labored. 'Of course . . . I can speak!' He shrugged. 'Of course!'

'That should serve you well in Hollywood.'

The grin hung on to his open mouth as he struggled to decide whether she was mocking him or not. 'Actually,' he retreated, 'I read English better than speak. Look . . .' He pulled an American paperback from his briefcase and continued in Spanish. 'I'm studying the formula. Formula is everything.' He passed it to her and she glanced at the back cover.

Ever read a popular mystery and thought to yourself: 'I can write better than that!' Now you can! We will teach you:

How to use clues to keep the reader guessing and the pages turning!

Twelve secret techniques writers use to hook the reader from the start.

How to structure your novel for a big Hollywood sale! It's easy!

She handed it back to him.

'My cousin in Los Angeles sent it to me,' he said as he returned it to the case, then he shook his head in misty wonderment. 'They stuff themselves with silver there!' The face of the literary enthusiast fell away, leaving that of the cool professional. 'I'm familiar with the case you're working on.'

'The Waterbury case?'

'Sí, Doctora. I work principally with Narcotics and Vice, but in a case like this, where a commercial quantity of drugs is found at a murder scene, Narcotics will often work with Homicide, to try to combine forces, so to speak.'

'You were one of the investigators?'

'Yes, Doctora.'

'I didn't see your name on the *expediente*.'

'I was working more as an intellectual author of the investigation. Others filled out the papers.'

'Ah.' She frowned thoughtfully. 'The intellectual author.' She couldn't help but be amused by his pompousness. 'Do you have some sort of theory?'

'Yes.' He sat down across from her. 'You've read the *expediente*.'

'Part of it. It's very long.'

'They all are. But you saw from the surgeon's report that Waterbury seems to have been beaten, then shot several times with the same gun, and then executed with a mercy shot to the head with a second gun.'

The brutal sentence washed over her. 'Yes.'

He continued in a monotone, his face taut. 'The theory is thus: Señor Waterbury was killed in a settling of accounts.'

'That's what Comisario Fortunato said.'

'And with good reason. But I have a way of seeing this murder that perhaps the Comisario doesn't have, another perspective, one might say.' He leaned forward, and she could feel a strange intimacy come over the room, the first whiff of intrigue that she had always associated with Buenos Aires, with rainy streets and trench-coats and German submarines. Fabian narrowed his eyes. 'We must look at this investigation from the point of view of a detective novel.'

She didn't have time to register her disbelief before he continued, his face transfixed by a dramatic squint.

'Our story begins at the theater of the crime. We can imagine Comisario Fortunato before the smoking automobile. A man is dead. The fabric of society has been torn, and only the Comisario can repair this damage by bringing the killer to justice. He examines the clues and tries to re-enact the crime in his head. In the case of Waterbury we have a body containing three .32 caliber bullets. All are haphazard: the thigh, the hand – a defensive wound, probably – the thorax and the groin. All at extremely close range, what we call "clothes-burning" range, undoubtedly fired by someone sitting beside the victim. Then, the final authoritative shot of the 9mm, perhaps a disposition of the case by whoever was in charge. I see a chaotic situation. A struggle. Unexpected, because it's very danger-ous to go shooting a gun in the back seat of a car. If you want to execute someone, the classic way is to take them out of the car and put them on their knees, or lay them on the ground. That way, you're shooting down, and the bullet won't go flying off and hit someone else. No, this was something more panicked. Unplanned.

Maybe it was a deal that went bad. Or maybe the intent was to intimidate him, and somehow it got out of control.'

He cocked his head. 'If I was writing this particular detective story, that would be my theory. Waterbury was killed without intention.' He flipped his hands to the side as if he'd stumbled across a brilliant solution. 'You should come out with me! I can tell you *many* interesting things! I can show you a bit of Buenos Aires. For example, have you been to San Telmo? It's a very special barrio, with many night clubs and a lot of music.'

'Fabian –'

He lowered his voice, his rooster grin turning secretive. 'And when we get to know each other better, perhaps I can tell you what my police story is about.'

She let a touch of annoyance into her voice. 'Forget it. It's not going to happen, Fabian.'

He dropped his head, his fingers to his brow. 'What a beast I am!' Looking up at her, his smile shining out from his cloud of contrition. 'I'm sorry, Doctora. You're exotic here, and it made me step out of my routine. It's not every day that a beautiful police woman from the United States shows up here in the provinces of Buenos Aires. Please forget what I said.'

'It's fine, Fabian.'

Fortunato came in without knocking, and Fabian looked embarrassed. 'Ah! Inspector Diaz!'

'Yes.' Fabian reached nervously for the knot of his tie. 'We were just going over the *expediente*. I was telling her that the crime looks chaotic. Not like a calculated execution. Because of the pattern of the wounds from the .32.'

Fortunato didn't move or speak, merely pursed his lips and looked absently at Fabian, before turning to Athena. 'That was something I wanted to go into tomorrow. First, you should review the *expediente* without any preconceptions and then we can start considering theories.' He looked disapprovingly at Fabian. 'But I see that Romeo has run ahead of us.'

The young officer crumpled like a napkin, and Athena felt sorry for him. Fortunato said, 'If you are finished for the day, Doctora, I can drive you to your hotel.'

'Why did you call him Romeo?' she asked in his car.

Fortunato spoke diplomatically, in that reassuringly calm way that she'd grown to like. 'Inspector Diaz has a certain taste for women. He has a pretty face and dresses well, as you can see. That's why we call him Romeo. It's *okay*. But, from time to time, Fabian confuses his role of policeman with his role of conquistador.'

'Don't worry; it's nothing I can't handle. Do you think he's really working on a police story to sell to Hollywood?'

Now Fortunato's worn face turned to a grandfatherly smile. 'I'm surprised he didn't tell you he's training to be the first Argentine astronaut.' He shrugged. 'It could be. If he wrote a story about the hippodrome, or the football stadium, now *there* he has a great deal of expertise!' She laughed and Fortunato went on. 'One thing you have to understand about the Porteño, the man of Buenos Aires. He's an actor. And to be a good policeman, you have to be a good actor. Because people want to see that policeman face.' They were stopped at a light and Fortunato turned to her to show her his *cara de policia*. He raised his chin and frowned, transforming himself into a picture of implacable authority as he beckoned with his fingers. 'You! Come here!' He glared behind the cold Fascist mask for a moment, and then broke into a smile. 'Thus it is, youngster.'

The eerie flicker of identities hung in the car before dissipating in the sunny autumn afternoon. 'So did Fabian work as an investigator on the case before?'

'Perhaps a little. Investigations are fluid. One works, one shares information. The truth is that the Waterbury investigation didn't go far because of the lack of an initial clue. This isn't the United States. Here, lamentably, there is a great lack of resources. We concentrate on the cases we have the best chance to solve. We can go to the judge's office and you'll see a heap of *expedientes* higher than Aconcagua.'

'I understand.'

'The *muchachos* tried. The vehicle was a stolen car with false papers. When they found the owner he had nothing to do with it.'

'But that didn't stop you from processing him for a traffic infraction.'

A sleepy irony came across the Comisario's face. 'Thus is justice. We're all guilty. Even Jesus Christ was processed for disorderly conduct.'

She couldn't help laughing and a rare smile opened up below his mustache. When they arrived at the Sheraton he turned to her.

'Look, Doctora Fowler. Perhaps you are tired, but often on the weekends I go to listen to tango at a particular place in La Boca. It's very typical of Buenos Aires. Not for tourists. It's called 17 Stone Angels. If you like, I can look for you tonight at your hotel.'

She beamed at him. 'It would be a pleasure.' She started to walk away from the car then turned back and bent toward the driver's window. 'One last little favor, Comisario.' He looked up at her attentively. 'I'd like to meet the judge who is directing this investigation.'

Fortunato's agreeable nod seemed to approve of her stratagem. 'At your orders, Doctora.'

She stood back and waited for him to disappear into traffic, paused another minute to be sure, and then summoned a taxi from the afternoon crush. She gave a reflexive glance behind her before getting in. Her next appointment was not on the official agenda.

CHAPTER 5

Athena glanced around the waiting room of the Instituto Contra la Represion Policial. In the dispiriting yellow light of a cheap floor lamp, ponderous leather volumes of the *Revista Juridica Argentina* traced the law back to 1936, along with somber gold-embossed walls of *Derecho Constitucional, Ley de la Republica Argentina* and other hopeful compendia of legal redress. A magazine on a coffee table featured a cover photo of two mostly nude women laughing with a handsome man. 'The Summer in Punta,' it proclaimed. 'Sand, Sex and Silver.' Several people sat alongside Athena, dressed in clean, cheap button-down shirts and with the rounder Andean features that typically belonged to the lower class. From their hushed sentences she gathered that they had enlisted the services of the Instituto in suing the policemen who had murdered their brother.

She'd heard about the Anti-Police Repression Institute from her mentor, a professor of Latin American studies at Georgetown. 'It's a setup,' he told her cheerfully when she'd called him with the news of her assignment. 'The local police will give you the runaround and the embassy will brush you off as politely as possible. Once you go down there and fail, everyone's done their duty and Senator Braden has to shut up about it and move the Free Trade package.' He relented from the cynical discourse. 'Go, listen, observe. When you get your feet on the ground, call these people. They're a group of lawyers that prosecute the police for civil rights violations. If you can interest them in the case, they might be able to get something going.'

His assessment had irritated her, but it seemed to be playing out just as he'd predicted. The FBI had been elusive, cancelling her appointment and promising to call back when they had 'a break in the schedule.' Her contact with the Argentine Ministry of Justice was an assistant to an assistant, and there was the insubstantial Wilbert Small, from the embassy. She'd be an idiot to think they took her seriously. Anger rose to her throat, then dissipated as she thought of the family sitting across from her. These were people with a *real* grievance. Naomi Waterbury had a real grievance.

The current edition of the newspaper lay on the table and she noticed that Carlo Pelegrini had again staked out a place in the headlines. *Pelegrini says I'm a Simple Mailman.* Pelegrini seemed to be a wealthy businessman who operated a private courier system. The previous winter, he'd been caught paying a bribe of more than twelve million dollars to government officials in exchange for an exclusive right to carry the national mails. Now, other businesses were coming to light. The article alluded to a network of ventures, worth billions of dollars, held by dummy corporations and off-shore investment groups. Pelegrini denied owning these businesses, denied that he received income from them, denied exerting an unsavory influence over politicians in the intimate circles of the President of the Republic. He was a simple mailman.

She scanned further down the page to a sidebar, headlined *The Gringos get in Line.* RapidMail, the American colossus of worldwide package delivery, was also said to be summoning its allies for their own move on the Argentine postal service, fronted by the Grupo Capital AmiBank.

The receptionist guided Athena to the office of Carmen Amado de los Santos. A tight little clutter of office furniture was stamped with the usual diplomas and an award from Amnesty International for service in the protection of human rights. Carmen Amado herself had long black hair and little round glasses, a slim woman of perhaps forty who, despite her professional gravity, could not resist wearing a skirt cut above the knees. She adorned her rich brown skin with a sliver of blue eye shadow and a tinge of rouge but, despite these feminine touches, all sense of coquetry dropped away when she began to speak.

'Doctor Fowler,' she said in a perfect, steely English, 'you've come to Buenos Aires to investigate the murder of a United States citizen.'

'Yes.'

'And the United States State Department has sent you here?'

'Yes. The family requested that the murder be investigated.'

She raised her eyebrows. 'That's interesting! We have never found the State Department to be so sentimental. What is your official job with them?'

The question flustered her a bit. 'I don't work for the government. I teach political science at Georgetown University, in Washington.'

'A full professor? At your age? You are what: twenty-six? Twenty-seven?'

'Twenty-eight.' She tried to say it nonchalantly but it sounded petulant. 'I'm an assistant professor, actually.'

'Ah! An assistant professor. Of course.' The lawyer leaned back in her chair. 'And what have they done for you here? They've given you the assistance of the FBI? Introduced you to the Minister of Justice?'

Athena swallowed. 'I'm mostly working with the Buenos Aires Provincial Police.'

'The police.'

'Yes. With a Comisario Fortunato, of the Brigada de Investigaciónes in San Justo. That was where the murder took place.'

The long-haired woman burst into a brief withering laugh. 'And has Comisario Fortunato been very helpful?'

She felt hemmed in. 'I think he's trying.'

'Then why are you coming to me?'

'Well . . .' Her professor had warned her that INCORP had an ideological bias, but she hadn't been prepared for this hostility. 'I do have some confidence in the Comisario, but I think even the police have limits.'

'I'm not sure what you are trying to tell me, Doctor Fowler,' Carmen said with a faint smile. 'Here we see the Buenos Aires police as tireless crusaders for Justice and Truth. Like the United States government itself.'

'Well . . .' Athena felt her face going red as she struggled for an answer. In her confusion she ended up mouthing something she knew was a lie even before she had finished saying it. 'I don't think they would send me here if they weren't serious about getting an answer to this murder.'

Carmen Amado gave her a friendly smile. 'Here is my advice, Señorita. I suggest you take a few cafés, do some shopping on Calle Florida and then, please, go home. Just go home. Go and write your report and get a citation from the State Department because here, we don't have time to entertain you. We are four lawyers against security forces that kill hundreds each year and abuse and extort money from tens of thousands. We are not interested in a phony investigation sponsored by the United States Department of State

43

for the purpose of convincing their own people of how virtuous they are.'

'But –'

'Go on. You don't need our services to please your employers.' She looked at her watch, then again at Athena. 'Please . . .'

Athena took a long breath but didn't move. She was close to bursting into tears, wavering between anger at the attack and the shame at having her motives stripped so bare. Carmen Amado had hit that one part of the truth so perfectly square that it momentarily eclipsed everything else. But it was only part of the truth, and if she couldn't get past it now then she might as well fold up the investigation and go home just as the lawyer had suggested.

'I think I need to make something clear to you,' she began quietly. 'I don't represent the United States government. I represent a five-year-old girl and a widow whose father and husband died a horrible death on a trip to Buenos Aires and came back as ashes in a plastic jar. That's who I represent.' She took a breath. 'And I assure you that woman has made every phone call and written every letter and begged favors from every stranger who would listen, all so that someone would come down here and find out why her husband was tortured and murdered in a country she's never even been to.' Athena felt a tear at the corner of her eye and brushed it away angrily. She could hear her voice fluttering up and down. 'And you're right! They deserve somebody better than me! I know that! Everybody knows it!' She stopped to compose herself again. 'But I'm the one who's here!' She wiped away another tear and then her voice was dead calm. 'So you tell me: should I go back and explain that you wouldn't help them because you don't like the United States government?'

The lawyer stared silently at her, shifted backwards in her chair. She considered a while, then took a packet of tissues from her desk and pushed them across to Athena. 'I'm sorry.' Her voice warmed up a little. 'Why don't you tell me about the crime. What was the victim's name?'

Athena felt relieved as she reached for the tissues. 'Robert Waterbury.'

She nodded. 'I remember that one.' She took out a cigarette and paused just before lighting it. 'It's okay?'

'Of course.'

Blowing a fog of blue smoke towards the open window: 'They found him in the car in San Justo, no? Shot several times, then

44

finished with a nine millimeter. That was the detail that captured me, the nine millimeter. That's the standard police bullet. Also, he was wearing handcuffs, which made me suspicious. You read the *expediente*, no? Do you remember the brand of handcuffs they used?' When Athena hesitated, Carmen said, 'Was it Eagle Security?'

'I think so.'

Carmen nodded. 'That's the brand the police use. Exported to them by one of your hardworking companies in New Jersey. The same company also sells them pepper spray, teargas, and metal detectors, also anti-riot gear, up to water cannons and armored trucks.' She smiled. 'But not the *picana electrica*, for torture. That is still *industria nacional*. In that respect, at least, we are resisting globalization.'

She waved the hand with the cigarette. 'But I'm sure your Comisario Fortunato told you this.'

Athena resisted the impulse to defend him. 'No, he didn't mention that.'

'All the same,' she said cheerfully, 'with fifty thousand nine millimeter pistols running around Buenos Aires province, there must be a few that don't belong to the police. What did the Comisario say?'

'The theory right now is that it was a settling of accounts between drug dealers. Or a drug deal that went bad.'

'Ah! The old "settling of accounts!" That's almost as popular as the "shot due to mistaken identity" line, and the classic "shot while attempting to escape!" They're very traditional in their literature, the police. They don't like New Fiction.' Her voice took on a girl-to-girl intimacy. '*Chica*, let me tell you about our defenders of the public well-being.'

She went down the list with the insistent cadence of a well-used speech: illegal imprisonment, torture, trigger-happy officers, and extra-judicial executions committed in cold blood. 'Eighty-eight percent of the population has a negative image of the police, and fifty percent fear them outright. Of every hundred robberies denounced, only one results in a conviction. Of every ten murders, three are solved. One quarter of all killings in Buenos Aires province are committed by the police themselves.'

'A quarter?' She tried to match that statistic with the half-dozen police she'd met in her day at the comisaria, and the face she came up with was the officer who had run over the dog and then shot it in the middle of the street.

The police, Carmen went on, had become a corporation, with an organized hierarchy and a sophisticated system of collection and distribution. Their loyalty was to the corporation, and officers suspected of disloyalty would end up marginalized, or even dead. 'In the last week, three policeman have been killed, all of them victims of "attempted robbery," while they were off-duty. That, *chica*, is a settling of accounts.'

Athena thought of the Comisario, with his kind face and his weary sigh. 'Well,' she tendered, 'don't you think there can be *some* good police?'

'No.' She could tell that the flat answer hadn't satisfied Athena. 'I tell you simply: no. Exemplary husbands, there might be. Loyal friends, gentle fathers. There must be. But not good policemen. And San Justo? Where your friend Fortunato is a Comisario? It's one of the most corrupt districts there are.'

Athena shook her head. 'But this man has investigated corrupt police himself. I think he wants to do good things. Maybe he's constrained by the system.' The lawyer didn't answer, and Athena went on hesitantly. 'But there are a few elements that make me uncomfortable.' She described the clues left unexplored, including the missing friend named Pablo at AmiBank and the phone number found in Waterbury's pocket: Teresa. 'It's frustrating, but since I'm here basically at their indulgence I'm not in a position to make any demands. I'm just hoping something will happen.'

The lawyer deliberated for a moment. 'Okay. *Athena*, no?'

'Athena.'

'Fine. Here is what I can offer you, Athena. If you will get the widow to retain INCORP as her representative, I can get a copy of the *expediente* and we can begin an investigation. But the papers take time. Perhaps you will have to return to Buenos Aires in a month.'

Athena's hopes spiraled downward again, and Carmen must have seen it. 'Or,' she added slowly, 'I have a friend who can perhaps help. He's a journalist who has written much about the police. A case like this might interest him.' She took out her address book and looked up a number, then dialed it: *Con Ricardo Berenski, por favor? De parte de Carmen Amado.* As she waited, 'Ricardo is half-famous here. Now he's working on an investigation of a businessman named Carlo Pelegrini.'

Athena recognized the name. 'I saw a couple of his articles.'

Ricardo had come to the phone and Carmen's voice became

playful. '*Amor*, I wanted to find you before Pelegrini's men do. *Sí, querido*. Every time I open the newspaper you're putting your foot in his ass. *Sí*. Look, Rici, I have a girl here from the United States investigating a murder of one of her countrymen. About four months ago. Yes, Robert Waterbury.' A pause. 'Me too. It had that odor . . .'

She made the arrangements to meet for a drink the following evening, then hung up and turned back to Athena. '*Bien*,' Carmen concluded, 'talk to the widow and we'll see.' She stood up and Athena stood up with her. 'And, *ojo*,' she said, tapping beneath her eye, 'be discreet.' She pointed to the phone, and Athena shuddered at her next words. 'They're listening.'

CHAPTER 6

The smell of the sulphur hissed into Fortunato's nostrils, and he set the votive candle next to his favorite picture of his wife. Marcela in black and white, at the age of twenty, a few days before they'd married at the Metallurgical Syndicate Hall. She'd just graduated from the teachers' college, a tall, big-boned woman with a lanky waist and fluid hips that he found intriguing and erotic for their strength as much as their feminine grace. He loved her handsome dark face, with its long Inca nose and framing tendrils of black hair. *Mi Negra*, he'd called her, or *India*. Her father had used his connections as secretary of the Union to get the hall at a discount, and had welcomed him into the family with a long toast filled with high-flown words and tears. As a cadet in the Academy, Fortunato was looking forward to a steady career and a decent pension at the end. The people had still liked the police in those days, before all that mess with the subversives made everything go rotten.

He looked around the room, whose objects implied his life in the same way that an *expediente* implied a crime. A portrait here or there, a souvenir *mate* purchased on a vacation to Cordoba. They were like pieces of evidence, but like all *expedientes* they lent themselves to a certain amount of fraud. Four little rooms in the suburbs of Villa Luzuriaga formed a paradoxical home for the Comisario of one of the most lucrative stations of the Buenos Aires police galaxy.

He went into the little kitchen and put a kettle of water on the stove. Maybe a *mate* would lift his spirits. He filled a gourd with herb and a silver straw, dousing it with lukewarm water and watching the pale green flakes swell. She could never bear to take her *mate* bitter, always insisted on sugar. *And cut me a little slice of lemon, Miguelito.* Now he drank it bitter every day.

He'd been severely depressed since Marcela's death, but it had started long before that when it first became apparent that her illness

48

lay beyond the power of doctors. The diagnosis had fallen, and when they went to the specialists in hope of some new information, it had fallen just the same, fallen again and again until it became inescapable. Marcela seemed to have accepted it before he did, counted her fifty-eight years as sufficient and prepared herself for the torture that would soon be meted out to her. For him, it had been harder to submit. He kept trying to make an arrangement.

'Old woman!' he'd said. 'They tell me there's a study that they're conducting in the United States that has had success . . .'

'And where are we going to get the money to go tramping around the United States? With your fifteen hundred pesos per month!'

'I'll borrow it,' he'd said, but he knew that with that stratagem she had trapped him. For years he had been accumulating money through his 'jobs' for the institution, and for years she had been refusing to acknowledge it. At home, he played the honest policeman.

It had been easy in the beginning. A traffic stop, some minor infraction either real or imagined. 'You just tell them the law,' Sub-Inspector Leon Bianco instructed him over a beer at La Gloria. 'It's up to them if they want to follow it.' And the law was always troublesome – there were the hours at the police station filling out papers, the inevitable check of *antecedentes*. And once *antecedentes* were examined, some tinge always came through. No one was ever innocent.

The problem was that Marcela did the family budget, and he didn't know exactly how to declare it to her.

'Look, Beauty, we have some extra money this month.'

'Extra? From where?'

He looked away and fought off a bashful uncertainty. 'It's a bit like this: with all the subversives around now, our jobs are much more dangerous than before, so sometimes individuals give us tips to keep extra careful watch over them.' It wasn't totally a lie: they did collect protection money from some of the businesses and factories.

'Oh?' Suspicious. 'Tell me from who? Who's giving you extra pay?'

'Marcela,' he said delicately, 'in the Institution, it's a little different from most jobs. They expect us to confront delinquents and subversives, but they pay us a miserable salary. So . . . To a point, we have to autofinance –'

Her face hardened and she recoiled from him, stepping on his

49

explanation. 'Don't start with that, Miguel! Don't even start! I didn't marry a corrupt policeman.'

He had tried to seduce her with appliances. First, a coffee-maker and, taking heart from that, a washing machine. A week later he arrived home to find an empty space where the machine had been. 'I gave it to the neighbor,' she said airily.

After that he stashed the money in a safety deposit box in the Banco de la Nación and bided his time. He began collecting from lottery sellers and pimps, devising meticulous schedules filled with names and check-marks. In three years he had ascended to the brigadas, the plain-clothes groups that conducted intelligence operations and mounted raids. He became expert in working with *buchones*, stool pigeons who could be reeled in on a moment's notice to face some ancient charge hanging over their heads. He unraveled auto theft networks and raided illegal casinos, bordellos, marijuana stockpiles. When he brought in a killer of three children the newspaper put his name on the front page and the mayor of Buenos Aires gave him a citation. Those were good operations; it was clear who the bad guys were. He noted the shine of admiration in the faces of the younger officers, imagined he could hear them discussing him as they lounged about the streets. 'That's the Fortunato who found the kidnapped girl in San Martin. It's he who caught the rapist that violated six women.' Marcela worried pleasingly for his safety. As far as she knew, he was the most incorruptible policeman in Buenos Aires.

The money kept accumulating. He'd assumed that when they had children she would see the way clear to use the money for their sake. But they had no luck with children, in spite of the tests and the prayers to the Virgin of Lujan. Their best hopes went away in a pool of blood when Marcela miscarried a little girl at the sixth month, in that long, bad year of 1976 when martial law came down and the army slapped Argentina senseless with a hard, flat hand. Then they offered him a different sort of work.

Sub-Comisario Bianco called him into his office. 'Miguel, we're going to pinch one of the subversives tonight at his house. Why don't you come and lend a hand?'

The Communists were everywhere in those days. Not only with guns, but, equally dangerously, in the labor unions and the university. They liked to hide behind the democratic institutions, talking of exploitation and class war, but now the military had decided to tear away the Constitution and show them what war was all about.

The target that night was a member of the autoworkers syndicate at the Ford factory. The factory manager, as a patriotic service, had identified him as a persistent troublemaker in labor matters and 'probably a Communist.' This was explained to Fortunato in a few sentences by Sub-Comisario Bianco, at that time with jet-black hair and a crisp military manner. The operation was to go to the house at three in the morning and grab him in his bed. 'You just follow along,' Bianco explained. 'Nothing's going to happen. He'll go quietly. He's got three children there.'

The subversive lived in a small apartment behind his parents' house, much like Fortunato's. Fortunato rode over with Bianco and three other agents in a Ford Falcon. It was summer, but they were wearing suits. They stopped outside the door and lined up, two of the men on either side of the door with submachine guns, while the rest of them drew their pistols and stood back and to the side.

Bianco stepped up to the door and pounded on it three times with all his strength. 'Open up!' he screamed. 'Police!' There was a sound of rustling inside, and a baby started crying. Bianco pounded again. 'Open it! Open it!' He stepped back, summoning his energies, and Fortunato thought he heard a timid voice say, 'I'm coming!'

Too late. Bianco fired a round into the lock and then hurled himself against the panel. The door burst open right into the face of the wife, knocking her down and bringing a gout of blood from her nose. Bianco was already beside himself. 'Whore! I said open it!' The other plainclothes men came flowing through after him, into the darkened bedroom with their guns drawn, shouting. They found two children cowering in the bed, along with the crying baby. The husband wasn't there.

'Where is he?' Bianco screamed.

The woman was crying. 'I don't know. He went to watch a football game with some friends!'

Bianco grabbed her by her hair and pulled her to her feet. 'Talk to me straight, whore, or you're all going in.' She stuck to her story, cowering, despite the blows and the threats and the gathering intensity of Bianco's fury. *For the love of God he went to a football game!* Finally Bianco lost his temper completely. 'Bring me the boy!'

A soldier brought out a little boy, perhaps six years old, and Bianco grabbed his arm, making him cry out. 'Where is your father?

Where?' He beat the child across the face with the flat of his hand and then gave him such a blow to the head that he went sprawling across the floor. Next he demanded the girl, a bit younger, and beat her as she cried out without comprehension. By now the woman was hysterical, but nonetheless seemed to know nothing about her husband's whereabouts. 'No?' Bianco demanded, beside himself. 'No?' He grabbed the baby from the woman's arms and held it upside down by its feet, swaying it back and forth slightly and delivering sharp slaps across its back. The baby, only a few weeks old, was screaming in its tiny hoarse voice, so far gone that it could no longer catch its breath. 'Where is he?' he asked, slapping the baby again. 'Where is he?'

At this the mother began to sing, naming his sister, his brother, his friends from the union, any possible place he might be, knowing only that he had gone out to watch a football game! That he was for River! That he sometimes bet five pesos! They called in reinforcements to raid the houses she had named and sat down to wait. Fortunato was ringing with shock, watching in disbelief as one of the plainclothes men began to catalog all the appliances and furniture in the little apartment. Twenty minutes later the husband came home and they arrested him without a struggle. Bianco made a phone call. In the end they took them all away, the mother and children crying softly. After that soldiers came in and started loading the furniture onto an army truck. 'See,' Bianco told him, dismissing his initial worries about the operation. 'Nothing happened!'

In the next days Marcela found him distracted and moody, and he finally unraveled the story as they sipped on a morning *mate*. 'They were subversives, of course, or at least, the father was . . .' He let the sentence trail off, and she didn't answer.

She sat silently for a half-minute, looking at the floor, then hid her face in her hands and shook. 'It's so horrible!' She sobbed for a minute without control, then took her hands away from her wet face. 'Don't get in with those people, Miguel! I'm begging you! Or someday . . .' with a shudder, 'you'll be the one beating the baby.'

He heeded her, ducking Bianco's summons for other *operativos* until Bianco finally stopped inviting him. The Sub-Comisario treated him with a tinge of scorn after that, as if Fortunato lacked the necessary masculinity to own up to the task. In contrition, he'd devoted himself to the three things required for advancement in the force: he collected money, he arrested criminals and he protected his friends. The field became smooth again. Now Bianco had ascended to Comisario General, atop the División de Investigaciónes, and he had taken his friend Fortunato up the ladder with him.

Fortunato finished his *mate* and went to his bedroom to dress for the evening. From the large wooden wardrobe he selected his best jacket, a fine Italian wool woven in large black and white houndstooth checks. Marcela had gotten it for his birthday twenty years ago at a high priced store in the center, even though he insisted they could get the same thing cheaper in the suburbs. He still remembered the jacket's magical radiance when he'd worn it out of the store, not realizing that two decades later the small lapels and bold pattern had gone ludicrously out of fashion. He matched it with a crimson tie and his black loafers, fished an old pair of cuff-links from a little box on the shelf. Peering into his wallet he was dismayed to find it a bit light. One should always have a bit extra for an evening out.

He pulled a screwdriver from his night table and quickly unscrewed the floor of the wardrobe, prying it carefully up from a thin groove he'd cut in the corner. Looking back at him from beneath the panel, in orderly rows of tight green bundles, sat half-a-million dollars in United States currency.

The money had accumulated almost by itself, secreted into the little space when Marcela was out. He had dispensed some of it to needy fellow policemen or to crime victims who especially moved him. The children near the police station knew him as an infallible source of toys and sweets. But still it kept piling up, nearly filling the compartment allotted to it so that soon he would need to start a new compartment.

What good had it done him, really? Even at the end, with Marcela, when he invented a new fiction of a special medical fund for policemen's families, she'd refused. 'It already *is*, Miguel. I prefer to die with dignity in my home, not chasing after impossible hopes.'

He sat on the bed, looking at the neat compartments into which he had divided his life. In the other half of the wardrobe behind the closed door, Marcela's clothes would be hanging just as she'd left them, her shoes arranged in tidy pairs at the bottom, her hats on top. Some men carried on affairs, or even had a second family in another part of town. His infidelity had been different; he had cheated with an ideal instead of with another woman, and kept faithful to the lie that they'd shared, the lie of the honest cop and his schoolteacher wife. And then had come Waterbury, and cancer.

He opened Marcela's half of the wardrobe and the scent of lilac powder came rushing over him. Fortunato wept at the sight of her dresses.

An hour later, he strapped on his Browning nine millimeter and left for the 17 Stone Angels.

CHAPTER 7

Athena was waiting for him in the lobby of the Sheraton in a white silk blouse, her face shining with a bashful eagerness. Appropriate, he supposed, for an evening with a man twenty-five years her senior. One wanted to be well-dressed, but not too alluring.

She seemed slightly nervous as they walked to the car. 'What a custom you have here, eating dinner at midnight!'

'Here we eat late, Athena. The trick is, you need a little siesta. Then you wake up, drink a *cafecito*, and there you are.'

They got into the Fiat Uno and headed down to La Boca. The autumn evening had a blood warmth, still retaining a trace of that humid softness that seasoned the air during summer. It streamed across Fortunato's face like a swath of velvet. The streets of Palermo looked exceptionally beautiful, with the plane trees casting out pale green platters into the canopy of branches that arched overhead. The splendid old townhouses gave the smaller streets an intimate sense of material contentment, as if the lives they held inside abounded in orderly but sensual comfort. The bigger apartment buildings in this bastion of the upper-middle class showed off well-lit lobbies behind walls of plate glass. One imagined cocktail parties served by a white-jacketed barman with slick black hair. Both sides of the street were lined with balconies trailing vines and houseplants, and from a few of them the blue exhalation of grilling meat was drifting upward. On nearly every corner a bustling neighborhood café threw a warm glow into the street.

'This is Palermo,' he explained to her. 'This is a barrio of the middle class and above, though lately it has become very fashionable.'

'It's beautiful,' the Doctora said.

'The Porteño enjoys the life of the street,' he explained. 'See all the balconies? People like to let the air flow in, to hear the sounds and to look out.'

He saw her watching the well-attired people who strolled tranquilly, or raised their glasses in the golden light of a restaurant.

'Forgive me, Athena, I'm very content that you've come and I have great hopes for our investigation, but I still do not understand why they have sent a human rights expert such as yourself and not someone from the FBI.'

The girl tried to be *piola*, but he could sense a stiffness in her explanation. 'I think that's internal politics, Miguel. The State Department found it more convenient to approach it as a matter of human rights because of jurisdictions and that type of thing.'

Fortunato relaxed. She really meant what the Chief had already said: the gringos didn't care. Why else would they send a woman with no authority and no credentials? 'Of course. There's always politics. But here is Avenida Corrientes.'

The street became a river of light. Theatrical posters displayed manic actors with comic smiles, and a dozen bookstores had rolled their wooden shelves onto the sidewalk. At eleven-thirty, the cafés were packed and lively.

'This is the theater district. As you can see, the people of Buenos Aires like to live fully. At one in the morning, it is the same.'

'Wow!'

'This is a city with its own culture,' he went on. 'There are many famous writers: Borges, Bioy-Casares, Julio Cortazar, Roberto Arldt.' Fortunato knew the names through Marcela's crumbling paperbacks. 'Also, Buenos Aires has its own music and dance: the tango. We have our own food, our own dialect, called *lunfardo*.'

They rounded the big white obelisk that pointed to the pink-infused sky, turned onto the Avenida 9 de Julio. 'This is the widest street in the world,' he told her. 'Fourteen lanes in each direction. Look there . . .' He pointed across the vast Plaza de la Republica to where an American hamburger chain had hooked two huge outlets onto the street amongst the restaurants and traditional businesses. 'That should make you feel at home.'

'People actually go there?'

'Sí, Señorita!' he said. 'There are every day more in Buenos Aires. And others like them. Also Wal-Mart and Carrefour: many big corporations from the exterior. Little by little they go eating the old businesses.'

They streamed down the 9 de Julio with a thousand other cars, some, he thought, with false papers like his, most others slightly out of order, with some little *coima* paid to get them through the inspection. Buenos Aires, the city of the *arrangement*. And he, a citizen in full.

She was looking all around. 'This is really marvelous, Miguel. Thank you for bringing me.'

'Now we're coming into La Boca. It's called La Boca because it's near the port, which was the mouth of Buenos Aires.'

Here the buildings became low and ramshackle. Many were armored with corrugated tin, two-story shacks without balconies or decoration, as if they'd been cut out of sardine cans. They looked tight and mean. 'These are *conventillos*. Here live many poor people. This part of the city can be a bit dangerous.'

They continued through the narrow streets, past fluorescent-lit cafés and dark wooden bars, huddles of rough-looking men with faces inclined towards televised football games. Fortunato parked the car and gave a little boy permission to watch it for him. '17 Stone Angels,' he said as they approached a single-story building. 'Look up there . . .'

He pointed to the roofline where a long row of the mythical beings looked down from amidst molded sprays of lilies and garlanded escutcheons. Some glared down with turbulent eyes and frothy beards, others smiled, laughed coyly, or turned their lips down at the impulse of some sorrowful mineral thought. Sixteen of them, progressing from sadness at one side to laughter at the other, the whole range of emotion that a life might encompass. Largest of all loomed the one over the entrance, the seventeenth, seeming masculine at one moment and feminine the next, its identity obscured by a blindfold that covered its eyes.

'The owner claims that they were originally carved for the *Palacio de Justicia* in the last century, but the official in charge of the contract found a reason to reject them. The reality was that he'd taken a bribe to award the contract to someone else. Somehow they ended up here.'

Athena stared up at the outsize statues. 'So the blindfolded one is Justice?'

'Yes,' Fortunato said with a trace of humor. 'Because she never sees anything.' Athena looked at him dubiously and he added, 'For the same reason, my wife used to insist that it represented Love.'

*

57

Fortunato had been coming to the 17 Stone Angels for decades now. He used to come with Marcela. Every Thursday they'd gone to the club in the barrio to dance, and every two weeks they had made the drive here, to La Boca, where the tango had been born, to dance and chat away the night with other regulars over bottles of red wine and soda. He didn't know exactly why they kept coming. Other than its grandiose facade, the place itself had little to set it apart from a thousand other poor bars in the city. Fluorescent lights bounded off plaster walls, while a mirror of tarnished silver doubled bottles of grappa and mysterious spirits that Fortunato suspected dated to the last century. Some immigrant carpenter had hammered the bar together a hundred years ago out of tropical woods from the North, without pretensions to beauty but plenty strong enough to support the slouch of a *guapo* coolly watching the proceedings or a body shoved up against it in a brawl. Uncountable *milongas* had been stepped out by easy women and questionable men, and Fortunato could still feel the presence, in the islands of stained white table-cloths, of that vanished demi-monde.

At midnight, Los Angeles de Piedra had just begun to percolate. Mostly older people, like himself, but also a sprinkling of curious young people who had discovered the place in the last couple of years. He hadn't been here since Marcela had gotten too sick to dance, some three months ago. Even so, he could see at a glance that everyone had found out.

'*Capitan!*' Norberto said as he came in the door. The owner kissed him on the cheek then continued talking softly with his arm around his neck. 'I'm so sorry about Marcela. All of us, we heard the news and we didn't know what to do! We thought we'd lost you! Did you get the flowers that we sent to the comisaria?'

'Thank you, Norberto. I received them. It was a comfort.' He turned to the gringa. 'Norberto, this is Doctora Fowler, a friend of mine visiting from the United States. She's here for some police matters,' he clarified, to allay any speculation.

La Doctora was examining the place, and from what Fortunato could tell she looked pleased. He couldn't get his balance with the gringa. She seemed very self-contained, vaguely prosecutorial, but at the same time he thought he could perceive a tenderness that animated her beneath that surface.

They conferred over the menu and he ordered them a mixed grill, 'the most Argentine,' and Norberto brought bottles of red wine and soda along with a small metal bucket of ice. La Doctora crunched on a bread stick while Fortunato poured out her wine and lightened it with a shot of soda. He dropped in an ice cube, then prepared the same for himself. At a corner table the musicians were downing coffee, whiskey and cigarettes.

He leaned towards her. 'There are the musicians, over there. A violin, a guitar, and a *bandoneon*.' She looked at him, puzzled, and he searched for the word. 'An . . . accordion. This is not a tourist place,' he said. 'The tourists go to Carlito's where everything is fine. This place is more . . . tango.' He told her the history of tango, that it had originated in the Andalusian tangos of the 1850s, then developed in whorehouses here in La Boca and in the southern suburbs at the turn of the twentieth century. Tango was a dance of the underworld, of pimps and prostitutes, of poor men losing their girlfriends to millionaires, of lost connections to the barrio, of knife fights between *guapos* –

'What's a *guapo*?'

'*Guapo* is *lunfardo* for a hard young man who uses a knife. Tango is full of *lunfardo*. It's going to cost you to understand what they are saying, but I'll help you.' He bit into a breadstick and continued his thought. 'Tango is all like that: about love, violence, memory . . .' He took a sip of his wine. 'Corruption. It has much that is dark and bitter, because life is thus.' He leaned toward her and hushed his voice. 'This here isn't the *best* tango – they're all spent here, you'll see – but this is the *soul* of tango, where it began.' He nodded towards Osvaldo, a man of about sixty whose shaved head and jet-black eyebrows enhanced the menacing aura that glittered from his gap-toothed smile and his gold chain. Fortunato leaned in towards Athena Fowler. 'That man over there. He's managed women his whole life. Also, he was famous as a knife fighter. Now he's getting old, like us all. He carries a little gun in his belt. The other with him is a *puntero* of the barrio. A dealer of cocaine. And it's all in the music. There's tangos about the pimp, and about cocaine. There's tangos about men like that' – motioning towards another table – 'sitting with their whiskey and their smoke, looking sad. There's tangos about bars like Los 17 Angeles de Piedra.'

Osvaldo the pimp saw Fortunato looking and raised his thumb towards him 'What do you say, Capitan!'

'Here in the battle, Osvaldo, as always.'

'I'm sorry about Marcela,' the pimp hollered across the room.

'Thus is life,' Fortunato said, returning to La Doctora.

'Everybody seems to know you.'

'I used to come here often.' He sat back, suddenly uncomfortable. 'My wife and I would come here to dance.'

Her face filled with compassion again. 'I'm sorry,' she said.

Fortunato shrugged. 'There are even tangos about the dead wife.'

The grill came, a charcoal brazier topped with ribs, a steak, a half chicken, a pork sausage, a blood sausage, tripe, liver and, as a special gift to him, a soft crispy piece of *mollejas*, the sweetbreads. Brown and purple and beige, meat colors, glistening with oil. La Doctora looked at it with amazement as Norberto stood it on their table. 'We can't eat all this!'

'This is a poor neighborhood. Nothing will get thrown away.'

The musicians took their places now and the guitarist closed his eyes and tuned his instrument as they began to eat. They launched into a *milonga*, a lively dancing tango, and a few couples got up and began moving across the floor. La Doctora was watching them. 'It's different from the tangos you see on television.'

'Those are show,' the detective said dismissively. 'This is tango of the barrio.' Luis and Yolanda were dancing, each of them looking to the side and keeping a stiff back as they advanced and whirled and retreated. Luis was marking her well, moving her from side to side, and never missing a step. They were light and fluid, perfectly entwined. 'Notice that the woman's steps and the man's steps are completely different, but they match perfectly. He advances, she retreats. She moves to the side, and he closes her off. In tango, the man rules. He leads her, but he allows her to be a woman.' He knew that in the United States, they saw things differently. 'That's how it is here.'

'My father could tango.'

'You don't say!'

Her father, it seemed, had been quite the dancer in his youth. At family gatherings he would put on his old records and teach her a few steps. Fortunato had the silly idea of asking her to dance, but just then the music ended and someone got up to sing. Gustavo, a retired sailor of at least eighty years, in a dandruff-covered black suit, mangling 'Silencio'. The withered old man sang with one skinny hand in front of his chest and the other trembling out at the side, stretching the dramatic notes like pieces of taffy. La Doctora watched with an amazed smile as he missed note after note.

'He's the worst!' Fortunato whispered under the music, 'but he's a friend. And he keeps singing!'

The song dated from after the First World War. It was about a woman who had seven sons who were all killed in the fields of France, leaving at last a terrible silence in the soul. As Gustavo was flinging his hand out for the climactic line, Fortunato felt a tap on the shoulder. Chief Bianco was standing over him, smiling.

'Miguel!'

'*Jefe!*' Fortunato rose to his feet.

The Chief was wearing his ivory dinner jacket, which meant he had come to sing. His wife, Gladys, stood behind him, stuffed into printed flowers. Fortunato made the introductions and everyone kissed. He invited the Biancos to sit down.

'I'm glad to see you out,' Gladys said sympathetically. 'We've missed you here.'

'Thus is life,' Fortunato answered, trying to inject the proper weight into the tired reply.

'Retard!' Bianco scolded. 'Why did you take Señorita Fowler to this place when Soriano is singing at Carlito's!'

'Ah!' Fortunato waved his hand. 'It's full of tourists.'

'You're right.' The Chief addressed La Doctora, knocking his fist on the table. 'This is the real tango! Without artifice or illusion!' He noticed the pimp and pointed at him. 'What say, *loco*?'

The bald man's teeth sparkled. 'Here listening to the maestros, *General*!' Nodding to Gladys: 'Señora!'

'And . . .' Bianco focused his square gold-framed bifocals again on La Doctora. 'How is Buenos Aires? How is the Waterbury case?'

'You're familiar with the Waterbury case?'

'Of course!' the Chief said. 'That case is known at all levels. We're very interested in seeing you and Comisario Fortunato solve it.' He got a pained look on his face. 'But you left very little time!'

'Leon is the Comisario General of the Dirección de Investigaciónes,' Fortunato explained. 'That's a position of some rank.'

La Doctora didn't react to his importance. 'What do you think about the Waterbury case?'

He turned to Fortunato. 'It was a matter of drugs, no, Miguel? Drug deals go bad all the time. One side wants more, or someone gets tired of waiting for his money. Possibly this Waterbury tried to get a lot of money fast, and he got in with people he shouldn't have trusted. That's common. The jails are full of retards who had a bright idea that couldn't go wrong.'

'But why would they kill him over cocaine and leave the cocaine in the car?'

'That was an accident,' the Chief said.

'Athena,' Fortunato added slowly, addressing her informally for the first time, 'the criminal world has much to do with chance. Outside of novels and films, there are few criminal geniuses. Often the plan is like this: go into the place, take out a gun, get the money, and go. Very primitive. Then things go wrong. Unexpected things happen. People appear without warning or the victim acts in unforeseen ways, and then things develop on their own account. What I mean is, we can't be sure that there was a clear motive for this murder.'

'What is sure is that we will do everything possible!' the Chief said firmly, dropping his fist on the table. 'The victim had children, no?'

'One daughter.'

'*Dios mio!*' Gladys said.

Bianco shook his head silently, lost in visions of revenge. 'A policeman can't make promises,' he said at last. 'But before this finishes . . .' He swiped the matter aside with his open hand. 'We shouldn't have entered into this subject. It puts me in a bad way, and I don't want to ruin the evening. Monday I'll get a copy of the *expediente* and we'll see if I can give a hand. Norberto!' the Chief hollered. 'Champagne. Get me the national. The *chica* must try the national, so she can see that we have nothing to apologize to the French for!'

Gustavo had rested and now launched into the sentimental 'Cafetin de Buenos Aires,' barking out in sonorous tones his melancholy recollections of the café where he learned about life.

'He's doing better with this one,' the Chief commented. 'He's warming up.'

The champagne came and they toasted La Doctora's arrival in Buenos Aires, then it was the Chief's turn to sing.

The sight of the Chief up there with his white performer's jacket always struck Fortunato as slightly humorous, even after these many years. Bianco cleared his throat and took a long drink of water. ' "Mano a Mano," ' he told the musicians sternly, and they launched into the classic, now some seventy years old. As the chief began

62

singing, his face took on a look of haughty strength, verging on arrogance. He was making a perfect *cara de policia*.

'This is one of the most classic,' Fortunato explained.

'I can't understand it.'

'There is much *lunfardo*. The theme is thus: the singer loses his woman to the rich playboys. She throws their money to the passing crowd like a lazy cat playing with a miserable mouse. The man is crushed, but he resists. He says, when you are old and ugly, and they've put you out on the street like used furniture, don't forget your friend, who will still help you with advice, a loan, or in any way he can.' Fortunato gave her a soft look. 'He still loves her.'

The gringa cocked her head and her guarded features warmed to the romantic sentiment. 'That's beautiful.'

'Yes,' he answered, 'it's beautiful.'

The Chief sat down to applause and launched into a long discourse on tango and the deleterious moral effect of *rockandroll*. The grill disappeared and Fortunato ordered more wine. The Chief asked Athena to dance and after some initial stumbles she repeated the basic step over and over again for two minutes. Fortunato enjoyed her bashful smile as he danced past her with Bianco's wife, and on the next number, as something inevitable, he took her in his arms. A formal approach, fingers touching, his other hand politely behind her shoulder. He tried to downplay his embarrassment by lading her with compliments and teaching her another step, and in their mutual discomfort she lost her enigmatic distance and became a young woman in a bar in Buenos Aires, dancing with a man old enough to be her father. For an instant, he wanted to kiss her.

They left at three, when the coffee could no longer hold off her exhaustion. The bookstores on Corrientes had closed and the furtive elements of the city were flitting in the darker passages. Gangs of street children at Plaza Misereres lounged half-naked and wild, looking for a victim, while the base of a grand statue crawled with spray-painted slogans against the International Monetary Fund. Athena hadn't said anything in a long time, and Fortunato's absurd situation came down on him again. Waterbury's murder. His wife's death. And him between the fangs of both those events. He looked over at La Doctora; her head had lolled back against the seat, her mouth half-open in the sleep of the innocent. She looked young and childlike as the shadows skated over her skin.

'It's so easy for you,' he confided softly. 'You eat a few beefsteaks, make your report and go home. Us, we have to go on living in this whorehouse.'

CHAPTER 8

The next morning Fortunato had a busy round of police work. An overloaded lumber truck had rolled over two months before and seriously injured a pedestrian. Now the insurance company wanted the *expediente* to disappear. 'Fifteen thousand,' Fortunato told their lawyer. 'And follow the safety regulations next time.' They'd picked up a *puntero* the previous day, and his lawyer had come in to make the arrangements before they officially recorded the arrest. 'Two thousand five hundred,' Fortunato said. Meanwhile, a string of burglaries on the western edge of the district indicated that someone was robbing on their own account, and Fortunato put Inspector Nicolosi on it. Nicolosi could be depended on to plod doggedly behind the criminals until an arrest was made. A good man, Nicolosi, but he had one defect that made it impossible to trust him: he was honest.

In the midst of it Fabian appeared at the door. Today he approached the fringe of respectability in a burgundy jacket with a black turtleneck, but a flashy bronze medallion hanging by a thick chain dispersed the effect.

'What's happening with the chain, Fabian?'

'The style of the Sixties is coming back, Comi. If I'm going to circulate among the youth and find –'

Fortunato held up his hand. 'No, Fabian. Save the verses for the adolescents at the dance clubs. I have things to do.'

'Precisely, Comisario, And for this, I have come to offer my help.' Fabian stepped into the office and closed the door behind him. He flashed a brief Romeo smirk. 'As you are a man that has many responsibilities, I thought perhaps I should help La Doctora with this matter of Waterbury.' He raised his hands defensively. 'Knowing, of course, that this is something to be approached, as you say, *tranquilamente*, and that you have your own sources of information,

I thought that in the spirit of, can I say, *entertaining* La Doctora, to show that we are good hosts, I could donate some of my time, perhaps familiarize her with the methods of the Buenos Aires police, with the city and its cultural treasures –'

Fortunato pointed to the door. 'Go, Romeo. Go.'

'It was a suggestion!' he said, backpedaling.

'Go.'

'She's a pretty girl, Comi!'

'Go!'

La Doctora spent the morning in the conference room looking over the *expediente*. Fortunato checked on her periodically to offer her coffee or answer questions. She was filling page after page with notes, an activity which made Fortunato apprehensive. In the afternoon they embarked on a round of field trips. First, they went to meet with Judge Duarte, who had been the On-Duty judge when Waterbury's body had turned up. Duarte had the manner for this job: fair-skinned and severe, about fifty, he spoke little and gave off an air of unshakeable integrity. He wore the accolades of the Sociedad Juridica and the Rotary Club on his office wall. But Duarte was no working stiff. He was clever at designing investigations which studiously avoided the obvious, or seeding them with technical violations that would invalidate the case in court. And when it was time for a case to go to sleep. Duarte could send it to the bottom more permanently than the *Titanic*.

His performance that afternoon reached its usual high standard. Even when La Doctora obviously overplayed her hand, calling on the righteous indignation of her government, Duarte didn't break character.

'Speaking on behalf of the United States,' La Doctora said, 'we are disappointed that so little effort was made to solve this case.'

A less disciplined man might have at least smiled, but Duarte even managed to reflect her outrage back to her. 'I too am disappointed!' Pointing to the huge stack of *expedientes* awaiting prosecution, some of which were earning him a healthy fee for their lassitude: 'But look at the case load they give me! All of these people are waiting for justice. Some of them are guilty and some, surely, are innocent. So on one hand, I have an unidentified body with chalks of cocaine and no suspect, and on the other some poor man, perhaps innocent, sitting in a *calabozo* for a year waiting for his trial. Whose case should I advance?'

He returned to the difficulties at hand: the lack of conclusive forensic evidence, the absence of witnesses or associates to provide information.

A trace of inquisitorial fire came to her eyes. 'Why weren't his old contacts at AmiBank interviewed? This *Pablo*: he might know something! Why didn't anyone call his wife to see if she had pertinent information? Those seem like the most basic elements of an investigation! Why weren't those things done?'

Duarte listened to her attentively, sidestepping the threat. 'What we need in this country are ten thousand more people like you, Doctora. Then, yes, perhaps we could get the resources we need. My voice is hoarse from asking for them.' He offered a truce. 'But now we have the undivided attention of Comisario Fortunato, a man of much experience and excellent reputation. Remember that the Comisario directs some forty men, yet he is taking time from his own investigative work and his administrative duties to render assistance to you.' He shrugged. 'And don't forget that as a consequence, someone else's case is sitting without attention.'

La Doctora seemed frustrated but she said nothing more. They exchanged stiff goodbyes and Fortunato brought her to the scene of the crime, now overgrown with a summer's worth of weeds and their blown stalks. Ferocious thistles and grasses reached to the waist, a little piece of the old pampa trying to reinstate itself on its ancestral lands. They got out and walked around. In the bright afternoon light the shuttered factories had lost their fearsome desolation. La Doctora put her hands on her hips and stared again at the spot where Waterbury had been finished, as if trying to insert the dark tableaus of the murder photos into the sunny lot. She strode out to the sidewalk and looked up and down the half-abandoned street. 'I don't know, Miguel.'

He could sense her frustration, and he thought for a moment she was going to make an open accusation about the way the investigation had been handled. She started to say something about Duarte and then held herself back, lapsing into silence. Things were not going well. She was showing an unpleasant determination to get beneath the surface, and if she became too militant she might complain loudly enough to bring in the FBI and the Federales.

'I live only a few miles from here,' the Comisario said at last. 'Why don't you come to the house? We'll take a *mate* and try to figure what direction to go next.'

*

He left the car on the street outside his kitchen window and returned the silent wave given by the woman across the way. Marcela had always had good relations with the neighbors, but things had gone rotten a few years ago when the police had shot one of the neighborhood teenagers dead under suspicious circumstances and Fortunato had appeared in the newspaper defending the officer. He'd had no choice, he told Marcela: a comisario had to back up his men. Besides, the boy had been up to *something*. When Marcela died, no one had come to offer him condolences.

He unlocked the door and they stepped into the cool, dim interior. He put a kettle of water on the stove.

'Is this your wife?' the young woman said from the dining room.

'Marcela,' he answered.

'She was a pretty woman. She looks like she had a good sense of humor.'

'She had a marvelous humor!' Fortunato said, remembering her big laugh. 'She was very rapid with jokes. And a very good dis-position. If you knew her you would say: 'What is this woman doing with this dead man?' She was a sort of antidote to my professional life, which can become very heavy, dealing with delinquents and crime all day. Do you want to hear some music?'

He went to his shelf and selected one of the black vinyl discs he and Marcela had collected over the years. Astor Piazzola with his so-called New Tango. He liked to tease Marcela by calling it Bad Tango, but the magazines said it had found a certain acceptance in the exterior, so he put it on.

'Astor Piazzola!' La Doctora exclaimed after the first few bars.

'My wife liked this disc,' he said. 'I prefer his earlier style, when he played with Anibal Troilo.' He wet the leaves of the herb with warm water, then added a slice of lemon.

'Did your wife work?' La Doctora said, floating before the pictures. She seemed to be examining the articles of the house casually, but with intent.

'She was a teacher. She taught primary school. Her students loved her. Even in the last year, we couldn't go walking without a student coming up to her, now grown up but excited, like a child: "Señora Jimenez! I was your student in the fourth grade!" And she'd say, like to a little one, "Ah! *Chico!*" and they'd leave so content! She was . . .' He wanted to finish with some superlative, but he felt himself being overcome and he let it trail off. 'Thus is life, young one,' he said at last.

He poured the first water into the *mate* and then sucked it out with the straw, spitting it into the sink. 'It's too strong at first,' he explained, then sprinkled sugar on top. He poured the second water, passing the frothy gourd to her. 'You drink all of it and pass it back,' he said. She put her mouth hesitantly to the silver straw and began sucking, looking like a little girl with a soda. 'There's a whole language to the *mate*,' he explained. 'Long ago, if the gaucho came to visit a young woman she would prepare him a *mate*. If she used old herb, bitter and half cold, better that he rides on. But if she made him a fresh *mate*, sweet and with foam, well,' with the trace of a smile, 'that was a bit more promising.'

She wrinkled her brow, the straw still between her lips. 'It tastes like grass cuttings!'

Fortunato rolled his eyes and muttered to the ceiling: 'Why did they send me this gringa?'

She laughed and then finished the *mate*, and he filled it for himself.

'Forgive me, Athena, but you said your father died recently of cancer. What kind was it?'

'The liver. He lasted about three months after the diagnosis.'

He shook his head. '*Terrible*. What was he like, your father?'

She thought quietly for a moment. 'You would have liked him. He was very modest. Very generous. He worked for an insurance company. Part of his job was investigating fraudulent claims.'

'Ah! A species of police.'

'In some senses. But he had problems at the end because his company was acquired by another company. The new company was much more aggressive in denying claims, even those he thought were legitimate. They forced him to retire when he testified against them in a lawsuit. After that, at sixty, his options were limited.'

Fortunato thought about it a moment. 'But he never regretted his decision, no?'

'Never.' Her gaze fell into a broken smile. 'But I didn't understand all that until later. I used to ridicule him for being a company man.'

'It's forgivable. Perhaps from him you get your passion for the truth.' He handed her the gourd again. 'Sometimes, when someone important dies, it makes one look inside and crystallize what one really wants to do in life. For you, being so young, at least the pain has this value. You still have time to act.'

'And you?'

'My father died when I was eight. Nothing clear remained.'

'What about your wife? Has her death made you reconsider anything?'

'Reconsider?' The question swelled in the intimate kitchen to an intensity far more profound than Fortunato had been prepared for. He recoiled from it, coming to his feet to fetch some cookies from the cupboard. 'I'm nearly the age of your father when he retired,' he said, bringing the packet to the table. 'At my altitude you only reconsider whether to have meat sauce or olive oil on your pasta.'

Athena took a cookie and bit it in half, tossing her head to the side. That part of the discussion had ended. 'As far as the investigation,' she began, 'I want to find out more about what Robert Waterbury was doing here before he was murdered. His wife said he used to see an old friend from his AmiBank days. His name was Pablo. If we could find him he might be able to tell us something.'

There she went with AmiBank again! AmiBank, who the newspapers said was a rival of Carlo Pelegrini! Fortunato remembered following Waterbury to a meeting at AmiBank during the surveillance. Athena was right: Pablo might indeed be able to tell them something. He took his mouth from the straw. 'And Pablo's last name?'

'She didn't know. Only Pablo something.'

'Does he still work there?'

'His wife didn't know.'

He cocked his head thoughtfully. 'It's a good idea. But there are many Pablos in Buenos Aires, and we don't know if this one used to work for AmiBank or another bank. We could perhaps check the AmiBank records of a decade ago, and make inquiries at their headquarters in New York. With time . . . Of course. You are here for a month? Six weeks?'

'A week. Officially.'

He turned down the corner of his mouth with the disillusion of one betrayed. 'It's very little.' He let it rest as he sipped the *mate*, then continued. 'But I see another way to proceed, that will perhaps be faster.' La Doctora raised her eyebrows hopefully. 'Let me speak to you frankly. Here in Buenos Aires, the technical facilities are very limited. It's rare that a case is solved with fingerprints and such things. More than that, a good policeman must develop his network of informants. It's a particular skill. And being of this barrio, working here many years,' he cocked his head, 'my sources are not so bad. I've already begun to make inquiries. Why don't you let me take several days to deepen the effort. Then, we'll see if we can turn something up that way.'

'And what am I supposed to do while you're doing that?'

He shrugged. 'Get to know Buenos Aires. Go to the Café Tortoni, which is a famous literary café over a hundred years old. Go to a show at the Teatro Colón. Visit the famous cemetery at La Recoleta, where the rich are buried.' He opened his arms. 'Swim in the waters of the city.'

CHAPTER 9

In the early evening buzz of Avenida Corrientes, amid the neon and the car horns that rebounded off the plaster finery of the last century, Athena counted down the numbers that separated her from Ricardo Berenski. Calle Brazil, Calle Paraguay. The handsome Argentines streamed past her, their faces turbulent or flirtatious or questioning. Emotions seemed closer to the surface here. People didn't look away as they did in New York or Washington, but locked eyes briefly, like a challenge or an enticement. It felt like a place where a person might fall in love any minute, but where everyone seemed to be nursing a broken heart.

She couldn't escape a furtive paranoia as she headed to her meeting with the journalist. Miguel would look poorly on this little side investigation, especially since she was pursuing it in secret. But he had said to swim, she thought, so she was swimming. It wasn't her fault if she'd strayed out of the shallow end.

The wide, spacious Café Losadas comprised not only a bar and café but also a bookstore, a theater, and a publishing house that printed titles on culture and politics. Behind its agricultural-sized spread of window glass men polluted notebooks with copious words, their eyes trained simultaneously on the elusive phantasm of their literary careers and the women going in and out the front door.

But Ricardo Berenski was no pretender. In the cult of investigative journalism that flourished in Buenos Aires, Berenski was one of the principal idols. Athena expected someone cinematic: tall and dark, with intellectual spectacles and a tweed sports jacket.

The real Ricardo made an almost comical impostor. Short, and saved from baldness by two islands of clipped reddish hair, he resembled the last self-portraits of Van Gogh, but smiling. His pallid skin and slightly bulging eyes made him look sharp-witted and excitable, an effect magnified by a quick gravelly voice that seemed always to be leading to a punchline. He hunched forward when he walked, craned his neck and squinted when he listened. His gnome-like presence defied weightiness, but in fact, Ricardo had splashed a lot of ugliness across the glossy faces of the major media.

When a former torturer of the Dictatorship published a book denying the allegations of his past, Ricardo arranged for him to appear on a national television show to promote it. What the torturer didn't find out until halfway through his earnest denial was that the other guest was one of his former victims, who lifted up his shirt and showed the audience the scars. Another time, Ricardo had arranged for an actor with a hidden camera to pose as a drug dealer and close a distribution agreement with the highest ranking comisario in Greater Buenos Aires. His book on police corruption had forced the chief of the *Bonaerense* into retirement and made a stink that had yet to dissipate. Informed people thought that the only thing keeping him alive was his fame.

'Do you ever get death threats and that sort of thing?'

'Ahh!' He tossed his shoulders disdainfully. 'If they call you on the telephone, that means they're not really going to kill you. I tell them, "*Andate a la concha de tu madre, hijo de puta!*" ' He stood up to kiss a passing friend. 'How's it going, beauty?' Sitting down again, eagerly sipping his second whiskey. 'But this with the police,' he continued, shaking his head, 'the complete corporatization, that comes from the Dictatorship.'

'How?'

'During the Repression, the army and the police had two motives. The first was to eliminate all thought that ran against the interests of the national elite and foreign capital. Very noble, no? The other was less exalted: simply to make money. When they took people away, they also robbed them. They had warehouses where they stored the belongings of the people they had murdered. They considered it their natural right in exchange for their heroic service to the fatherland. And the police of today, the big ones, were created during that era. Now they're more sophisticated. They rent themselves out. They were involved in the bombings of the embassy of Israel and the Jewish Relief Society that killed hundreds of people. Also they have very fluid relations with Carlo Pelegrini and his private security businesses.' He tipped his glass to his mouth, looking past her towards the door. 'But what is this about Waterbury? That's what we came here to talk about, no? Carmen told me you think it might have been a police assassination – nine millimeter, handcuffs, the burning car. All the classics of the genre. The cocaine we can explain away as planted to mislead the investigation, because you told me on the telephone he had no history of drugs. Who's the judge?'

'Duarte.'

He threw back his head. 'Duarte! Now we've passed from genre to parody.'

'What do you mean?'

'We call him *Sominex*, you know, like the pills, because he's so good at putting cases to sleep.'

Athena put her face in her hand. 'This is too much.'

Berenski laughed, pounding her on the shoulder. 'Strength, *chica*! Strength! Now you're in the game! And the Selección Argentina doesn't play by Northamerican rules. What more have you got?'

'I have a phone number taken from his pants pocket and a friend who he knew from his days at AmiBank ten years ago.'

'AmiBank. Ah, this is interesting! And the police never investigated them?'

'No.'

'Now, yes . . .' He tilted his face upward and sniffed the air, circling his hand slowly in front of his nose. 'I smell that odor of shit! Give me the number before we go. I have a friend who sometimes traces these little things for me.' His next words pricked her like an electric shock. 'You know, I met Waterbury once.'

'You met him?'

'At the Bar Azul, in San Telmo. San Telmo is a barrio a bit, artistic, let's say, with little experimental theaters that mix Nietzsche and Marcel Duchamp and the complete works of Eric Satie played backwards. That type, the demi-monde, and many go to the Bar Azul after the shows. Thursday night they bring in a tango group and play tango with half-price whiskey. That's where I met him. He was going around with some French tango dancer. A woman absolutely disagreeable. One of those people who know nothing about anything, but they're so certain of it that they dominate the conversation. But very pretty. And the girl could dance. Waterbury was a bit of a trunk, but she found someone who could dance the tango and then her whole demeanor changed. She was a character we used to see around in the bars: half-actress, half . . . I don't know, she circulated in odd things. We called her *La Francesa*, but I think her name was . . . Paulé.'

Athena felt uncomfortable as she thought of Waterbury going around with a young French dancer while his family waited for him at home.

'I knew her because a friend of mine, an actress, or, better said . . .' He lifted his arms gaudily, '*artiste*, knew her and *La Francesa* invited us to their table. There was another woman also, a slightly older woman, but very well-maintained. I think she was of some money, because we were drinking champagne and she was the one who kept asking for more. The best, eh? Dom Perignon. Veuve Cliquot. The *nacional* was an insult to her. She and *La Francesa* got into an argument about which champagne was better, and things turned ugly. *La Francesa* was trying to bank on her expertise as a native Parisian, but the older woman finally tired of her and said, "Yours is a Paris of shopgirls and waitresses. What do you know of champagne?"' Ricardo lowered his voice and leaned forward. 'Then she says, "If you're so at home in Paris, what are you doing selling your cunt in Buenos Aires?"' He raised his eyebrows. 'At this, *everything* went rotten! *La Francesa* calls her a wrinkled old pig in that little French voice and walks out, and Waterbury's left planted there with this rich woman, holding on to his champagne glass like a lifesaver in the middle of the ocean. He and the woman left a minute after that.'

'Did you talk to Robert Waterbury?'

'Very little. To be honest, Waterbury impacted me as a bit confused. He said he was a writer, but he hadn't published anything in some years. He told me he'd come to Buenos Aires to research another book. And when he said this he and the rich woman looked at each other, and of course, one always speculates. The whole episode was a matter of some thirty minutes.'

'Who was the woman?'

'That I don't know. Tamara, Teresa . . . Something with a "T."'

Athena felt a surge of excitement. 'Teresa?'

'I think, yes.'

'That phone number I told you Robert Waterbury had in his pocket when he was murdered had the name Teresa written with it! The surgeon found it before the autopsy!'

'Did you call the number?'

'Not yet.'

Now Berenski was peering at her intently, but at the same time considering something else. 'Don't call it. Let me trace it first. Then we'll go forward well-armed.'

'What about the Frenchwoman? Paulé. Could we talk to her? We could go to the Bar Azul tonight, if you're not doing anything.'

He held up his hand. '*Tranquila, amor*. Don't give the number such importance. If I walk out of here and some drug addict puts a cork in me, will your telephone number in my pocket tell them who murdered me?' His lips twisted into a sideways grin, '*Bueno*, if that happened they'd arm the biggest party in the history of the Buenos Aires police, but looking at it theoretically . . .' He shrugged. 'We'll see. Of *La Francesa* I don't know. She's not on the scene these days. Maybe she went back to her land.'

Athena watched him go at his drink again, and took a slow sip of her own. She was thinking about her afternoon with Miguel and his promise to intensify his efforts. 'Ricardo, do you know a Comisario Fortunato? In San Justo?' She handed him Fortunato's card.

Berenski furrowed his brow. 'In Investigaciónes, eh?' Tapping his glass absently on the table. 'Yes. He's older, very soft, very smooth. I met him once. One of his men uncovered some cars with phony papers, and they followed them back to a comisario in Quilmes. More than this, I don't know.'

'He's my main contact with the police. To me,' she pictured his melancholic smile, 'he seems very decent. Do you think I can trust him to investigate this crime?'

'Trust him?' Ricardo wagged his head to the left, and then to the right. 'You can trust him up to the point where you can't trust him. He's police.' He considered something, then, on the verge of a proposal, changed his mind. 'No,' he muttered, 'I can't put you in with him.'

'Who?'

Taking in a long breath: 'I know a sort of specialist on the police in San Justo. He would know all about your Fortunato. But I'll tell you directly, he's a criminal, and for this he has a relation with the *cana*, the "cops." '

'You know him from your investigations?'

'No.' Ricardo scratched nervously at his nose. 'I know him from the *Ejercito Revolucionario del Pueblo*, of the Seventies.' For the first time Ricardo seemed serious. 'The last of our revolutionary dreams. Then I woke up and went into exile for eight years. I worked more in the informational part, producing *The Red Star*. But this *muchacho*, no. He was really a warrior type. Very valiant. Very dangerous. *Very* dangerous,' he repeated, awed by his remembrance.

'He killed a heap of *Fascistas*. When the ERP kidnapped General Lopez and subjected him to a revolutionary court, it was Cacho who executed him. Don't look so shocked, Lopez was an *hijo de puta*. Murderer. Torturer. Thief. He deserved to die. But to kill someone defenseless, in cold blood . . .' He tilted his head, blew out a puff of tension. '*Muy pesado*.' Very heavy. Now Berenski shivered, and his voice took on a troubled mix of sadness and what sounded almost like shame. 'But it went bad for him, just like it went bad for everyone. They killed his younger brother, an adolescent that had nothing to do with politics. They killed his wife. They captured Cacho, they tortured him . . . And there's a bit of a shadow among us that survived the war, because now he's working with the same people we fought against.' He shook his head. 'I don't know. Of that war, some survived intact and some survived broken. Cacho is broken.'

'But you'll introduce me to him?'

The journalist shook his head. '*Bueno*. Between Cacho and me, it's complicated. Sometimes he gives me information. But at the same time, he gets very aggressive. Resentful. I think it's disagreeable for both of us when we meet.' He shook his head, looking at the table. 'The man is bent.'

CHAPTER 10

Fortunato did his best to look enthusiastic as he strode through the musty smoke of La Gloria to meet with the Chief. Bianco had just gotten a haircut that day and his white hair had been razored into fine clean edges. Fortunato could smell the barber's lilac water as he leaned in to kiss him. To Fortunato's relief Bianco had left the monkeys at home.

'*Tanguero!*'

'Sit down, Miguel. Sit down!'

A whiskey and a small steel tray indented with peanuts and olives had already been laid on the table next to a liter of beer, and Fortunato noticed two cigarette butts bent into the ashtray. Julio Sosa was crooning his operatic rendition of 'Verdemar' over the radio, and the Chief tuned into it for a moment after they sat down as if listening for something he'd missed before. At last he frowned.

'I've never liked Julio Sosa,' the Chief said. 'He's too sweet.'

Fortunato grimaced. 'He's for the women,' he said, then thought, *better said, he* was *for the women*. The elegant voice that boomed around the dark bar had been recorded thirty-five years ago. Marcela had been an admirer of Julio Sosa. He used to pretend to be jealous of Sosa, of the fine suit and debonair hairstyle that Sosa wore on the covers of his record albums. *Julio! Julio!* Marcela would tease him. *I'm going to leave you for Julio.*

The Chief continued. 'Take someone else, say *El Polaco*, to sing this song, and given the same song, it's going to have that tang of whiskey, with a more complex feeling. This,' he motioned around the dim ether that hung in the decrepit interior of the bar, 'this is just a lullaby.' Fortunato said nothing, still thinking of Marcela. 'And,' the Chief began, 'how are we going with this matter of the gringa?'

It relieved Miguel to get on the theme, because he was on the theme already by himself, wondering again about Waterbury's missing friend Pablo whom Athena kept mentioning. Pablo. AmiBank. And that note in the papers about AmiBank and Carlo Pelegrini.

But they were talking now about the gringa. 'Look, Leon, the matter is thus: we have to give her something.'

Elena came with another steel dish, this one filled with tiny breadsticks and little pink rounds of sausage. 'Bring me a whiskey, *amor*,' Fortunato said quickly.

'Why?' the Chief continued when she'd left. 'Why can't you just put on your idiot face for a couple of weeks and let her go home?'

'She's not so retarded, Leon. We went over to see Duarte a few days ago. She was asking things like,' imitating her ingenuous voice: ' "Why didn't anyone talk to the wife? Why didn't anyone talk to his contacts at AmiBank?" '

'And Duarte?'

'He defended himself! All that verse about *la justicia*, the scarce resources, the usual,' Fortunato said sourly. 'But the *chica* wasn't buying that merchandise.' Fortunato worked a cigarette out of the box and picked up the Chief's lighter.

'So you went back to the theme of the *narcos*?'

Fortunato finished pulling the flame into the tube before answering. 'Of course! But then she says, again, "I still don't understand how drug dealers would kill him for drugs and leave six chalks of pure cocaine in the car!" '

'But I told her –'

'Yes, you told her, and I told her too, but don't be so sure that we're the only ones making *cara de gil* here.'

The Chief twisted his mouth downward, knocked his knuckles absently on the table a few times as if to clear his head.

'Yes,' Fortunato said acidly. 'I think we can say that she senses a certain lack of professionalism in the management of the *Caso Waterbury*.'

'*You* were supposed to manage it, Miguel!'

'I *was* managing it! Domingo's *merquero* was shot with his own gun, did you forget that? Did you want him turning up at the hospital with a bullet wound? I took him over to one of our clinics. I managed it!' The Chief frowned, and Fortunato felt himself looking once more at Waterbury's shuddering corpse, felt Domingo's smug babyface invading his mind again. *You calmed the hijo de puta,*

79

Comi. He pushed it away, tasted the sour fizz of the beer. 'Look, Leon, *something*, we have to give.'

The Chief nodded. 'You're right, Miguel. As always. She's been talking to the Instituto Contra La Represión Policial. She also met with Ricardo Berenski.'

Fortunato said nothing, but the feeling of betrayal burned at his ears. Everybody knew Berenski. His book had created a surge of literary activity in the Buenos Aires police as the entire force had rushed to see whose name appeared in it. For a while they'd had a picture of Berenski taped into one of the urinals. Other photos made their way to the shooting range. 'When did she meet with Berenski?'

'Two days ago, at the Losadas, on Corrientes.'

Fortunato nodded silently. He'd seen Athena yesterday, had even asked her *What have you done in Buenos Aires? Where have you gone?* and recommended her a music store with a good tango collection. She hadn't said a word about Berenski.

The Chief went on softly, comprehending. 'Don't take it so seriously, Miguel. That's how they are. They talk, they exchange their little complaints . . .' He threw a limp hand, clicked his tongue. 'Nothing happens. But I want to close this and get her back to her land before Berenski starts trying to sell newspapers with it. What it means is that you're going to have to tell her a story. I think we need to deepen the drug theme. Maybe it was a clumsy play, but that's what we have right now and the chalks have already been introduced as a prop.'

Fortunato made an effort to calm the unpleasantness in his head. They had an investigation to conduct, a case to solve. He turned the details over in his mind. 'Fine,' he said after a pause. 'But if we're going to tell a story, we need characters.'

The Chief smiled, back to his old self. '*Che!* I've got just the man!'

CHAPTER 11

Enrique Boguso had never been a very thorough criminal, but he tried to compensate for his poor planning skills with a brutal decisiveness. He styled himself a bold improviser, able to coolly murder his way through the occasional untidy situations that resulted from his less-than-meticulous preparation. As insurance, he provided information to the police and they turned their attention elsewhere. Finally, though, he'd gone too far, committing a crime of such singular horror that even the police lost their patience.

An aficionado of the Repression and its death squads, Boguso read avidly the human rights reports and often imitated their methodology in his own crimes. On his fateful night, the twenty-five year old and a friend had broken into the house of a bricklayer in Quilmes with the information that he had a fortune stashed in his wall. Boguso had brought an electric prod and other accoutrements of the Dictatorship and proceeded to torture the family one by one, strapping them to the bed with a black hood over their heads. But the story, its thousands, and the nights of cocaine and whores it promised, had been illusory. The criminals turned up two hundred pesos in the course of murdering both parents, and in a dispute over the spoils Boguso's partner had shot him in the leg. They'd arrested him at the hospital the next day, sentenced him to perpetual chains in a remarkably speedy trial, and now he awaited his final disposition in a holding cell at Comisaria 33, in Quilmes.

Number 33 had a reputation for yielding a good sum, and a few years ago Fortunato had passed up the chance to buy a spot as its comisario for only seventy-five thousand pesos. The Comisaria had recently undergone a complete facelift. Its century-old walls had been re-plastered and re-painted and a second floor was under construction, with new showers, lockers, a kitchen and a bunk room. One sparkling white cell, which the Comisario referred to as 'the honeymoon suite,' had been freshly installed for preferential prisoners, still unused. The Comisario proudly showed off the new interrogation room, one of a very few that had a two-way mirror for observation.

'*Epa!*' Fortunato exclaimed. '*Estilo* Hollywood!'

'And we had to do it all ourselves, without a penny from Central,' the Comisario said, with a touch of rancor. Vast portions of the police expenses were paid with money that came from nowhere and flowed through the station without the encumbrance of accounting. Comisario 33 had spent, by the Comisario's reckoning, more than a hundred thousand pesos on restorations, but these would never become official and no government assessor would ever ask questions. That the police could consistently operate with a fraction of the budget truly necessary gave them a certain degree of indulgence among the politicians who controlled the official purse. It was a little arrangement between the institution and the government.

Despite the industriousness of the workmen, the *calabozos* where the prisoners were temporarily held had escaped improvement. They lay at the back of the building, running along a narrow hallway of grim unpainted concrete blocked off from the rest of the station by a heavy grid of iron. The acid stench of urine and excrement swelled out of the cells and through the iron bars, and Fortunato instinctively breathed through his mouth. In a long file were six steel doors with little rectangles cut out at eye level. A small strip of bars at the top and bottom let in a modicum of air and the only light. The cells were dark and wet, cold in the winter and sweltering in the summer.

For Boguso, this *calabozo* was a privileged resting place, one he paid dearly for. Boguso had spent years as a *buchon* for the police, and he knew that once he was transferred to the prison where his informing had sent so many others, the definition of 'life imprisonment' would likely be short. Five hundred pesos per month paid to the Comisario had kept his hopes alive for some sort of permanent arrangement, but the money would run out soon and Boguso had lately noticed signals of distraction from his not always faithful wife.

Bianco had already set things up between Fortunato and the Comisario of #33, who now unlocked the grate to the *calabozos*. As they walked along the dim putrid corridor of cells, Fortunato heard various shufflings in the dark behind the iron panels: four young thieves had been arrested the night before and their arrest records were making the long slow trip from Central. The Comisario opened the cell at the end of the line and in the rancid gloom Fortunato saw Boguso hunched up on the concrete platform that served as a bed. A few pieces of a disgusting white substance that Fortunato recognized as soggy bread sat on the urine-soaked floor below him.

The Comisario addressed him in an impersonal tone. 'Stand up, Boguso.'

The prisoner slowly came to his feet and Fortunato got a better look at him. The wild black curls Fortunato had seen in the paper had been shaved to a bristle, and the man's eyes focused on them with the instinctive flinch of a victim. His hands hung limply together in their cuffs and a wet stain spread down his thigh.

'Clean him up,' Fortunato said.

Upstairs in the new interrogation room, Fortunato gave Boguso a cigarette, sent one of the sub-inspectors for a *mate* and a kettle of water. 'Sweet or bitter?' he asked Boguso politely.

'Sweet,' he said. And then, perhaps emboldened by his freshly scrubbed state, 'With a slice of lemon.'

'*Con limón*,' Fortunato repeated, and the Comisario tactfully followed the sub-inspector out the door.

Fortunato flicked his lighter and lit Boguso's cigarette. Boguso had to raise both hands to bring it to his mouth and Fortunato could see a ring of sores on his wrists beneath the manacles. 'They're keeping you in cuffs?' he solicited, as if surprised. The Comisario had already told him that they'd had some problems with Boguso throwing his excrement at one of the guards.

Boguso nodded, his eyes turned down at the table.

'That doesn't seem necessary. Maybe I could talk to the Comisario for you.' He let Boguso take a few more puffs of the cigarette, let him fill up with the good feeling of the nicotine. He noticed that Boguso had a nervous twitch in his left eyebrow. 'Do you know why I'm here?'

'I have no idea,' the killer told him.

'I'm here to help you.'

Boguso laughed, but his game face couldn't completely surface from the weeks of solitary confinement.

'You're not such an easy person to help, Enrique. You made yourself half-unpopular with your last stunt. The hoods, the electric prod . . .' He shook his head. 'The newspapers spent a river of ink on how your crime was the harvest of the Dictatorship.'

A weird pride slopped across Boguso's features. 'I read them.'

'The human rights groups had a fiesta with that escapade. And the people who weren't crying about human rights were asking why we didn't just shoot you when we arrested you. Then Berenski reported that you were a *buchon*, protected by the police, and that made everybody look bad.' Fortunato leaned back. 'No, amigo, you shit yourself with that last one. And you shit on the Institution.'

'It was Tello's idea to kill them. I told him –'

Fortunato held up his hand. 'No, Enrique, let's not enter into that theme again. It already *is*. What I've found in life, though, is that even when you think you're at the bottom, it can always get worse.' The murderer looked skeptical. Fortunato shrugged. 'They send you to Rio Negro,' nodding his head almost sadly, 'it's worse.' The naked, fresh-shaved face flinched very subtly, but Fortunato noted it. 'They'll kill you there,' he said sympathetically. 'No. They'll rape you, and then they'll kill you. Did you read that last report in the paper? Some poor *buchon* bled to death through his asshole.' He sighed, threw his hands gently to the sides. 'As I said, Enrique. I can help you. But I need a little favor.'

Boguso looked at him warily.

'There was a gringo killed a few months ago in San Justo, and we need to find the killer. It's political. Something of pressure on the government.' He swirled his hand airily. 'You know how they are.'

'They're *hijo de puta*!'

'They're very *hijo de puta*, but for whatever reason, the gringos took an interest. It would be helpful if you could illuminate the case for us.'

The pigeon seemed to search his information, then said slowly, 'You want me to denounce someone?'

'Yes. I want you to denounce Enrique Boguso.'

Boguso's mouth fell open. Even his long history of relations with the police hadn't prepared him for the bizarre demand. 'You want me to take responsibility for a murder I didn't even do?'

'Sí, Señor.'

Fortunato watched Boguso try to grasp it. The eye seemed to be twitching a little bit faster. 'Look,' the older man reasoned, 'is it such an extra burden? Your first one was when you were sixteen and once you got your clean adult record you did it again. After this last pair, I don't think one more fake killing will make much difference. It's already perpetual chains, no? We give you the *expediente* to study, you sing your little story for the judge, the gringos write their report and everybody's happy.'

'And me? How am I happy?'

'Well, Enrique. You help us and we help you. Isn't it always like that? I think we could improve your accommodations, at least. Keep you someplace a little cozier, with conjugal privileges. And in a few years, when all the noise goes away, who knows? Someone might find a technical error in your conviction. Or you might escape somehow, or get pardoned.'

'It's *way* crazy, hombre.'

Fortunato hesitated, letting a long philosophical pause elapse before he spoke slowly and distantly. 'Yes, son. It's crazy. But it's a crazy world, no? A world of illusion, where the best actor rules.' He sighed. 'Think about it. I can find someone else if it's too heavy for you. Buenos Aires doesn't lack for people with complicated situations.'

'Way crazy,' the killer murmured.

The Comisario came in with the gourd full of steaming herbs and a little steel teapot. The sub-inspector carried a sugar bowl and a lemon.

'Everything friendly?' the Comisario asked.

'He's a prince, this guy!' Fortunato put another cigarette in front of Boguso. 'Take it.'

Boguso sipped the *mate* as Fortunato discussed with the Comisario the various renovations and the petty disputes and annoyances around the station. When Boguso's straw gurgled Fortunato would sprinkle some sugar on top and pour a few more tablespoons of hot water onto the herbs. After a while he stood up and went to the door. 'Fine; I have things to do, Vincente. Can I chat with Enrique again in a few days?'

The Comisario played it perfectly. 'You'll have to buy a plane ticket. They're transferring him to Rio Negro tomorrow.'

Boguso twisted up towards the Comisario as if hit with one of his own electric shocks. 'What?'

'I got the order from the Direction of Penal Services yesterday. They want you in Rio Negro.'

'You sold me, you whore! I've been paying you five hundred pesos a month . . .'

The Comisario slapped him on the back of his head and the *mate* went spilling across the floor. 'Shut up, *boludo*! I didn't tell you to murder the bricklayer and his wife! I tried to help you as much as I could, you heap of shit. It's out of my hands!'

Boguso made a reflexive motion to stand up and the sub-inspector grabbed him by his ear and sat him in the chair again, then back-handed him hard across the face with a dry impact that resounded off the walls.

'Oh, this is very inconvenient,' Fortunato said quietly. 'I'm afraid I wasted your time, Vincente. I'm sorry. If he's going to Rio Negro . . .' He put his hand on the knob and opened the door.

'Don't mention it, Miguel. It's a pleasure to see you.'

Boguso screamed in panic. 'Wait, Comisario! Wait!'

'It already *is*, Enrique. I came too late. I'm sorry.'

'No! Don't leave! Let's chat some more, Comi! I'm for you. Anything you want! Comi!' The prisoner's tormented face was now twitching uncontrollably, and for some reason Fortunato thought of Boguso's victims, the bricklayer and his wife, and the ugly spasms that must have transfigured their faces when Boguso had applied the electric wires to their testicles or breasts. And he thought of Waterbury again, his face in shock from the devastating wounds inflicted on him, and suddenly Fortunato felt a sensation of disgust at Boguso, wished that he could draw his nine millimeter right there and put a round through his remorseless, feral head and walk calmly out the door and keep walking, to his home, to Marcela, to some distant green place where everyone was a stranger and he had no past. Instead, he motioned for the Comisario and the sub-inspector to leave the room and calmly picked the *mate* up off the floor. He sat down across from the panic-stricken murderer and said, 'And, son; shall we work together?'

Over the next four days Fortunato had the pleasure of spending many hours with Boguso, who had been moved to the clean white VIP cell at Comisario #33, complete with lights, a toilet and a sink. It had done him well; he looked rested and he devoted himself to his studies wholeheartedly. Fortunato wrote out his story, along with all the details he would need, and gave him a photocopy of the *expediente* so that he could familiarize himself with the other evidence and declarations that had been made. The location and angle of entry of the bullet wounds, the make and color of the murder vehicle, details of Waterbury's clothing and appearance. They even took him to the crime scene one night to memorize those extra details that only an eyewitness would know.

In a strange way, it was like a piece of theater in which the part of Miguel Fortunato was played by Enrique Boguso. According to the script, a missing accomplice had fired the .32 caliber bullets into Waterbury's legs and groin and chest, and he, Boguso, had delivered the *coup de grace* to Waterbury's head with the nine millimeter to end it. Bianco procured Fortunato a clean nine millimeter Astra taken off a dead bank robber and he fired a bullet into a side of beef. A sympathetic clerk at the evidence room at the Brigada de Investigaciónes never noticed when he changed that bullet for the one that had transfixed Waterbury's skull. Boguso was more than happy to wrap his fingerprints all over the 'murder weapon,' after which Fortunato brought the Astra to his house for safekeeping. For Boguso's accomplice they pulled from their files a Uruguayan criminal who hadn't been seen in Argentina in five years.

Fortunato coached Boguso and quizzed him on his progress each day, listening with dread as the killer repeated the horrific details one at a time. In the daydreams and nightdreams that came to him more and more frequently, his own self became confused with Boguso, with victims in hoods, with calm men sipping coffee while they rested between applications of the electric prod. He'd never hated any of the criminals he'd prosecuted, but he'd come to hate Boguso in a way that he found hard to conceal. He dreamed of killing him, of watching his face twist in pain as he crumpled backwards and down. He, who'd never wanted to kill anyone. Boguso came to represent all the unknown people who had gotten him into this: the Chief, always glib and cheerful with his tangos, Domingo the sadist, Vasquez with his *merca*, and a host of shadows who remained out of sight in the upper reaches, beyond harm. In the distant upper reaches of the pyramid, vague and aloof: Carlo Pelegrini.

For his own part, the closer Boguso came to mastering his material the cockier he grew. 'Amigo Fortunato,' he'd say, 'let's talk about what happens after I'm convicted. I want to know more specifically when I'm getting out and how much money I'll have waiting. All these promises flying around in the air,' he shook his head distastefully, 'it's not good business.'

'Don't be too clever, Boguso. You'll make more problems for yourself.'

'And how do I know you won't cut me as soon as it's over? *Killed while escaping, committed suicide in his cell*, crap like that. That's the oldest cop trick there is.'

He rested his hand lightly on the murderer's shoulder. 'It's business, Enrique,' he said. 'In business you don't kill your partner.'

The explanation sounded weak even to him.

CHAPTER 12

The *remisero* glanced at the piece of paper Athena showed him and looked at her doubtfully. 'It's complicated, that neighborhood.'

'That's where I need to go.'

He muttered something, then motioned her into his car and set out into the cement streets, his tires thumping softly over the asphalt expansion joints. They quickly left the little stores at the center of San Justo and made their way deeper into the exurbs of Buenos Aires, past modest houses fortified with fences and barred windows. The 'For Sale' signs showed the losing struggle to stay in the middle class. 'They're all looking for something smaller,' the cab driver said.

The occasional desultory business interrupted the modest houses: a butcher, an ice-cream shop that also sold tickets for the *quinella*, a sickly-looking hardware store. They passed the uninterrupted brick wall of an abandoned factory. 'Here they used to make televisions,' the driver said, 'but it's been globalized, thanks to your friends at the IMF. Now we have Sony and Sanyo. Over there, in that other block, they made electric fans. Also globalized. They couldn't compete with *los chinos*. I know because I used to be their accountant.'

The *remisero*, it turned out, had a degree in economics from the University of Buenos Aires, and the rare presence of an American ear made him voluble. 'Thus the neo-liberal model, Señorita. The glory of Free Trade as imposed by your experts from the universities of Chicago and Harvard and promoted by the global corporations. Cut the importation duties, open the market to foreign corporations, privatize state enterprises. Then, when the national factories go broke, the multi-nationals can write in their annual reports that they have conquered a new market. Thus is the game. But don't worry: when they're finished with us, they'll do the same thing to you.'

'What do you think is the solution?'

He spit out a dry laugh. 'A long brick wall and a few good machine guns.'

Something on the street caught her eye. 'What's happening there?'

Three men had pinned someone in a sports jacket against a white plaster wall. One of them, in a blue jogging suit, cuffed the victim on the head and spat on him, then pulled several bank-notes from the man's wallet and threw it on the ground. The window was open and she could hear the assailant in the jogging suit cursing as they passed. He slapped the man across the top of his head once more and turned to face the *remis*, fixing her with a glare so malevolent that she turned away. The driver punched it through the inter-section.

'It's troublesome, this barrio,' he said. '*Globalizado.*'

He dropped her at the corner she'd requested and drove off. The even files of small working-class houses died out here into unfinished brick walls and vacant lots, with yellow dirt footpaths lapping at the street. A few meager dwellings squatted behind weedy lawns and hopeful little plantings of hibiscus or avocado. A guard dog barked through an iron fence a hundred yards away. At three in the afternoon, the cracked and crumpled sidewalks buckled footless down the block.

Athena took out the piece of paper Ricardo had written for her and tried to orient herself. Cacho's house sat behind an empty lot with no address and Ricardo's diagram was ambiguous. She ambled hesitantly down the street, then returned, stopping before the concrete slab of an aborted construction project. Behind it she could see a brick wall with a few strange slit windows in it. She heard a car approaching behind her. Before she realized it, the car had pulled over to the curb and disgorged three men who quickly closed in on her. In the next second, she recognized the blue jogging suit, the dark, frightening rage. He tilted his chin up and glared. 'What's happening with you? Eh? What are you doing here?'

She glanced up and down the street but the only movement was the dog several houses away, throwing itself against the iron fence. 'Excuse me,' she said, sounding overly polite even to herself. 'I'm looking for someone. Perhaps you can help me. Do you know Cacho Rivera?'

One of the men laughed, the other kept her targeted in his harsh black glare. 'On whose part?' the jogger said.

'On the part of Ricardo Berenski. It's a personal matter.'

He stared at her over a long, unpleasant pause. She'd place him in his late forties. His black hair and dark skin stretched over sharp features and a prominent nose that had been broken and set back crookedly. With his shaggy hair shot with gray, he might have been an aging hippy, but he had nothing relaxed or benevolent about him, and the wrinkles and small irregular scars around one of his eyes layered a patina of violent experience over his face as though something inside was burning through to the surface. He had a hairspring intensity about him. '*Bien*,' he said at last. Turning to his cohorts, '*Muchachos*; as we said, eh?' They melted off towards the car and he motioned towards the brick building. 'Let's talk inside.'

She followed him around the corner to a heavy metal door, which he unlocked and opened for her with a small polite gesture of welcome. She hesitated a moment before entering the isolation of the dim room. He was Berenski's friend, right? She went in and he locked the door behind them.

The room had a cool, stony smell, despite the heat of the day, and was surprisingly clean and well-furnished. The smoothly finished plaster spread from floor to ceiling like a fresh sheet of paper, interrupted by various expensive wall fixtures and several paintings and drawings in neat glassed-in frames. A leather sofa faced an oversized television screen, along with two stuffed leather chairs. A stack of unopened boxes containing video cameras stood in the corner. She noticed that the windows were barred and shuttered with steel, and that four or five gun ports like those seen on armored cars had been set into the walls below thick strips of bulletproof glass. An assault rifle leaned against the television set.

He motioned towards the leather sofa and she settled nervously into the cool squeaking cushions. 'Who are you and why did Berenski send you to me?'

She spoke as if they were sitting in an office somewhere. 'I'm Doctor Athena Fowler. I'm trying to find out about the murder of a United States citizen and Ricardo thought you might be able to help.'

It seemed to annoy him. 'Then maybe you should go and talk to the Mothers of the Plaza de Mayo. We've got thirty thousand people murdered with the best wishes of *Tio Sam*, and their families want to know what happened, too! That's the reality here in Argentina.'

She kept her voice level as she answered, though her blood was pounding. 'Reality is wide and deep, Señor Rivera, and we all have our feet in it. If you want to talk about injustice, let's start with you and me. Why did you have that man against the wall ten minutes ago?'

His black features coiled at her question, then suddenly eased. He laughed. 'You're very fierce, friend of Berenski. Would you like a drink?' He poured her a glass of red wine. 'Soda?' he asked politely.

'Please.' He squirted some seltzer into the wine. The astringent bubbles of the mixture writhed on the surface of her tongue, refreshing her. Athena had to listen carefully to understand him: he had a thick barrio accent laded with *lunfardo* she knew wouldn't be found in any Spanish dictionary but, despite the slang and the coarse-sounding inflections, his speech betrayed the uneven polish of self-education.

'So, tell me how you know Berenski. Are you a journalist also?'

'No. I'm a teacher at Georgetown University, in Washington DC.' She told him how she'd met Ricardo, not hiding the lack of support from the embassy or the FBI. She knew that in Cacho's world the cardboard faces of official standing were of no importance, and the chance to speak honestly refreshed her. 'The victim had a wife and daughter,' she finished, taking a line from her encounter with Carmen Amado. 'That's who I represent.'

He went on quizzing her casually about where she was staying, her contacts in the city. Something about Cacho's physical presence exhilarated her: she could sense in him a man who had played it all many times before and was capable of doing so again without a second thought. *He's very dangerous*, Ricardo had warned her. *He killed a heap of Fascists.* At the moment, pulling open the steel shutters to let in the mid-morning light, he seemed tidy and domestic.

'So tell me about this murder,' he said, sitting down on the leather chair across from her, 'and why you've come to me.'

'The victim was a man named Robert Waterbury. He was murdered in this neighborhood.' She watched his face for a reaction but saw only a steady attention. 'Ricardo said you know a lot about what happens around here.'

He tipped his head. 'I heard about that one. They made shit out of some gringo over on Avellaneda. They burned the car, I believe there were a few chalks of *milonga* . . .'

'The police thought it might be some sort of settling of accounts related to drugs.'

'And Ricardo agreed with them?'

'No. He thinks it's more complicated than that.'

Cacho didn't voice his opinion. He seemed to be calculating something. 'And how does it go with the police? With whom are you working?'

'With Comisario Fortunato, of the Brigada de San Justo.' She watched his face but Cacho displayed nothing. 'Do you know Comisario Fortunato?'

Cacho squinted as he reached for the soda bottle and sprayed another shot into his glass. 'Very little. I know him more than anything by his reputation.' He drew his head back and peered at her intently, then changed the subject. 'You're an athlete, aren't you?'

The sudden appraisal surprised and flattered her. 'I'm a runner.'

'Of what distance?'

'Marathons.'

He raised his eyebrows as he considered it. 'I could tell you were an athlete by the way you move. The way you sat down on the couch. You dominate your body. Some people are like that.'

'You're very observant.'

'In my profession, one has to be observant. Observe, gather information. That's the difference between the fuck-ups rotting in the Tombs and those of us breathing the free air. That, and luck. But now you've interested me in this gringo who got cut. What was he doing in Buenos Aires? Why would someone cut him?'

'He was a writer, looking for background material for a new book. It could be that he put himself in something by accident.'

'Without doubt.' He clicked his tongue scornfully. '*Boludo!*' Retard. He shook his head, then took a fresh breath. 'You see, Athena, I'm the one asking for information from you. Forgive that I've wasted your time.'

She felt him wriggling away from her. 'That's fine. But you said you knew Miguel Fortunato by his reputation. What *is* his reputation?'

Cacho hesitated, threw his shoulders up. 'He doesn't have fame of being a torturer. He doesn't mount those little *operettas*, where they set up a *muchacho* with a job and then kill him in a phony shoot-out. He's a good man. Taking into account that he's police, of course.'

She looked for a delicate way to phrase it. 'Is he . . . Does he make *arrangements* with people?'

'*Chica!* He's a comisario!'

'Which means what?'

His look signaled that answering such a stupid question would be a waste of breath. 'I'll tell you this: he knows how to investigate. And he knows the barrio very well.'

The validation, such as it was, heartened her. So maybe he'd compromised a little to reach his position. Maybe he'd had no choice.

The criminal sat watching her with his legs crossed and his chin resting on his hand. She had a sense of her own exoticism in his life, just as he felt exotic to her. She'd never met a revolutionary before, or *terrorista*, as they'd been called at the time. 'Ricardo said you two know each other from the Seventies.' She stopped, then prompted him. 'That you were in the *Ejercito Revolucionario del Pueblo* together.'

He looked irritated, assessing her with an acid look. 'Yes. Us and some six hundred retards against forces of security that numbered 400,000. Our average age was twenty-three.'

The thought of a few hundred youths arrayed against an entire state gave her a depressing sensation of hopelessness but, at the same time, a certain awe for the man in front of her, as if he were the incarnation of something profound and mystical. 'How could you join a cause that seems so . . . impossible?'

'Ché won! Fidel won!' The tough barrio accent gave way to a more philosophical remove. 'It's not a thing of the numbers. It's a way of seeing. You're the vanguard of the Revolution, the sacred Liberators fighting for the People. The side of Good. Of Justice. Of Historical Destiny.' He shrugged. 'Stupidities like that.'

He made a bitter little show of teeth. 'I'll tell you how it was, *Profesora*, so you can write it up for your classes. Our leader, Santucho, had been defying the statistics for so long that he lost contact with the reality. In his mind, we would triumph because of our wills of steel. Win or die for Argentina, that was our slogan. He imagined that the masses would rise up to support us, that our six hundred conscripts were the beginning of sixty thousand. That was the dream. But they tortured our sympathizers and murdered our families and in the end it was they who ambushed us, they who had the stronger intelligence. It was a ring of iron that Santucho couldn't break with his transcendent thought.'

Her eyes drifted past the vapors of sad history to the pile of stolen video cameras. He went on in a sonorous voice. 'We had too many amateurs, people with shaky hands and bad judgement. Those are the ones who get you killed. Then begin the meetings where your contact doesn't show, or where you drive past the safe-house to find a plainclothes cop or a pair of *milicos* smelling up the whole block. Your friends start to fall. Clara falls, Luis falls, the Buffalo falls. This one is taken prisoner at his mother's house, another is killed in a gunfight; some you never find out what happened, they're just gone.' He continued the soft hypnotic eulogy. 'Claudio falls, Carlos falls, Elena falls, Billy falls. Mario falls, Rodolfo falls, Oscar and Juana, *el Pibe Loco*, Sandra and Silvia and Mauro and Nestor. They all fall. All of them.' Resentment stiffened his voice. 'But Ricardo doesn't fall, because Ricardo's out of the country. Because Ricardo ran to Mexico.'

He fell silent and Athena could tell that his mind had gone back twenty-five years, to long-dead people who gazed back at him with smooth hopeful faces. And he, with all the skills of the brilliant guerilla gone adrift, his own fall so utterly complete. She remembered what Ricardo had said; that some survivors were intact and others broken. Her last question was so awkward and intrusive that she didn't dare phrase it as a question. At the same time, she couldn't keep from saying it.

'So you left the Revolution.'

He frowned at her. 'Didn't you hear me? Did I go into exile?' He sat upright. 'In 1975, when they killed Santucho and all the little hens scattered for Mexico and Switzerland, I stayed planted! I kept hitting the banks and the comisarias until I was the only one still standing.' He practically spit. 'I never deserted the Revolution! It deserted me, revolution of shit!' He became hard again, contemptuous. 'I'm a criminal! That's my political statement! Tell *that* to Ricardo! I did my service to *La Revolución*. I brought the final justice to one of the worst *hijos de puta* that they had, a murderer of dozens, of hundreds. I did it! And you? You can't even find the killer of one! All you do is make ornaments for the oppressors with your clever little reports!'

'What kind of political statement is it to cooperate with the police who were hunting down your friends twenty years ago?'

The challenge blanked him, and then a murderous fury blossomed in his face. She was afraid in that instant that he might get up and hit her. 'Who are you, to come here asking these types of questions? You talk about matters of life and death as if *you* could

95

judge *me!* Don't be so confident! Don't imagine that your passport protects you here! That was the mistake of your friend Waterbury!'

She fought down her fear. 'What do you know about Waterbury?'

He glared at her for a few seconds and then let out a disparaging hiss. '*Qué concha brava!*' What a bold cunt. He looked to the side and then a cool impersonal manner dropped over him like a cloth. He stood up. 'Ricardo sent you so I attended you. Now I have things to do.' She followed him to the door and he unlocked it for her. 'Wait at the kiosk on the corner and I'll call a *remis* to look for you there. And don't mention me to anyone.'

As she walked out she turned to him and extended her hand. He had something dark and luminous about him, like obsidian. 'Thank you for meeting me, Cacho.'

She could see the forces working away behind his harsh agonized face, the struggle between the disinterred revolutionary and the hardened criminal. At last he took her hand, then leaned over and gave her a last cologne-scented kiss. 'You're *brava*, friend of Berenski. You don't know what disillusion is yet. I'm talking to you from the other side. Stay here a while in Argentina. After, we'll revise our accounts.'

CHAPTER 13

The problem now, Athena thought as she waited for the Comisario in the conference room, was how to tell Miguel that she wanted to bring Ricardo Berenski into the investigation. Elements of the Buenos Aires police had thought highly enough of Berenski to threaten to kill him, and she hadn't yet sculpted a good excuse for why she had sought him out behind Miguel's back. Nonetheless, Berenski had turned up a stunning bit of information: the number in Waterbury's pocket had belonged to Teresa Castex de Pelegrini, the rich woman that Berenski had met with Waterbury that night six months ago, and the wife of Carlo Pelegrini. Fortunato's authority and experience could help now, and she'd decided to bank on her gut feeling about him. On some unquantifiable level, he wanted to see this through and, as if in confirmation of this, he had announced over the telephone that he'd finally come up with something 'of great significance.' When he'd summoned her here for a briefing she'd felt like calling up Carmen Amado to tell her that yes, there was an honest cop in Buenos Aires.

A familiar voice interrupted her thoughts.

'Athena, the Goddess of Love!'

Fabian filled the doorway with his smile, his ash-blond curls as perfect as if he'd just come from the beauty salon. He wore a sports jacket of eggplant-colored suede, matched by a maroon shirt and an olive tie with gold and purple stripes. The combination so surprised Athena that she didn't bother to correct his mythological error. 'Interesting jacket.'

'It's unique, no? With this color? At first I thought No, Fabian. No. But after . . .' He made a discerning little frown, like a chef adding ingredients. 'I calm it a little with the shirt and balance it with the green . . . It remains half-dignified, no?'

'No.'

'Ah!' he said, easing into the room and bending down to give her a patchouli-scented kiss. 'You are bitter chocolate!' He put his hand over his heart and broke into an old song, looking deeply into her eyes: '*El dia que me quieras . . .*' stopping after the first line. 'This is by the immortal Carlos Gardel, that died tragically in an accident of aviation in 1935. I, personally, hate tango, but you can't argue with Carlos. Every day he sings better!' He slid into the seat across from her. 'I can't stop thinking about your case. That one of Robert Waterbury.'

'You're very much the thinker!'

He accepted the ironic compliment with a wave of the hand. 'I was reading in my screenplay book last night and I found something that might be useful.' His face became nearly mystical with the power of his insight. 'At this point, I think you must consider the Chief. Have you thought about that?'

She wasn't sure how to react, and Fabian plowed on. 'Because in the movies, it's always the chief that did it. The hero's partner is killed, and then three quarters of the way into the plot it's always "My God, it was the chief all along!" Don't tell me you haven't seen that a thousand times.'

Athena looked at the clownish policeman, unsure of his intent. 'Are you talking about a particular person, Fabian?'

'Of course not!' he answered, with a fatuousness that incited suspicion rather than allaying it. 'That would be inconceivable! I'm talking of concepts, of plot mechanisms. But if you have no other ideas and you're here, why not? Moreover, the idea that some sinister chief committed the crime is much more interesting than this tired hypothesis of drugs, of the settling of scores. At least, from the cinematic point of view.'

'Your joke is in very bad taste, Fabian.'

He dropped his smile. 'You're right. The truth is, I feel sorry for you. It's difficult to come to a foreign country and try to solve a crime like this. There's much frustration. But I would like to help you. What I suggest is this: after work, privately, without telling the Comisario, you and I should go and make some inquiries. To survey once again the crime scene, see if some clue has been missed. Then there is dinner, with one of our excellent red wines, and we should visit some interesting bars in Palermo and San Telmo, to familiarize you with the ambiance of the events. There is one that is *very* interesting called –'

'Fabian –'

'El Gaucho Maricon –'

'Fabian! I don't think that would be appropriate –'

'Doctora,' he interrupted her, leaning close and speaking in an urgent near-whisper, 'you are in Buenos Aires! The city where love and death never stop changing their thousand beautiful masks!' He suddenly let go of the poetic approach. 'Am I too transparent?'

'I knew boys in high school who were less transparent than you.'

'Ow!' He winced. 'Now, you hit me hard, Athena! My ego has shrunk to the size of a coffee bean.' He stood up and broke into a smile. 'Thus is life. No? I give you the number of my cell phone.' Extracting a card from his pocket. 'If you need help at any moment you can call your friend Fabian. Until then . . .' She felt his curls tickle her skin as he kissed her cheek. He stopped in the doorway, shaking his finger at her. 'You're going to like my police story. You don't know it yet, but you're going to like it.'

The sight of Comisario Fortunato's weary face pasted in his drab office dispersed the queer cologne of Fabian's games. He gave an officer a few pesos for coffee and enquired about her previous days in Buenos Aires. Had she passed them well? How was she occupying her time? She answered blandly as he stacked some papers on his desk, something about meeting with a few people, enjoying the cafés. She was eager to find out what he'd uncovered.

'*Bien.*' He put the papers to the side. 'I have good news for you. After we spoke I asked all in the brigada to inquire among their sources for information about Waterbury. This was not so simple; many times the *buchones*, for reasons of their own, are not eager to chat. As this is priority one, we did it, and thankfully it rendered quite a bit. It seems that one of our informants heard another criminal boasting about killing a German and, following that line, it turned out that it was not a German after all, but a Northamerican. It's not sure yet, but it seems that we already have the killer in custody.'

Athena felt her heart beat faster but she said nothing.

'It seems that one of the material authors of the crime is a delinquent named Enrique Boguso, that has already been processed on a different murder that he committed after that of Robert Waterbury. We think he is close to a confession.'

99

'Why did he do it?'

'The motive still isn't clear, but, as we suspected, it had something to do with drugs. Waterbury wanted to buy a small amount, and then they decided to get clever: It's not known yet. Let's see if it gets clearer in the next few days.'

As glad as the news made her, she felt cheated that it didn't involve a connection to Teresa and Carlo Pelegrini. Chiding herself: she was complaining because the murder was too mundane? And yet . . . 'There's something I need to tell you, Miguel. Something of interest to the case.'

'What, young one?'

She felt timid before Fortunato's kind eyes. 'I went and talked with Ricardo Berenski. He's a journalist, perhaps you've heard of him.'

Fortunato rubbed his chin. 'He writes about sports, no? About *futbol*.'

She almost laughed with relief. The Comisario's features had never seemed so endearing. 'No. He's an investigative journalist. I went to him just to get another view on the case.'

Fortunato looked open and expectant. 'And . . . ?'

'We traced a phone number in Robert Waterbury's pocket on the night he was murdered. I wrote it down from the *expediente*, but I forgot to mention it to you.' She blushed as she lied, ignoring at the same time the fluttering question of why the Comisario hadn't traced the number himself. 'It seems to be the personal number of Teresa Castex de Pelegrini. The wife of Carlo Pelegrini.'

Fortunato cocked his eyebrows a little. 'Pelegrini? The magnate?' He'd already traced the number to Pelegrini's house, but had left it at that in the hopes that everything would die down. Now, though, with Berenski involved, he couldn't ignore it. The investigation had just broached a new barrier, and he had no choice but to go with it and improvise. 'Interesting. What did your friend the journalist say?'

'Nothing, yet. We tried to call her but we didn't get anywhere. I thought perhaps the authority of the police could open things a bit. If we need to listen to the line, or something like that.'

Fortunato took his time in replying. Berenski knew much about Pelegrini, maybe more than anyone outside Pelegrini's own circle. It would be helpful to know what Berenski knew. And there was still the matter of the name *Renssaelaer*, the last little god whom

Waterbury had invoked as the possible cause of his suffering. Besides, better to manage Berenski than to let him go around loose. 'Let's do this, Athena. Telephone the Señor Berenski so that we can combine for a little chat. Not in the station; something informal. Tell him it could be of interest to everyone.'

They met at the Café Losadas again. At mid-morning the big room was quiet except for a half-dozen people browsing among the books. Berenski greeted Athena with a kiss and the two men shook hands, then there was a little impasse at the booth as neither man wanted to sit with his back to the door. Berenski won out and she slid in next to Fortunato.

The Comisario gave Berenski a quizzical look. 'You wrote that piece about the corruption among the *futbol* referees, no?'

'That was I.'

'You did well, *chico*. But tell me, did you see the last SuperClassic? Where Morelo refused to call that foul in the last minute? In your opinion, was that dirty, or no?'

'Morelo is dirty,' he said in his croaking voice. 'But in that instance, the call was correct.'

'No! You're for Boca!'

Ricardo shrugged. 'River should have paid Morelo more. Then he would have seen that foul with microscopic clarity. But Comisario!' He hunched his shoulders comically, his palms upturned as he burst out enthusiastically, 'It's Argentina! What are you drinking, *amigo*? I invite you with the money I won on the SuperClassic.'

Fortunato took an espresso, bitter, while Athena took hers with a dollop of whipped cream. Berenski accompanied his with a shot of scotch. Fortunato admired his whiskey-in-the-morning style: he played it all, the *muchacho*. The journalist took out a palm-sized notebook and a black fountain pen gleaming with gold.

'What an elegant pen!' Fortunato said admiringly. 'They pay you well.'

Berenski held up the instrument, examining it with satisfaction. 'It's fake! Made in China. The watch, too. I'm fanatic about fake things! One can be ironic without saying a word!' He leaned in, croaking confidentially to the policeman, 'There's a little store on Bolivar called *Todo Falso*. All of the best names, but fake! Now I'm trying to get one of those autos with duplicated papers that are circulating everywhere. Maybe you know someone . . .'

Fortunato laughed. 'You're an *hijo de puta*!'

'What can I say?' the journalist grinned as he rocked back in the booth. 'I am! But there's much to discuss. Athena already told you about the telephone number?'

'Yes. It was interesting.'

'The number was registered to one of Pelegrini's corporations, but it was listed as being at his residence in Palermo Chico. When I called it a woman answered to the name Teresa, but then she marked me as a stranger and cut the line.'

'Even being Castex, that doesn't mean it has something to do with the murder.'

'Of course. But I think it would be interesting to have a chat with the señora, no?'

Fortunato rubbed the stubble along his jaw, nodding. 'It's a good idea. But such people are not so eager to talk. I would have to get an order from the judge to compel her, and I'm not certain the evidence justifies that sort of measure. The judge is Emilio Duarte. He's very strict about matters of the Constitution.'

'Ah, Duarte,' the journalist said casually. 'He has a good reputation.'

Fortunato couldn't tell if Berenski was just flashing another fake accessory with his remark about Duarte. He chose not to agree or disagree. 'I should tell you that we've found information that leads in another direction. It could be that we already have the killer.'

'Yes? Who?'

'Perhaps you remember him: Enrique Boguso. He was the one that killed the bricklayer and his wife in front of their children in Quilmes three months ago.'

Berenski wrinkled his nose with disgust. 'I remember it. They used electric shocks. 1970s style.' He touched the pen to the notebook. 'Enrique Boguso, no? And who was the informant?'

Fortunato put his hand over the pad. 'Amigo Ricardo, we're a bit premature here. We're still mounting the case. I'm speaking to you confidentially, as a friend of La Doctora.'

'It's fine, Miguel.' He capped the pen with a counterfeit click and put it away. 'But tell me: how would it happen that someone like Boguso, a brute of the outer barrios, crosses with a foreigner like Robert Waterbury who was staying in the center and mixing with rich people like Teresa Castex de Pelegrini?'

Fortunato explained patiently the theories of the drug motive and Waterbury's gathering of atmosphere for his book. 'Neither is certain yet.'

'This book,' Berenski answered back, 'that's another thing. It seems that Waterbury was a very lazy writer.'

'What do you mean?'

'Most writers have a journal, or some manuscript that they're torturing. Especially if they are gathering atmosphere. Athena says that there was nothing like that mentioned in the *expediente*.'

That detail had bothered Fortunato also. He turned his hands upward sympathetically. 'Perhaps that was the problem: he had no notes because he had no ideas, no hopes. For that, he turned to drugs.'

Berenski sat back. 'Still, it's curious.'

'Yes. But let's return to the matter of Pelegrini. I read some of your articles before I came, but it's a turbid business. It escapes me. What's going on with Pelegrini?'

The waiter materialized and clacked the order onto the table, slapping the bill onto the spike, which Berenski drew towards himself as he looked into the thick glass tumbler. To Fortunato he seemed to be using the liquor to stall, uncertain as to whether he should enter deeply into the theme of Pelegrini. Finally, he looked up with a new air of sobriety. 'I'll tell you now, because this is coming out now anyway. It's thus: Pelegrini is involved in a war right now. On one side, you have Pelegrini, the President, and various military who are tied into the vast network of businesses that Pelegrini says he doesn't own. On the other, you have the Minister of Economy and the Governor of Buenos Aires, acting for the gringos.'

'What do you mean?' Athena asked. 'What does the United States have to do with it?'

'Because RapidMail wants the Argentine Postal System.'

Athena wrinkled her brow. 'RapidMail? They're just a courier service.'

Berenski laughed. '*Chica*, you see the little striped box and you think they're like a McDonald's of the sky. But RapidMail has origins that are half-obscure. It was started by Joseph Carver, ex-agent of the CIA. Carver began his transport career in the Vietnam War, where he ran questionable cargos in and out of the Golden Triangle, *estilo* Iran-Contra, but before they had to go to all the trouble of convicting someone and then pardoning them. He made some very good friends there, including other CIA agents and your ex-president. All the *muchachos* returned home with money to invest, and thus began RapidMail.'

Ricardo hesitated as he watched someone who'd come in the door. 'Fine. Twenty-five years later, they notice a fat fish called Argentina. The country is for sale, and they decide they want to buy the Post Office. Think of it: a discount price, guaranteed profits written into the contract by force of law, rate increases without end. They can take it all over, or just take over the profitable parts and leave the rest to the people. Who's not going to be interested in that business? So they start to arrange it, using Grupo AmiBank as their front because the Grupo has all those golden connections that smooth the course. Except Carlo Pelegrini already has the same idea, and he also has very good connections, and six months advance. When RapidMail's men show up to begin negotiations three of Pelegrini's *pistoleros* pull them over on the way in from the airport. They take out their weapons and they courteously dis-invite them from the party. An embarrassing lack of hospitality on the part of the *patria*, no?'

Fortunato opened his hands. 'It's a disgrace!'

'So Joseph Carver makes some phone calls. He calls his friend the ex-president and he calls an acquaintance at the United States Chamber of Commerce. He starts to talk and talk about this corrupt Pelegrini, and about the Argentines who will not open their markets. It's a violation of the sacredness of Free Trade! Suddenly Pelegrini is under investigation by the DEA, by the FBI. There are complaints before the World Trade Organization and very serious chats between Ovejo, our minister of Economy, and the United States ambassador. Ovejo travels to Washington to talk with the vice-president. Suddenly, Ovejo is attacking Pelegrini at all sides. On television, in the newspapers, in his private offices. "We must open the country to more foreign investment!" he says. "We must stop this corrupt man and cancel his extortionate government contracts!" ' He turned to Fortunato. 'He's like Morelo of the SuperClassic: The gringos paid him enough that he would start calling the foul.'

'What does Pelegrini do to defend himself?' Fortunato asked.

'That scandal of Ovejo's brother-in-law? That was investigated and mounted by Pelegrini. With the help of the Buenos Aires police, eh? When that failed, he tried to use his inside men to design bid specifications that would make it impossible for anyone but himself to win the contract. The same thing he has done for years. But this time it's not certain he will win because the Grupo is also at work there.'

'How do you get all this information?' Athena asked in amazement.

Ricardo laughed. 'Everyone believes in a free press when it comes to airing the misdeeds of their enemies. You would be surprised at my sources.'

Fortunato rubbed his mustache thoughtfully. 'And tell me, Ricardo: have you heard the name Renssaelaer?'

The journalist leaned back in his chair. He looked slightly distressed, and it took him some time to answer. 'William Renssaelaer. He's the chief of all Pelegrini's security operations. He came here as an attaché to the American embassy during the Dictatorship and stayed. He directs everything that constitutes security for Pelegrini, from his bodyguards to whatever intelligence Pelegrini is gathering from the government or from his corporate rivals. Why do you mention Renssaelaer?'

'It's a name that I saw floating in the newspapers, nothing more.' The Comisario frowned down into his coffee cup, weighing Berenski's strange reaction to the name Renssaelaer. 'All this is very interesting, Ricardo, but still I don't hear anything that would connect Pelegrini to Waterbury. Not enough to issue a summons to Teresa Castex.'

'Waterbury worked for AmiBank, which is the parent of Grupo AmiBank, on his first stay in Argentina. No, Athena?'

'That's what his wife said.'

Fortunato shook his head. 'But Waterbury worked there long before all this between the Grupo AmiBank and Pelegrini.'

'Yes, but perhaps his friend is still there. And then, we have the phone number in Waterbury's pocket, connecting him to the intimate circle of Pelegrini.'

Fortunato covered his anxiety with a thoughtful silence, glancing down for a time at the sludge in his coffee cup. Berenski was very *piola*, very crafty, and he probably had other contacts who might become interested in the case. He had ended the careers of a lot of police. He, Fortunato, would have to move much faster to stay ahead of Berenski. 'If the Boguso lead ends up dead, I'll make my best case with Duarte to revise Teresa Castex's telephone records and summon her to the station.'

'*Excelente*, Miguel. But one little thing more . . .'

Berenski now began to ask him, in a nonchalant way, about the goings-on in the barrios north of Buenos Aires. Fortunato spotted his game immediately: being of the south, Fortunato might not mind tipping a few cards on his northern rivals. The journalist teased out the details with a comic bravado that made it enjoyable, like being shaved by an expert barber, and Fortunato dropped him little clues about car theft and the sale of *expedientes* that he hoped would cripple the aggressive actions of the *brigadas* of the north. Berenski laughed as if the deceits were stunts in a screwball comedy, laughed and made notes with his fake fountain pen. Fortunato gave him a few broad clues and then mentioned his next appointment. When they got up to leave the journalist snapped the cap on his pen and offered it to the policeman. '*Amigo* Fortunato, take this little souvenir, as you were admiring it.'

'Ricardo, no!'

'It's nothing, *querido*! I have twenty just like it at home! *Por favor!*' Berenski clasped the policeman's shoulder and looked him in the eye, grinning. 'You can use it to write up the Waterbury report.'

They parted company in the pounding traffic of Corrientes, and Fortunato walked silently at Athena's side, looking weary in his tan sports jacket and drooping gray mustache. The amiable chat with Berenski had raised her confidence in the detective and she felt a wave of affection for the man as she glanced at his large ungraceful figure. 'Miguel,' she said, 'I want to ask you a slightly delicate question.'

He looked over at her earnestly. 'Whatever you want, daughter.'

'You were telling Ricardo about corruption in other parts of the police. But what's happening in your own jurisdiction?'

He stopped walking, startled by the question, and she was afraid from his silence that she had offended him. He looked at her silently and thoughtfully, and she sensed that he was preparing to reveal a private shame. 'Athena. Corruption, there always is. Like that one over there . . .' pointing at a young *Federal* at the corner. 'His salary is six hundred pesos monthly, and yet he must continually confront the worst of society. There arrives a time when he starts to feel that he deserves something extra. Bites of ten pesos, twenty pesos.

Picoteando.' He made pecking motions with his fingers. 'I don't condone it, but thus it is. It's very difficult to stop.'

'What about at higher levels?'

He looked at her without speaking for a moment. 'This is a strange line of questions. Why do you ask?'

'I'm trying to understand all this. People keep telling me how corrupt the police are, how they fear them. But when I look at you, I don't see that. I see someone very dignified, very sincere. And I just can't reconcile it.'

The Comisario faced her without saying anything, and though his features didn't move a strange tremor seemed to work beneath the surface. He put his hand gently on her back and steered her forward, and she felt as if he were scolding her until he said, 'The truth is, I've seen some things.' He glanced towards the young *Federal* and stopped talking until the light changed and they'd crossed the street. 'Once I remember we assaulted a lottery stand. A *narco* was using it to parcel out cocaine and we sequestered some three kilos. Except when I read the *sumario* later, it was only one kilo.'

'What did you do?'

'That's always the question, no? These are people you work with every day. Sometimes your life depends on them.' They'd reached the temporary wooden wall of a construction site. Someone had scribbled the words *Ovejo – Asesino Gringo!* 'I went to one of the other men in the assault and I said "*Che*, we grabbed three kilos, no? The *sumario* says one." And I knew I'd hit it right on, because he put himself a little fierce and he says, "What's happening with you, Fortunato? Are you going around with a scale now?"'

'And what happened?'

Fortunato answered without looking up from the ground. 'I acted the *boludo* and didn't say anything else, then they transferred me out of Narcotics and into Homicide. And now here I am, at your service!' They stopped at the corner in a clutter of businessmen and legal functionaries. Only two blocks from the *Palacio de Justicia*, the narrow street was lined by bookstores filled with legal primers. There were volumes on forensics and constitutional law, divorce and custody, civil suits, product liability: everything to make a just society. The presence of so many books about law in such a corrupt city struck Athena as ironic at first, but then, people never stopped hoping. Just like the scandals that Berenski and others continually turned up: there were always new ones, but always people willing to risk it all to expose them.

The Comisario must have been basking in the same line of thought as they silently traversed the city. 'Look, corrupt ones – there's always a few. But you can't see everything divided in two: good and evil, honest and dishonest. It's artificial. Because also in the mix there's loyalty, there's friendship. There's the obligation one has to the family. And so evil gets mixed with good. In reality, there are very few men who are truly evil.'

'It's not the evil people that do most of the damage in this world,' Athena said. 'It's all the good ones who help them. I read about these corporations that cook up trade and finance laws that destroy Third World countries. I read these human rights reports, filled with the most horrific kinds of abuse. And I ask myself' – glancing over at him – 'what makes a decent person become an accomplice? Because if that sort of evil could be stopped, that helpful evil, there would be no Hitlers, no Stalins, no biological and nuclear weapons designed to kill indiscriminately.' She became bolder as they stepped into the Plaza de la Justicia. 'At a certain point, you have to say that those who help are evil, too.'

The policeman remained silent as they continued to his car, and again she feared that she'd gone too far. 'I'll drop you off at the Sheraton,' he said at last. 'I have another meeting in an hour.'

Fortunato left her at her hotel and headed through the grandiose canyons of the center toward the familiar province where he lived and worked. Without intending to, he found himself steering toward the vacant lot where Waterbury had died. His eyes moved along the wall of the factory up to the single window in the corner where the caretaker lived. The window had been opened and the flowered curtain ruffled over the sill in the autumn wind. What did the caretaker know? What other witnesses might be waiting to come forward? Some late-night pedestrian, or a homeless person living in one of the empty buildings nearby? Even with no witnesses, he could feel the abstract presence of a spectator: the universe, Athena, himself, viewing it again and again in his memory. Waterbury looking at him over the seat, grabbing onto him with his eyes as if at the last shred of kindness in the world. I have a wife and daughter . . . Fortunato rolled on through increasingly desolate streets, adrift not in the hard white light of the afternoon but in the two dark hours last spring when he had made the brief and terminal acquaintance of Robert Waterbury.

CHAPTER 14

Fortunato knocked on the metal door, loud enough to be heard but retaining a shade of politeness. Not pounding, like a cop. After that he put his hands out to the sides, making it obvious that they were empty without holding them up in the air. '*Ché*, Cacho. It's I, Fortunato.'

The locks clattered and the door swung open. Cacho stood there in blue jeans and a sweatshirt, looking at him with his usual expectant hostility, waiting for him to speak. 'It seems we have a mutual friend,' Fortunato said.

'Who?'

'The famous gringa.'

'*Who?*'

Dismissing the feigned ignorance. 'Stop swelling my balls and let me in! We already know! She came two days ago, in the morning. It's not a big thing!'

The criminal seemed to be considering whether to keep denying everything or to let him in and find out what he knew. He finally stood aside and Fortunato came in.

The windows facing the street still languished behind steel shutters, but those facing the courtyard let in the pleasant afternoon sun. The oily smell of pan-fried meat from a late lunch hung in the air. 'You fitted it out well there. A clear field of fire out that side all the way to the street, you can escape from that side door without being exposed. The little tower in the front . . .' He nodded. 'You didn't waste your time in Cuba. And inside,' nodding approvingly at the expensive furniture, 'very nice. It's best to steal quality.'

Cacho said nothing.

Fortunato looked him over. He didn't have a gun within reach. He could kill him now. It wouldn't be a murder profoundly investigated. A bold man would do that, a man who had confidence and resolve. But was he that type of man? Like, for example, Domingo, or Bianco? And what type of man was that, finally?

'Are you following her?' the thief asked.

'I'm her custodian. Assisting her in the investigation.'

Cacho gave an acrid little smile. 'Yes, it's neat business all around.'

Fortunato nodded noncommittally, kept circling the room and looking at the paintings and the music collection. Argentine rock, foreign rock, a few tangos sprinkled in. '*Tangos Bajos*, by Melingo. I heard he's good.'

'I would make you a recording, but that would be a violation of the artist's rights, no?'

'Cacho, Cacho.' Fortunato shook his head wearily. 'She's an interesting girl, La Doctora. She's obsessed with these issues of Truth and Corruption and all of that. Typical Northamerican. Such a good eye for all the immorality beyond their borders.'

Cacho reacted impatiently. 'Look, Miguel, to cut it short, I banked you. I didn't claim to know you personally, of course, but by reputation you are an impenetrable fortress of integrity.' He flicked his head to the side. '*Bien*, perhaps not impenetrable, because she's not so stupid. But at least only semi-penetrated.'

'Thank you for your generous assessment.' Fortunato saw from Cacho's reflection in the window behind him that he had a pistol stuck into his pantwaist after all.

'One doesn't sacrifice an associate of so many years.' Cacho scratched his chest. 'They gave you the hide to eat on that one, amigo. I knew that when you told me Domingo and Vasquez were coming with you. Then you killed the *boludo* as if you were some adolescent with a rented gun.' Cacho twisted his features in distaste. 'An innocent with a daughter!'

'You, Cacho? Is that you? Who administered The People's Justice to General Lopez so long ago?' The detective kept circling, filing away the details of the room. 'How many innocents did you kill? *Boludos* that took a policeman's job for the pension, that couldn't even spell the word Capitalism. Very few know your history, Cacho, but I do. I've even read about you in books! Under your old name, of course. But as you say, one doesn't sacrifice an associate of many years.' Assault rifle, gun ports in the walls. Probably an arsenal hidden here somewhere. A door leading out to a courtyard, a stairway from the kitchen to the second floor. 'You're right. It's lamentable, the accident. But it was Domingo's fault. He brought

Vasquez. Vasquez went crazy. If you had come with us when I asked you it would have happened differently.'

'Don't put me in your whorehouse, Miguel. Killing some idiot writer –'

'I didn't kill him!' Fortunato heard the weakness in his own voice. 'It was Domingo and Vasquez! It wasn't me!' Cacho's silence goaded Fortunato on. 'What's Vasquez saying? Is he going around singing to the whole world?'

'I don't mix with Vasquez.'

Fortunato's voice was getting louder. 'But what do you hear? What are your *muchachos* saying? Because I tell you: I didn't kill the gringo!'

At that moment a pot clanked in the kitchen and Fortunato took a few steps towards it. A woman wearing nothing but a T-shirt was holding a *mate* in one hand and kettle in the other. She ducked out of sight up the stairs. Cacho's hand had moved to his back hip.

'It's time to go,' the criminal said. 'You're upsetting my guest.' He opened the door and stood next to it.

Fortunato moved to the opening and stepped into the afternoon sunlight. The flat neutrality of Cacho's voice offered little comfort. 'I didn't say anything to the gringa That's one thing you don't have to worry about. Of Vasquez, I can't guarantee anything. This is your matter, Miguel. You created it. If you need to settle accounts with Vasquez and Domingo, that's your business. I'm clean in this one.'

Fortunato thought he saw in Cacho's hard black eyes the faint disgust that the innocent have for the guilty. 'No, hombre. You are very far from clean.' He gave Cacho his back.

'Miguel!'

He turned around.

'I'm sorry about your wife.'

He couldn't tell if the criminal was mocking him or if he was trying to offer genuine consolation for an old associate. He raised his hand in a tired wave and walked away.

CHAPTER 15

'A delinquent like Boguso is sub-human,' the Comisario of #33 was saying as he led them through the station. 'A career delinquent with an abnormal personality. Drugs, auto theft, robbery. When he was sixteen he killed a boy in another gang. Now he's here for torturing and killing a couple in front of their three children.' The Comisario shook his head, disgusted.

'Too much *merca*,' Fortunato said.

The Comisario grimaced. 'The boy was twisted before he ever took his first noseful of *merca*. Torturing the children in front of the parents, then the parents in front of the children. For two hundred pesos!'

He guided Athena and Fortunato past the clean white empty cell that Boguso occupied and up to the interview room. The wooden stairs gave off a faint smell of varnish.

'All reformed,' the patron said proudly. 'Afterwards, I'll give you the tour.' He unlocked the door to the observation room and Athena walked into the dark closet-like space with two metal chairs similar to the ones at her kitchen table back home. The Comisario of #33 sat down beside her and she looked for the first time at the suspect.

She had trouble reconciling the man in front of her, slouching alone in orange coveralls, with a man who would brutally murder and torture. Undersized and skinny, he sat in the chair with his manacled hands folded together on the table. His stubbly black hair revealed several scars lying like little white worms along his skull, and his knuckles were covered with black tattoos, but his thin, young face looked surprisingly composed and receptive.

Fortunato came in followed by a clerk. The clerk sat at the table with a pad and Fortunato pulled a chair directly across from the criminal at a distance of about a meter and settled into it.

'Do you know why I'm here, Enrique?'

'Yes. Over the gringo,' the suspect returned. He had a higher voice than she expected, slightly reedy.

'That's right. The one we talked about three days ago, Robert Waterbury. And have you been physically pressured or threatened?'

The criminal shook his head. 'No, Señor.'

'Have you been coerced in any way?'

'No, Señor.'

'Enrique, we are referring to events that happened the night of October 16, last year, one week before that matter with the bricklayer and his wife. Correct?'

'Yes.'

'Why don't you tell me again what you were doing that night?'

The killer went into a description of drinking beers at a club called the Liverpool, in San Telmo. He'd been with a friend that they called *el Uruguayo*, whose first name was Marco, last name unknown. They'd taken various *papelitos* and some small chalks. Did they take them to sell? Yes. Had they sold at the Liverpool before? Yes, many times. How many papers? How many chalks? About forty *papelitos* and . . . he hesitated, six or seven chalks.

'And can you describe for me the *papelitos*?'

'They were of blue metallized foil, about two centimeters on each side.'

Athena remembered the blue cocaine packets from the *expediente*, and hearing them cited so precisely by the criminal lent a strange authority to the mass of documents she'd spent so many hours examining, as if they themselves had created Boguso and his actions. The door to the observation room opened and Athena looked up as Judge Duarte walked in, putting his fingers to his lips and shaking hands with her and the Comisario of #33. *Sominex*, Berenski had called him. He seemed wide awake now as he stood in the darkness watching the confession.

Boguso continued, describing the events as any young man might describe a boring night out with a friend. They'd fallen into conversation with Waterbury and the gringo said he was researching some book that he was writing. They'd given him some *merca* to sample, then told him that they had a better quality in the car. While Waterbury was in the bathroom, Marco, the Uruguayan, said, 'The gringo has a lot of *mangos, viste*? Let's take him and get money from his credit card,' because it was a thing that Marco had done once before. *You keep them all night and drive them around to different bank machines and make them withdraw the limit at each one.*

Athena kept trying to imagine Waterbury being stupid enough to go outside with Boguso and the missing *Uruguayo*. Even as literary research into the Buenos Aires underworld, it seemed a strangely reckless move for a former banker with a family and mortgage payments to consider.

Boguso went on with his story. At the car Marco had taken out the gun and put on the handcuffs, then they'd pushed him to the floor of the back seat.

'And Waterbury didn't resist?'

Boguso gave a light shrug. 'He resisted a little, but we hit him a few times and he went along. We told him that after we finished with the credit cards we would let him go.'

'Did you have the intention of letting him go?'

'I wasn't really thinking about it,' Boguso explained easily. 'I was just thinking about the money. It was, like, a job.'

The callousness of the words would have angered Athena if the whole tone of the confession had not felt off-kilter. She knew from other research that stories of inconceivable cruelty always brought their own surreal atmosphere, but something else felt strange about this confession: Boguso seemed almost cheerful.

They'd taken eighty pesos from his wallet and then tried the credit card at a bank on Avenida Regimiento de Patricios, only to have it be overdrawn on the first try. 'Marco got angry. He thought the gringo was giving us the wrong identification number, and moreover, he was half-crazy from *milonga*.'

'By *milonga* you mean cocaine?'

'Yes. He was snorting from the chalks, which were pure, and he hits the gringo and says "*Hijo de puta*, are you trying to screw us?" And then I hear him beating the gringo with the butt of his pistol.'

'You are driving?'

'Yes.' Boguso glanced in the direction of the observation mirror. 'A 1992 Ford Falcon sedan, colored metallized gray, with an interior of light brown. Marco had a .32 pistol, I believe the ammunition he used was Remington, I had a nine millimeter in the glove compartment, an Astra, and I was using cartridges of the make Federal –'

Something too rehearsed here! It was too much detail, too fast, in the very language of the *expediente*! She glanced across the dim closet toward the Comisario of #33 and the judge, expecting them to return her look of skepticism, but the two of them watched without flinching. Was it just her? After all, here was a man confessing to a murder six feet in front of her face. People lied to proclaim their innocence, not their guilt!

Comisario Fortunato reacted to Boguso's rush of strangely wooden description. 'Slow down, Enrique. What happened then?'

'I heard the gun go off and Waterbury made a terrible scream: he was shot in the hand and I think the body.'

Fortunato questioned him a bit more sharply. 'But you told me the gringo was lying on the floor. How could you see it?'

Boguso hesitated, then went on like a student with the right answer. 'I couldn't see the gringo. But I could see Marco, and how it all turned out after.'

Fortunato nodded and Boguso went on with the description: how they had panicked and driven him to San Justo, how the Uruguayan, in a frenzy, had shot him several more times and how, arriving at the vacant lot, he himself had finished Waterbury with the nine milli-meter.

She felt the Comisario of #33's hand on her shoulder, as if shielding her from the impact of the murder's final moments, but it wasn't the brutality of the words that bothered her, but rather their perfection. By the time he had finished she knew for certain that his testimony was full of lies, no matter how well they matched the record. Maybe he'd been involved in the murder. Maybe he'd even fired the final shot, but something bigger was being neatly interred in this flawless confession, and she knew no one was going to help her dig it up. Her stomach began to churn. If she took part in this sham she became little more than an accessory to Waterbury's murder.

When Fortunato joined them afterwards in the Comisario's office, he seemed exhausted by the recounting of the crime. His shoulders slumped and at first he didn't fully involve himself in the conversation with the Comisario of #33 and Judge Duarte. They discussed the whereabouts of the Uruguayan and the procurement of a search warrant for Boguso's apartment so that they could sequester the murder weapon. Judge Duarte, with an uncharacteristic zeal, promised to have the proper papers by the end of the day. Athena brought up the matter of Teresa Castex de Pelegrini's phone number but the three men discarded it as a bit of errata, complimenting her on her admirable persistence. 'She's already half Inspector,' Judge

Duarte said, but when she began to voice her other objections Duarte lost patience. 'Doctora Fowler, when I have a confession that perfectly supports the physical evidence, I don't go inventing reasons why it couldn't have happened that way! We're in the real world here, not the university.' She blushed. When Fortunato drove her back to the Sheraton, he tried to console her with an invitation to go and get the missing Astra the next day.

She paused before she got out, steeled herself. 'Boguso is lying, Miguel.'

He kept looking at her with his silent, attentive face. To accuse Boguso of lying after Fortunato had signed off on his story was to accuse Fortunato himself of lying. She backtracked. 'I don't know if it's all lies or just partly lies, but there's something wrong here. I can't . . .' She looked away and then back towards Fortunato's gleaming brown eyes. 'Miguel, it's lies. I can't go back and tell Robert Waterbury's family that I heard the truth. You know he's lying.'

She thought she saw the Comisario swallow and stiffen in his seat. 'It was strange,' he agreed, slightly off-center. 'But a murder like this, that's not for money, not for passion . . . It defies you.' The weight of the afternoon seemed to bear down on him all at once and give his words a tired, plaintive tint. 'Even when the killer is rotting in Devoto, you can never put things back in balance.' He added in a low, wounded tone, 'If I had the power to undo the wrongs –'

The bullying scream of a car horn behind them vaporized the blue moment. The horn let up for a second, then issued a second blast, along with a stream of curses. Fortunato shrugged. 'It's a world of insults.' Pulling the door closed. 'Let's see how the murder weapon comes out.'

They managed that *operativo* with Inspector Domingo Fausto, the fleshy, slightly sinister officer who had run over and then dispatched the dog the previous week. Something aloof and frightening about the man: the way he pretended she wasn't there. They raided the apartment without incident; they even had Athena stay and watch the wife while they searched the other room, finding the gun under the mattress as Boguso had indicated. The wife and Athena had a conversation about the price of domestic appliances in the United States. A message from Ricardo Berenski waited for her at the Sheraton, but he didn't answer his phone. Meanwhile other pressing matters prevented Comisario Fortunato from meeting with her again.

In deference to her schedule they expedited the ballistics tests on the Astra and matched them with the bullet the following day. By now the weight of the physical evidence lent an irresistible momentum to Boguso's testimony. Judge Duarte put out an order of capture on the missing Uruguayan, although Fortunato admitted that he might have fled back to his own country by now. If so, he assured her, he would see the extradition through. She tried again to reach Ricardo to tell him the resolution of the case and to say goodbye, but still without success. She did reach Carmen Amado de los Santos at INCORP, who received the news of Boguso's confession blandly. 'How convenient that they already had the killer in perpetual chains,' she said. Her tone implied that she'd expected nothing more from the *Bonaerense* and their lackey from the United States.

As the matter of Robert Waterbury's human rights drew to a close, her anger began giving way to resignation. Boguso had satisfied the police and he would satisfy the State Department, and now the name of Athena Fowler would be high on the list when the US government was looking for someone to observe an election or oversee an aid package. However happy the US government might be, though, there would be no such easy sale to Naomi Waterbury. All she could tell her was that she didn't really know.

As she made her reservations to return to Washington, Athena felt for the first time a sense of futility in her own future. Behind all the satisfactory explanations she would parrot back to Washington, Waterbury's mysterious transit through Buenos Aires kept smoking and sputtering through her thoughts. A French *artiste*, a billionaire's wife, arguments about the quality of champagne shouted over a tango: it seemed a life apart from everything she knew. She'd be leaving that enigma here, though. The author's last journals, if they existed, would never be found, and the only other sources were the memories of people whose extravagant voices she would never have time to collect. Robert Waterbury's final lunge at success would dissolve into the infinity of unfinished tales that would henceforth compose her Buenos Aires, her Comisario Fortunato, her life.

Miguel took her out one last time – to Carlito's Bar to listen to Melingo, one of the acclaimed new voices of tango. The Comisario wore the same comical-looking houndstooth of the week before, now with a gray ascot that gave him a sense of old man's bravado.

She had expected him to be in good spirits, but his moods shifted rapidly during the course of the night. At times he was his old self, translating the *lunfardo* for her and playing the tour guide about Argentine customs, at other times his gray mustache and thick cindery brows hung slack and deserted across exhausted features.

'What are you thinking of, Miguel?' she asked him after one long pause. 'Your wife?'

He looked up slowly, lifting his lips into a ponderous smile. 'The truth is, young one, that there are times when one feels abandoned.'

She reached across the table and touched his hand. Whatever his role as a policeman she couldn't help caring for him. 'Miguel. Your wife didn't abandon you. It wasn't her choice.' She had difficulty voicing her next thought. 'And I'm not abandoning you, Miguel. There's limits for me.'

'No,' he murmured. 'There are times one feels abandoned by one's self.'

She didn't understand him and the only explanation he gave was to lift his glass of wine and soda and wordlessly toast to nothing.

CHAPTER 16

He went alone to the Sheraton the next morning, without the need for an entourage to bolster his image, just as she had dressed in blue jeans for the flight back, no longer needing a professional gloss. She looked young and fresh at the check-out desk. He smiled as he approached her, overcome by a surge of affection. He touched her on the shoulder and she looked up at him. 'Miguel! I knew you'd be early! You're in a hurry to get rid of me!'

'No, daughter. Never believe that.' He bent down and kissed her on the cheek, his sight filled for a moment with the filaments of her straight golden hair. For some reason his mind roved back to Marcela, and the emptiness of his house.

Athena cast off the moment. 'You'll have to say goodbye to Ricardo Berenski for me if you see him again. I couldn't reach him.'

'Of course. I think Señor Berenski and I have much to discuss.'

He excused himself and Athena finished settling the bill and wandered over to the door to wait for him. Outside she could see Palermo Park shining brilliantly in the morning light, overlooked by the wrought iron balconies and lushly carved facades of the buildings that surrounded it. She wanted to memorize it and keep it fresh as an antidote against the regularity of her life, but she could feel the stately black railings and molded adornment of the city began to fade as soon as she looked away. She had played the game in Buenos Aires, had gone along without any accusations or denouncements, just as she had played the game to get sent here in the first place. Now she was taking back something counterfeit, whose report would become the official truth and would lead to a career burnishing official truths, like a content provider to some corporate website.

She heard someone calling her. 'Athena! Athena!'

To the left she saw a striking green sports jacket, and immediately recognized Fabian coming towards her at a quick pace. He wore his usual open smile, gave off his usual aura of handsome availability. 'Doctora!'

She couldn't help but be glad to see him. 'Fabian!' She stepped into the circle of his cologne and exchanged kisses.

'Today you depart!'

'Yes, unfortunately.'

He grasped her arm and squeezed it eagerly. 'But I had something to tell you about the Waterbury case! I was reading in one of my screenwriting books last night, and I think I found a structural element that is critical to this investigation.'

His persistence in this conceit annoyed her. 'Fabian. It already *is*. Boguso confessed. We found the murder weapon and they've put an order of arrest out on the other murderer.'

'Yes, but to me, this doesn't feel like the end of the story. You know? It feels more like Act One, where, just as everyone is about to accept the obvious answer to the crime, the detective finds some new piece of evidence that sends the plot in another direction. So let's think: what new clues are there? What clues don't fit in?'

She looked at this strange man in his gigolo clothes, and his theatrical grimace copped from a low-budget rendering of Sherlock Holmes. Fabian played life like a football game, and though she had tired of his tricky passes and feigned injuries, she couldn't resist. After all, she would never see him again. 'Fine, Fabian. Here's one: the mortuary found the telephone number of Carlo Pelegrini's wife in Waterbury's pocket? How's that?'

Fabian slapped his forehead. 'Of course! The billionaire is inescapable! And there must be a multinational corporation, like a bank. A Northamerican bank, because it's for the Northamerican market and you have to have a few Northamericans for interest, like yourself, and Waterbury. This is incredible! It's just like in my film!' He shook his head, beside himself. 'I'm going to tell you about it now, but you have to promise not to steal it. Promise? Because it also belongs to my cousin in Los Angeles; we're both depending on this to get rich. He's already working on it. It starts out with the voice-over of the failed writer, desperate to rescue his career and his family with one best-selling *Policial*.'

Something strange was happening. Fabian put aside his jester persona and began to speak in English. It was tippy and heavily accented, but she could tell immediately that the words had been carefully learned, as if they belonged to someone else. '*I realized on the long flight down that there comes a time when one's imagination has consumed everything else and begins to devour its host. Yet here I am in Buenos Aires, with a stack of primers about police procedure and three cheap handbooks on How to Write a Mystery, making my last ridiculous play.'* Fabian tipped his head and fell silent behind an unnerving smile.

An odd falling sensation came on her, as if all of the lobby were slipping away. 'What are you trying to tell me, Fabian?'

Fabian's unsettling expression didn't change. 'Here the story becomes a bit complex, Doctora. That's what you must do in Act Two, deepen the plot, as in the formula. If you don't, they shit on you. Like in Waterbury's second book. He didn't follow the formula and they threw it to the wolves. And that was the last of a series of disappointments that sent him running to Buenos Aires, into the path of that final nine millimeter bullet.' He took a breath and let it out in a long nasal breeze, looking directly at her. 'I have read the declaración made in Comisario #33, and I can assure you that my version is a thousand times more entertaining and, unlike that of Enrique Boguso, based on a true story.' He bore in on her with his eyes, and for the first time she could see his *cara de policia*, a different one than Fortunato's old-fashioned Mussolini face, more devious and sardonic, now changing again into the seductive young leading man. 'Shall we take a coffee?'

Fortunato came up on them and Fabian greeted him with his old good humor. 'Comiso! Phenomenal!'

The Comisario didn't completely hide his annoyance. 'What are you doing here, Fabian?'

'I came to have a chat with you both about the Waterbury case. It seems that new evidence has come to light. There's much more to this than what Boguso has told you. I think we must re-open the case.'

Fortunato didn't react for a few moments, then he dismissed it with an exasperated sigh. 'Leave it, Romeo! Don't swell my balls with this nonsense!' Looking at his watch, 'It's almost eleven, Athena. Allowing time for any unforeseen inconvenience –'

Fabian implored him. 'Comiso! What inconvenience? There's another flight tomorrow! I know the perfect café close by. We can sit and take a *cortado*.' He smiled at the Comisario. 'Don't you want to find out the truth?'

Athena was staring fixedly at Fabian, whose parrot-green jacket now looked modern and sophisticated beside the dull camel wool worn by Comisario Fortunato. She could sense a rivalry between the two, the clash between one man on his way up and another, perhaps from this very instant, becoming obsolete. She could sense Fortunato's embarrassment and something that might have been fear, but she had to take sides now. She turned to the Comisario. 'I'll fly tomorrow, Miguel.' She nodded at Fabian, who once again basked in theatrical grandeur. 'Fine, Fabian. Let's see what happens in Act Two.'

PART TWO
WATERBURY'S LAST PLAY

CHAPTER 17

'The character of the desperate novelist is a cliché, is it not? All that well-worn despair and tiresome financial difficulty. And yet, from time to time we have no choice but to find ourselves living those clichés. Like you, Doctora, as the crusading guardian of human rights, or the Comisario here, as the hardened policeman trying to solve his most difficult case. The image of things overwhelms us and turns us to its will. That, it seems, is what happened to our Señor Waterbury.

'The *boludo* had enjoyed some success in the publishing business. His first book, *The Black Market*, emerged in twelve countries and won various prizes. He'd sat on literary panels, given interviews, seen his words in foreign alphabets.

'But success was cruel to Robert Waterbury in a strange way; it made him lose all fear. He had been flattered and greeted with that tone of reverence that seduces all writers: *Ah, Robert Waterbury! You wrote* The Black Market*!* A fatal voice, one that washes away the foundations of the real world. He heard the call to take his place among the Great Ones of Literature. A quick look at the accounts of his predecessors would have warned that the odds were against him, but in the world of Destiny there are no statistics. He left his position at the bank and moved, with his family, to South Hampton to struggle with his next book. He was a novelist now. He would say that when he met people, feeling slightly embarrassed by the grandeur of that word: *novelista*.

'With time, though, that mythical life began to call in its loans. The wife was injured in a car accident and could not work for six months. His house needed a new roof. His car gave up and he bought a new one, banking on the income from his next book. He began to borrow from his retirement savings.'

*

'None of this intruded on *Indigo Down*. He regarded it as his masterwork, structured around the idea of the world as a vast sacred text, a landscape of nouns and verbs whose secret prophecies hung just beyond reach of the characters that stumbled through them. After four years and eight drafts he sent his agent the new novel. But by that time the world had not only ceased waiting for the next work of Robert Waterbury, it had forgotten who he was. And disgracefully, the market for mystical illumination turned out to be rather disappointing. After seventeen submissions his agent got him a modest advance.

' "Ten thousand dollars!" he told his agent. "I could wipe my ass with that!"

' "Maybe you'll make it back on royalties," his agent said, without much belief, and then, "Hold on, I've got another call."

'To console himself Waterbury read about the tribulations of great writers in the encyclopedia. Dostoyevsky, who began his career by being condemned to a firing squad. Cervantes, in and out of jail, passing his last years as a guest of a rich friend. Kerouac, the most tragic, whose first book had been his masterpiece. Most great writers' biographies ended "died poor," "died a drunk," or "committed suicide." Even this was of little consolation, because a simple trip to the bookstore reminded him that the majority of writers never became great, simply died in unread obscurity, failed commercial ventures without a myth to hold on to. The possibility that he belonged to this final sad category terrified him. The silver-plated tones with which people had once addressed the distinguished author had worn away, leaving only the dull base metal in which was stamped "Failed Writer."

'So our Señor Waterbury arrives in Buenos Aires with a pair of sports jackets and a suitcase full of good clothes he'd worn ten years ago when he used to work for AmiBank. The plan was simple: to write something formulaic, without a hint of literary or moral ambition. "Commercial," as the publishers put it. Keep the language simple. Populate it with beautiful women and handsome men. Start out with a murder and leave a trail of bodies all the way to the finale. It would be a thriller of international finance and larceny, set against the background of a country struggling in the wake of a murderous military dictatorship.

'Of that world, as we know, Waterbury had a particular knowledge. A specialist in finance, he had been sent to Buenos Aires for two years by AmiBank to help tidy up the unfortunate loans of the Seventies and Eighties. In those years, the bank had loaned billions to dictators and thieves and had taken the whole country as collateral. Waterbury arrived in the second phase, where the bank was trading its bad debts for our state-owned enterprises. Telephone companies, copper mines, the national airlines, dams, highways, electric utilities: all were up for sale on the kind of easy terms negotiated by officials who kept numbered accounts at AmiBank's offshore subsidiaries. It was a good system, a system that worked, endorsed by American economists and the International Monetary Fund. Waterbury had taken part in this fiesta by helping arrange juicy packages for AmiBank's investors.'

'Fabian,' Fortunato interrupted, 'wait a minute. Where did you get this information?'

'All writers keep a diary, no? In the case of Waterbury, a very meticulous record of his time in our beautiful Buenos Aires. And, working from these, my cousin and I –'

'Enough of the cousin! Do you have this diary?'

'And how did you get it?' Athena added.

Fabian raised his hand. 'Afterwards, I'll tell you. But can I offer you another coffee, Comiso? Doctora?' He shouted across the near-empty café. 'Lucho! Three cortados more.' The waiter nodded, and Fortunato noticed that even downtown, which was Federal Police jurisdiction, he didn't bring Fabian a bill.

'*Bien*,' Fabian said, putting down a glass of soda. 'We see Waterbury arrive in Buenos Aires and take a room at the Hotel San Antonio on Calle Paraguay, a downtown office district that at night turns into a haven for prostitutes. The San Antonio dates from the Thirties and, though it is small, the marble stairways and gleaming brass rails of the Reception still retain a certain discreet elegance. Waterbury considers his room: a small wood-paneled cube with a bit of gilding around the mirror and the smell of old lacquer. He tries with some difficulty to imagine himself working within the waxy pool of light cast by the desk lamp. He pulls several books from his suitcase and begins to look them over. "Write a Bestseller!" proclaims one cover. "Seven Steps to Mystery" offers another.'

'Those were the books you showed me!' Athena threw in.

'But of course! How could I make up titles like those? But I continue. As he looks at these books, Waterbury feels a sense of great insignificance come over him, and the room begins to squeeze him. He has no plot, no victim, no main character, only the idea of an Argentine detective on an implacable search for the truth. But what kind of detective? What hidden truth? Maybe he would be an older man, weary, fatigued, near retirement, like Comisario Fortunato. A man for whom the lifelong pursuit of justice has come up short. Stop!'

Fabian raised his hand and gave a low-lidded smile. 'I know what you're thinking! You are thinking that my story is one of those literary confections that ends up being about itself. That I'll put in a Fortunato and an Inspector Fabian and then, "My God, here we all are, in a story written by Waterbury himself! How brilliant!" That's the classic, no? Like Roberto Altman did in that film *The Player*, you saw it? Or that other movie, with Travolta? No, *chica*, that old trick goes all the way back to Cervantes, in the second half of *Don Quixote*.' He reached for one of the coin-sized cookies on a saucer in front of him and popped it into his mouth. 'No, señoritas and caballeros, don't worry yourselves: I have too much pride for that old trick, and so did Waterbury, who at this moment is preparing for a bad night in Room 306 of the Hotel San Antonio.

'Our author pulls out his first novel, stares at the picture of himself six years younger, when he still had that easy smile of success. He can only bear a quick glance at his second novel, with its portrait of him in that overly dramatic "Please-take-me-seriously!" style that overpopulates the liquidation racks like prisoners who, in the face of irrefutable guilt, endlessly proclaim their innocence. He flops on the bed and stares up at the ceiling. He needs background. He needs contacts. Atmosphere. And though he doesn't want to admit it, he needs someone to take him seriously.

'His only connection is an old friend from the bank, a certain Pablo, with whom he had worked ten years ago. At that time they'd both been bachelors, cutting elegantly through the crowded sidewalks of the financial district, trading looks with beautiful women and polishing the understories of loans worth hundreds of millions of dollars. You can see their type still, walking down Calle Florida or at the Plaza de Congresso – this year's selection of handsome young men who'll make a good catch for the right woman: a ticket to security, the upper class, vacations in Europe and Punta del Este. They're enchanters, easy to smile, but also wearing well the look of gravity that befits a man of responsibility. A life of gold, *amores*, that by definition can only be temporary but that has a deceptive sense of permanence to those who are living it.

'Ten years ago Pablo had the kind of Latin looks associated with actors or singers. Straight black hair, long lashes, an even face with pale skin. As a rising executive with a bright future in finance, he'd attracted both eligible young women and influential men, as Waterbury himself had been attracted to him. And not just to Pablo's looks but his voice, an intimate, smooth baritone like polished copper, full of humor and a certain philosophical tinge that gave even simple statements an aura of carefree comprehension. Pablo stood out as a person going somewhere, and people wanted to be remembered by him when he got there.

'Waterbury also hopes to be remembered. He has not spoken to Pablo in four years and waits nervously as the secretary at Grupo AmiBank relays his name. In a moment, Pablo's welcoming voice cuts through all the years of separation.

' "*Ché*, Roberto! My famous novelist friend! Are you really here in Buenos Aires?"

'The phrase "famous novelist" sends a twist through Waterbury's chest, but his old friend's warmth reassures him. He explains that indeed he has taken up residence at the Hotel San Antonio with the idea of researching and writing a detective thriller set in Buenos Aires. The two give brief recountings of their marriages and children, then Pablo interrupts the conversation.

' "Don't tell me anything more, Roberto! Let's meet as soon as possible! This very evening, if you can! Come to my office at five and we'll go for drinks."

'Waterbury cuts the line, content. Pablo sounds exactly equal as in the days when they'd conspired on massive financial packages during the day and more delicate, more sensual packages in the evening hours. He hoped Pablo wouldn't notice he was still wearing the same suit.

'As Waterbury arrives at the Grupo AmiBank headquarters the river of secretaries and businessmen is flooding into the streets at the close of the day. The crystal windows of the cafés are full of elegant encounters and the walking street of Florida has a sense of busy ease. Grupo AmiBank's lobby is a jewel of marble and steel, set off by a naked colossus squeezing a globe. Waterbury asks for Pablo with his gringo accent, and the guards become respectful. Pablo is one of those from the tenth floor, for whom a driver is always waiting after work.

'An old man in a red jacket drives the elevator, croaks out its arrival at the penthouse. There is paneling of rich tropical wood, and a secretary out of a fashion magazine, with her long blond hair and her robust breasts. She greets Waterbury like an old friend, *Señor Waterbury*, and leads him through a glass door into a hallway with a carpet as deep and white and soundless as snow.

' "Robert!" Pablo says his name in English, with only a trace of an accent. He comes to his feet, still very much the Latin playboy, his jet-black hair untouched by gray. As they clasp hands he embraces Waterbury and kisses him on the cheek. Even in his elevated position Pablo's voice has not abandoned that ability to make one instantly feel intimate and welcome. Waterbury feels privileged to be in his presence.

'The office itself is dignified without being too ornate. The paneling, the flat cloud of carpet, wide immaculate windows that look out towards the muddy gray Río de la Plata. On the big wooden desk Waterbury sees a gold pen and the backs of picture frames. Against the wall a glass cart holds a dozen liquors and a seltzer bottle.

' "I'll prepare you a drink! Scotch, no? I'm sorry I don't have your Glenbangie, but I hope you'll sacrifice yourself and drink Señor Walker as a favor to me." Pablo speaks in the English he perfected in a year in the AmiBank office in New York, and Waterbury answers the same way.

' "What a memory you have!"

'Pablo takes a few cylinders of ice from the silver bucket and snaps them into the glass. "How would I forget your favorite? You, the great Scotch snob, who forced me from bar to bar insulting the selection? Eh? You ruined me! And then in your book you said it all tasted like poison, *hijo de puta*!"

'Waterbury laughs. "That was the character speaking, not me!"

' "Ah! Look how he denies it! As if you were working for the government! Soda?"

' "If it's only Johnny, you'd better add some soda."

'Pablo shakes his head in mock despair and splashes soda into the carved crystal. He pours one for himself and sits across from Waterbury on the thick brown leather couch. He takes a moment without saying anything, overcome with the simple pleasure of seeing his old friend. "You look good, Robert. It seems the years have treated you well."

'Waterbury dodges the urge to deliver a long recounting, instead puts a pleasant face on things. "I can't complain. I was lucky in finding my wife, I have a wonderful daughter. I won't say it's been the easiest ten years of my life, but I guess having an easy life wasn't my priority. Meanwhile, here we are drinking whiskey. Life is kind!"

' "Thus it is, hombre. I've also been fortunate. But tell me about your wife. What is your daughter's name? Did you bring a photo, I hope?"

'Waterbury has left the photo in his room. His wife is a pretty woman, but the picture he's brought was taken in bad light from a bad angle, and though the child looks luminous his wife's face came out bloated and fat, a false image that gives him little pleasure. Pablo's wife, on the other hand, shows up marvelously in the photo on his desk. Named Coco, she poses on Ipanema beach in a bikini and long gleaming brown hair.

'They talk a bit more about family and then Pablo takes on a serious look. "And the writing. It goes well for you?"

'Waterbury, while a poor liar, has a certain capacity for half-truths. "You know, Pablo, for a writer, it's only going as well as the next book, but I think Buenos Aires will render up something good."

' "I read *The Black Market*. It was excellent. I wanted Coco to read it but she doesn't read English."

' "It came out in Spanish!"

'The financier looks embarrassed. "I must have been in New York at that time," he says doubtfully. "I don't remember seeing it."

'Waterbury feels that twinge of failure again. The Spanish rights had been sold for a modest amount to a publisher in Madrid, and he doubted the distribution had been extensive.

' "And what about your second book? I never heard from you about it."

'His stomach tightens. "It wasn't very commercial. It was called *Indigo Down*."

' "What an unusual title! What was it about?"

' "It was about these strange prophetic messages that start appearing in the newspaper. A kind of advertising campaign. And my idea for promoting the book was to actually place those ads in real newspapers, to make the whole thing play out as it did in the book, in the real world." Waterbury shrugs.

'Pablo stares at him, uncertain of whether his friend's idea is genius or absurdity. "And what were the messages about?"

'Waterbury feels his face going a bit pink. "Corruption. Good and evil. The ads are attacking the wealthiest citizen in the city, exposing him level by level, promising justice." He takes a sip of his whisky. "But the editor left for a better job and the company backed out on the promotion agreement . . ." He shrugs. "It's a fucking endurance test, Pablo. It's about how much disappointment you can take and still keep trying."

'Pablo chuckles, then shakes his head. One might think that Waterbury's book about an international capitalist who takes on a conscience about the half-dirty nature of his work might cause some inquietude on the part of the director of the Grupo AmiBank, but the financier gives that theme little importance. "The truth is, I admire you, Robert. You threw off your position at the bank like an old pair of shoes and made yourself brand new. There are very few who have that capacity of renunciation. The rest of us hide in our shells like turtles, peering out." He hunched his head in towards his shoulders. "Perhaps *this*, oh, maybe some day *that*." Letting up again: "I see you as a sort of guerilla of the spirit, like those misguided leftists of the Seventies."

' "Didn't most of those guys die miserably?"

' "*Bueno!* You don't have to take the metaphor that far! The point is that you have the courage to challenge the status quo." Laughing again, that exhilarating, intimate laugh that wraps itself around Waterbury like an embrace. "And now you are here! Tell me about this Buenos Aires book. What is it about? Can I help you with it in some way?"

' "It's not all clear yet." Waterbury isn't sure how much he should really tell his friend, sitting, as they are, on the top floor of the Grupo Capital AmiBank offices. "I'm imagining it as a murder mystery, involving finance, corruption . . . That sort of thing."

'Waterbury watches Pablo's face for any sign of displeasure, but the financier looks pleased and attentive. He asks: "And who is the victim?"

Fabian, on posing the last question, leaned back and rubbed his chin. 'It's ironic, no? That Robert Waterbury was writing his own future in his journal, without even realizing it. But in a sense we're all thus, writing the book of our own lives, where we are, infallibly, the principal character and whose ending we never know. Our fantasies become our destinies. For that reason I imagine that death must have come as a great surprise to Waterbury. And one from which he had difficulty maintaining an editorial distance.'

Fortunato felt a haze of anguish rising from Fabian's last remark. He remembered Waterbury's look of near-irritation that he'd been pressed into something so ridiculous as a kidnapping. Later, when fear had stripped away everything else, the look he'd given him over the seat. *Protect me.*

Athena interrupted his musings. 'Fabian, I missed my flight for this. If you have Robert Waterbury's journals then why don't you just give me a photocopy?' She sweetened the pot with an inviting smile. 'Then we could discuss something more pleasant over dinner.'

The Inspector laughed, shaking his finger at her. He turned to Fortunato. 'She's half-*piola*, the girl, eh? I think Buenos Aires is infiltrating her soul!'

Fortunato moved only his eyebrows. 'Let's make her an Inspector.' He knew Athena would never trick anything out of Fabian, but by listening he could already make the first deduction. First, Fabian had Waterbury's diary, or a copy. Though a youth of great verses, the story and philosophy seemed borrowed, maybe even studied for future use in his conquests. These were the observations of a mature and thoughtful man, who had already lived his share of corruption and failure. A man like Robert Waterbury.

Fortunato mustered his most dignified face, sensing at least a momentary safety in his traditional role. 'Speaking seriously, Fabian: if you have the diary, better that you produce it. I don't know what the judge will say about these irregularities.'

'And with good reason, Comiso, with good reason. But that is for afterwards. For now, I continue with my little story.'

'So Waterbury is in the office of Grupo AmiBank, no? And his friend Pablo invites him for dinner. "I have cleared my schedule," he says, "but unfortunately our two-year-old is sick and my wife cannot join us. So it is just you and I. Like before!" With dinner still three hours away, they have no hurry. Waterbury asks his friend about his career.

' "Me? You know how it is, Robert. One goes on working for the company, but if one is industrious, various opportunities arise to manage a few things for one's own account. I have a partnership in an importer of electric appliances. Also, a few *acciones* in a real estate venture near Punta del Este."

'Waterbury hears in the name of the Uruguayan resort the tell-tale shuffle of laundered money. A river of underground silver from Argentina has surfaced as luxurious chalets and tennis clubs up and down the Atlantic coast of that beautiful country, the fruit of unpaid taxes, secret percentages on government contracts, and assorted "commissions." But this is his friend Pablo, and he should be happy for his good fortune. Now Pablo gets a mischievous look on his face, almost like the old days, when they'd talked about their conquests. He glances at his watch. "I have an idea. I'll take you to one of my little ventures. You'll be surprised. But you have to keep it private. Okay?"

'He picks up the telephone and speaks a few words, and then they are stepping into his car, a gray Mercedes sedan with polarized windows, driven by a silent, middle-aged man who, between his words of courtesy and his opening of doors, radiates a quiet malevolence. The locks click shut, and they slide through the grand commotion of Avenida Corrientes with the windows closed to all sound. Waterbury can see the huge white granite obelisk of the Plaza de la Republica growing larger in front of them, and then all twenty-eight lanes of the massive 9 de Julio spread out like a vast agriculture of metal and glass, the widest boulevard in the world, washing through the marvelous city as if for some great purpose. The balconies of the apartments have gone green with potted plants, the blocks of buildings seem endless and permissive, and the feeling of Buenos Aires comes back to him again. A city of lives infused with intense sadness and equally intense beauty, where generosity, love and corruption never stray far from each other, and where one can always trace the mark left by the edge of the knife. In that nostalgia for a fantastical Buenos Aires floats Waterbury.

'They get on to the autopista 25 de Julio and the city flows past beneath them. Streets and avenues bear the dates of famous events of the revolution. They've passed from the 9 de Julio 1816, when General San Martin defeated the Spaniards at the Battle of Ayacucho, to the 25 de Julio in 1806, when Cordoba had risen up in arms against the Viceroy in the first abortive stirrings of independence. The plazas bear all our greatest hopes: the Plaza de la Republica, the Plaza Libertad, the Plaza del Congreso. But also, leading to these plazas or inextricably connected to them by other names, are the streets honoring our dictators and murderers: Julio Argentina Roca, president and famous exterminator of Indians. General Fernando Sarmiento, who had said that the blood of the savages would be good fertilizer for the soil. Along with those, the streets named for famous oligarchs, corrupt politicians, soldiers in dubious wars, composers, artists, authors, tango singers, the countries of the world. The jumbled city plan condenses all human aspirations and failure into an address book of times and events. Huge and shimmering, real and more than real, all of Buenos Aires has become a vast tale unrolling before him.

'After half an hour they are reaching the limits of the Capital, that imaginary ring where Buenos Aires gives way to *Provincia*. At that line the Federal Police cede to the Provincial, civic governments become parochial and informal. The buildings are smaller and less grandiose, the rents are lower. The driver follows the railroad line for a while and then pulls over at a plain brick building with a furniture store at the bottom.

' "Here we are," Pablo smiles, still secretive. He keeps talking as they approach a wrought iron door that covers a second door. "I got into this about one and a half years ago, and it is my most profitable venture. I keep it quiet for obvious reasons, but I know you'll find it amusing, so I'm showing you. This is the business of the future, here. It's high-tech."

'He unlocks the second door and they climb a stairway between clean white walls. At the top, Pablo enters a code into a stainless steel keypad and the door beeps twice. He pushes it open and motions for Waterbury to enter.

'The room is some seventy feet long, painted crisp and clean. The windows are covered with black cloth. Half of the room is a series of metal racks burdened with computers and electrical cords. In the room's center a man in his twenties is sitting at a console of computer monitors with a thermos and a cold wet *mate*. He has an open book in front of him.

' "How's it going, *chico*. Everything fine?"

' "No drama whatsoever, Señor."

'Waterbury looks around the white room and the clean polished wooden floor, unclear what the place is. Pablo motions him over towards the monitors. "I'm proud to say that we have one of the few websites in Argentina that is actually making money."

'Waterbury comes over and when he sees the first monitor he

looks away for a moment, embarrassed, then looks back at it. Two naked men are kneeling at either end of a naked woman. On another screen he spots the words "Sexo Ardiente!" and "Chicas Argentinas Calentadas al Rojo!" Below the words, a woman in leather chaps and a wide flat gaucho hat is bending over a saddle.

'"We get most of the content from Los Angeles, but our big attraction is the Argentine girls. We do theme pictures, like the gaucha there. Or holding a *mate*. It's our market niche."

'"How much do you pay them?" Waterbury asks, looking at the willing smile of the woman in the chaps.

'The businessman tips his head as he thinks. "Five hundred pesos per session. Sometimes more. Sometimes a little less. I don't have anything to do with that part. There's a photographer and all that. Most of the girls are prostitutes, so for them it's easy work at a better price than they can get on the street."

'He has the technician pull up the screen that shows the hits per hour. "There's a calculus for relating the hits per hour to gross sales. All we need to do is keep increasing traffic, and the money increases in step. Right now we're only selling subscriptions and a few special pay per views, but next month we're going to expand to shipping hard goods: videos, magazines, sexual aids. That area over there will be the warehouse and shipping department. We're also negotiating a strategic partnership with a company in Los Angeles to expand into the entire Latin American market. It's crazy, no?"

'Pablo goes on explaining as they descend the stairs again. "Three hundred thousand pesos per month, and growing every day. It's a *caramelo*! Modest capital investment, low overhead. I financed it through the World Bank!" He laughs, clapping Waterbury on the shoulder. "It's business, my friend! Don't look so shocked. I thought you would find it amusing."

'They are back in the protective capsule of polarized glass, heading to the center again. They go to a restaurant in La Recoleta very new and very *de moda*, called La Rosa Blanca. A place where famous musicians and artists mingle with the blessed rich of our capital. Helena de Schutte owns it in partnership with two others. Maybe you've seen her name in the magazines lately: the Helena de Schutte that people say is the mistress of Carlo Pelegrini. Since all this scandal with poor Señor Pelegrini, I'm sure it has affected her business. That is to say, there has been a considerable increase.'

*

'But let us return to Waterbury, who crosses the gleaming threshold with the unpleasant anxiety that he might have to pick up the check. Dining out is a privilege he and his family have long since abandoned, and the obligation of paying for a meal that could easily run, he can see from the orchids on each table, to three hundred pesos worries him. Maybe he betrays himself, because Pablo touches his back and says, "I invite you to everything tonight, Robert. This is a special night. We are celebrating that we are whole, that we are on our paths and that we are together."

'As the warmth and affection in Pablo's words wash over Waterbury he has trouble understanding what Pablo sees in him. They were friends and colleagues for two years, and maintained a lazy correspondence for six years after that. But they had never shared any near-death experiences, had not been thrown in jail together or even made a long trip. He imagines that in Pablo's eyes he is a successful author, the man who quit the bank and made good, and thus is exempt from the conventional measurements of material success. And yet, he doesn't doubt Pablo's sincerity. He knows that we Porteños are a sentimental people, for whom the obligations of a friendship are a privilege and not a burden.

'La Rosa Blanca is in an old carriage house, now stripped down to the brick and expanded with vast panels of uninterrupted glass. A waterfall courses down a rock wall at one end, then flows through the restaurant to the pond that lies just outside the open end of the place. Crystal glitters everywhere against the rough brick background, ornamented by pretty young hostesses in silk who merely stand around and glow.

'Waterbury sees them and thinks *pretty girls glowing like incandescent lamps*, hears the cascade slapping along its course and thinks *the water slapping on the rocks*. He is working again, beginning the venture which he hopes will save him. With that thought and the presence of his friend, he starts to swell. His best books are ahead of him. Yes. When they write the legend, this will be viewed as his down and out time, the desperate period so many great writers go through on their way to immortality. And he could use this restaurant, with its elegant princesses and its swans, could even use Pablo somehow. He has the sensation not of making up a story as he goes along, but of making up his life as he goes along, as if through his will he has produced this elegant scene and his own presence there.

' "They say this belongs to the mistress of one of Argentina's richest men. A man named Carlo Pelegrini."

'This is before Don Carlo's name became a regular entertainment in the local editions, so Waterbury only raises his eyebrows, without feeling much impact. He doesn't know that soon his life will become very much involved with Don Carlo. That strange doors will open.

'They are given the formidable menu. Waterbury is washed from one island of beautiful script to the next, dizzied by the descriptions of the foods on offer. He wavers between the rack of Patagonian lamb and the thick filet mignon in a sauce of mushrooms and champagne. Pablo orders Margaritas made from a rare Mexican tequila and fresh crab legs flown in from Tierra del Fuego.

'What do friends talk about after so much absence? Always three things: what they are doing now, what they have done, and after that, to dust off the fates of friends and colleagues that they have carried as mental curios across the years. The talk moves to their former work together at the bank.

'The deal Waterbury closed with Pablo involved the national airline. You remember, Athena, the airline whose ex-employees were beating drums on the Avenida Santa Fé the day you arrived? It was a perfect circle of business: AmiBank sold a half-billion of their uncollectable Argentine government debt to a Spanish group for a fraction of its value. The Spaniards in turn used that half-billion in debt to pay the government for the people's airline. How content everyone was! AmiBank got cash for its uncollectable loans, the Spanish got the national airline at a great discount, and the government of Argentina got a pat on the back from the International Monetary Fund for reducing its debt. Of course, certain government functionaries negotiating for the Argentine side quietly received "commissions."

' "I always wondered about those terms. They were a little too good to us. They were way too good, as a matter of fact."

'Pablo opens his mouth and laughs without making a sound. "Don't tell me you have forgotten so soon, Robert! Free Trade for all countries! No more government industries! That was the war cry of the ones who held the notes. And if you don't, well, we send your currency to hell and you have twelve thousand percent inflation! Besides, the airline was inefficient. It was giving only a tiny bit of the profit it should have made."

' "But the Spanish have basically shut it down, haven't they? I read that they absorbed all the best international routes and sold off the assets. They plundered it." The writer goes quiet for a moment. "We fucked them, Pablo. We fucked the entire country."

'Pablo looks defensive for a moment, then shrugs. "We guessed wrong! How were we to know?"'

Fabian leaned back, smiling. 'So easy, no? To calmly throw one's hands in the air, *Ah! What misfortune! But it wasn't my fault!* How many times have we heard that, eh, Comiso? *It went out of control! The victim acted badly!* Easier still when the men providing the excuses are dressed in such elegant suits and bear the credentials of the finest global institutions. One compiles an *expediente* that always points to one's innocence, because the benefits of finding in one's favor are riches, status, a pretty wife, while to find on the other side, well, one may end up like Robert Waterbury.

'But such thoughts do not trouble Waterbury now; he is lost in his Destiny. The night has become a series of places separated by the interior of Pablo's German automobile. At the Jockey Club they sip their drinks beside a tray of caviar, surrounded by pictures of horses. At the Millionaire's House they play snooker in the billiards room of a classic mansion. Pablo's tastes have changed in the last ten years: the bars are now elegant and tranquil, the acquaintances that greet him have grown older, more petrified with dignity. Before, Pablo had always been deferential and solicitous of such men, addressing them with a winning obsequiousness. Now, in a way Waterbury can't quite quantify, he speaks to them as an equal. Suave and masterly in all currents of life, Pablo has become the fulfilled promise of every promising young man, a personage that Waterbury finds every bit as mythical as his own role of the desperate novelist.

'In this atmosphere any confession is possible. In the back seat of the moving auto, gray shadows slide over them like the fronds of a primitive jungle: "The truth is, Pablo, that it's been very difficult. My financial position is tenuous. The first book did well but the second was a flop, and in this business, one flop is all it takes to go back to the bottom of the pile. After that you're a known quantity, and that quantity is failure. I'm making my last play, Pablo. That's the truth. This is my last play. Maybe I should have just gotten a job or something, but I couldn't. I couldn't surrender."

'He watches Pablo's face and is seized by the sudden fear that having heard this, his friend will lose faith and extinguish the magical force that animates this night. Pablo is completely in his own thoughts, his eyes gleaming in the street lights and then falling again into darkness as they pass. "It's a strange search, Robert. One that I will never make, because it is not my character. But I understand it. I will bank you, amigo. Thus are friends." And for Robert Waterbury, the globe continues spinning.

'In the last hours they arrive at the tiny Bar Azul, in San Telmo. It is one of those theme bars, where instead of a simple drink one is thought to need entertainment. The theme is that everything in the bar is blue, even the lights, which render everyone ghostly and mysterious. At other times they change the lights to red, or to white. It fits the clientele, a confetti of marginal theater people, film-makers reeling out experimental films that no one will ever see, supposed writers, painters aspiring or already failed and musicians without work. All know each other and thus buttress each other's fierce pretensions about their world of Art. It's a place of pierced noses and tongues, where those with light hair dye it black, and those with black hair dye it purple and those with purple hair shave it off entirely. It won't last long; but for the moment it is very *de moda*, and Pablo finds it amusing.

'On Thursday nights they play tangos in between sets of rock, a half-ironic return to the past which amuses the denizens of the place. It is strange to see them with their tattoos and their metal, listening to the scratchy orchestras of Carlos di Sarli and Oswaldo Pugliese, artists whose *bandoneons* have been silent for fifty years. What tango is playing? It must be "Por Una Cabeza," because in American movies when they want tango in capital letters they always use that one. In *Schindler's List*, that scene when Schindler meets the Nazis? "Por Una Cabeza." And that movie with Al Pacino where the blind man dances with the beautiful woman? "Por Una Cabeza." Always "Por Una Cabeza," or "El Choclo," because gringos know nothing about tango.'

' "Por Una Cabeza" is a pretty tango,' Fortunato defends. 'You can't argue with Carlitos Gardel.'

'Fine.' Fabian threw out his hands. 'I concede that point, Comiso. Every day the *boludo* sings better! So, when Pablo and Waterbury arrive, we'll say that the immortal Carlos Gardel is winding through the tragicomic verses of "Por Una Cabeza," lamenting once again the failed romance that lost the horse race of love by only a head.

Okay? At that point perhaps Pablo is overcome by that voice of the 1930s, he says, "Enough whiskey. Let's drink champagne."

'Waterbury will wonder later whether the champagne somehow attracted the girl to the table like the bubbles in a magic cauldron. She is passing by and happens to glance at them and come over. She has light hair, which in the Bar Azul is blue hair, cut short and sharp, and pale skin that glows aqua along the slim length of her naked arms and legs. Her one-piece dress sparkles with sequins and ends at the middle of her thigh. She's a pretty woman, with delicate features and a slim, small-boned body that nonetheless has a certain ampleness that attracted his attention. Strangest is that Waterbury feels he recognizes her. She glances at them, then looks a second time more intently, before continuing on her way. Waterbury next sees her standing beside Pablo, bending down to him and speaking above the music. "Aren't you going to invite me to join you, shameless one?"

'Pablo laughs. "Forgive me, Señorita. Please . . ." He stands up and pulls a chair out for her, sliding it in beneath her as she seats herself like a bird settling in to a nest. She gives Waterbury an ancient smile, Waterbury quivers slightly inside as he returns it. The feeling of familiarity won't leave him.

' "Paulé," she says.

' "Is your accent German or French?" he asks.

' "French!" she answers. "I'm insulted that you even ask me that! The Germans have an overbearing accent in their Spanish, as if every word is a heavy object and they are beating you with it. The French always capture the correct meter." In truth, she speaks rather badly, a careless salad of genders and tenses, but she doesn't seem to know it and laces it all together with a spoiled coquetry. She signals a passing waiter. "*Ché mozo!* Another little glass, please."

'Pablo is making one of our gestures at Waterbury, gathering his fingers together and shaking his hand up and down, as if to say, *Que loca!* She turns to him in the midst of it, but isn't bothered. "And you, Pablo. It's Pablo, no? I remember because I am Paulé, which is the French version. Pablo!"

' "Yes."

' "How's life?"

' "Life is a river in the Amazon, Paulé. Rich and tranquil and sensual, and always leading to someplace mysterious at the next turn."

143

' "Perhaps for you, my love, life is a river. For others life is a sewer, filthy and mean and always going down a hole." She touches Waterbury on the arm. "And for you? How is life?"

'The champagne must have affected him. He considers his books and his flight to Buenos Aires. "Life is a quest."

'She gives his answer a weary arch of her eyebrows. "A quest for what?"

'Waterbury thinks for a short time. "To unite the world of the imagination with the world of the senses," he says at last.

'She nods. "Fine. I see we have an intellectual at the table. Thank you, Messieur Rimbaud."

' "And what is it for you?"

'She looks at the bottom of the champagne that Pablo has just poured for her. "It's a quest . . . to get at the place where all these bubbles come from. Salud!" She takes a sip, frowns at the bottle in disappointment. "The Cordon Rouge always has too much taste of lanolin!"

'At this Pablo throws his hand to his forehead. "She's impossible, this woman!"

' "Not impossible," she corrects him. "Just improbable."

'Waterbury watches the improbable woman who has improbably invited herself to their table. She seems to know Pablo and he can't escape the feeling that he knows her.

' "And what do you do?" he asks her.

' "I'm a dancer. I dance the tango. I'm also an actress, and I do some modeling."

'At this last Pablo seems doubly amused.

' "How did you end up in Buenos Aires?" Waterbury asks.

' "You've heard of Virulazo, haven't you?"

' "He was one of the great dancers of tango," Pablo explains. "Very famous."

' "Virulazo and his wife were dancing in Paris, and I met them there. I was a student of dramatic arts at the Sorbonne at that time. From them I learned the tango, and I returned to Buenos Aires to continue my studies. For a time, I danced at the Teatro Colón. I also maintain a studio of psychiatric dance pedagogy."

'Waterbury asks what that is.

' "It's my own creation to help people learn about their inner psyche through theater and dance.'

'Pablo pretends to take it very seriously, but Waterbury can see

144

the arch expression lurking behind his "How interesting!" Paulé says to him, "You're a businessman, I know. What about your friend from the United States? Is he a businessman too?"

' "No," Pablo says with real pride. "He's a novelist. He's here making investigations for his next novel."

' "How pretty. And have you published anything?"

'The writer sums up the languages and the prizes in a slightly bored tone of voice.

' "Oh!" She turns and looks at Waterbury, her face suddenly losing its disdain and seeming genuinely impressed, like a student of literature at the Sorbonne. At that moment Waterbury recognizes her with a shock that makes him feel faint. She is the woman he'd seen on all fours with a man at each end on the computer monitor at Pablo's internet site. The dissonance between the burning image from the website and the real person in front of him blanks his mind. Beneath those clothes is that body, with the same mouth, the same buttocks. One could say that Waterbury had finally succeeded in unifying the world of the imagination with the world of the senses, only to find himself astounded at the unexpected result.

'Having entered into the dominion of the imagination, though, Waterbury is pulled still further inside. A man comes over and asks Paulé to dance. She accepts, and as Waterbury watches her follow him to the floor he cannot resist seeking the woman in the photo beneath the glittering one-piece dress and the high-heels. The man has curly black hair and a small mustache, a cinematic *tanguero* in a button-down gray shirt and pleated black pants. Waterbury imagines him fucking her in a picture. He clutches her to him, and to the tune of "El Choclo" they begin to spin and lean through the complex steps of the dance. Their faces are severe. They look past each other, a thousand kilometers apart. Each of them do completely different steps, out of the hundreds of tango steps, and yet they match perfectly. They lean together, they pivot, he slides his foot in a crescent while she turns her knee. The man leads and the woman follows, and yet so tightly are they bound together that no one can say that he truly dominates her.

' "The girl dances!" Pablo says, and Waterbury nods, astonished behind his glass of champagne.

'She returns to the table when the music ends and she begins to ask him about his books. Waterbury is still cowed by the photo of her with the men, but her face becomes that of the young student at the Sorbonne. "And what were your books about?"

' "*The Black Market* was about an international banker who goes on a business trip with his wife. The wife disappears and he starts to look for her, but then he starts running into all these dead people. What it turns out is that he's in the Underworld, and only when he confronts the lies about his life and his work can he get out again."

' "It was excellent!" Pablo adds.

' "The second, *Indigo Down* . . ." He feels almost embarrassed at the memory. "It's about an advertising campaign. It was tied in with the Bible, prophecy, things like that." He discards the book. "Now I want to write one about Buenos Aires, a thriller type. Something they can fit into one of their little niches."

'She has heard the bitterness in his last statement, nods thoughtfully, and to his surprise he feels she understands his life. "It's difficult, no? To aspire? It brings one a world of problems."

'Pablo offers her a ride home. She lives in the center, not far from the Hotel San Antonio, where the tight walls of Robert Waterbury's room are waiting for him. Pablo drops them off together at the hotel, says goodnight as discreetly as a banker, then dissolves his night-colored car into the ashes of the evening. Waterbury contemplates this piece of woman in front of him, this student at the Sorbonne, this *tanguera*, this whore that fucks two men in front of a camera. The memory of his family insinuates itself, and besides, she might ask him for money and it would be strange. He walks her to her tiny apartment on Calle Suipacha. She shivers in her silver dress, in the silver dawn, and ducks into the door looking like the girl in all the tangos who grew up in the barrio and then became a toy of playboys and the dollars that they throw to the passing crowd. *La Francesa*. They exchange a kiss on the cheek, perfume mixed with smoke, and he floats back between the weary faces of the buildings. Thus ends his first night in Buenos Aires.'

Fabian leaned back in his chair and gave a little toss of his head, seeming to tire momentarily of his role of entertainer. The other two said nothing. The Waterbury case had spiraled irremediably into a kaleidoscope of brilliant facades, and they could only stagger unsteadily among its images.

Athena looked around the room. The café had begun to clutter up for lunch, and white-jacketed waiters were threading the busy air with steel platters and siphons of soda water. Gazing at the mahogany paneling and heavy wooden refrigerated cases, Athena felt as if they could all be far in the past, debating the *Caso Waterbury* in a timeless *noir* atmosphere of cynicism and lies. No use to ask questions; even the Comisario, slumping in his worn sports jacket and staring out the window, had withdrawn into a cigarette. She couldn't blame him. Fabian was turning his investigation upside down and laughing at all his own jokes while he did it, but the unspoken object of his laughter was the Comisario himself.

Fabian spoke first, lighting up again. 'Are you getting hungry?' he asked them. 'Because I, yes. Why don't we order something? I invite you both. I suggest the puré de papas and grilled beefsteak.' Looking at Fortunato. 'You can even get it Uruguayan style, with a fried egg on top, in honor of Boguso's mysterious accomplice!'

The Comisario gave him a deadpan look. 'Gracias, Romeo. I woke up this morning thinking that I needed more irony in my life.'

Fabian reached above the crowd and called out 'Lucho! Lucho!' and summoned him with a wiggle of his fingers. 'Three *menus*, amigo, the bifé with a fried egg and ham on top, *al Uruguayo*. Also a tomato salad and a bottle of the house *tinto* with soda. *Bien?*' The waiter hurried off and Fabian settled back contentedly. 'I continue:

'The next day Waterbury devotes to wandering, the simple gorgeous pleasure of being in a foreign city that offers up its coffee and its elegance like a bouquet. October has come over Buenos Aires, injecting a fresh promise in the branches that comb the air with new leaves. For Waterbury, coming from an October of autumnal decay in the higher latitudes, the spring feels miraculous, infusing him with hopes that the new book will save him at a single stroke. He wanders the city that he remembers, past Retiro station to the elegant apartments of La Recoleta. He sits in parks and plazas, he stops for an espresso or a triple sandwich with the crusts cut off. At all sides he's assaulted by our famous beauties, now using the excuse of the spring sunshine to turn loose their sensuality. As he sits in the cafés and dreams of the book he'll write, he waits for the plot. Something set in the atmosphere of the wealthy upper-class, whose nineteenth century mansions rise behind iron fences in the splendid little barrio of Palermo Chico. He dreams of gleaming North-american four-by-fours and private jets, of the dignified facade of massive riches built upon decades of fraudulent business deals and mafia tactics. In fact, he is dreaming Carlo Pelegrini without even knowing it, dreaming the future that will soon be chasing him like a train chasing its tracks. He is certainly dreaming of Paulé.'

'Fabian, *por favor*!' Fortunato broke in. 'Stop swelling my balls with your verses! If there is a connection between Waterbury and Pelegrini, tell me plainly and let's go on! I have things to do!'

Fabian slapped himself gently on the forehead. 'You're right, Comiso. My cousin in Los Angeles keeps telling me the same thing. This is where the literary types always go wrong. They can't understand that the world doesn't care about their themes or their graceful little phrases. But now I see why they keep doing it – there's a certain pleasure in saying this has meaning or that has meaning, when the truth is that none of it has any meaning.' He rolled on over Athena's protest. 'No, *chica*. You can read a thousand masterpieces with a thousand philosophies, and when it's all over you eat your pizza and drink your beer and do whatever you would have done anyway. The Comisario here isn't going to strip off his clothes and give away all his worldly possessions because of a sudden illumination he buys from the bookstore. A conscience like that, yes, is fantasy.'

Fortunato had tired of being used as an example. '*Mira*, Fabian,' he began coldly, 'I'm fed up with . . .' The chirping of his cell phone interrupted him and he held up his hand for silence. 'Fortunato.'

One of his inspectors had found a youth who had broken his leg in a soccer game and he and a lawyer wanted to write it up as a traffic accident to collect the insurance money. There was the question of shares. 'Do I have to wrap you in a blanket and give you a baby bottle?' Fortunato growled at him. 'Manage it yourself!' He hung up the phone, and Fabian started talking before he could resume.

'I was only making the point, Comisario, that metaphor, hidden significance, it's all *verso*.' Cocking his eyebrow with a smile. 'Better to stay with the formula.' He turned to Athena. 'But we are discussing Robert Waterbury, no?

'*Bien*. The novelist spends a week taking in atmosphere, reading the local magazines and following the scandals in the newspapers. He tries to outline a story in his journal, but all he has are a selection of characters that seem to him rather stereotypical and uninteresting, but which he imagines are the kind of characters that will make him money. This not-so-noble goal empties him of inspiration.

'But Pablo has promised to be helpful and Pablo is a friend of iron! He introduces Waterbury and he makes phone calls on his behalf, always presenting him as "the novelist from the United States," and Waterbury in turn carries a copy of his first novel to all his appointments, flashing his jacket photograph like a carnet. He's getting background on contemporary politics, he says, or he's getting background on the Dirty War. He works his way from friend to friend, each of them gracious and ready with their version of the world.

'At his home, though, things are going badly, and troubling advisories flood into his brain in the worrisome telephone calls of his wife. His daughter falls from the swing set and needs two thousand dollars' worth of bone setting. A dozen checks have been returned by the bank, and his wife has borrowed money from her brother to meet the latest mortgage payment. Worst of all, his agent, who has grown more and more elusive since the failure of his second book, informs him that he'll now be handled by a new young face at the agency. "You need someone passionate about your career, Bob, and I think that in this respect you would be better served by an agent with a fresh outlook." The rejection devastates Waterbury, a professional judgement on his ability even to write something cheap and commercial. For some days he is too depressed to continue his research.

'And just at that moment when it seems most impossible, when he has come to see himself through his agent's eyes and realize that the dream that made him abandon his prosperous career has finally abandoned him, Paulé appears at the desk of the Hotel San Antonio. It is evening. She is wearing a slim one-piece black dress that is slit from the knee to the thigh. "Why didn't you pass by my apartment?" she scolds him.

'The truth is, he hasn't been able to get her off his mind. At night, he fantasizes about her pornographic performance and in the day she comes back to him in fugitive glimpses of dance or of that deep comprehension reflected in her simple phrase, "It's difficult to aspire, isn't it?" He has walked past her apartment several times, imagining the scorn she would feel for him if he appeared. Moreover, he loves his wife, who supports him, and his child, for whom he is the world. For those reasons, he has not called her. But now she is before him in all the crooked luxury that the city can offer.

' "I've come to take you for tango lessons. It's essential for your investigations!"

'He surrenders to the dream. It whirls him away in a taxi and by the time they reach the *Confitería Ideal*, he is a writer again, in the embrace of the tango that directs his steps, smelling always of tobacco and perfume, erotic, over-warm, his hand feeling slightly sweaty against hers. "*Boludo*, you're stepping on me!"

' "Forgive me!" he says. "I have two left feet."

'Paulé laughs. "Don't worry. Now enter again. First, to the side, then together, yes, now three steps – You're knocking me over, you idiot!"

'Everyone at the *Confitería Ideal* already knows Paulé. The *Ideal* is one of those ancient pastry shops from the Year Zero, all dark wood and marble tables and stained glass panels in the ceiling. Only a few survive now: the Tortoni, el Aguila. The old 1920s typescripts and the cast-iron cash registers always bring on a cloud of nostalgia, like something from a childhood you never had. In a ballroom upstairs they give tango lessons six days per week, and thus Paulé gathers a few pesos. Waterbury can see in the longing glances of many men that Paulé has a following. Lonely old widowers with gray hair and threadbare suit jackets, shy public servants with two left feet. Waterbury feels awkward in front of their anguish, regrets it, but he leaves it behind for the intensity of the woman in his arms. He keeps his hand on her back, feeling her skin shift beneath the cotton fabric, imagining her sandwiched between two men, a woman eager to do anything and completely available. And yet: how can that image be this woman in front of him? He makes a misstep and she shoves him backwards. "Stop flattening my toes!" She sees Waterbury's stricken look, the angry glances of her fellow teachers, and she slides back into his arms, her breasts and stomach close to him as she puts one hand on his shoulder and the other out to the side, waiting for his grasp. Half-hopelessly: "I'm the worst teacher. I know. Let's try again."

'He invites her for a snack downstairs. It's only seven in the evening: too early for a real dinner. Paulé orders a campari and soda with crescents, and Waterbury an *empanada*. As soon as the waiter turns his back Paulé starts in.

' "You're here because you're desperate, aren't you? Don't be embarrassed: I have a nose for it. I am the Patron Saint of

Desperation. Like the Virgin of Lujan . . ." she tilts her head ironically, "but not a virgin."

'Waterbury plays it off. "What makes you think I'm desperate?"

' "Your family is at home. You're staying at a cheap hotel. Your books are out of print – I checked it on the Internet."

'*And I checked you on the Internet!* Waterbury feels like answering, annoyed at her presumption.

' "Maybe you have other money," she goes on, "but I don't believe so. No, I can see you are living out that tired myth of the desperate artist. What is your book in Buenos Aires about?"

'Waterbury trusts nothing about her, resents her disagreeable nature and her rapid, accurate observations. A woman like this deserves a vague answer. "It's a sort of thriller."

' "Come on. A thriller about what? Who are the characters? What is the plot?"

' "I'm still deciding that. That's why I'm here."

'The Frenchwoman indulges herself in a smug little nod. "And what are the themes? Is it once again about the imagination and the world of the senses, like your last book? Some important moral issue?"

'His irritation at the woman before him becomes his anger about the book. "This book will have no themes! It's going to be an empty stupid thriller that does nothing but make me money! I'm killing everybody this time, and when the smoke disappears I expect to be sitting on a mountain of silver! Period! I'm a content provider now: I fill shelves for media corporations."

'Paulé doesn't flinch. "So you are telling me that your first book didn't sell well and your last book was a failure, and that's the fault of the readers, because they only want easy things, cheap things, with violence and romance and sex. And this has embittered you, no? Because you thought you deserved better." The dancer goes on coldly in the face of Waterbury's silence. "But perhaps you didn't deserve better! Perhaps the one thing you refuse to consider is that your books simply weren't that good! That they were mediocre as literature and mediocre as entertainment?"

'The author is dizzied by her insults. "Don't you think I consider that every single day?"

' "Yes, perhaps that's it. They were not quite good enough for literature, and not shallow enough for cheap entertainment, and while this world may reward the great and disabuse the truly bad of their illusions, the merely adequate who are silly enough to aspire, it will punish them, and drag them through the mud by their own dreams. And you get tired of trying to do something great, and finally . . ." her eyes flicker to the side as she goes on, "you accommodate yourself to whatever meaningless pornography will pay your apartment. These are things that I know, Robert, because I am the Patron Saint of Desperation, of the visions that assassinate your life."

'The Frenchwoman leans her elbow on the table and rests her chin on her palm, staring at him with her gray eyes across the eighteen inches of marble between them. Her flat finish gives no clue to whatever emotion lies behind it. "I will be your muse." '

'And through Paulé, Waterbury begins to meet another group of friends. Bohemians ten to twenty years younger than him. Jugglers and mimes who pass a tin can at Palermo Park, surly musicians with bangles hanging off their faces, film directors with rich parents, actresses, intellectuals, angry painters, resentful writers who have yet to publish a book. They meet at the Bar Azul, go to theater productions in basements or apartments, drink bad wine, snort *merca*, fuck each other on filthy sheets in old high-ceilinged apartments whose windows let in dirty traffic noise and glimpses of angels carved in stone. Waterbury is too old for them, but his cachet as a foreign novelist gets him in, and Paulé never fails to polish his reputation. He has books in translation and an agent in New York, while they are primping themselves behind "underground" productions and little books published "for a select audience." And though he doesn't want to admit it, his acceptance by this tedious circle bolsters him.

'In this flock of crows Waterbury sits and listens, fills his journals with their smoke and shallow dramas while he drinks espresso and takes up tobacco in his neighborhood café. Now Waterbury, who never failed to read his daughter to sleep, wakes up at noon, eats dinner at eleven and crosses the night on a regimen of coffee and cocaine. He is loading up his credit card, giving his wife half-truths about his research in weekly conversations that have become a bit uncomfortable. She tells about the little girl and the lovable things she does. He stays silent about the parties that flow from bar to apartment to dance hall, about the cocaine. But the book is taking shape, he assures her. A very vague shape.

'Paulé, to his surprise, asks nothing of him. She annoys him with her pompousness, but the flashes of jaded tenderness beneath her impersonation of *La Francesa* intrigue him. He guesses her age between twenty-eight and forty, depending on the time of night, but like everything else about her, he doesn't inquire. The picture on Pablo's internet pornography site haunts him. He walks her to her apartment with an ache in his groin but refuses to go inside, knowing it would be impossible not to fall. And what diseases might she have? he asks himself. And what might he be getting into? And most of all, when his mind isn't fogged by her erotic image, he thinks of the effect on his wife and child, who would forever have this strange unwholesome *danseuse* in the room with them.'

Fabian abruptly clicked his tongue, mugged a sardonic little expression of shame. 'I'm sorry! Perhaps you are tired of hearing about Paulé. Maybe she is just a diversion, to keep things entertaining. But I see Lucho is coming.'

The waiter appeared with three steaming plates, the beefsteaks concealed beneath a heap of ham, fried egg, red pepper, and melted cheese. '*Al Boguso*,' Fabian joked. Lucho set the wine bottle and siphon on the table while Fabian busied himself adding corn oil and vinegar to sliced tomato salad. They started eating as Fabian told Athena about Montevideo, the fabled 'gray city' that had stopped in time some fifty years ago and lingered across the Rio de la Plata as the sleepy alter-ego of Buenos Aires. 'Provider of discreet financial services and elusive fugitives.' He mentioned his Hollywood cousin's brushes with various stars, and how he had a connection to a famous director, and this led him again to the matter of his screenplay, inextricable, in its turn, from the story of Robert Waterbury. He held a tomato on his fork and gestured with it. 'Now, as I warned you at the hotel, the next part is inevitable, because every thriller must have some fabulously wealthy man. He should have a questionable past, and, as the book is set here in Buenos Aires, he must have contacts with vicious *milicos* related to the anti-subversive war. With this in mind, we consider again *el Señor* Waterbury.'

'Waterbury is working the chain of contacts that he has made through Pablo. Because Waterbury, though yes, a bit desperate, is not so stupid. He's knowledgeable about economics and contemporary Argentine politics. He has traveled widely. He begins to show up at dinner tables and *asados* even without Pablo, and always with questions. "And what was your experience of the Seventies? And what is your opinion of Perón?" He is Waterbury, the erudite foreign novelist, and if no one has actually read his novels, he still has his copy of *The Black Market* to flash.

'One night he is drinking whiskey with a retired naval officer and another man who was briefly the Minister of Economy during the last days of the dictatorship. The name of Pelegrini comes up. "He should meet Pelegrini," the ex-minister says.

' "Pelegrini!" The idea strikes the old officer as ridiculous at first, then he considers it, looking at the bowl of his pipe. They are sitting in the oak-paneled library of a townhouse in Palermo. "It would be interesting, no? Pelegrini is a phenomenon." He shakes his head. "No! Pelegrini hates journalists. One of these days he's going to put a bullet in one and set loose a shitstorm."

' "But Roberto is not a journalist," says the former politician. "He's a novelist. He's irrelevant. What difference would it make to Carlo to spend a half-hour with him?"

' "It would be interesting for you," the admiral agrees to Water-bury. "But the issue is that Carlo is half-paranoid about journalists. They persecute him, and there were already some incidents."

' "What kind of incidents?" ' Waterbury asks.

'The ex-minister frowns. "They were exaggerated things! Such and such journalist gets assaulted and he tries to blame it on Don Carlo. Or an apartment is vandalized, and it must be the fault of Don Carlo. The problem is that there are many journalists with bad intentions, and they'll say any lie to call attention to themselves."

' "Like all these lies about the anti-subversive war," the admiral continues. "We save the country from the subversives, and then the leftists spend the next twenty years making *us* the villains and the terrorists the heroes." He finishes with a reprise Waterbury has heard many times among the discredited rightists of the old days: "We won the war but we lost the peace."

' "What does Pelegrini do?"

'The two older men look at each other. "He has a range of businesses," the former minister says slowly. "For example, he owns a courier service, like your private services in the United States. Also, he has an interest in the Customs warehouses at the airports and ports in Argentina, where people importing goods must put them until they clear customs. In partnership with some officers of the navy, like Juancito here."

' "Aldo!"

'Aldo clucks his tongue. "It's public information, Juan! It already passed through the newspapers." To Waterbury: "It's a completely legitimate deal. I presided over it, so I know. It's a heap of contracts this high, and every one of them with the appropriate signatures of the Ministry of Interior and the Armed Forces. But it has become fashion to attack Pelegrini, especially these days, while he's trying to make an arrangement with the national postal service."

'Waterbury can feel a chill coming from the naval officer's corner, and he tries to reassure him. "Juan, the reality doesn't matter to me. I fabricate my own reality. I'm only looking for atmosphere. The sound of a voice, what kind of clothes a person wears; things like that."

'The ex-minister takes up the idea. "What I would suggest, then –"

' "No, Aldo," the other interrupts. "Better that no! What is he going to find out in a half-hour? Carlo's not going to talk."

' "Not to talk, Juan. To observe." He turns to Waterbury. "You can go and see. he has a beautiful house in Palermo Chico, mansion type, of the old style. He has very pretty things. Moreover, he's a very interesting man to talk to. A philosophical type. He reads Borges to put himself to sleep."

' "Aldo!" The admiral shakes his head. "Pelegrini is a man of great weight! And with this mess of Grupo AmiBank . . . Better that no!"

' "Let's help the boy," the economist says. "It's our contribution to Art! Will you call him, or should I?"

'The admiral takes a sour look. "You call him! And make it well-clear that he's not a journalist." He looks at Waterbury and his tone mellows back to the luxurious hospitality he'd displayed before Pelegrini entered the conversation. "Roberto, I wish you much luck with your novel. But when you publish it," the old face tries to put some humor behind the request, "please don't put my name in the acknowledgments."

'Palermo Chico, as you may know, is a little slice of wrought iron and mansions lying among the wide green parks near Retiro station. These palaces were built when a peso was a peso, so fresh that you could practically smell the cattle and the wheat that gave them birth.

The mansions loom up three stories in cut stone, not regular stories, but the old style that rise five meters into elegant moldings and frescos painted by artists imported from France. Oval windows peek out from among artfully cut tiles, and immaculate gardens set off the proud colonnades of the front steps. They are houses that invite grand entrances, and many have been turned into embassies. The rest belong to the tiny circle of people who can pay to maintain them. Carlo Pelegrini has a mansion there, on Calle Castex, which is, by coincidence, the name of his wife: Teresa Castex de Pelegrini.

'Waterbury has been advised of all this by the ex-minister, and advised simply to look and listen and not bring up the subject of Don Carlo's business dealings. Above all, he should try not to appear as a journalist.

'The mansion stands on almost an entire city block, with a high brick wall maintaining the privacy of the lower floors. A guard buzzes the visitor through the wrought iron gate and accompanies him silently to a small stone guardhouse near the front entrance. The mansion itself looks like one he saw on a documentary about Napoleon, a massive construction of graceful beige stone under a cap of black slate.

'Waterbury is nervous. An unexpected rainstorm soaked him as he strolled from the subway stop and water is dripping down the back of his neck. He thinks of canceling the interview, but he knows he'll never get another chance. Poor Waterbury's heart is fluttering as he enters the guardhouse.

'The hut contains two men with walkie-talkies and a pair of Ithakas leaning in the corner. Both wear large black sunglasses, one of them moves forward to confront him. He is about Waterbury's own age but has obviously taken a very different path in life. He seems a man of little philosophy, with a cool face that has never expressed doubt. Waterbury doesn't know it, but this man is Abel Santamarina, the chief of MovilSegur, one of Señor Pelegrini's several private security companies. Santamarina was processed in 1984 for twelve incidences of torture and extra-judicial execution at the Banfield Pit, the clandestine detention center of the Federal Police during the anti-subversive war. Pardoned in the general amnesty of 1985, he now offers private security to Don Carlo and his many businesses.'

Fortunato spoke up. 'What does he look like, this Santamarina?'

'As it turns out, Waterbury described him with great care afterwards. He said he was well-developed in the shoulders and chest, very intimidating, with short colorless hair and eyes caught in that uncomfortable mix of brown and green, so that when you look into them they refuse to become one or the other.'

Fortunato thought about the man he'd met a few weeks ago with the Chief. 'A good description,' Fortunato said. 'Very artistic.'

'So the man looks at his clip-board, and he says with some distaste, "Robert Waterbury. Journalist."

' "I'm not a journalist," Waterbury corrects him. "I'm a novelist."

'The guard ignores him. "Journalist. Do you have any recording devices?"

' "No."

' "Wireless devices? Cellular telephone?"

' "No."

'Santamarina looks directly into his eyes, as if he can spy the thoughts whirling around Waterbury's brain. Whatever he sees, it is insufficient. "Lift up your arms."

'Waterbury complies and Santamarina begins to run his hands along his ribs. By now a third man has come in with a Doberman on a chain. Waterbury looks the dog in the eyes, the dog growls at him, and Waterbury takes a tiny but critical step backwards. He stumbles against the desk, where the little spike that holds message papers stabs him in his behind. He cries out and lurches forward again into Santamarina, who is at that moment running a metal detector along his legs. It happens at once: Waterbury cries out, Santamarina curses, the dog leaps up and grasps Waterbury's wrist between his teeth.

'In five seconds the guard has choked the dog away, but a stain of red has sprouted along Waterbury's torn sleeve. "What's happening with you, *loco*?" Santamarina berates him. "What's your problem?"

'The blood drips onto Waterbury's jacket and his eyes are tearing up. Santamarina looks at him with distaste and gives him his own handkerchief. He seems to remember that Waterbury is a guest. "Be more careful, *che*," he says in a tone not quite apologetic. "We get all kinds here, you know. There are many interests who would like to harm Señor Pelegrini." He brushes off the writer's shoulders, claps him on the back. "Go ahead, boss. Keep the handkerchief."

'The other guard walks him silently to the side entrance. The glass doors are gleaming behind a floral grille of exquisite wrought iron. The doorknob is a swirl of brass. Inside, the rich maroon carpet of the foyer leads to a quarter-acre of gleaming black and white squares. At four-thirty in the afternoon, with the sky overcast and the curtains half-drawn, the dimness is dispersed by glowing chandeliers and art nouveau floor lamps shaped like lilies. A butler in a white evening jacket looks at Waterbury's bloodied handkerchief. "Señor Waterbury. What happened? Is there something I can get you. A towel perhaps?"

'Waterbury catches the spectacle of his soaking hair and ruined suit in the mirror, seeing himself from the outside, as an impostor and a failure. He wrestles against the urge to turn around and leave. "A towel and a comb, thank you. I'll wait here."

'In a few minutes he is more composed and the bleeding has stopped. The butler takes him across the expanse of chess-like marble past the grand entryway, with its oversized double doors leading out and its helix of marble stairs ascending into the inner reaches of the house. Above him a fresco depicts a sky bordered by pink clouds, on which Phoebus guides the chariot of the sun. The furniture dates from the Twenties and Thirties, is impeccably upholstered in rich floral brocades and gleaming striped silks as if waiting patiently for the entrance of Carlos Gardel and his orchestra in black tuxedos. From the wall smiles an insouciant young peasant man lounging in a Dutch afternoon of several hundred years ago. They pass through this large room into a smaller room that appears to be for smoking, with leather chairs and pictures of racehorses and hunting dogs. At the far door, the butler knocks and then opens it, announcing, "Señor Waterbury is here, Don Carlo."

'Over the butler's shoulder Waterbury can see a formal dining room, with gilded molding and a magnificent chandelier on which every prism glitters. The butler steps aside and Waterbury sees a man and woman seated at a long gleaming table. The man is wearing a blue sweatshirt which goes well with his head of thick silver hair, while the woman, in a white silk blouse with a gold brooch, imposes a slight formality on the scene. It seems to Waterbury almost as if she's dressed for his arrival. Waterbury places her in her late forties, with tightly drawn hair dyed to a timeless chestnut. Her pleasing features seem slightly nervous – or perhaps eager. This will be Teresa Castex de Pelegrini.

'The man rises and smiles at him, shaking his hand. His sharp blue eyes make immediate and deep contact with Waterbury, who is awed by the magnate. "I'm Carlo Pelegrini," he says warmly, "it's a pleasure. And I present you my wife, Teresa Castex." The friendly expression changes to one of concern. "Your hand is bleeding! What happened?"

'The writer remembers Don Carlo's hatred of journalists and decides not to complain. "The dog was a bit nervous. It's nothing."

' "No, amigo, it's not nothing! How can it be nothing?" He turns to the butler, who is waiting at the door. "Nestor! Tell Abel to wait after his shift is over. I want to know why my guest is arriving with blood on his hand."

' "It's already stopped, Señor Pelegrini. Don't worry."

'He raises his hand. "This can't pass here! We will need a doctor to look at it. And your jacket . . . Afterwards we'll arrange it. Nestor, bring the Señor another handkerchief. And what else? A coffee? A drink? Perhaps a sandwich?" He dispatches Nestor to fetch coffee and sandwiches, signaling him also to wheel in a cart covered with liquor bottles. Waterbury notes that Don Carlo's accent is slightly drier than the traditional Porteño voice, giving him a masterly patrician air despite his informal attire. "So, you've come to Buenos Aires doing some journalism?"

' "No. I'm not a journalist. I'm a novelist."

' "Of course! You are Robert Waterbury."

'Waterbury smiles accommodatingly, unsure whether Pelegrini is mocking him, but the billionaire goes on. "*The Black Market!*" he says, waving his hand. "Genius! It's genius! That moment when the dead friend finally confronts him." Don Carlo looks distantly into space and recites the key line in Spanish with the perfect blend of comprehension and sadness: *You are an expert on debt, but no one ever told you about memory, which is the same. They are both things that linger from the past, and they both arrive at a point where they can no longer be negotiated.* He shakes his head in admiration. "*Excelente*! I wanted to stand up and applaud! That mix of business and psychology and metaphysics . . . Genius! I read it two times!"

'Waterbury listens in complete astonishment. Any writer would feel gratified to have his work resuscitated in such vivid colors, but coming from one of the wealthiest and most mysterious men of an entire country, the effect is as exhilarating as an unexpected inhalation of chemical solvents. Amidst the spectacular strangeness of the moment, Robert Waterbury feels shame at abandoning his literary scruples for something base and mediocre. He has the brief sickening feeling that perhaps when he came to Buenos Aires he left the best part of himself behind.

'Don Carlo continues with his critique. "You hit the international banks perfectly: they're a pack of jackals! But *Indigo Down*," he grimaces, "it was very . . . heavy. All that about justice and corruption . . ." He grimaces again. "A bit swollen."

' "*Indigo Down* was different," Waterbury protests. "I wanted to write a sacred text."

'Don Carlo gives Waterbury one of those deep smiles. "With yourself as God, no?"

'Waterbury laughs. "Perhaps, Señor Pelegrini, but with the knowledge that, as with all gods, the majority of the people would not take me very seriously."

'Now Teresa Castex speaks up, a bit stridently. "I preferred *Indigo Down*. You didn't run away from difficult themes."

'There is something vaguely sardonic in Pelegrini's voice. "Of course, Teresa! Teresa is the one who discovered you. We were vacationing in Barcelona when she picked up your book, and something about it captured her –"

' "It was the image of the lost wife," Teresa says.

' "For me it was those metaphysical themes," Don Carlo continues. "Borges, too, swims in those matters of memory and existence, though yours is more sensual and his is more on the side of the ascetic."

'Waterbury, who normally hates to be compared with anyone, takes the compliment to heart. "So you two are great readers?"

' "I, a little. It's very difficult to find time. But Teresa, yes," he waves lightly in the air, as if at a mosquito, "she goes around a lot in the arts."

' "People who can write a novel amaze me," she says. "You have to imagine a whole world. It seems like something impossible."

' "No, Señora Castex. What is impossible is to stop imagining the world."

'Don Carlo laughs as Nestor arrives with a warm washcloth and a towel, followed by a maid with a silver coffee service. At Don Carlo's request Nestor removes Waterbury's torn and soaking jacket and returns with a fresh white polo shirt with a famous brand name on the label. Waterbury slips it on in the smoking room then returns to his coffee.

'They talk some more about literature, with Don Carlo guiding the conversation and his wife inserting the occasional opinion. She takes advantage of a brief silence to inquire, "And what are you doing in Buenos Aires, Robert? Are you writing a new work?"

' "Yes. I'm doing the initial research."

' "And can you say what it is about?"

'Waterbury has good reason to be shy. Pelegrini was even then making the occasional appearance in the newspaper linked to matters of contraband and money-laundering, and Waterbury doesn't want to display any interest in such things. "This one is going to be a thriller type, set here in Buenos Aires. Something more commercial."

' "Of course, Robert. Even artists need to eat!"

'As in a work of theater the butler enters with a tray of little cakes, which they eat as they discuss the themes of literature and art. As Teresa Castex is telling of Rodin's stay in Buenos Aires, Don Carlo's cell phone distracts him and he excuses himself to the next room. The acrid conversation curls out like smoke beneath the door, and Waterbury hears the words "Grupo AmiBank," slapped harshly alongside the phrase *hijos de puta*. When Don Carlo returns his mood has changed. His pleasantries seem like a crust floating on a pool of lava, and Waterbury knows that it's time to go.

' "But look," Don Carlo says, mustering one last show of warmth. "Your jacket is ruined. Why don't you go with Teresa and she can help you buy a new one. No, amigo . . ." Waterbury feels Don Carlo's arm around his shoulder, can feel with equal intensity the force of his smile. "I insist."

Fabian looked down at his steak, of which he had only taken a few bites in his rush to tell the story. 'Look at this! I'm talking, and this poor *Uruguayo* is getting colder and colder.' Fortunato felt that he gave him a particularly smug grin. 'We can't let him go to waste, no?' The young detective began ostentatiously to cut and eat the steak, conscious that his companions were watching him. 'Skinny!' he called across the room to Lucho. 'Another beer!'

Athena rose abruptly. 'Don't start again until I get back,' she warned. Fortunato watched her recede towards the bathroom and then lit a cigarette. Fabian went on eating as if he were alone.

'Why, Fabian? Why didn't you tell me this before?'

The young man held up his hand until he finished chewing. 'Until now I've been checking out the information. I needed to be sure. A matter like this, you don't want to throw it all to the four winds without being completely right. Besides, you said you didn't want me on this case.' He cut off another piece of steak and popped it into his mouth.

Fortunato kept his *cara de gil*, his idiot face, firmly in place, just as Fabian was wearing his. That Fabian was revealing all this, after Boguso's confession had effectively settled the matter, meant that he had heavy people behind him. Fortunato spoke as casually as he could. 'But Fabian, with all due respect for your literary abilities, let's skip to the end of your story. Do you have evidence that it is someone other than Boguso?'

Fabian refused to tip his hand. 'We will talk of Boguso when we reach that part of the script. My cousin in Los Angeles . . .'

Fortunato cut him off, raising his voice slightly as he would speak to an officer of lower rank. 'Stop swelling my balls about the cousin! What I want from you –'

'You want the truth! I know!' He shrugged, took another bite. 'But do you really, Comiso? Truth is such a brute. Like King Kong, it doesn't notice who it crushes. Lies, on the other hand . . .' He cocked a smile at him. 'They're a little more humanitarian.'

Fortunato felt as if a cannonball had gone through his stomach. Fabian knew something, and the fear that had started at the Sheraton Hotel had been intensifying with every mention of Pelegrini's name. Along with the fear though, something equally cutting: Fabian could answer him in his own time, or not answer him at all, because in the space of two hours Fabian had gone from a subordinate to a superior, a member of the fashionable set, while Fortunato had become a lonely old widower living in a shabby little house in the suburbs, trailing off towards an undistinguished retirement. He, who'd risen cautiously through the ranks of the Buenos Aires police without ever arousing a shred of suspicion. Who'd earned public citations from the mayor, and private respect from the Chief and all the others who had benefited from his thirty years of orderly business. Now, to be dictated to by this low-level inspector!

The thought whipped through his mind of killing Fabian, and the silent image of Fabian crumbling to the floor transited his brain like the flapping of a bird's wings.

As if in answer Fabian wiped his mouth with a napkin, said quickly as he looked over Fortunato's shoulder, 'Stay tranquil, Comi, and the storm will pass over your head.' Speaking across him, 'Ah, here she is!'

Athena sat down and took a drink of water. 'Okay. I'm ready for the next installment of your . . .' she swirled her hands in the air, 'whatever this is.'

'Very well, Doctora. But before I continue with the next part, do you know much about Carlo Pelegrini?'

'Only what I read in the newspapers.'

'Ah, the newspapers!' The inspector turned his face to the Comisario, seeking agreement on the old gripe. 'There's no limit to the malice of those journalists, no? Pointing out that Pelegrini has a private postal system and a part ownership of the Customs warehouses, and claiming that he maintains a force of private security operatives estimated at nearly two thousand armed men. For this reason journalists such as Ricardo Berenski like to use the term "A State within the State," as in that headline in *Pagina /12* last week.'

He turned to Athena. 'And Berenski is the worst of all, isn't he? With those insinuations about money laundering, and his exposition of Don Carlo's attempt to take over the National Postal System? If I were Berenski, I think I'd walk in the shade for a while. He already makes much of his exile during the Dictatorship: these boys working for Carlo Pelegrini are the type who he was fleeing from. Raul Huaina Gomez, also called The Peruvian, ex-integrant of the Allianza Anticomunista Argentina that assassinated more than three hundred people before the military took over for them in 1976. Pardoned in the Amnesty of 1989. Hugo Gonzalez, called The Tiger, denounced by human rights investigators for twenty-six incidents of torture during his military service at the Escuela de Mechanica, and also child theft, extortion, robbery and rape, pardoned by the Law of Due Obedience in 1992. Abimael Zante – you remember him, Comiso, he was in one of your task groups at the Brigada of Quilmes for a while.'

Fortunato nodded, the unpleasant recollections of Zante returning to him. 'I had him transferred to Vicente Lopez to get rid of
him.'

'Thus the security apparatus of the esteemed Carlo Pelegrini. Very
wholesome, no?'

Fortunato kept his eyes trained on Fabian and his perfect blond
ringlets. He'd never seemed so dedicated to wholesomeness in all the
juicy squeezes he'd armed at the racetrack and in the discos. 'So,
returning to the theme of the victim . . .'

'Of course, Comiso. Forgive me.'

'La Señora de Pelegrini arranges to meet Waterbury at a brilliant café
in La Recoleta, where Waterbury groans over the price of a coffee.
The little silver trays and tableware make perfect accessories for the
well-wrapped clientele. Teresa Castex strides in and kisses him in a
mist of perfume and sits down for a coffee. "I hate this café," she
says. "It's quite pretentious, but it's an easy place to find and my
driver can wait outside with the car."

'Without the jewelry of the massive Mansion Castex, she seems
much like any upper-class woman in the room. As Waterbury will
observe in his journal that night, she's a woman on the unkinder half
of the forties, with stiff brown hair and a thin voice that seems
always on the verge of a complaint. She had once been beautiful in a
delicate way, but over the years her slight body seems to have dried
and hardened like an Inca mummy, with sharp rigid shoulders that
thrust out of the top of her blouse and hands like spiders. Her skin
has stayed youthful, well-cared for by spas and surgery, but her
bright silk scarf and Tiffany jewelry cannot alleviate the permanent
frown that pulls at her mouth. She gives the impression of perfectly
dressed unhappiness.

' "And Robert; what do you think of Buenos Aires?"

'Waterbury expresses his awe that so much beauty has been
blended with so much corruption and horror.

' "Oh, that," she shrugs. "It is no longer news to us." They chat
about literature for a while. Teresa Castex is partial to the French
Symbolists, whom she reads in the French. "But Carlo is crazy for
Borges," she adds. "It's a bit incongruous, because he's so much in
the commercial world and Borges is so abstract."

' "Those of Borges are more puzzles than stories."

' "Exactly. I think for him it's like a game: if he can solve the story, he has equaled Borges. He's very competitive, Carlo."

' "It seems he's done well. Your house is beautiful."

' "The house is mine," she says with a trace of venom. "It's the Castex Mansion and I am Teresa Castex. Perhaps those two words, *de Pelegrini*, make me his property, but the house still belongs to me."

'The intrigues within other people's marriages never make for light conversation, and Waterbury retreats from the subject. They return to literature.

' "It's very special to write a novel," Teresa says. "I've always wanted to write one, but I lack discipline. I sit down, but it all feels futile. Who am I to contend with the masters? Am I a great spirit?" Her face is a little bouquet of admiration. "Perhaps you are, Robert. I could sense you were different from reading your book, and then from your visit at our house. Maybe, in some small way, it is destiny that we meet. We'll see."

'Waterbury isn't sure how to react. Destiny is a surface that has proved rather slippery for him. Her coffee arrives with the perfect pat of tobacco-colored foam lingering against the white china. To his relief, she pays the bill.

'They stroll down the Calle Santa Fé, past gleaming shops with famous names. In an Italian clothing store they examine the light-weight suit coats of spring, looking for a replacement for his old one.

' "Linen, no!" Teresa protests with indignation. "The only place to wear linen is if you happen to be in a Renoir painting. Other-wise, it wrinkles." He tries another in navy blue. "Oh, Robert, you look very handsome in that. Perfect for author appearances. Why don't you get that one, and try on this other one made of silk and cotton."

' "Teresa! You can't buy me two!" But then he feels the cool slippery weight of the jacket, notes the sheen and the little universe of sage and tan within the intricate weave and a little rat-voice tells him that he may not get another chance. She insists on buying neckties, a belt and a pair of khaki pants. He stops her at the shoes.

' "But Robert, you can't go around in those dead dogs you're wearing! Don't be ridiculous!"

'He looks down at the polished-over scuff marks of his old wing-tips and accedes to the shoes. By the time they walk out she has spent five thousand dollars.

'She suggests that they lunch while the store completes the appropriate alterations, and Waterbury is surprised to see her lead them into the same restaurant he had visited with Pablo a few weeks before, La Rosa Blanca. Again Waterbury is besieged by that fear of having to pay the bill. After all, she's just spent several thousand dollars on making him look rich; he should try to act the part. He looks fearfully at the menu larded with French words and ingredients from far-flung places.

' "They take your head off here!" Teresa grimaces. She leans towards him. "I'll just put it on my husband's account. He's an investor in this restaurant; he bought it for his mistress." She sees that Waterbury is uncomfortable. "Don't worry, Robert; there will be no drama. She's only here at night." She finishes with a poisonous little twist, "That's when she does her best work."

'Waterbury again is reluctant to become the confidant of Teresa Castex and wonders, as they order, what spirit of auto-immolation would bring her to her rival's dinner table. He tries to leave the thought behind as they chatter about clothes and their favorite places of Europe.

' "So, Robert, excuse me if I intrude." Teresa is looking at him over a glass of white wine. "Of the artistic part, no doubt remains: you're an excellent writer with the chance at becoming a master, which very few have. But let's speak about the part, shall we say, less romantic. The economic element. Did it go well for you?"

'Waterbury too has drunk a glass of wine. Now the slightly brittle aura of Teresa Castex has softened, and Waterbury feels an allure that he will stereotype as the "jaded patrician." Maybe it is because she admires his books, or perhaps it is the presents she has bought him, but the moment becomes suddenly intimate and private, as if the little table is at the center of a whirlpool. "The truth is, Teresa, that the economic part has been very difficult."

'La Señora Castex begins to question him as to the specifics of his situation: whether he has savings, debts, what advance he expects to get for his next book. The level of detail surprises Waterbury but he doesn't feel he can refuse her. Finally she leans forward and smiles like a teenager. "I say all this because I have a proposition!"

'Waterbury goes cold, but at the same time feels a thrill.

' "It's thus: I have always wanted to write a book, but I have no talent. All the same, year after year, I keep perfecting it in my mind. It has much passion, and intrigue. Much corruption and even murder. It's the perfect story of Buenos Aires that you are looking for. I have always wanted to write this novel . . ."

' "But you only need write it!" Waterbury gushes, not really believing himself. "A pencil and piece of –"

' "Robert. Let's talk seriously. I told you I have no talent in novels, and if I write it no one will publish it. It would just be a waste of time. But if you write it," she arches her eyebrows, "that would be another story, no? If you write it, it will travel all over the world, it will be an important work. And moreover, I tell you it is just the story you are looking for. Very commercial." She smiles with her eyes half-closed. "And you can put in as much sex as you want to."

'It takes Waterbury a few moments to dissipate the laughing gas in his head. She is proposing something illicit and slightly dangerous, so very in tune with Buenos Aires that some ironic part of him wants to laugh at the perfection of it. He hesitates to ask her to clarify the scheme, because maybe this is the best part right now, when it is all fresh possibilities. Waterbury has heard a thousand times the phrase "I've been writing a book in my head for years," and a whole industry of ghost writers gorges itself on the egos of politicians and businessmen who want to garnish their accomplishments with the elusive title of Author. So perhaps now Teresa Castex wants to see her musings enshrined.

' "What's the book about?"

' "Afterwards I'll tell you. First, don't you want to know more about the arrangement?"

'The "arrangement." Waterbury recognizes well that dignified word Porteños use for bribes or kickbacks. *Arrangement.* "Okay."

'Beneath the business tone, her blue eyes are gleaming with something that makes Waterbury slightly uncomfortable. She rests her elbows on the table and lowers her voice as she speaks. "I will pay you two hundred thousand dollars to write a complete manuscript of this book for me. Deposited in the bank of your choice, of course. There are good ones in Uruguay, where the banking secrecy laws are very good. Two hundred thousand, eh? It's not so bad. And you won't have to pay taxes."

'Their arrangement would be the following: They will meet every three days and discuss the plot and the characters. Between their meetings, Waterbury will write another section of the manuscript. Perhaps twenty pages. In approximately six weeks, they will have the first redaction and he will receive the first third of his fee. After that, he can stay in Buenos Aires or return to his home to polish the further redactions. On its acceptance by his publisher, he will receive the greater part of his fee. Teresa Castex de Pelegrini would have her name on the cover as a co-author.

' "It can be in small print," she says. "Or even a *with*. Robert Waterbury *with* Teresa Castex."

'Two hundred thousand dollars, plus whatever he got from the publisher!

' "Have you talked this over with Carlo?"

' "Of course!" she answers. "He thinks it is a marvelous idea. Why don't you come to the house tomorrow for lunch, and we can begin! I'll have a contract ready for you when you get there." La Señora senses his hesitation. "And of course, an advance of ten thousand dollars." '

Athena put her cup down. 'Wait a minute, Fabian. What is Robert's wife doing all this time? She never told me anything about Teresa Castex or two hundred thousand dollars. If Waterbury's wife was so desperate for money, you would think he would send her part of the ten thousand, or at least mention it to her.'

Fabian conceded the point lazily. 'Of that matter I can only speculate. It's a weak point in the script, we might say. Perhaps Señor Waterbury was ashamed about the new phase of his career. Or perhaps he didn't want to mention his relationship with la Señora Castex, with its not-so-respectable implications. Without wanting to presume, Athena, many married men prefer to keep their relationships with other women secret, even ones that are completely appropriate.' Fabian smiled saucily. 'Thus they reserve the opportunity for the relationship to become inappropriate later on.'

Fortunato put his hand to his temple and growled in his low voice. 'Enough, Romeo. You're giving her a bad impression of the Institution.'

Fabian sighed, said to Athena, 'Comisario Fortunato is a man of very strict moral sensibilities. When Fortunato entered the force, it was all orderly. There was a sense of mission. Now, I fear, we're a little more lax.'

Athena was losing her patience. 'Fabian, I'm here about a murder. I need something a little more concrete than this . . . this *verso*.'

Fabian slouched backwards. 'The telephone records, *querida*. Afterwards I will show you the exact details of all the calls made to the Castex Mansion from the Hotel San Antonio. We've had them for some time –'

She leaned forward and cut him off in a voice of barely suppressed fury. 'We? She glanced angrily at the Comisario as she spoke. 'You're saying this was discovered during the investigation and no one told me?'

'Don't blame Comisario Fortunato. We felt it better to create the appearance that his investigation was going nowhere, and thus to be able to penetrate more profoundly into the matter. In fact, the Comisario's diligence of the last week has forced us to move more quickly than we intended.'

'What *we*? Is this you and the Comisario? You and your cousin? You and some imaginary Hollywood producer?'

'I can only tell you that there was a parallel investigation by another branch of the forces of Security. Someone of Pelegrini's stature attracts interest at the highest levels. Lamentably, I am not authorized to reveal more than that.'

Athena's eyes gleamed angrily and Fortunato shifted away from her gaze, trying to hide his own confusion. He felt the blood drain from his head as he considered Fabian's latest claim. If the Servicios de Inteligencia were investigating the link between Pelegrini and the *Bonaerense*, it went far beyond Bianco's ability to protect anyone. In that case, it became a question of who Inteligencia was backing: Pelegrini or his enemies in the government. On the other hand perhaps Fabian was working for the Federales. In that situation, Bianco might have enough influence to make Boguso remain as the murderer, if the matter stayed quiet. He thought of Fabian's reassurance: *Stay tranquil, Comi, and the storm will pass over your head*. Sí, amigo, just as it passed over Waterbury's head.

Athena had sat back in her chair and turned her sullen mask of a face towards the other side of the room. Finally she seemed to master her frustration. 'Go on,' she commanded. The Inspector gave a little hitch of his shoulders and arched his eyebrows at the Comisario as if to say *thus are women, no?*

'And so our Señor Waterbury becomes a regular visitor to the Castex mansion, wearing his brilliant new clothes. The master of the house can rarely be found during the day. The two authors meet in a private upstairs study and La Señora de Pelegrini tells him the heroic tale which she has decided will be Waterbury's redemption.

'It seems there was once a woman, a very wealthy and cultured woman who grew up in fine French boarding schools and a big mansion in Buenos Aires. The woman was happy. She loved France, loved drinking a *pastis* at a sidewalk café and discussing art and literature with the intellectuals and artists of the city, who gave much weight to her opinions. She lived the excitement of the May 1968 uprising in the arms of a young Socialist. "At this part," Teresa says, "I think we should put in some scenes of the woman and the Socialist making love. As a way to symbolize the sense of liberation of all sorts in those days. I would see them in an iron-framed bed, with a picture of Che Guevara in the background." Her face begins to soften, and she shifts her legs. "The woman is on top of him and he is caressing her . . ."

'Waterbury interrupts her. "Let's fill in the details later, Teresa."

'She continues: But this *affaire du coeur* was not to be. Her father did not approve and cruelly cut off her allowance. Rather than create discord in her family, the brave young woman left her lover to his exalted Workers and returned home to Buenos Aires. Her penitent father regretted his overbearing manner and rented her an apartment next to the exclusive cemetery of La Recoleta where, from her window, she could see the flagrant angels of the family tomb.

'That was the year 1970. Argentina danced between civil and military governments like a person standing on a hot griddle. The dream of the Left in Argentina lacked the *joie de vivre* of its French counterpart. The subversives had begun robbing and kidnapping, and the young woman made an attractive prize. Even so, she became involved with a member of the Revolutionary Workers Party, a handsome young engineer from an excellent family who straddled the border between the legal world and his *compañeros* of the People's Revolutionary Army. "If you want to, you can put in more sex here," Teresa says, "to show the fires of youth as a metaphor for the passion of politics." She smiles and lowers her voice. "For example, they are in an elevator, and in a moment of inspiration she opens his zipper and takes out his penis. He reaches under her blouse and puts his warm delicate fingers around her breasts . . ."

'La Señora stares fully in Waterbury's eyes as she describes the scene in the elevator and the writer feels his face flushing. If yes, a bit brittle, Teresa Castex is not without a certain sensual appeal, and they are practically alone in the huge house, with all its closed doors and vast quiet spaces. Waterbury's mind skitters through the possibilities as he jabs the pen back and forth in his notebook. The elevator scene ends with a simultaneous explosion of pleasure and Teresa Castex subsides for a moment into a nostalgic bliss. After, she touches Waterbury's arm and says, "I hope I did not give you a shock, Robert. We are both adults, no?"

'Fine. One day the boy stopped coming, and the woman never found out why. Perhaps he'd gone over into the clandestine life, or been forced into exile. He never answered his phone or came to call again. The woman was very sad. Later, when all the unpleasantness of the dictatorship came out, she saw his name among the lists of the Disappeared. "That's the tragic part," La Señora clarifies.

'The woman mourned him, but at a lovely party she met a young man from Cordova. Young and handsome, with cutting blue eyes and a confident voice, he attracted her from the start. "You can name him Mario."

'Mario sold expensive computer systems for an American company and had the salesman's gift for being liked. He spoke earnestly and knew when to laugh and when to listen. Aware that the conquest of this very desirable woman could not proceed without the conquest of her father, Mario captured the old man with his charisma and unfailing courtesy. Mario had risen quickly within the company, a man with a great future. Everyone fell in love with each other and a magnificent marriage was celebrated in the ballroom of the Alvear Palace.

'At that point Don Carlo knocks on the door, and Waterbury closes his journal.

' "Here are the writers!" Don Carlo greets them, then exchanges kisses with Waterbury and with his wife. He leans his weight on the corner of the desk and shines on Waterbury the radiance of those blue eyes. "And what is this work about?"

'Waterbury feels uncomfortable, wondering what his patron really knows about their arrangement. "We're still deciding," Waterbury answers. "But it seems to be a kind of love story."

' "Ah! Beautiful! I am already in a hurry to read it!"

'Having turned on him the fierce warmth of his gaze and voice, Carlo Pelegrini goes back to his business.

'It takes several days for Waterbury to tell the news to Paulé. He uses some of his advance to take her to a French restaurant in Palermo to celebrate his new possibilities. "Two hundred thousand dollars?" she says. The huge sum of money seems to undo her, as if her mind is clicking frantically to determine how she might also get hold of a fortune so easily. "She won't pay you."

' "She'll pay me. That's not what worries me. What worries me is that it's a bit complicated."

' "She wants to fuck you, right?"

' "Don't be ridiculous," he lies.

' "How 'ridiculous?' You're a handsome man. A distinguished author, looking pretty in the new clothes she's bought you. It is ridiculous to think that she does *not* want you in bed." Paulé half-closes her gray eyes. "*I* would want you."

'Her trick with the eyes, even if it's a joke, brings back the picture of Paulé that he can't get out of his mind. He puts it aside and recounts the tired narrative that Teresa Castex has burdened him with. The dancer doesn't answer at first, devoting herself instead to a round critique of the food. At last she says in a business-like way, "*Bien*. As your patron saint I advise you to take the money. Do whatever she wants. Whatever, eh?"

' "And write this shit?"

'She wrinkles her nose. "That's what you came here for, isn't it? To write shit?" He notices the bitterness in her voice. "Listen well, Robert: You left your position at the bank because you wanted to live it all out –"

' "I left the bank because I was tired of being part of a criminal enterprise!"

' "You are not that Good! You left because you had that fantasy in your head of the great artist, or the ruined artist, and now you've reached the part of the fantasy you hadn't foreseen, the part where you make some money and save your silly hide. Don't boot it out of reach while you're bending over to pick it up!" Her stern face is full of disdain. "Be like your friend Pablo: he never worries about where his silver comes from!" Waterbury is not prepared for her anger, cannot know if her goading is sarcastic or sincere. He guesses only that the struggling Paulé resents the huge sum of easy money. In spite of her tango lessons and her references to psychiatric dance pedagogy, he wonders exactly how she maintains herself. Before now he had always been careful to avoid the subject. "How do you know Pablo anyway?"

' "He owns an adult website and I posed for pictures. He came to watch."

'Waterbury hadn't expected her to admit it so boldly, and her complete casualness silences him even as it sends a dose of blood coursing between his legs. Pablo had denied being part of the pornography itself, and though the little lie disturbs Waterbury, he also feels a bit of envy. "So, do you . . . Are you a prostitute?"

' "I'm a model!" she says with fire. "And an actress! And a dancer!" She pauses, raising her eyebrows. "Exactly as you are a writer."

'The last comment fells him. Paulé's irony is usually quite direct, but in this case he can't tell. He seeks the refuge of a cigarette, but the little tube doesn't do him much good. He asks two coffees from the waiter and leans back from the square of white tablecloth. "What are you doing in Buenos Aires, Paulé? You've been here four years. Why do you stay?"

'She blows out a little puff of scorn then hangs a bitter smile on it. "That's your arrogance, Robert. You think you're the only one with an imagination."

' "Why do you stay in Buenos Aires?" he asks her again.

' "Here, there is tango."

'Waterbury understands. In France she is merely Paulé, a pretty woman with mouse-colored hair and a magical capacity in a dance that departed from fashion fifty years ago. Here in Buenos Aires Paulé is *La Francesa*, the dancer of tango, just as he, Waterbury, is still *Robert Waterbury*, the Northamerican writer. Here, in this place of memory and illusion, they can still close their fingers around the last rags of their fantastic dreams.

'Again, Waterbury walks her to her door, and again he lingers at the entrance. "Do you want to have a last drink of the night?" she asks him.

'They say that a good marriage takes one out of the fire. One has someone to make love to, who knows what one wants, without the need for the rituals and the wondering. During his eight years with his wife Waterbury has been glad to escape the fire, but with his family ten thousand kilometers away, the flames have come for him in the form of this glittering *Francesa*, who burns without being consumed.

'She is waiting now for his answer, the china skin of her face tinged gray with shadows. He envisions the drink and all that would

173

follow, says yes, but no, and they look at each other with a smile that shows that all is known between them. "Fine," she says. "I'll let you go."

CHAPTER 18

'Waterbury sets to work the following morning and writes the first pages of Teresa Castex's book. At his request she has given him photographs and flyers of the era, a copy of *French Vogue* from decades past, other trivia to give him the feel of the times. He intuits that Teresa Castex wants to rewrite her life into a story much grander than it has really been, with herself more adventurous and romantic and her husband perhaps a bit more dutiful. The work lacks inspiration, but the author puts together some twenty pages by the time of their next meeting and provides La Señora de Pelegrini with a copy. Her eyes are shining as she clutches the little stack of papers and reads her own character in the paragraphs: her adventures in Paris and in a Buenos Aires of urban guerillas and stern military men. Her excitement makes the leaves tremble in her hand. "Perfect!" she says. "You have captured exactly what I was looking for!" With that, she continues her story of the wealthy woman and her husband.'

'Mario, the woman found out over the next five years, was even more clever than he appeared to be. An excellent salesman, yes. He made friends rapidly and signed extraordinary contracts with the military, with financial institutions and the leading businesses of the country. He paid special attention to the middle ranks, those faceless men who shaped the specifications for bids and wrote the contracts, who could create overwhelming advantage or insurmountable obstacles with a few tiny lines of print. Mario was thoughtful and discreet, and he never forgot the names of these men's wives and children.

'La Señora de Pelegrini looks over at Waterbury, who has halted his pen above the page. "Aren't you writing this down?" she asks him.

' "It's just that it's a very abrupt change of direction."

' "Oh. We're just getting started, *amor*. Didn't you say you wanted to write a thriller?" She crosses her arms and narrates into the still air of the room.

' "March of 1976 arrives. Perón is dead and his widow Isabella is floundering through the last farcical year of her presidency. The *golpe* comes and the Generals stare down from the podium. Now the money began to flow in from the northern hemisphere like weather. The foreign bankers could lend with confidence, because in the documents signed by the military and their economic functionaries, the entire nation of Argentina will be the collateral. What a paradise! Loans guaranteed by the government, cumbersome financial regulations loosened: an excellent climate for a man with good contacts, a man who never forgets your wife's name.

' "By that time Mario had come to have great influence. In some branches of the National Bank and the Ministry of Public Works the entire middle range of bureaucrats were secretly on his payroll. When contracts were to be bid, one allocated an extra seven percent for Mario, who would apportion it most usefully. And those who didn't take that friendly lunch with Mario, or have a comfortable chat with him over a drink at the Jockey Club, would find themselves always left standing on the outside of the deal. Mario offered clever ways to hide the money overseas, and to circulate it back into Argentina through secret partnerships in his growing web of businesses. Mario came to dominate trucking and package delivery. He built on his wife's fortune, buying cattle farms and meat packing plants and government concessions to manage the airports and the harbors. With more money he opened more businesses, with more businesses he had more contacts, and with more contacts he could pay more bribes. Thus he rose to create his stinking corrupt empire, and to decorate it with pretty young girls who looked at him as if he were a great man!"

'La Señora de Pelegrini etches a few more specifics. How Mario used sabotage and violence to destroy his competitors in the trucking business, and blackmailed his package delivery rivals into selling out to him. She tells how he organized his friends in the Armada into a secret offshore corporation, then used their influence to procure huge contracts supplying beef to the armed forces. She begins to name names, including that of the admiral who provided Waterbury with his introduction to Pelegrini.

'Waterbury looks up from his notes. "Wait a minute." He feels the project veering off into a confusing and perhaps dangerous quadrant and is unsure whether he wants to hear more. At the same time, it is too early to refuse a prize of two hundred thousand dollars based on a bit of gossip. "Let's return to the wife," he says. "What is she doing all this time? Does she suspect what's going on?"

'La Señora at once relaxes into a happy nostalgia. "Ah, his wife! His young beautiful wife is lost in the splendor of motherhood, dutifully caring for his most precious possessions. It is she who must manage the servants and oversee the nannies. She is the one who must sort through the flood of invitations and social obligations that a family of such importance is burdened with and, of course, maintain her position as a leader in the world of Arts. After Fiorella comes the birth of Edmundo, and then Alicia. Her life is busy and blissful, until, like an astronomer sensing the gravitational pull of a dark hidden moon, she feels the presence of mortal sin intrude upon her life."

'Waterbury looks up from the page. "Mortal sin?"

'She turns to him. "Of this, we'll talk the next time. I think I've given you enough to fill twenty pages, no?"

'She accompanies Robert Waterbury through the empty rooms of the Castex Mansion and retrieves from the front closet a sealed cardboard box. "I prepared these materials to help give you a sense of the times." As he walks to the car Waterbury can feel Abel Santamarina examining him with his strange light eyes.

'At his room he opens the box. Editions of *La Prensa* announce the *golpe de estado* that brought in the Dictatorship, and small articles clipped from the financial newspaper detail the business transactions of obscure corporations. Again there are magazines of the Seventies and Eighties, a cassette of popular music of the time, a dried rose coming apart in an envelope, a silver rattle, a picture of a tomb in La Recoleta and a book of poems, privately printed in a luxurious leather-bound edition, written by a poet who hides her identity behind the filigreed initials "T.C."

'Waterbury surveys this strange *expediente* of Teresa Castex's life with pity. Her poems are odes to "Arte" or "Amor" that crumble in a heap of pretentious references. "Oh Art, my lover, why have you ravished me and left me sitting in the wastecan like an invitation from a social inferior?" He senses Teresa's boundless aspirations, desires which he knows will forever suffocate beneath her narrow spirit and non-existent talent. He begins to think of what she has told him in a different light, the story of a trivial woman who gradually discovers the depths of corruption within the man closest to her and so begins her own awakening.

'Waterbury begins to write, and to his surprise, it comes easily to him. A magnate, an ingénue, a background of theft on such a massive scale that it can only be called business. *There* are the revolutionaries and the corrupt politicians, *there* the complicit functionaries of the United States, as he himself had been. The tango, the pompous facades, the racks of cow bones suffering over hot coals: it all whirls around him and becomes the city itself, so that when he walks in the streets they are the streets of his book, the bitter taste of coffee is of his book. Waterbury writes without thought, crashing through ten or twelve pages at a sitting where before he would only write three. The vain and shallow Teresa Castex becomes a woman torn between her own material security and the knowledge that she has become part of an evil cancer that includes her in its filthy web. Shall she expose it, and risk the luxuries and status it accrues to her? Or shall she close her eyes? Thus Waterbury extracts his novel from the frivolous clucking of Teresa Castex.

'At the same time, distant footsteps are pacing in the background of Waterbury's brain. There is something a bit dirty about this arrangement. As a guest of Don Carlo, he is a traitor. As a friend of Teresa Castex, he is a user. And as a foreigner balancing between a rich and ruthless magnate and his angry wife, he is a cursed *boludo*. In his latest encounter with Don Carlo he has noted a tension that worries him. He meets with Pablo at his office to ask for advice.

' "With Carlo Pelegrini? *The* Carlo Pelegrini, of MovilSegur and all the rest?"

' "Yes."

'Pablo swivels his head downward to the white carpet, letting out a long rich breath. He is silent for a surprising amount of time before he looks up. "Does he know you are here?"

'Waterbury feels a little flutter of anxiety. "No. Why?"

' "Pelegrini . . ." He shakes his head. "How did you meet Pelegrini?"

' "Some friends gave me an introduction, and then things developed." The writer mentions the admiral and the former minister of economy, then recreates his little tango with Teresa Castex and her version of her own life and the life of "Mario."

'Pablo nods, and for the first time Waterbury sees his carefree features dulled down with worry. "You shit yourself, *hermano*."

' "What do you mean?"

' "Pelegrini is heavy. He has a security apparatus directed by ex-repressors of the Dictatorship. He has many turbid businesses. Don't mix in with him."

' "I'm already in, Pablo! I have a contract for two hundred thousand dollars. We can live for four years on that. It buys me the time to write a real book."

' "Don't put yourself —"

' "I'm just a fucking novelist! What's more useless and ineffectual than that? He has nothing to fear from me!"

' "It's not what you *are*, it's what he *thinks* you are. Moreover, to play games with another man's wife, here in Argentina, is always dangerous. This isn't a culture where the two men shake hands and talk about philosophy."

' "Don't be ridiculous. I have a wife!" His protest feels weightless even to himself. He wonders if Pablo knows of his continuing friendship with Paulé.

' "That's fine! You don't have to convince me. But be careful, Robert." He clears his throat. "And one more little thing: better that you don't come to this office again. From now on we meet outside."

' "What do you mean?"

'His friend speaks delicately. "Robert, I tell you this as a friend, and it must be kept in absolute confidence. The theme is thus: The relationship of Grupo AmiBank with Pelegrini these days is a bit tense. There's a species of competition, let's say, between the Grupo and the Pelegrini interests. If Pelegrini sees you coming here and meeting with me, well, he might have the mistaken idea . . ." He puts up both hands to close the matter. "Better that *no*, Robert. My advice is that —" '

Fabian's sentence was interrupted by the sound of Fortunato's cell phone. The Comisario took it from his pocket. 'Fortunato.'

The Chief's voice boomed through the tiny holes. 'Miguelito! How goes it, *querido*? I called to see that La Doctora left well-content. Did you give her the certificate of appreciation?'

Fortunato could feel Fabian and Athena trying to interpret the call. 'No.'

The little voice sounded surprised. 'You forgot to give it to her? What happened, Miguel? Now we'll have to send it.'

'*Mira*, this moment is a bit inconvenient. I'm in a reunion with Inspector Diaz and a colleague from the United States, the Doctora Fowler. It's a matter of some priority. I'll call you afterwards.'

Fortunato waited a few seconds then said agreeably, 'Perfecto!' and cut the line. He threw a dismissive little pout to his companions. 'Continue.'

Instead Fabian rose from the table. 'With your permission,' he said, and looked towards the back of the restaurant. Fortunato's bladder had been insisting for some time, but he'd suppressed it, unwilling to leave Fabian alone with Athena. Now he stood up and followed the Inspector to the bathroom. A mistake: the tiny bathroom felt crowded and he had no choice but to talk to Fabian's back as he waited his turn. Fortunato stared at the expanse of parrot-green cloth, its collar concealed by the cascade of blond curls. If one wanted to commit a murder, this would be a good way to set it up, except in this case there would be no alibi or escape route. Too early to say whether Fabian was attacking or supporting him, or if Fabian knew he had committed the murder at all. He wasn't sure where to start.

'I congratulate you, Fabian. I don't know how much of this is true, but on a cinematic level, it's a great success.'

'That's the important part, Comiso,' Fabian said to the wall. 'When they make the film I'll try to get you named as a technical advisor. Thus we can spread the money a bit between colleagues, as is the tradition.'

'The thing that bothers me is that you didn't put me up to this beforehand. Combining forces we could have arrived much more rapidly. I had heard that the Federales were arming an investigation.'

Fabian adjusted himself and then turned to the Comisario, who was blocking the door. He forced a stiff pleasantness onto his face. 'With your permission, Comiso. I don't want to be rude to La Doctora.'

The lunch hour had ended and the waiter scattered another round of little white cups on the table. Fabian had accessorized his plumage with a small cigar he'd bought at the counter and now he hung it in the air between them and cocked his head as if he were listening to the smoke. When the Comisario sat down he began again.

'*Bien*. Waterbury has written more than thirty pages in three days. He prepares a copy for La Señora and arrives at the Castex Mansion at the appropriate hour. Unexpectedly, Santamarina, the ex-torturer, intercepts him at the security post and surprises him with a full search. He revises Waterbury as if he has never before visited the

Mansion Castex, then takes his portfolio and empties out the papers, carefully surveying their contents. Finding the sheets that tell the story of Mario's rise to power, he rewards the author with a stare of violent contempt, then puts the manuscript in a paper bag and guides Waterbury towards the house. The butler does not meet them at the door. Instead Santamarina himself leads him through the long silent gleam of the mansion, past the frescoes and the smiling Dutch peasant. There is a smell of floor polish, of lemon. Don Carlo is waiting for him in the smoking room, ensconced in the aroma of leather and tobacco. Above him hangs a photograph of a racehorse that was put to sleep before he was born.

' "Ah, Robert. Sit down! Sit down, amigo." The magnate wears a button-down shirt of cream-colored silk, crossed by an iridescent gray tie loosened at his neck. The jacket lying across the arm of another chair makes Waterbury suppose that he has come home from his office for this meeting.

'Waterbury creaks into the leather armchair that Pelegrini has indicated. "Teresa isn't here?"

' "Yes, she is here," the businessman says, "but she's busy at the moment. She asked me to receive you myself."

' "Oh!" Waterbury says. In the room with them now is the fictional Mario, and the tales of Mario's beatings and extortions hover in the air. "It's an unexpected pleasure."

'Don Carlo nods to Santamarina and the bodyguard places Waterbury's pages beside him and moves wordlessly out the door. "And," Carlo says glancing at the words. " How is your project with my wife?"

'Waterbury feels the vague sting of an accusation, tries to steady his voice as he answers. "It's going well."

' "And does she have great potential as an author?"

' "*Bien*," Waterbury says, trying out some old *verso*, "in literature there is nothing absolute. An excellent book in the literary sense may sell poorly, and be considered a failure, while a mediocre book may sell a million copies." Don Carlo is still pinning him there with his eyes. "So, as to her potential, that's a disposition that I can't really make, especially not before the book is finished."

'Don Carlo stares at him silently for a time, then turns his attention to the manuscript and begins to look through it, saying at the same time, "So long since I studied English, and then it was technical English, of the kind needed to read service manuals and write invoices. Not fine English, like this." He examines the page. "Ah, look at that! *Extortion*. It's the same in Spanish. *Extorción*. And here: *bribe*. That's a *coima*, no?" He continues reading for fifteen minutes, without excusing himself or apologizing, knowing that Waterbury will sit quietly and wait for him. "What's this?" he says. "*Blackmail?*"

' "*Chantaje*," the writer answers him softly.

' "Ah, *chantaje*, of course. And here is *liar*, that means *mentiroso*, and *arrangement*. That means *arreglo*, no?" Carlo looks up and Waterbury can see the veneer of his smile wearing away. "This Mario is a real *hijo de puta!*"

'The writer swallows, feeling the heat rise to his face. "Yes. That particular character isn't very straight, but he's operating in an environment where that's demanded of him for success. At the end of the book he changes."

' "But how? From what I see here he is beyond change! He has a standard of living based on extortion and bribery. Such people can't change. Especially when they are part of a corrupt system. You have to kill them!"

'Waterbury begins to speak and his voice rises and breaks. "You know, Carlo, it's not up to me to judge my characters. I just try to present them. A novel needs a full array of characters, and . . ." he tries an intimate little shrug, "somebody has to be the bad guy, no?"

'The magnate drops his smile and cuts him off. "Don't play the *boludo* with me. Do you think me so stupid?" He puts his anger away and takes a softer line. "To the point. At the start, I was happy that Teresa had a project, because the truth is that since the children are gone she is a bit lost. She has paranoid fantasies of this and that. Do you understand? I indulged her fantasies because I thought that this might be a sort of therapy for her. But this," he holds up the manuscript, "this is an insult!"

' "It's just a character —"

' "Yes, just a character with businesses like mine, that worked at a computer company, like I did. It's an insult and a violation of my confidence in you! I welcome you into my house and in return you encourage my wife to defame me with this confection of lies she has invented from the newspaper! This doesn't go! It doesn't go! Not for a novelist or anyone else!"

'Poor Waterbury cringes into the squeaking leather cushions

without an answer. Pelegrini goes on lashing at him. "She told me she already gave you ten thousand. Ingrate! Take that and don't ever come back!" Pelegrini rips out a little laugh. "Did you think a writer of the last ranks, like yourself, could legitimately make two hundred thousand dollars writing a book? You're dreaming! Only in a dirty deal like the one you made with Teresa, where you take advantage of an unstable woman, only thus could you make that much money with your *supposed* talent. And if it was only I who thought so, you wouldn't be here in Buenos Aires working a cheap confidence trick and trying to pass yourself off as a grand literary success!"

'The author doesn't feel his body, only the lurid pink distress of his mutilated sense of self. He can only sit and wait for Pelegrini to finish annihilating him.

' "This doesn't go any further. You understand? If any part of this ever appears anywhere, in fiction or in any other form, no amount of money in the world will be enough to justify the consequences to you and your family. And don't make any mistake: I can find you here, at the Hostal San Antonio – or there." Pelegrini recites Waterbury's address in New York and the name of his daughter's school, then lapses to a silent glare.

'Waterbury has no answer. He fumbles to his feet and stumbles out of the smoking room. Santamarina is waiting for him, puts his hand on his arm as he directs him across the spacious chesswork of tiles and the glittering chandelier. There is no Teresa Castex and her lucrative vanities, no inspired literary thriller, only the warm spring air of Buenos Aires, the straining Doberman of the custodian, the high black gate and then the unsteady sidewalk. Two blocks away a flock of black taxis gleam like cheap hearses in the sunlight.'

'Waterbury falls through the afternoon in a state of shock. His fabulous landscape has withered in front of him. Buenos Aires streams past his window with its glorious stone angels and verdigris domes, but all has gone gray and lusterless. His easy salvation has evaporated and left him groaning with debt and shot to pieces by Don Carlo's devastating assessment of his talent and his character. Maybe it is his own corruption that has brought him to such a pass. If he had refused La Señora's offer at the beginning he could have kept a steady course and written a book, rising and falling on his own merits. As it is, the sudden elevation and crash has left him feeling like he can give no more. He passes the hotel clerk with a wave and hurries to his room, throwing himself on the bed. On the tiny desk his books on writing a bestseller laugh at him, and he writhes in an agony of self-hatred and futility, a man who has failed himself and his family, a fraud, a liar, a pretender to literary achievement on the level of Teresa Castex herself. He is out of place on all sides. To stay in this empty and mocking city feels like torture, but to return home now, as a failure, impossible. He lies there as at the bottom of a smothering black pool, but into the dim room comes the buzz of the desk clerk. "You have a visitor," he says. "That French woman."

'A tiny crack of light seems to open. "Send her up," Waterbury croaks, and he gathers the resolve to rouse himself from the pit. She is, he tells himself, the Patron Saint of Desperation. He hears the elevator hum and clank, and then the knocking at his door. She stands there in her black dress and a little handbag. It's tango night.

' "What a depressing room!" she says, looking past him. "If I lived here I would have put a bullet in my head two weeks ago!"

'Waterbury's smile dies out before it can complete itself and the dancer eyes him more closely. "What's happening with you?" she asks. "You look like your wife just sent you divorce papers!" She strides into the room and puts her handbag on the desk. "It's not for so much, *amor*! With all that money from La Señora de Pelegrini you can find a woman half her age!" This does not cheer him, and she realizes that something is wrong. She speaks more softly, her gray eyes crystalline and wise beneath their slashes of liner. "Robert! Tell me what's happened to you!"

'He lifts his hand as if to answer but before any words can escape he finds himself crying without control, finally buried by the years of frustration and failure, humiliated in his last attempt to be clever in his business and his art. *La Francesa* puts her arms around him and holds him but he goes on crying, clutching her as if she was the incarnation of every hope he once had for Buenos Aires, or himself. She pats him on the back and murmurs small incomprehensible consolations without knowing even what he is crying about. That it is all right, that she is here, that it will all pass, that the moon and the stars will still be shining when it is over. At last he takes a deep breath and sits on the bed, relating in a choking voice the events that have stolen away his hopes for easy salvation. She listens without interruptions, a grimace of discomfort crossing her face when the writer finishes with Pelegrini's brutal summary.

'The silence sits there for a half-minute as she holds her chin and watches him. She shakes her head sadly. "It looked so easy. It floated your way and when you tried to capture it you found it was nothing more than a little ball of smoke."

'She gives a long sigh. "Listen to me . . ." She kneels in front of him and puts her hand on his knee, her gray eyes wide and sympathetic. Her voice is soft and low, almost a hum in the quiet afternoon sun. "You came to Buenos Aires to make your last play. But Teresa Castex is not your last play." Her face is only inches away from his. She is nearly whispering. "Life is your last play, and it is happening right now. All around you. All at one time."

'The moment overpowers them. He is kissing her, feeling her thick glossy lips and her unfamiliar tongue, smelling as always the odor of smoke in her hair, and her perfume. Without remembering how it happened he is on the bed with her, horizontal, holding her black-dressed body close to him as her arms writhe slowly across his back. He has forgotten his wife, or rather, he has abolished her and his daughter to a remote planet which he knows he must visit again in the near future but which for the moment is only a shadow. The dream is like a fever now, even more intense for the knowledge that it has reached its full bloom and as such has already marked some unknowable endpoint. Nothing exists but this dark room, this woman, and around it the idea of a city called Buenos Aires built not of bricks but of the infinite illusions of its citizens and the aspirations that are forever receding before them.'

Fabian leaned back in his chair and shook his head ruefully. He seemed almost serious. 'It's a disappointment, I know, that Waterbury would be unfaithful to the wife who waits for him. Bad news to carry back to the widow. But thus it happened. Waterbury fell, as we all fall, to our own desires for things real or things imaginary. We can't help it: that's what pulls us on. You, me, the Comisario. For Waterbury, it was the flesh, or perhaps, looking more profoundly, the vision and the flesh made whole.' Fabian shrugged. 'There are others who do much worse for much meaner reasons. Was it worse that he slept with *La Francesa* or that a decade before he devoted himself to extracting money from the country for AmiBank? I suppose it depends who you ask, no?' He slapped his forehead. 'See that? Here I am going around in these *boludeses* again! I can't resist!' He puffed. '*Qué tonto!*' He looked at his watch. 'Fine, we are reaching the end now. Both I and Waterbury have little time left.'

'The next morning *La Francesa* returns to her room and Waterbury decides to look over the manuscript that he has already written. The first twenty pages of the Señora's history can be easily condensed. That of the French Socialist is disposable, but the part about the young engineer and revolutionary who disappears, yes, there is something of value. And that of the magnate, the disagreeable Mario, in his progress to corruption, yes, a most interesting story in that. He is considering all this when he hears a knock at the door.

'Teresa Castex presents herself dressed in the manner of a schoolgirl in a gray skirt and white blouse. The feeling of recaptured youth is strengthened by her hair, which she has released from its tight bun to flow down over her shoulders and her back. There is a too-brilliant smile on her face, almost childish above the expensive leather portfolio that she presses to her chest. "I told the boy at the desk that I wanted to surprise you!" she explains, glancing around the room at the chaotic bed sheets and the general disarray.

'Waterbury feels immediately uncomfortable, both for the unusual state of animation of Teresa Castex and for the memory of his last encounter with her husband. He invites her in and throws the bedspread unevenly over the humped-up sheets. "This is half-Bohemian, Robert! You should have used some of your advance to get a better room."

'She goes on with her comments about this part of town and other hotels that he would find more congenial to the project, and he answers her without much grace. Finally she puts the leather case on the desk and sits down. Her eyes are bright and nervous, her voice too gay for the occasion. "So, I decided we would have our normally scheduled session at your room today, to perhaps bring a different ambiance to the story."

'An air of delusion has come over the dim lodging. Waterbury half-sits on the windowsill. "Teresa. Do you know what happened with your husband yesterday?"

'She plays the *gil*, but badly. "Yes, I was indisposed yesterday. Forgive me; I should have called you in advance. He told me that you chatted."

' "It was a bit more than a chat. He looked at the copy of the manuscript and he told me that if I continued in any form he would make me regret it."

'She begins to get angry. "Why did you give him the manuscript? He has nothing to do with it!"

' "I didn't give it to him! The security guard took it away at the gate when I got there. What did you tell him about the book?"

' "He has nothing to do with it!" La Señora says again, flaming with indignation. "This is *my* project! It is *my* life and *my* novel, and he has no right to say what will happen with it or what its contents will be! I am Teresa Castex! Of the Mansion Castex! I am Castex!" To Waterbury's silence she commands: "Take out your journal and let us begin! Where were we? That was it! It was mortal sin, the mortal sin of adultery that the filthy Mario has entered into at the back of his innocent wife and children!"

'The writer is not prepared for the situation that is developing before him. He doesn't move and Teresa Castex says "Come on! Take out your journal! Carlo does not control everything I do!"

'He tries to be calm. "Teresa. Your husband made his threats very clear."

'Her face is flushing pink beneath the makeup. "To the devil with my husband! Your contract is with me! I paid you ten thousand dollars! Did you forget that? I demand that you begin right now to redact our book!" Her command has no effect and she sees that she has blundered. Her face collapses. "He has nothing to do with this! Nothing! This is *my* project! Robert!" She comes to her feet and lurches across the floor to Waterbury, and his vision is filled with her tight-skinned old features made young. "Don't let him do this to us!" She leans in to kiss him and he hears the clicking of her neck bones. He remains like wood and inhales her perfume. Her lips are thin and timid at first, then they grind away desperately at his mouth without bringing it to life. She leans back and regards him with a face of pure torment. "Forgive me," she whispers. "You don't find me attractive."

'Waterbury lies to try to comfort her. "It's not that, Teresa. Of course I find you attractive. But I have a wife and daughter in the United States."

'The skinny woman moves away. "Of course. How silly I am! It's written on the back of your book!"

'The confusion now fills the air completely. Waterbury does not know why his life has suddenly become so rotten with deception. Just a few weeks before he was a desperate but honorable man.

'The wounded Teresa Castex, failure as both an author and an adulteress, can tell him nothing.

'She stands motionless, her hands pressed to her temples, then pounds her fists down through the air. "He has devoured my life! He has taken over my house and my social standing. He has belittled me in the eyes of my children. And now he is trying to take away our work, our relationship! He is pure corruption!"

'She reaches into her portfolio and subtracts a little packet of papers. "*Bien*," La Señora says a bit formally, "this is the material for the next section of the book. You must decide whether you will let my husband frighten you away from our book and your two hundred thousand dollars. I will await your call." La Señora de Pelegrini leaves the papers on his desk and closes the door behind her.

'I suspect that at that point Robert Waterbury was already under surveillance by Pelegrini's men. In the movie version, I see a twenty-four hour surveillance, effected by weary men who wait for hours for him to emerge from his hotel and then follow him at a careful distance. A shot of a man sipping at a *mate* in his car, a man pretending to read a newspaper. They are studying his habits and his social contacts. Does he carry a cell phone or pager? Is he armed? All of those things. Pablo's warning has come too late: Pelegrini already knows about his visit to the Grupo AmiBank, and he knows that Waterbury was once an employee of the bank. Perhaps before his wife appeared at Waterbury's hotel room, he still believed his threat alone was sufficient. Who can say with certainty? What is certain is that Waterbury didn't realize the true danger he was in before he opened up the packet that Teresa Castex had left on his desk. At last, his dreams have become his Destiny.

'He pulls out the papers and there it is. Correspondence, transcriptions of telephone conversations, documents from banks located in the West Indies. And with it, a description in Teresa Castex's handwriting of transactions between certain officials and her husband that leave no doubt about her husband's intentions towards the Post Office. In black and white he can see the fifteen million in bribes that Pelegrini was distributing to the Post Office officials and to various members of the government for the purpose of securing the right to take over the public mail system. In the hands of Pelegrini's rivals at AmiBank, such information would be dynamite.'

Fortunato frowned. 'Have you seen these papers, Fabian?'

Fabian held up his hand to stop their questions. 'Afterwards we'll talk about that. But you see now why Pelegrini had to act. It's the classic. Waterbury knew too much. The documents showed the clear course of the money from Pelegrini to an offshore bank, and from there to accounts in the name of certain postal officials and fictitious companies that then invested their money back in Argentina. But all this was exposed by Ricardo Berenski and the others in their articles about Pelegrini. Surely you've seen them, Comisario.'

'I've seen them.'

Fabian lifted his palms towards Athena. 'The biggest scandal in months! Though, of course, it was surely uncovered independently of Waterbury.'

'Fine. So what happened next?'

'Robert Waterbury becomes nervous, but also confused. That the Señora de Pelegrini would expose her own husband shocks Waterbury, though he understands what a depth of ancient resentment it comes from. He only wishes she had not chosen him to be her confessor. Now, yes, he begins to feel insecure. A part of him would like to go home. Another part is drawn to stay, to live out a few more weeks with Paulé and with his manuscript, to live this fantasy made real. In just a short time of intensive work he can complete the first redaction and then leave it behind forever: his affair, his blunder with the Señora.'

'Did he see any signs that Pelegrini was after him?' Athena asked.

'That we will never know. At this point the journals of Robert Waterbury end, and I can only speculate on the rest. I see Carlo Pelegrini questioning his wife about her visit to Calle Paraguay. It is uncertain how much she tells her husband, but her sobbing complaints move him from resentment to action. The order goes out to his security apparatus, who have been conducting the surveillance. I see three or four men arming the *capacha* with two automobiles. They would need some experienced men, but they find themselves lacking in the last days and one of the men decides to call on an old friend, Enrique Boguso, who is a bit erratic, but willing to undertake such a mission for not very much money. Here the first mistake. What is the mission? To intimidate Waterbury into compliance. Pelegrini suspects that his wife has revealed too much about his business affairs, and so it has gone beyond a matter of jealous husbands and disobedient wives. Waterbury must be shocked into permanent silence, even after he has returned to the United States. For this, he must experience a level of fear that will wake him up with a jerk for the rest of his life.

'The night of October 30th comes. Waterbury goes to eat at a restaurant around the corner at approximately eleven o'clock and leaves the restaurant shortly after midnight. A building is under construction and they park their car next to a container piled with shattered wood and plaster. Waterbury comes around the corner. He walks beneath the scaffolding, as he has other nights, and two of the men corner him there. It's the logical place. Boguso has a hose filled with little balls of lead, and he silences the writer with a blow to the head.

'I see Waterbury in the auto, confused by the blow, confused by his situation. How could this be happening to him? He is only a writer. He guesses about Pelegrini and he wants to talk to the magnate, to dismiss his worries and assure him that his relationship with Teresa is only platonic. It all seems rather absurd, but at the same time, frightening. He has already been beaten a bit, and held on the floorboards of the car with handcuffs on. What might happen?

'For some time they drive, gradually making their way to the outer suburbs of Buenos Aires. Waterbury asks questions that are answered with a blow or an insult. Perhaps he is thinking of his wife and daughter, wishing he was home with them. Or perhaps he is thinking of *La Francesa*, or Pablo, or of what an interesting story this will make someday. I suspect that some part of Waterbury is still apart from his circumstances. They come to rest at a vacant lot on Calle Avellaneda, in San Justo, and Waterbury is pulled erect on the seat. He looks around at the abandoned neighborhood and now an ugly sense of reality begins to swallow him up. The dark windows, the apathetic weeds. A lost place, apart from all mercy. Perhaps it occurs to him, "This is the kind of place where one takes a bullet in the head." I imagine now that remorse comes over him. For the vanity of Teresa Castex, for his affair with *La Francesa*. For all the silly dreams that dissolved the life he had with his wife and daughter and made Buenos Aires seem more golden and more real. Because what is it now? The filthy gray light, the cheap swaggering by men who hit him while he is in manacles. Waterbury has tried to be stoic, to reason, to joke, to plead, to say nothing, but no approach will change the men.

'Now his captors are losing control. Empty little papers of *merca* scatter to the floor and the atmosphere in the car has an electric feel, like that bitter smell of ozone around a red neon sign. The intimidation of Waterbury becomes an entertainment for the kidnappers. Guns are waving in the air, guns are pressing into his balls and then without reason a gun goes off and the last cord of sanity snaps. Waterbury panics and reaches out. Another explosion, then another. Waterbury is screaming, bleeding from the thighs, the balls, the hand, the chest . . .'

'Enough, Fabian,' the Comisario snapped.

The Inspector ignored him. 'Finally Boguso takes up his nine millimeter Astra and walks around to the back door. The killer –'

'I said it's already enough.'

'I'm almost finished, Comisario.' He looks at Athena. 'The killer leans in, he raises the pistol towards Waterbury's head –'

'*Enough!*' the Comisario shouted. 'What's happening with you? Is this entertainment? You're so content! What good luck that a man is murdered in an empty lot! What diversion!'

The uncharacteristic outburst halted Fabian; he dropped his gaze to the table. A stupid thing for Fortunato to do, but it had escaped by itself, the reaction to the long afternoon of mockery and in-sinuation. And then, to see the murder playing out in front of him again, acted out by the stinking Boguso . . . Fabian might know nothing or he might know enough to put him in perpetual chains, and after two hours listening to him he still couldn't tell. Fortunato released the tension with a sudden flush of stale air. 'Forgive me, Fabian. I lack your ironic distance.'

Fabian's eyes glittered briefly, but Fortunato couldn't tell what that meant. 'It's fine, Comisario.' He cocked a smile. 'With good reason.'

Fortunato felt another curtain of dread flutter through his body, then his cell phone sounded. 'Fortunato.'

Chief Bianco's panic traversed half of Buenos Aires and erupted from the handset. 'Boguso retracted his confession!'

'What?'

'This morning. He's implicating Carlo Pelegrini as the intellectual author!'

Fortunato answered slowly. 'And what others?'

Bianco ignored the question. 'The matter is, Miguel, that this is a very delicate time! Other things have happened . . .' The Chief stopped himself, but his nervous complaint kept ringing in Fortunato's head even after he pushed on. 'Where are you?'

'In the center, near Corrientes.'

'I want you to come to my office immediately.'

'Forgive me, *Sargento*, but I'm occupied right now. Thank you for the information. I'll call you for the papers. *Está? Perfecto!*'

Fortunato hung up the phone and looked at the two of them. He didn't know what to say so he simply raised his eyebrows. It already *was*. He looked at Athena. 'That was Central. Enrique Boguso recanted this morning. He implicated Pelegrini as the intellectual author. As Fabian must have known when he met us at the Sheraton this morning.'

Athena turned to the blonde Inspector, her voice inquisitorial. 'You already knew?'

Fabian sighed. 'It's the truth: I already knew. But, as you were about to leave and we had to eat lunch anyway . . .' He shrugged. 'I thought I would give you the film version. I am, yes, a bit eccentric in that respect. But even so, this will all come out in perfect form, with evidence and photocopies and a pretty *expediente* stamped with all the rigor of the Law. I just wanted to save you the trip home.' He dropped his grin. 'Seriously, Athena, the truth is this: Robert Waterbury was killed by Carlo Pelegrini because of the questionable relationship with his wife and the information about his bribes to try to secure the Post Office contract.'

Athena's face was as hard as ice. 'Who squeezed the trigger? And don't lie to me this time!'

'Enrique Boguso killed him, with two accomplices. One is Abel Santamarina, Pelegrini's chief bodygurard. We believed the other is fugitive in Paraguay.'

Her green eyes roved irritably over Fortunato before returning to Fabian. 'Why wouldn't Boguso confess this in the beginning?'

'To betray Pelegrini is a death sentence. Boguso looked for a way to stop the investigation before it touched Pelegrini and his chief of security. Thus he might at least go on living even in prison, and probably with the hope of Pelegrini's help in arranging a quiet parole in a few years. Now . . .' Fabian shrugged. 'His future is not so very brilliant.'

Fabian precluded any more questions by looking at his watch. '*Carajo!* The afternoon is escaping me. Athena . . .' he leaned down and quickly kissed her. 'I'll call you at the hotel. Comiso,' he gave him a little salute, 'we'll see each other.' Backing away from the table with a little grin. 'Don't worry about the bill. I'll arrange it later.' With that, he fluttered out the door and onto the sidewalk like a flake of green confetti in a parade.

Athena watched him go, sipping at the last of her soda water, trying hard to conceal her resentment. 'What do you think?' she asked in an even voice.

Fortunato shrugged. 'Much must be true. Either that, or he has a grand career ahead of him as an author.' He paused. 'Berenski had it right. He mentioned the missing diary.'

'But how would Fabian get it? And who would be doing a parallel investigation? The Federales? Besides, if it's true, where are the documents that he claims Teresa Castex gave Waterbury? It seems like those would be enough to bring down the government.'

'Athena, at this altitude I don't even want to guess. Did Boguso assassinate Robert Waterbury?' He swallowed before laying out the lie. 'I believe, yes. But that of Pelegrini's woman and this *Francesa* . . . I don't know more than you.'

There was a short silence as Athena let her thoughts drift out the big window. 'What bothers me is that he has no feelings about it at all. It's just a game to him.'

Fortunato allowed himself the luxury of taking out a cigarette without answering. He could feel that he had lost her trust, but he had to put that aside for the moment. In the last two hours, everything had changed. Fabian's group was running things now. They wanted the man at the top of the pyramid, and as long as Boguso held up in the role of material author, they might spare the rest along the way. But Boguso would never hold up. Fortunato scratched a flame from his lighter and squinted through the smoke. Some detached part of him realized that it was only a matter of time.

He and Athena lobbed desultory comments back and forth for another twenty minutes, though with Fabian gone the waiter no longer came to offer them anything. In the end Athena threw a few bronze coins on the table and they walked out.

Fortunato listened absently to Athena as he drove her to the Sheraton. She was asking all the relevant questions about Fabian's story, but in a half-hearted disconnected manner, as if she didn't really expect answers from him. As he fended her off he was thinking about the one discrepancy of Fabian's narrative that stood out above all the others for him, a discrepancy that only an intimate witness to Waterbury's last hours could pick out. Throughout Fabian's long story, with its personages both expected and unexpected, a single name had been left out, a name that Waterbury himself had uttered in the half hour before he died, suspecting that he, and not Pelegrini, might have brought down on him the terrible events of that night. Berenski too had blanched at that name. Another Northamerican, with a long history in Buenos Aires: William Renssaelaer.

They arrived at the hotel and Athena paused with one leg out the door. Fortunato felt a pang at seeing her leave. 'What are you going to do?'

She turned to him. 'I suppose I'll try to extend my stay.'

He smiled. 'At least it will be good to have you around a bit longer.'

She ignored his attempt at irony and swung her other leg out of the car. The Comisario felt a stab of panic as she began to shift to the pavement.

'You know who we should talk to?' he said brightly. 'Ricardo Berenski. He's the expert on Pelegrini, and he knew something of what was going on between Pelegrini and the RapidMail/AmiBank group. Maybe he has some idea about the missing documents of Teresa Castex.'

'I have his number,' she said noncommittally. 'Adios.'

He watched her walk towards the entrance of the Sheraton, a flood of grief and loneliness sweeping over him as it had when the morgue had taken Marcela's body away. He felt his throat clogging up and he fought back the sorrow. It was too much. Too much of explanations that explained nothing, of disdainful looks. Too much knowledge of Robert Waterbury.

Athena turned back and looked towards Fortunato from the door of the Sheraton, regretting her harsh departure in spite of herself. The car was still there: he was sitting at the wheel staring straight ahead. She thought of going back and saying something, but she considered the whole stupid sham of an investigation and turned back towards the lobby. She was done with Fortunato.

In truth, she'd known since early in Fabian's speech that she would be calling Ricardo Berenski as soon as she left the café. She would tell Ricardo the details and he would laugh and laugh, and within thirty seconds he would have some new insight, a possible lead, and a friend he could contact to corroborate a detail. Ricardo would straighten things out.

By the time she reached for the telephone to call him, Ricardo Berenski was already dead.

PART THREE
FORTUNATO'S LAW

CHAPTER 19

The killing had been done in classic style: wrists wired together, a single shot to the back of the head and the body set on fire and left smoking at the dump among the stinking potpourri of garbage. Burying the body would have been easy, but the killers wanted not to conceal the mutilated corpse, but to expose it to the world. A throwback to the days of the white terror, when the Allianza Anticomunista Argentina had made showy murders the most effective sort of postcard: bodies would turn up at roadsides, dumps, sprawling face down or sunwards with that embarrassing tactlessness of the dead.

Berenski's assassination hit the media with a noise few people could have predicted. After years of intimidation, beatings, and menacing phone calls, nearly every journalist in Argentina staked out Berenski's charred body as a battleground in what they felt was a desperate struggle for survival. Berenski had gone after the police and the most powerful politicians in the country. He'd turned up the story of Carlo Pelegrini. If Berenski could be killed with impunity, any of them could be killed, and the last line of resistance to the perversion of what had once been a prosperous country would dissolve. Even in the general population it was understood that the battle over the dead journalist had become a struggle for the country itself, for with Berenski and his colleagues lay the last hopes of an honest government, and no matter how many times the dream was annihilated, that earnest longing remained stronger than all the futility that enveloped it, and it moved events before it.

The death topped the headlines of nearly every newspaper in the country, and special reports broke in on melodramas and variety shows. Berenski's comic smile gazed from every tabloid and television screen, emphasized by the stunning picture of the blackened corpse curled up among sour vegetables and crumpled plastic bags.

The television and radio aired clips of Berenski interviewing famous villains of the past – the former Chief of Police protesting an accusation of murder for which he was later convicted, an indignant Minister of Justice denying the bribes he'd taken. These lies cast an aura of parody over the earnest statements of the police about their eagerness to solve the murder. The Governor of Buenos Aires called a press conference to name a special task force to solve the case. Athena noticed Comisario General Leon Bianco standing in the background wearing the same frown of resolve as when he'd sung 'Mano a Mano' at the 17 Stone Angels.

The police started their investigation by smearing the victim. Berenski had bounced a check the week before so the question of financial difficulties was raised, and this was carefully expanded to insinuate that Berenski might have been murdered by someone he'd been trying to blackmail. A man stepped forward to insist that he had sold Berenski cocaine, and another, who claimed to be one of the journalist's sources, said that Berenski boasted of mounting something 'that would bring him much silver.' A real estate agent in Punta del Este testified that Berenski had come into his agency looking to buy an apartment at the beach, something in the range of $200–300,000, far beyond his modest salary.

The journalists fought back. They exposed the cocaine seller as a longstanding police informant, and placed Berenski in Buenos Aires the day that the realtor claimed to have spoken with him in Uruguay. Berenski's picture began to appear everywhere, a silent indictment of the torpid investigation. Journalists on television held a photo to the camera, press conferences given by film stars or sports heroes included Berenski's face in the background or pasted to the podium with the words 'Remember Berenski.' The dead man's image curved around telephone poles and mocked the powerful from train stations and magazine kiosks On the news programs or interviews where his picture didn't appear, the quick phrases could be heard, 'And on this day the 7th of April, let us remember Ricardo Berenski, assassinated two days ago and still without a solution.' 'On this 8th day of April, let us remember Ricardo Berenski . . .' By the 9th of April Carlo Pelegrini's name began to appear in the press beside that of the murdered journalist as the prime suspect, followed, in the mutterings on the street, by the Buenos Aires Police.

By luck, the case fell during the turn of Judge Faviola Hocht. A steely woman in her fifties, descendant of Spaniards and Austrians, she had the reputation of being incorruptible and unappeasable. They called her *La Gallega* for her peasant-like brutishness in the pursuit of truth; she refused to make deals and spurned offers of 'consultancies' from the companies and law firms who opposed her. She had her own investigators and her own arrangements with the police. Though she could not always get a conviction or, given a conviction, insure that the criminal would go to jail, everyone in Buenos Aires knew one thing for certain: *La Gallega*'s investigations left ruins in their wake.

Certain forces began to agitate to remove her from the case. It came out in the press that Judge Hocht had been a personal friend of Berenski's and, according to the accusations of her enemies, one of his covert sources. Editorials attacked her as a political operative and questioned her competence. Even the President of the Republic, who shed a tear as he remembered the noble Berenski in an interview, privately directed his appointees in the Justice Department to scour the Constitution for a reason to move the case out of *La Gallega*'s jurisdiction. The soccer game of the *Caso* Berenski moved up and down the field, cheered by the crowd and misdirected by its corrupt referees. Berenski himself probably would have bet on Pelegrini.

Fortunato had found Berenski's death waiting for him on the afternoon newsstand, a few hours after the long talk with Fabian. He'd stopped for cigarettes on his way to meet the Chief and there was Berenski's face filling a quarter of the front page, with another photo of his carbonized body below. The shock of it left Fortunato floating on his feet. He drifted there in the first horrible novelty and then, as he walked slowly back to his car with the paper spread out below him, a physical sense of disgust came over him. He remembered Berenski's laugh and the joy he took in his fake possessions. Berenski understood that they lived in a counterfeit world, where a counterfeit God forgave all fraud. Berenski with his comic appearance and his shamelessness. Now they'd turned him into burnt meat.

'Who was it?' Fortunato inserted quietly into the dusty gloom of La Gloria's back room.

The Chief gave a little laugh. 'Who wasn't it? They could have held a raffle for the privilege!' He watched Fortunato carefully as he made the joke. 'Why that face? What's Berenski matter to you? It was inevitable that someone was going to cut the *puta*.' With a smirk: 'Probably it was the directors of his newspaper. Look what business they're going to do now!'

The Chief leaned to the side and signaled through the door at the barmaid. 'Skinny! Two Eisenbachs!' He settled back down. 'The problem is that even dead he's making problems. All of this *Who killed Berenski? Who killed Berenski?*' He squinted with distaste, waving his hand across his nose to disperse the imaginary stench. 'The problem is that when the journalists see Pelegrini's name on Boguso's new tale, it's going to make our situation a bit more *caliente*.'

Fortunato didn't answer the Chief's understatement. The scratchy minor chords of bygone violins singed the dark air of the worn café.

The Chief continued in a lighter tone. 'The good news is I read a transcript of Boguso's new story. He mentions a Uruguayan and Santamarina, but there's not a word about police. It appears that whoever is behind this mess is only after Pelegrini. It only remains for Santamarina to keep his mouth shut.'

'And if they offer him a deal?'

'He won't take it! He's not that type. He'll wait tranquilly until Pelegrini can get him loose.'

'And Renssaelaer?'

The Chief pulled back, and Fortunato thought his perplexity looked real. 'What Renssaelaer?'

'He's the head of security for all Pelegrini's organization. Waterbury mentioned his name before he died. Something of "Renssaelaer sent you," that we should tell Renssaelaer he had nothing to fear.'

Now Bianco looked genuinely disconcerted. 'I know nothing of this.'

Fortunato reflected on the increasingly bloated list of people whose silence he depended on. 'I should go and talk to Boguso alone.'

Bianco plastered on an embarrassed little grin. 'That's another thing. The investigation has now changed from a simple homicide to *organización ilicita*, which means it is under the jurisdiction of the Federales. They moved him to a federal comisaria. It doesn't mean we can't speak with him, of course, but there are certain inconveniences. Moreover, now he insists he won't talk without his lawyer.'

Fortunato absorbed this with a slow nod. 'Who's paying the lawyer?'

The Chief shook his head. 'Now we're arriving, Miguel. His lawyer is with the firm of Ernesto Campora, the brother of German Campora, the Chief of Intelligence. He took it without charge. From what you've told me, I suspect that your Inspector Diaz belongs to that group.'

Fortunato squinted. Federales. Campora. The case was slipping out of their control. The waitress appeared and inserted two beers and a saucer of green olives into the silence. Bianco indicated the glasses. 'Drink! Relax a little.' He pinched one of the olives and began working it in his jaws while Fortunato rested his fingertips on the cool surface of his schooner without lifting it to his mouth.

'It's political, hombre,' Bianco went on, extracting the olive pit. 'Ovejo, the Minister of Economy, wants to run for president, but the President isn't so eager to give up his job. The more filth they throw at Pelegrini, the dirtier the President gets, even if it never goes to trial. It's a round business, because Ovejo represents the interests of the IMF and foreign capital against the local interests. You can be sure he's getting it back on the other side. That's how it is, and, disgracefully, we're in the middle of the two whores.'

Fortunato felt anger surging up out of his chest. 'I wasn't in the middle of anything. You put me in the middle –'

Bianco cut into his sentence sharply. 'Don't start whining now! The Institution has done well for you. You want to say that you can't return the favor once in a while?' The Chief lowered his voice but continued with a stiff face. 'Some operations go well and others go badly. You have to face up to them. A policeman must be hard! Resolved!'

'I want the truth about this, Leon. All of it. You owe me that.'

The Chief curled his mouth and looked down at the little mound of olive pits on the table. He exhaled and settled back into his chair. 'Pelegrini wanted to squeeze Waterbury. The *why* isn't clear: something of the wife, as your Diaz suggested. Pelegrini arranged it through Santamarina, the one you met here a few weeks ago. You know the rest.'

'The man was completely innocent!'

Fortunato's reference to the crime seemed to puzzle Bianco. 'What does that have to do with anything? The *puta* was up to *something*, or he wouldn't be dead right now. He was going around with Pelegrini's wife.'

'You told me he was blackmailing him!'

The Chief shifted under Fortunato's glare. 'One or the other. What does that matter?'

Fortunato recognized in his mentor's face the same blank disregard he'd seen twenty-five years ago when they'd raided the family of the Union representative and carried away every trace of them. He swallowed. 'To me, it matters.'

'Then you shouldn't have fucked the whole thing up!' Bianco wrinkled his nose. 'What's going on with you? Eh? What's going on? This isn't time to be mounting little colored mirrors!' He caricatured Fortunato's heavy manner: "Poor writer! He was going around with a rich man's woman and ended up dead!" Are you crazy? People die every day. You, me, we all die! You're drowning in a glass of water, Miguel!' The Chief stopped arguing abruptly and looked anew at Fortunato for a second, as if assessing him. 'Forgive me, Miguel. I get mad, and . . . There's much frustration.' He shrugged the rest, then looked to the side for a moment. 'Don't worry. I'll cover you, like always. Everything will be arranged. In two weeks, no one will remember who Robert Waterbury was.'

Fortunato didn't answer, but he knew that certain things could never be arranged. Waterbury was dead, his wife a widow and his daughter an orphan. And he, Fortunato, had fired the final shot.

Bianco shouted a greeting across the room and another officer came over and began discussing the Berenski murder with great relish. Fortunato gave a numb greeting when the Chief presented him, absently shaking the man's hand then letting his gaze drift off to the Argentine selection of 1978, the fiercest year of the Dictatorship, when they had hosted the World Cup and won and the crowds had gone dancing in the streets while dead bodies washed up on the shore of the Rio de la Plata. Alone again with Bianco, the Chief's glossy confidence: 'Relax, Miguel. Everything will solve itself.'

CHAPTER 20

The final erasure of Berenski's infinite laugh affected Athena more than she would have expected. After the meeting with Fabian she had left a message on Berenski's machine, then flung herself on the bed to try to figure out how she would package a one-week extension of her stay to the people back in Washington. She'd turned on the television without sound, and as she placed a call to the embassy the afternoon news program began to roll out a series of photos and news clips of Berenski, contrasting them with a strange blackened mannequin lying at the feet of a half-dozen detectives. She gasped, turned up the volume, and when the worst hit her she sat on the bed and began to sob with horror and grief. One had to cry over Berenski, who laughed at all the lies yet never forgot who they really hurt. In his comical way he was a thousand times the fighter of Argentina's medal-plated generals or scowling commandos.

She wanted to talk to someone – Carmen de los Santos, Berenski's family – but she was peripheral to all these lives, a tourist in other people's misery. She switched channels until she found another version of the murder, watched the sober face of the Federal Comisario as he spoke of *la investigación*. After an hour she lay on her back, considering the strange lunch with Fabian and his story of Robert Waterbury. To her surprise, the telephone rang. Wilbert Small, from the embassy.

'How's our star investigator?'

'What do you mean?'

'I heard they've got Robert Waterbury's killer in custody.'

She considered the dubious claim, then wondered who had called the embassy. Probably not Miguel Fortunato. 'News travels fast.'

'They know we're interested. I'm impressed, Athena.'

She tried to fight off the compliment but it got to her anyway. 'I wouldn't say it's completely settled yet, Bert.'

'Not settled? I heard they've got a signed confession.'

'You mean *two* signed confessions. That's something we need to talk about. I need to extend my stay here.'

'That, Athena, is exactly what I called you about. But I've got some other news: the FBI wants to meet with you tomorrow at nine.'

The announcement surprised her. She'd been trying to get in with the FBI since she'd arrived two weeks ago, and they'd always been too busy. 'What's it about?'

'Oh, I prefer to let the FBI do their own talking, but I know they've heard about your work and they probably want to debrief you before they take it on.'

A surge of pleasure filled her. The FBI! Once the FBI came into the investigation they'd start pulling so many strings that Fabian's head would pop off. 'That's great!'

'Hey, you came down here and kicked some fanny and word gets around. Why don't I swing by tomorrow at eight-thirty and we can walk over together. That'll give me time to tell you about the job offer.'

'Job offer?'

'You may be doing a lot more investigating. See you tomorrow!' he said coyly, and hung up.

'Wow,' she said quietly, then opened up one of the tiny bottles of liquor on the shelf and poured it into a glass. She leaned her arm on the small table near the window and looked out at the rooftops and balconies around her. The cityscape looked dreamy and mythical in the saffron light of late afternoon, like a day from 1920 that had been kept in a hatbox and now spilled across the TV antennas and clotheslines. She didn't know exactly what to think except that everything she could have hoped for or imagined was coming to pass. The thought of Ricardo Berenski merged with the alcohol and bathed everything in a golden sadness. At least, she thought as she opened another little flask of liquor, he would have approved of the results.

The offer Wilbert Small made the next morning in the Sheraton's coffee shop was so perfect that it felt unreal. Over two hundred American citizens were languishing in Latin American jails, Small told her, on everything from drug charges to traffic accidents. She would be part of a team that investigated them case-by-case and made a recommendation about repatriating the prisoners.

'Are these people innocent?'

Small chuckled. 'Frankly, most of them are guilty, and the best they can hope for is a nice clean cell in the States. But some of them committed minor infractions and didn't know how to work the system. They don't belong in prison. They need an advocate and you'd be that advocate. You'd travel all over Latin America investigating in much the same way you did here. Does that interest you?'

She laughed. 'Does it interest me?' She laughed again. 'Of course it interests me!' She took the smile off her face. 'What are my chances of getting the job?'

'I'd say . . .' he reached for her breakfast check and signed it for her, 'you've practically got it already. Especially with a recommendation from the FBI.' He looked at his watch. 'We'd better roll!'

She'd been too enthralled by the job to bring up the matter of extending her stay in Buenos Aires, but if the FBI was calling her in to consult, it went without saying that she'd be staying on. She couldn't help but enjoy being squired through embassy security. Everything first rate: clipped Marines, bulletproof glass, intercoms. And outside, a line of visa seekers winding off around the block. The FBI agent met her in a nondescript conference room with a big wooden table and Old Glory hanging in the corner. Athena put his age at mid-fifties, with the thinning gray hair and staid blue suit of a successful insurance executive. Her new colleague. She caught the trace of an accent as he introduced himself as Frank Castro.

'Cuban?' she asked.

'Yes,' he said. 'No relation.' Castro brought out a yellow legal pad and an expensive-looking fountain pen. After ordering coffee from an Argentine assistant he closed the door and opened up a slim dossier. His manner of speaking was short and dry, and seemed to demand short, dry answers.

'So tell me about your investigation,' he began. 'Has local law enforcement been cooperative?'

'Fairly cooperative,' she answered. She was excited but she wanted to keep up a professional front. 'I've been working with Comisario Fortunato of the Buenos Aires Department of Investigations.'

'The *Bonaerense*,' Castro affirmed. 'Tell me what you've done.'

'We started out by reviewing the *expediente*, then we visited the crime scene. A week after I arrived, Officer Fortunato heard through an informant that someone had bragged about killing a foreigner, and that led us to Enrique Boguso, who was already in jail for an unrelated double homicide.'

'Who was the informant?'

'Fortunato didn't say.'

Castro nodded.

Athena went on. 'Anyway, Boguso confessed to the murder, which he said he committed with another man, a Uruguayan.'

'And his name is . . . ?'

'Marco. It's in his *declaración*. According to them, it had something to do with cocaine, and there were several chalks of cocaine at the scene. A day after Boguso confessed, he changed his story. He said he'd been paid by someone named Santamarina, who manages security for Carlo Pelegrini, who's a big –'

'I know who Carlo Pelegrini is,' Castro interrupted. 'Why'd Boguso change his story? His conscience bothering him?' Wilbert Small laughed.

She noted something perfunctory and slightly sardonic about the agent's attitude. She struggled to keep the defensiveness out of her voice. 'The police interpretation was that he thought Pelegrini could help him if he kept his mouth shut.'

He gave a skeptical look. 'Do you think they beat the second confession out of him?'

'I was present at the first one, and in that case I'd say definitely not. There is a piece of evidence that supports the Pelegrini connection, and that was that the coroner found Carlo Pelegrini's wife's phone number in the victim's pocket.'

'Is that in the *expediente*?'

'Yes.'

Castro nodded and made a note on his yellow paper.

The agent's impatient manner had begun to make her nervous. She told a condensed version of Fabian's story. Castro inquired about Fabian's name and wrote it in his notebook, then asked a few follow-up questions. He didn't seem particularly interested in the answers. At last he put his pen down.

'Let me tell you where we're at on this, Doctor Fowler. We've been interested in the Waterbury case for some time, but local law enforcement has been uncooperative, to say the least. We've asked four times for a copy of the *expediente* and every time they've found a new excuse for not handing it over. This morning we finally got a copy.'

'Interesting timing. Do you think Pelegrini is really involved?' she asked.

'I wouldn't be surprised if Carlo Pelegrini is behind it. Between you and I, we've linked the Pelegrini enterprises with money laundering and some other activities that affect the security of the United States. In my mind, he's overdue.'

'And what would be his motive?'

'Well, your friends in the police department seem to think that Waterbury was fooling around with Pelegrini's wife. That might have been motive enough. Or maybe she gave Waterbury informa-tion that could hurt Pelegrini, as you said. Tried to play him off against her husband. That'll get a person dead. At any rate,' he said briskly, 'you've done an excellent job in re-energizing this investi-gation.'

'Thank you.'

'An *incredible* job,' Small added.

Castro looked her in the eye with a business-like frankness. 'At this point, we'd like you to return to the States and brief the victim's family on what you've found out. We'll go forward from here.'

He'd said it so plainly that it took her a few seconds to fully understand. Wilbert Small shifted in his seat. 'You mean . . . I'm done?'

'You're done. We've already talked to the Buenos Aires police and let them know that we'll be handling the investigation directly from here forward.'

'You've done a first rate job,' Small said warmly. 'Now we need your skills in other arenas.'

She was still confused by the bluntness of it. 'I have to say, this is all a bit sudden. I mean, I came down here to resolve this case, Agent Castro, and I wouldn't say it's quite resolved yet.'

Castro answered blandly. 'This case could take months to resolve. Maybe longer. Tracing it back to Pelegrini is going to take a full-fledged investigation and a lot of training and expertise.'

'But . . .' She found herself trapped in his viewpoint. It *could* take months. She *had* no real expertise.

'The other factor,' Small broke in, 'is that your other job is starting in less than a month. You need to go back to Washington and go through the formalities, get briefed on everything. You probably need to square things away with the university, don't you?'

'I understand that, Bert, but . . .' She stopped speaking and sat there absently for a moment. An ugly thought was taking shape in her mind. Maybe it was the agent's perfunctory interview, or the FBI's sudden interest in the case now that Pelegrini had been accused. Berenski's words came back to her. *He's like Morelo, of the SuperClassic: The gringos paid him enough that he would start calling the foul.* Now the FBI was calling the foul, eager to go after a man who had committed the double offense of being an enemy of justice and an enemy of certain American corporate interests. For reasons still unclear to her she'd flushed out admissions that might eventually lead to the truth about Robert Waterbury's murder. Her job was to walk away with her accolades and her pats on the back while the FBI tied everything into a tight little package and hung it around Pelegrini's neck. That's the way the system worked: you write the report, you take the promotion, you leave the responsibility with someone higher up the chain. And one day you found out you were Miguel Fortunato.

She closed her eyes for a moment and then turned to the agent. 'I'm sorry,' she said in a low, steady voice, 'but this is just not acceptable.'

'What's not acceptable?'

'I'm not done here. I'm not leaving yet.'

There was a confused silence. 'No, Miss Fowler,' Castro answered. 'You are done here. And you *are* leaving.'

She looked from one closed face to the other. Small sat uncomfortably, offering no help, while Castro seemed irritated and impatient. 'What is this, Agent Castro? For two weeks you won't return my phone calls, and suddenly Pelegrini's name pops up and you're all over it! What's the deal here?' He eyed her coldly. 'This isn't about Waterbury's murder at all, is it?' she continued. 'It's about getting Pelegrini. Who are you working for here, Mr Castro? RapidMail? Did they come in and brief you, hint around that there might be some consulting fees in it for you down the line if you're extra diligent? Maybe a little security contract after you retire?'

Now he was visibly angry. 'Who do you think –?'

'Oh, I'm sorry! I shouldn't question your integrity. RapidMail probably just worked this all out in Washington and handed the orders down from there.' She swiveled around. 'How about it, Bert? Did AmiBank grease the wheels back home? Is that why we're all sitting here?'

Agent Castro's voice was leaden with contempt. 'Why don't you just take your conspiracy theories back to your friends at the university, Miss Fowler. This is the real world. You're finished here.' He looked over at Small and the two of them came to their feet.

She felt everything slipping away from her and there was nothing she could do about it. 'Okay! Let's all stand up! Fine!' She rose. 'I know all about RapidMail and Grupo AmiBank and even William Renssaelaer, who used to work out of this very embassy and is working for Pelegrini now! I know all your filthy little corporate games. Ricardo Berenski told me everything!'

This caught the FBI man by surprise, and for the first time she saw a trace of uncertainty in his features. 'When did you talk to Ricardo Berenski?' he asked quickly.

'That's none of your business! You can read about it in the fucking *New York Times*!'

The mention of the newspaper seemed to calm Agent Castro, as if she'd overplayed her hand. He fixed her with a faint smirk and said quietly, 'Dream on.'

The embassy worked fast at rolling up the welcome mat. When she returned to the hotel she was asked politely to re-register using her own credit card, and with that gesture she knew that she had no reason to expect more assignments from the State Department. She imagined that by now Wilbert Small had telephoned Fortunato to strip her of whatever meager official standing she'd had. She tried not to think about the job offer she'd just thrown away; that train of thought led straight to hell. Instead, she remembered Berenski and Carmen Amado, people who didn't give up, and Naomi Waterbury, who had given up everything. Folding now wasn't an option.

She stared at the ceiling and squeezed her temples. She would need to corroborate Fabian's story, to pull out his fictional cast and find out what was real. Starting with Teresa Castex. A woman who wouldn't be eager to meet with an investigator, and could muster a wall of lawyers and bodyguards in a matter of minutes.

The idea came to her suddenly, and though it seemed absurd at first, as she began to work out the mechanics it started to feel completely appropriate. She took a deep breath and placed two international phone calls, one to New York, and the other to Los Angeles. 'Suzanne! This is Athena. I need a favor.'

CHAPTER 21

Athena only had to leave one message with Teresa Castex before she received a return call on her new cellular line. It was a voice of luxurious petulance, lathering her ear with honey. 'I'm enchanted to receive your call! I'm so glad you found me! The truth is that I've wanted to talk about Robert for some time, but here it's so difficult to find someone who understands these matters. Is this your first time in Buenos Aires? *Fantastico!*'

She suggested they meet at the Café Tortoni, a beautiful old confitería in the center where the literary elite had once convened. The Tortoni had changed little since the 1890s: its gilded walls were giddily dressed with mirrors and red velvet, while crisp waiters in white jackets moved efficiently between the marble tables. Period photos and yellowed newspaper clippings told of readings by Borges and Victoria Ocampo seventy years earlier, while other doors led to private salons and a spacious expanse of billiard tables. German and Japanese tourists read guidebooks over cups of coffee.

Fabian had described Teresa Castex de Pelegrini with superficial accuracy, but she still turned out to be an entirely different Teresa Castex than the one Athena had imagined. Far from being Fabian's brittle woman wrenched by an unrequited love, Teresa Castex's beauty had weathered rather attractively, and it crossed her mind that perhaps the unrequited part of the relationship was Fabian's invention. Slim, around fifty, with artful dark-blond hair and the proud carriage of a model, she was no Inca mummy. She spoke in English to a woman she knew as Suzanne Winterthur, of Avondale Publishers.

'I was desolated by Robert's death, Susana, desolated! We were collaborating on a fantastic new work, as you know, and just as we approached the heart of the story that terrible event happened. Fortunately, we had already talked about the ending, so I can be of great help to your project. You may not know it, but I have been a writer since before this sad affair with Robert.'

She fished two small books out of her soft leather bag and put them on the table. Each was leather-bound and embossed with gold leaf, obviously self-published. Athena opened one of the volumes to the middle and felt herself blushing after reading the first few lines. The poem appeared to be the thoughts of a woman in the midst of a frantic orgy. Another involved a woman waiting in a limousine for her lover. *Me masturbo con tu imagen* . . . Athena nodded appreciatively and opened the other book. This one was more tame: a book of poems with titles like 'The Boy on the St Germain des Prés,' or 'The Florentine Handbag.' They seemed to be existential ruminations on various shopping expeditions Teresa had made.

She swallowed to clear her throat. 'Your style is really . . . unusual. Are the North American rights still available for these?' Athena asked.

'Oh!' She waved her hand, unable to contain her pleasure. 'Later we can discuss such things. I give you these as a gift. But let's talk more of this Waterbury project. What do you need from me?'

'Two things: some biographical information and some idea of how the novel was to finish.' Here Athena let a look of embarrassment come to her. 'I'm ashamed to say it, Teresa, but publishing is still a business and we have to listen to the marketing department. They want to use the background of the author's death to sell the novella.'

This seemed distasteful even to the wife of Carlo Pelegrini. 'They want to use his assassination to sell the book?'

She shook her head somberly. 'It's a corrupt business, Teresa. But at least this will get your efforts out to a wider audience. The marketing department sees this as some sort of "artist on the way down" story. You know, with the drugs and all that. There's always something very compelling about an artist who destroys himself just as he's creating his greatest work. Look what it did for Van Gogh! They've even had an offer for the movie rights. Of course his wife was furious, because she said he never used drugs . . .' She shrugged. 'That's why I was hoping you might know something about his last days here.'

Now Teresa Castex became wary, took out a cigarette to hide behind. 'Of that death . . .' She let it trail off, shaking her head. 'It's a bit confused.' Something passed across her face. 'He wasn't killed for drugs.' She halted on that fat invitation and glanced around the room, then leaned forward. 'The police killed him.'

The claim made Athena flutter inside. That hypothesis had surfaced early on and if she'd never completely believed it, she'd never completely dispelled it either.

'The police?'

'I tell you this in confidence, because few know it. But that is the truth, it was the police.'

For the first time since they'd met, Athena felt Teresa Castex was being genuine. 'But why would the police kill him?'

She needed little urging. 'This will not make a very pretty addition to his legend, but if you would like to know, I will tell you. You see, Robert became involved with a woman here. A French prostitute of the lowest order. She claimed she was a tango dancer, and acted like a woman of twenty-five, but I am sure she was closer to forty. She must have come from the slums of Paris to make her fortune here in Argentina, where she would be exotic. I saw through that, of course, but Robert, he always had a more romantic view of the world. He wanted to see her like a character that appears often in tango, of the Frenchwoman adrift in Buenos Aires. So he fell in with this romanticized view of her, and became involved in her affairs.'

'What about his wife?'

A flash of knowing bitterness. 'You are young, Susana, but when you reach my altitude of life, you will understand that a man who was struggling, like Robert, is susceptible to that sort of thing.'

'But how did that get him in trouble with the police?'

'You see, the police control the prostitutes here, either through the pimps, or directly. This Frenchwoman belonged to the police. She saw Robert simply as a way to get money, but as happens sometimes, I'm told, Robert began to want to save her from her chosen occupation.' She pulled her mouth to the side. 'He was half-retarded in that aspect. He threatened to expose the policeman, and the policeman decided to get rid of him. After, of course, they mounted a little sham of an investigation, but in Buenos Aires . . .' She puffed some air and looked at the ceiling.

'Do you know what policeman this was?'

Her eyes widened. '*Chica*, if I knew, he would already be in jail! I know this much only because Robert confessed it to me in the course of our creative sessions. I felt sorry to see him go down that path.'

'But if Waterbury needed money himself, how much could this prostitute get out of him?'

'Maybe it was not so much . . .' The Señora's face filled with disdain. 'But for that pretentious little whore, enough.'

'And do you know where I might find this woman?'

The question seemed to strike Teresa Castex the wrong way, and she retreated into a suspicious silence for a moment. 'Why do you ask that?'

With a nervous little jump of her hands that felt like a huge gesture: 'Oh . . . For more background. The ambiance of the book.'

Teresa became pleasant again in a less casual way. 'I understand. But let's talk about the book. Do you have the manuscript with you?'

She felt a slight vertigo. 'I don't. You see, our trade division decided to go ahead with the book last week, and since I was already in Chile on other business they had to send it by courier. Unfortunately, it seems to have gotten lost somewhere between here and New York.'

The older woman gave a smile that seemed uncomfortably wide. 'But my husband owns the delivery service! Just give me the receipt and we'll have it by tomorrow morning!'

'Great!' Athena said. 'I'll give it to you before we leave.' She hurried ahead. 'I haven't seen the manuscript, but evidently he had finished about one hundred and fifty pages.'

'Tell me where he left off. I didn't see him for almost a week before he was killed, and from what you say he made great progress.'

Athena hesitated for a moment. According to Fabian, the book had traced the relationship between a billionaire and his wife as he climbed the ladder of corruption to the top. But Fabian had said a lot of things. Teresa Castex was watching her with an ominously encouraging grin.

'Well . . . As you know, the book was tracing the career of a businessman and his wife. He was a bit, I would say, opportunistic.' She went as far as Fabian's version allowed, watching Teresa Castex's face for some indication of her success but encountering only the same pleasant attentiveness. 'And at the part we left off, there was some issue of bribes paid to the government . . . It was inconclusive.'

Teresa Castex didn't lose her faint smile. 'Who are you?'

'I don't understand your question.'

Teresa Castex shook her head. 'That's not what our book was about at all! Our book was about corrupt police who try to blackmail a businessman. They want to make him a bed for the murder of a journalist and a writer, and they even hire a whore to come in and try to trick his wife. But the ending is thus: the woman is an amateur! She can't even tell the right story, and the wife knows she is a liar and a whore! That's what our book was about! It's realistic, no?'

Athena felt her mouth drawing outwards to a stupid grin, reacting without will to Teresa Castex's false cordiality.

'So comic! Who do you work for? Ovejo? AmiBank? Or do you work directly for RapidMail? They are so jealous that an Argentine might own the business they think should belong to them!' She stood up to leave, and Athena noticed a large man in a dark suit and sunglasses coming towards them.

'You disgust me!' Castex went on. 'You'll do anything to get at my husband! No lie is too low! Why do you come to me when you're the ones who killed him!' She snatched the books off the table, then picked up the waterglass and dumped it into Athena's lap. There was a shock of icy cold, and then Athena felt the moisture running down her legs.

'And for your information, I am a writer on my own merits! I do not need Robert Waterbury to authenticate me!' Now she picked up the other glass of water, but before she could empty it Athena sprang to her feet and grabbed her hand.

'Excuse me,' she said in a low, venomous English. 'You must have mistaken me for your fucking doormat!'

'Your mother's cunt!' the other woman murmured in Spanish.

Athena twisted the glass from her hand and flung the water into Teresa's face with such force that it splattered the two files of tables behind her. She saw the water dripping from the Señora's make-up, heard the complaints of the patrons behind her, then felt herself knocked off her feet by a wall of dark cloth. She tripped over her chair and clattered into a brass flower pot that banged to the floor like a clash of cymbals ringing in the final note of a symphony. Teresa Castex was standing above her beside her bodyguard, shaking her finger. 'You people killed him! You killed Robert to make a bed, *puta*, and you can write that in your report!' She stared after them as they stepped out into the sunlight.

When they were gone a waiter came over and brushed the soil off her career-girl outfit. From behind her she heard someone make a hissing cat sound, and the low laughter of men. She was soaking wet and speckled with potting soil. Her lie had been uncovered, and in almost every way her little *operativo* had been a failure. But as she left the gilded walls of the Tortoni her mind had suddenly opened to a possibility that felt lurid and monstrous, yet oddly plausible in a cold, corporate way: Waterbury's killer had been working for AmiBank.

CHAPTER 22

Comisario Fortunato, meanwhile, was settling in to what promised to be a very bad day. He had told Fabian by telephone to come to his office at nine in the morning, but the Inspector hadn't shown. When he'd picked up the morning paper Pelegrini's name appeared across the front page in large letters across from a photo of Berenski's grieving widow. Below it, in a sidebar, the phrase 'Pelegrini also implicated in murder of Northamerican.' After that came the FBI.

Agents Castro and Fosbee coursed across the threshold like two blocks of cloth topped with wooden faces. A federal comisario from Central accompanied them. The Federales had sold it as an inter-agency liaison session, but Fortunato knew at the first handshake that it was an interrogation. He ordered the requisite coffees and forced himself into his expression of solicitous calm.

'You're ahead of us on this investigation, Comisario Fortunato, so I want to ask you some questions that you probably know the answers to.'

'At your orders,' Fortunato answered.

They started out with the usual simple queries: how long had he been a police officer, what divisions had he worked in? Stupidities about the case they could know from reading the *expediente*. They were casual about it, but he knew the method. They wanted to see what gestures and vocal inflections he used when he told the truth. After they established that, they began to heat it up a bit.

'The victim was found with handcuffs of the same sort used by the Buenos Aires police,' the older agent, Castro, said in his Caribbean-tinged Spanish. 'Moreover, the fatal bullet, according to the coroner, was a nine millimeter round, a round which is used by the police. Did you ever investigate the possibility that there might have been police involvement in this case?'

'*Bien*,' Fortunato began. He knew not to raise his hands to his face, or to look sideways as he spoke. But to interject a little word like *bien* to buy time, that was a mistake. Better to answer directly, without evidence of thinking too much. 'That of the handcuffs and the bullet certainly raised our suspicions, but at the same time there are other sets of handcuffs and other nine millimeter pistols in the hands of non-police. We did a survery of private security companies in the capital and found eight firms that use this variety of handcuffs.'

'I didn't see that survey in the *diligencias*,' Castro said.

Fortunato made a puzzled expression. 'It should be there. If not, I'll get you a copy.'

The federal comisario came to his aid. 'Sometimes that happens,' he explained to the Northamericans.

They didn't seem convinced but they didn't press it, so Fortunato continued. 'One also can't ignore that these cuffs also end up in the hands of people who have nothing to do with law enforcement. I don't think that the presence of the cuffs necessarily indicates the police.' He swallowed. 'It's a similar case with the nine millimeter shell. The victim had been wounded four times with a .32 caliber round, a cheap pistol used very much by common delinquents here in Buenos Aires, and as you pointed out, finished with the nine millimeter, which also circulates among the criminal element. The Astra nine millimeter used by Enrique Boguso is in wide circulation, as well as those of the marks Liama, Smith and Wesson, Ruger, Beretta, Browning and many others.' The men were listening without expression, and Fortunato grew more confident in his story. This was the one piece of evidence he had sealed perfectly. 'For the doubts, we did a ballistics test and, as it turned out, the bullet matched the Astra nine millimeter that the suspect Boguso indicated to us as the murder weapon.

'I saw those tests,' Castro said, 'but there was a problem with them. Some of the pictures of the bullet don't match the bullet that's in evidence now.'

Fortunato wrinkled his brows. Had they found a set of the original pictures in a file somewhere, or were they bluffing him? 'You don't say! I haven't heard anything about that.'

'Haven't you been leading this investigation?'

The two hard-cop faces stared back at him, men who had a lifetime of experience separating lies from truth. 'Of course, but one has to assume that the *expediente* is intact. If the evidence has been compromised, I'll look into it immediately. But I can assure you that when the evidence left my office, everything was completely in order.'

The FBI men didn't answer, merely stared at him. Finally Agent Castro spoke. 'The coroner's report showed a piece of paper in the victim's pocket with a phone number registered to Carlo Pelegrini. And yet your investigation made no effort to trace that number. Why not?'

Fortunato reached up and scratched his forehead. A bad move. Very bad. 'Of course we traced it. But as you well know, surrounding any murder are a mountain of clues, many of which have nothing to do with the murder itself. We knew about the Pelegrini phone number –'

'It's not in the *expediente*,' the younger gringo said.

'You are correct, Agent Fosbee, and the reason is thus: the police must follow the instructions of the judge in mounting an investigation. Sometimes, though, to save time, we do things outside of the judge's strict orders, and these results may be found in our files, though perhaps not in the *expediente* itself. In the case of the phone number, we had reliable information that Enrique Boguso committed the crime, and during the course of questioning, Boguso confessed. Now, he has changed his story, and thus the matter of the telephone number assumes new importance. As we go on deepening the investigation –'

The senior agent interrupted with his annoying rudeness. 'Can you think of a reason why Boguso would change his story so suddenly?'

'None. This was a very recent and surprising turn and I have not yet had the chance to question the suspect about his change. As you know, San Justo has no scarcity of crimes to investigate, and the Waterbury murder, being already more than four months old, must take its place behind those that are a bit fresher.' He decided to poke back. 'To be honest, Señor Castro, it's only recently that the Federales and the FBI have taken an interest in the case, for reasons that remain a bit mysterious to me.'

Castro didn't answer. The session dragged on for a few more questions, then died out in a round of cardboard handshakes. They were lying, so was he, and everyone knew it but said nothing. It was a matter of respecting each other's professionalism.

Alone in his office again, Fortunato's mind swarmed with a dozen strategies for fending them off. He would need to conduct a survey of private security companies in Buenos Aires and forge a trace of Pelegrini's phone number as if it had been done months ago. He would need to check the photos of the bullet in all copies of the *expediente* that he could locate. But couldn't the Federales find out easily that the surveys and the traces had been ordered that very day? Didn't they have their own copies of the *expediente*? No, he thought, sinking into his chair and running his hands along his scalp to soothe his brain. No, it was impossible. Once the journalists got involved, and the inevitable beatings by the police, Boguso's story would crumble, and the investigation would begin again with a new ferocity. And someone would talk, because people like Vasquez or Domingo always had to brag, and youngsters like that hippy driver, Onda, to confess their wonderment. No, only Bianco could save him now. Or Pelegrini.

He picked up the newspaper and leafed through to the crime section, where he found the last disagreeable surprise of the morning. There in the small print, among items of little importance: *Two robbers . . . shot by police in Quilmes last night . . .* He sensed it even before he read the rest of the brief paragraph and could envision the entirety of the event from the sketchy resumé. *While fleeing the Kiosko Malvinas . . .* Probably a clandestine lottery office, or some other repository of cash. The door would have been jimmied open by previous arrangement with the police for the usual 70/30 split. Two robbers stuffing money into a bag, disordering the office for the sake of appearance. To their surprise, three policemen and a burst of thunder behind the building. The dull points of lead cutting through the body, and then a finishing shot to the chest. Someone pressing a pistol into a dead man's hand, pulling the trigger. By the time Fortunato reached the names he could have filled them in himself. Of the deceased: Rodrigo 'Onda' Williams. Among the responding officers: Domingo Fausto.

The first reporter called his office an hour later. He didn't take the call, of course, but he recognized it as the first raindrop of the coming storm and it sent a new twist of anxiety into his stomach. When the receptionist told him that the Doctora Fowler was on the line, he couldn't help but feel that a reprieve of some sort had been granted. The feminine warmth of Athena's voice comforted him. Since Marcela's death he'd had no antidote to this world of men and their stratagems. If she wanted to meet with him, he would for once allow himself the fool's pleasure of taking it at face value.

He listened to Athena make her pitch in the coffee shop of the Sheraton. It was a good story about Teresa Castex: leave it to a gringa to come up with something so cinematic. Nothing crucial had come out of it – that Pelegrini's wife would suspect the police rather than her husband was a common deception of human nature. What it might reveal, though, was the thinking in the Pelegrini camp that Pelegrini's enemies were behind the new investigation, and that someone in the police might be a convenient suspect. For that reason, the news did not comfort him.

'I think I've got a way to find the Frenchwoman,' Athena went on, 'and I've already located Pablo Moya at AmiBank, as Fabian claimed.'

'Then what do you need me for?'

She sighed. 'I don't feel comfortable trying to get up to Pablo Moya's office. I think I'd do a lot better if someone with authority came with me, like you.' She softened him a little with a hint of the admiring female. 'You can show the badge, give them that routine of "Don't fuck with me, I'm the police!"'

Fortunato had to smile. 'Don't give me that *verso* of the little girl in distress. I already know you.'

'See, you're a thousand times more *piola* than me.' She shrugged. 'I don't see any problem with you helping me, Miguel. It's your job to investigate the crime. And, besides, I'm not sure the FBI has the authority to take me off this case. I answer to Senator Braden.' She changed tack, her face settling. 'Do you really want to leave this case with Fabian and the FBI?'

He considered it as he sipped at the weak Café Americano she'd poured him from the thermos on the table. Athena was right, there was a certain advantage in pursuing the case with her. He might find out something useful, something the Chief or Pelegrini might be able to defend themselves with, and defend him at the same time.

'And you know something, Miguel?' she continued. 'The FBI, Fabian, the Federales: they don't really care about Robert Waterbury. They have their own agenda.' Her voice became sharper. 'I want the people who killed Waterbury to *pay*! You saw what they did to him! I want all of them, not just Boguso or whoever couldn't make a deal. I want *all* of them! All the way to the top! And forgive me for my presumption, Miguel, but I know that underneath all the lies surrounding this investigation, from both my government and yours, and underneath all the . . . the . . . shit surrounding what it takes to be a comisario in the Police of Buenos Aires, you do, too. Don't you?'

Fortunato swallowed, unable to answer, and something of disappointment and hurt flickered through her eyes. He could tell by the strangely childlike plaintiveness with which she said her next words that there was more at stake for her than solving the case. 'I need you, Miguel. Now, I really need you.'

He looked at her smooth young face, perhaps not even thirty. He should have said that to make everything right by Robert Waterbury was an impossibility, and that even if it wasn't, he could never be the person to do it. Unless he was the one person who could. He leaned back in the booth and took out a pack of cigarettes, lit one, and watched the smoke stream out from the extinguished match head. He looked up at her. 'What's your plan?'

CHAPTER 23

They left his car parked illegally on Cordoba and headed along Florida. The street had been closed off to automobiles and converted into a giant sidewalk, filled now with pedestrians breezing past café windows and pausing at kiosks to peruse magazine covers stamped with the face of the embattled Carlo Pelegrini. He walked along it now with Athena, toward the Grupo AmiBank building. Better to show up without an appointment, surprise him.

They turned into the sumptuous wood-paneled lobby, past a somber-looking custodian with a 9mm pistol: probably his service pistol, Fortunato thought. The Comisario flashed his badge at the two men at the desk, said with unassailable matter-of-factness, 'Good afternoon, *muchachos*, I'm Comisario Fortunato, of Investigaciónes, San Justo. I'm here to speak with Pablo Moya, on the tenth floor. This is my colleague Athena Fowler, an assessor for the United States Department of State. I'll announce myself.' He walked on without waiting for them to call, Athena following. By luck the elevator was waiting for them and they stepped in without looking back. Thirty seconds later they exited into the plush white carpet of the tenth floor. Fortunato still had his badge out. He knew they'd already announced him. 'I'm Comisario Fortunato of the Department of Investigations, Provincial Police of Buenos Aires. This is my colleague La Doctora Athena Fowler, working on behalf of the FBI of the United States. With Señor Moya, please.'

'Señor Moya is in a meeting now . . .'

Fortunato put on his police face, tilting his chin up and speaking with a voice of total command. 'Now he has a more important meeting. What is your name?'

The woman quavered a bit. 'Maria Foch.'

'Señorita Foch. Connect me with Señor Moya, immediately. This is a police matter.' She put him on the line and Fortunato became instantly cordial. 'Señor Moya, forgive the disturbance. I'm Comisario Fortunato, of the division of Investigaciónes in La Matanza. I happened to be in the neighborhood so I took the opportunity to make a little visit. I'm with a colleague from the United States who is attached to the FBI and we would like to chat with you for a few minutes . . . I know you are busy. If you prefer, I can call the judge and arrange something more formal at the comisaria, but I thought this would be more . . .' Fortunato listened. 'Perfecto! In a minute, then.' He glanced at Athena, tossed his head with the faintest trace of smugness on his kind face. The door buzzed and they walked through it.

'Comisario Fortunato! It's a pleasure!' Señor Moya had already come from behind his desk and strode across the room towards Fortunato with his hand extended.

The Comisario took the warm wide hand and then presented Athena to him. Moya's eye lingered with a special warmth that emitted a gentlemanly seductiveness, and Fortunato speculated that Moya, with his long lashes and square build, was accustomed to smoothing his way through life with a friendly smile. Some faces, he thought, were constructed according to a destiny that their owner went on discovering little by little. Like Moya's, created to decorate money, or his own face, that everyone found so sympathetic, ideal for imparting tragic news and concealing other people's fraud.

They sat down and Fortunato started in on the usual questions – much as the FBI had done with him the day before – with a cordial conversation about Moya's work and his family. The banker answered expertly: formal, but always as if on the verge of weaving some friendship, so that Fortunato kept feeling the urge to break down and see things the way Moya portrayed them. Life, the banker's tone implied, was an important affair, to be managed among *hombres* but not taken too seriously. He had something boyish and exuberant about him that hung beneath his polished exterior, almost naughty. Fortunato could see why he'd made it to the tenth floor. As they talked, the Comisario couldn't help noticing the soft sheen of Moya's charcoal suit and his mesmerizing silk tie of olive and gold that shone and shifted as he moved.

The 'regulars' dispensed with, Fortunato started in earnest. 'Señor Moya; do you know why we are here?'

Moya became slightly more grave. 'I imagine it is about Robert Waterbury.'

'Why do you say that?'

'Because the others were already here, a comisario . . . Perez, I think, and a sub-comisario . . .' He searched the air for an answer, then dismissed it. 'It escapes me. But I had the impression this was a Federal investigation, not a Provincial one.'

Fortunato ignored the little sting. 'The murder took place in San Justo, so it is my jurisdiction. The Federales have taken an interest in it because of the theme of *organización ilícita*.' Grimacing, 'But those are semantic questions, Señor Moya. What interests us all is to find the people responsible for the crime.'

'Me more than anyone. Robert was a good friend.' He opened his hands and Fortunato saw a nostalgia descend on him, along with a genuine grief. 'Very cultured, very kind. An excellent writer.' Pablo looked down at his desk for a moment, disturbed. 'He didn't deserve that end.'

Fortunato's mind was invaded by the image of Waterbury covered with blood. He swallowed. 'No one deserves it. Can you tell us more about your relation with the victim?'

The banker regained his balance. '*Bien*. We were friends, with all that implies. We met some ten years ago when the bank sent Robert here to work on the privatization of Aerolíneas, and when he returned, he asked for my help in meeting some people in Buenos Aires for his book. He was researching a novel.'

'Who did you introduce him to?'

Pablo thought about it, then seemed to reconsider. 'You know, Comisario Fortunato,' he said politely, 'I answered all of these questions two days ago for the Federales. I suggest that you could save time by simply reading my declaration.'

'I always prefer to hear them directly.'

The executive concealed any annoyance he felt, uncrossed his legs to dispel his irritation and leaned back. 'He wanted to meet people of money, to see how they lived, how they thought. I tried to help him.' He gave them a few names which Athena copied into her book. 'But these were informal meetings, without any motive besides socializing.'

Fortunato nodded. 'And tell me, Señor Moya, do you know of a man named Carlo Pelegrini?'

'Of course! The businessman who paid bribes to get control of the Post Office. He's in the newspapers every day. Now he's associated with this Berenski murder, no?'

'Thus say the newspapers,' Fortunato shrugged. 'Tell me about the relationship between Carlo Pelegrini and Robert Waterbury.'

Pablo looked towards the liquor cart as if considering whether to offer them a drink. 'I don't know much about that. I think he became friends with the wife, Teresa Castex. He got in with her and . . . I don't know. It became strange. Robert was a writer of some reputation, as you know, and she was paying him to help her write a book. Something of that type; a bit rare. I told him not to put himself in with her.'

'Why did you tell him that?'

'Because Pelegrini is heavy and she is his wife. One doesn't need to be a mathematician to solve that equation.' He cocked his head thoughtfully towards Athena. 'I've sometimes thought that perhaps Pelegrini had him killed because of the wife.'

Fortunato rubbed the stubble of his chin. A variation of Fabian's theme, but keeping his own name conveniently out of the forefront. 'And what was the relationship between Grupo AmiBank and Carlo Pelegrini at this time?'

'The same as now: nothing.'

'You weren't rivals for control of the Post Office?'

'*Bien*, I suppose that an adversarial relationship is still a relationship.'

'And did Señor Waterbury ever mention any anxiety about Carlo Pelegrini to you?'

The banker lowered his eyelashes for a moment. 'We arrive at that theme.' He looked up. 'The Federales also asked. Robert came to me and told me that he was writing a book with Pelegrini's wife. The details to me seemed half-rare.' He waggled his hand dubiously. 'Moreover, this was a sensitive time for Pelegrini. Berenski had just begun to expose his bribes in the Post Office case. If he saw Robert coming to the AmiBank office . . .' He shook his head, and his voice rose into a furtive protestation of innocence, though no accusation had been made. 'I warned him that Pelegrini might misinterpret his visits here, that it could be complicated.' He rested his elbows on the desk and rubbed his forehead as if to erase some memory. 'I suppose it was my fault for not acting with more force to stop the situation. But how could I know that he would kill him?'

Fortunato was finding it hard to read the man. His words had an undertow of deep emotion, but at the same time something about the testimony struck a false note. He tried to inject some sympathy into his voice. 'There's evidence that even the murderers did not foresee killing him. It seems to have been an intimidation that went badly.'

'All the same,' Moya began, but he couldn't seem to finish his sentence. A mixture of grief and embarrassment took the form of a cloudy smile on his silent face.

Fortunato glanced over at Athena. She was staring intently at Pablo Moya, as if she too had detected the ambiguities of his explanation. It was time to fish a little. The Comisario cleared his throat and shifted in his chair. 'Señor Moya,' he said in his soft, calm voice, 'do you know a Mr William Renssaelaer?'

Moya gave the slightest flinch backwards. 'No. No, I don't know the name.'

The old Comisario noted the opening, and used an ancient ruse. 'That's interesting. Can you think of a reason someone would tell me that they saw you with William Renssaelaer?'

Now the banker began to fidget nervously with a gold pen. 'Where? At a party?' He waited for an answer but Fortunato remained silent. 'Because I might chat with anyone at a party, without ever learning their name.' He tried to sound relaxed and helpful but the smile kept flitting through at inappropriate moments. 'The truth is that in my position one is invited to many social events and meets many people. So, could I have been seen talking to someone who associates with Carlo Pelegrini? Of course! I might be talking to anyone!'

It was a blunder worthy of a television detective show, and Fortunato moved in on it. 'Now you say that William Renssaelaer is an associate of Carlo Pelegrini? But you just told us you didn't recognize the name!'

The banker's boyish face began to fall into disarray. 'I was speaking hypothetically! To say that one meets the entire range of society!'

Athena addressed him for the first time, using her most elegant voice. 'Particularly when one operates an internet pornography site, as you do, Señor Moya.'

The banker stopped talking and rocked backwards in his chair as his mouth came soundlessly open. He crossed his fingers over his stomach, uncrossed them. 'Well . . . I have investments in high technology ventures through a limited partnership, but I'm not up to date on the particulars.'

'You're lying, Pablo. You're the owner of an internet porno site and you've even watched them film some of the scenes. It's strange, no? One can launder money and sell out the country and one's status will go up. But operate a pornography site or consort with prostitutes and everyone looks down on you. Especially one's wife and daughter.'

'Are you accusing me –! Where did you get this nonsense?'

'Robert Waterbury told me.'

Now Pablo's confusion overcame him. 'Robert? When?'

'When he was alive, of course. You see, Pablo, I also was a friend of Robert's. So I have a personal interest in this.' She inclined herself towards him and her eyes narrowed to match her low, nearly whispered voice. 'I'm going to the bottom of this matter, and if I have to pull you down with me, that's fine. It's fine! Now tell us about your relationship with William Renssaelaer, or I swear to you your website will be only the beginning.'

Fortunato was surprised by her sudden attack, and by its success. Pablo had become a jittery replica of the suave *caballero* who had welcomed them into his office.

'My personal business . . .' he began.

She was implacable. 'Don't even say it! You can tell us about William Renssaelaer, or you can start getting calls from the boys at *Pagina / 12* tomorrow morning.'

Moya sat paralyzed by her ultimatum, but at last he became angry. 'Get out of here! Get out!' He rose from his seat. 'This is typical of the police, to come in and accuse the innocent! Give me your card, Comisario! It's Fortunato, no?' He scribbled it on a pad. 'And you, Señorita.'

She stood up, calm as a sheet of steel. In that moment Fortunato loved her. 'I'm Athena. You can remember me simply as the one who ruined you.' She closed her notebook and headed for the elevator.

Fortunato started after her, but Moya cut him off at the door of his office and planted himself in the corridor to spit one last defense at Athena's back. 'I have nothing to be ashamed of! Nothing!'

Fortunato looked into the livid face, only a half-meter from his own. A deep confusion was working in the dark eyes, as if part of Pablo Moya was appalled that he would be standing in a hallway hissing lies at a woman's back. His features melted into a look of profound anguish, which he turned absently to the Comisario.

'We'll see each other,' Fortunato told him.

'Why William Renssaelaer?' Athena asked when they'd reached the street again. Calle Florida at rush hour was like a river running through two cliffs of concrete and glass. The sound of footfalls on pavement was all around them, festooned with conversations, the calls of the newsmen, beeping cell phones.

Fortunato kept walking beside her. 'Because it was the one name that did not appear in Fabian's story. It was a stray bullet, but did you see how it hit him? After that he wouldn't answer any more questions. He had more fear of talking about this Renssaelaer than to be exposed for his pornography venture.'

'But why would he know Pelegrini's chief of security?'

'Thus the question, daughter.' Fortunato's mind was working furiously as they strode down Florida. There was a relation between Renssaelaer and Pablo Moya, executives of two supposedly opposing factions. But was it connected to Robert Waterbury's murder? Now this, yes, was an interesting investigation.

For the first time since the night of the kidnapping, Fortunato felt the world begin to open up to him. He was still free, still flowing along this beautiful stream of life, with its furtive aromas of coffee and cologne drifting across the muffled footsteps. Athena walked beside him, immersed in thought. At last they were working together to solve the Waterbury case. 'You played it well, Athena. You gave him a *bife* he won't forget!'

'I don't like his type.'

'So I noted!' He enjoyed her look of pleasure. 'I saw you biting your tongue that first afternoon when we passed the Aerolíneas demonstration.'

She looked at him. 'That obvious?'

He rolled his eyes toward the pink heavens. '*Chica!* It's only the left that takes an interest in human rights. Will you really expose his pornography site?'

She looked contentedly over the crowds of Porteños exiting from their workdays. 'Oh, I may find some deserving journalist at *Paginal 12* and give them Pablo's website address.'

He stopped her and put his finger to his lips, 'Shhh!' He cupped his hand to his ear. 'I think I hear Berenski laughing.'

They turned up Calle Lavalle to go to the Café Richmond for a snack. The marquees of a dozen movie theaters hung over the narrow walkway in a blaze of colored light, and Fortunato lost himself in the discussion of the case. On the periphery, his own role in the murder was waiting for him with its dark consequences, but he would settle up with that phantom later. Over sandwiches he agreed with Athena that Fabian had been trying to lead them to Pelegrini. They considered the possibility that he was working for the Federales and that the Federales were being driven by Minister Ovejo and Pelegrini's other enemies in the government. 'Or maybe Fabian's working for AmiBank on the side.'

'But why would he expose Moya's website if he worked for AmiBank?'

The Comisario raised his hands. 'Because he's a *hijo de puta*! He feels more clever that way. Fabian is half-criminal, and that's typical for them. They feel powerful when they can manipulate someone. As to him working for AmiBank . . .' He was speaking a little too freely, perhaps, but he didn't care at the moment. 'A good inspector that does some favors can get a job in private security for four or five times his police salary.' He shrugged, pulled out a smoke. 'It's the same in your country, no? They work for the government, then they get a fat job with a corporation. Then they're back in the government, and they get an even fatter job. Look at your present administration. They're all in arms and petroleum.'

'Don't encourage me in that line. I've been trying to behave myself.'

A smile crept out from under his mustache. 'And what do we do now? It could be that there's a relation between Pablo Moya and William Renssaelaer, but we don't know what it is. The opinion of Teresa Castex isn't useful. For the sake of argument: why work so hard? Why not stay tranquil, drink a pair of *mates* and watch the wolves tear Pelegrini to pieces? Even if he didn't kill Waterbury, he's guilty of *something*!'

She feigned a look of admiration. 'You're so rigorous with your ethics, Miguel!' Serious again. 'I have a feeling it wasn't Boguso.' She looked away as she said it: 'I think it was someone in the police.'

A chill passed through Fortunato. 'Why?'

She shook her head. 'I don't know. I can't get rid of the idea. The nine millimeter, and what Teresa Castex said . . . Sometimes things don't have any sense, but they *are*.'

He took in a long breath and looked past her for a while. 'There remains *La Francesa*,' he ventured at last. 'But that's not so easy. We don't know her last name or what she looks like.'

'We have a picture.'

'How?'

Athena gave him a little pat on the shoulder. 'I got it off the internet.' She passed over a photo of a woman's face. A pretty woman with short straight hair of a nondescript color, small eyes and nose, her mouth rounded into an 'o'. The face had an intense erotic expression which, with the rest of the body cropped out, looked strangely painful. Fortunato recognized her from the week he had surveilled Waterbury.

Athena went on. 'I thought I would go around to all the tango schools and try and find out where she is. If she's trying to stay hidden, people might be more willing to tell a foreign woman than a local comisario. I've gotten the impression that the police aren't universally trusted here.'

Fortunato smiled. 'Look how she shits on the poor Institution! Typical leftist!' He chuckled. 'You're right. If you find her, call me.' He took out a few pieces of money and put them on the table, then stood up. 'I, too, will make some inquiries.'

CHAPTER 24

Fortunato hadn't returned to the Hotel San Antonio since the night of the squeeze, and he'd kept the investigation clear of the place. Now the unseasonable autumn heat had turned the air as warm as blood, and he could feel the moistness inside his jacket as he approached the yellowed light that poured out the glass doors of the lobby. He'd stared at this door for hours when they'd been arming the *capacha*, and it felt strange finally to go inside – like diving into a pool of water after seeing the surface a thousand times. The tawny marble of the reception looked sallow under the light, and Fortunato noted a streak of verdigris metal polish on the brass along the counter.

He recognized the clerk, a bored young man who had his eyes glued to a football match on a tiny television, as he had the night of Waterbury's misfortune. He worked the midnight to eight shift, probably earning just enough to keep him in spending money if he lived at home with his parents. The young man looked up at him dully, the hopeless expression of a man marking time in a marble cell. One had to fish sometimes, to examine a face and divine its capacity for corruption or fear. Thus a good policeman. He guessed that this face would respond to either.

'Good evening, young one.'

'Good evening, Señor.'

'Who is it? River and Independientes?'

'Sí. Independientes has them four to two.'

'*Puta!* I put twenty pesos on River!'

The young man kept one eye on the screen. 'Better to put twenty pesos on the referee. He's killing them.'

The Comisario sighed. 'There's no honor in Argentina. *Mirá . . .*' His voice radiated a sense of calm professionalism. A boy like this wouldn't ask to see identification: he knew it would only get him a *piña* or at best some long hours at the station. 'I had a few questions to ask you about the night the gringo disappeared.'

The boy's face took on a look of dread and he glanced quickly towards the door. He turned back and looked warily at Fortunato. 'I already told everything I know.'

In a kindly voice: 'Of course, son, but I'm conducting a separate investigation. Don't worry; it's all in conformance with the law.' Fortunato dug into his pocket, pulling out a roll of bills and pausing as he watched the clerk's reaction. 'I suppose the police have come by recently?'

The clerk glanced at the door again, unsure of what was happening but encouraged by the sight of the money. 'Yes. Yesterday and the day before.'

'Which ones?'

'Federales and those of the *Bonaerense*.'

'Do you have their names?'

The clerk hesitated, perhaps wondering for the first time who he was talking to. Fortunato maintained his look of expectation, and the clerk took several cards from a drawer. Federales: a comisario from Homicide, and a sub-co from the local station. Officers of some rank. There was a certain seriousness to the investigation now. The other card, of the *Bonaerense*, struck him like a familiar slap. Domingo Fausto, Inspector. Checking their trail. The cruel beefy face flashed across his vision; he put it out of his mind. 'And what did you tell them?'

'The truth. That the Northamerican was out when I came to work and he never returned. That I finished the shift without event.'

Fortunato nodded his head approvingly, his voice warm and sympathetic. '*Bien, muchacho*. And no other guests came that night?'

'There were some, but I don't remember well. That was six months ago.'

Fortunato nodded. 'The registry, please.'

The clerk produced a large ledger book with names in it. Most were couples, without the identification numbers or passports required by law. He made an automatic mental note that he could squeeze the owner for that omission, then concentrated on the names again. All common last names, their stays lasting only a few hours. He'd expected that.

A whistle came from the television as the referee called a foul against River. Fortunato glanced at it with annoyance. 'Lower the volume.' He waited for the clerk to comply. 'You rent rooms by the hour here?'

'Some. The girls come over from Reconquista. But it's tranquil. We never have any problems.'

'Do you remember anything unusual about the clients that night?'

'No.'

The policeman pulled out a photo he'd brought with him. 'Do you remember seeing this man?'

Two black brows moved together. 'Yes. Yes. *Un tipo* "Rock Star." He came in with a girl around . . . twelve-thirty, one in the morning. Not long after I arrived.'

'How did he act?'

He shrugged. 'When they come in here like that, it's not to introduce themselves and make friends with the guy at the reception. He came, he signed, he went upstairs with the girl and he left two hours later. See . . .' He pointed at the check-out time in the register, then squinted. 'But if I remember well, the woman left first. I wondered what he was doing up there the last hour.'

So Fabian had been alone in the hotel for at least an hour while Waterbury was taking his last ride. *Puta!* 'And was he carrying anything when he left?'

'I think he had an athletic bag.'

The detective nodded, then asked a few more questions about the woman, gathering only that she wasn't one of the regulars and that nothing about her stood out. The clerk knew nothing else. If Pelegrini's men had come in to search the room later, they must have done it on a different shift.

'Fine. You did well, young one. Fortunately, in our department there is money in the budget to reward citizens like yourself.' The Comisario limbered ten hundred-peso notes from the roll, probably two months' salary for the clerk. He handed them over but kept his fingers on them. 'But I want you to forget you saw me. The element of surprise is critical to the investigation.'

The clerk put his hand over the bills and pulled them across the counter. 'Don't worry, Uncle. You don't exist.'

Fortunato nodded with the faintest hint of chill. 'Good. If you keep your word, I'll know. And if you don't,' his face lost all expression, 'I'll know that, too.'

Once outside, Fortunato staggered through the night. He had

236

suspected that the journals had been taken from Waterbury's room, but if Fabian had gotten them *while the squeeze was happening*, he had to have known about the abduction from the start! How? Through Domingo? A sense of shame and anger mixed within Fortunato. All of them plotting behind his back! Like when the colonels and lieutenants plotted behind the generals' backs in those barracks uprisings. And him the stupid *gil*, playing the commanding officer!

The rage to kill someone swept across Fortunato and left him with his heart pounding and his fists clenched. The incident in the vacant lot in San Justo had removed the concept of murder from the realm of idle fantasy. He pushed the notion aside and concentrated on the problem. Fabian knew he'd abducted Waterbury and that he could do nothing but wait and hope while others were making a bed for Pelegrini.

Fine. The situation was developing. One had to pursue it more profoundly now, at a level where things were closer to the blood. He opened the door to his car and looked at his watch. One in the morning. He put in a call to Cacho.

CHAPTER 25

As he'd expected, the former revolutionary was far too wary to meet him someplace private: that kind of caution had kept him alive when an entire country was hunting him. He recommended a café in the middle of Ramos Mejia, a pizzeria large enough to guarantee some empty space around them in the dead hours of the afternoon the next day, but too central to allow someone to cork him without a dozen witnesses. Fortunato drank a whiskey as he made his proposition, and Cacho refused him before he could even get to the price.

'I'm not putting myself into this, Fortunato. I already told you that. Look for someone else to pick up Vasquez. Ask Domingo.'

'I'm doing this apart from Domingo. It's private.'

'Even more crazy. Look for someone else.' The thief stood up.

'Cacho, don't be so hard. It's just to talk with him.' He saw the man hesitate. 'I'll give you two green sticks.'

'Twenty thousand? To talk? You could have him cut for that money, and buy the widow a new car afterwards. What's happening, Miguel? What does Vasquez know that's worth twenty thousand?'

Fortunato shrugged offhandedly. 'Maybe he knows why Robert Waterbury was killed.'

Cacho shook his head of gray-streaked black hair. 'I already read about the *opereta* with Onda. Very nice, Señor, but no thank you. That's not my business. You want to talk about stolen televisions, call me.'

'Maybe he can tell us who killed Ricardo Berenski.'

Fortunato's words halted Cacho at the edge of the table, and the Comisario could see he'd hit something. 'You two are old *compañeros*, no? Berenski worked in Propaganda for the ERP; that's well-known. Berenski kept up the struggle, in his manner. That's why they killed him.'

'What would a *merquero* like Vasquez know about that?'

'Sit down, Cacho. Chat a little more with me. We're old friends now. I know your crimes, you know mine. There's little to hide. But of that night, of the gringo, it's not like it seems.' The criminal sat down and lit a cigarette. Fortunato looked over his shoulder and went on in a confidential voice. 'I fired the last bullet. That's the truth. But it was Domingo and Vasquez that shot him up first. When I fired, it already was. I did it because . . .' He hesitated, remembering Waterbury's agony, the look he'd given him before everything had gone bad. He'd been lying so long he had to work to try to muster the sincerity of the truth. 'I did it because he was suffering. Vasquez shot him in the balls, the thigh. Domingo shot him in the chest.' Fortunato felt his voice cracking as he remembered the night. 'There was no alternative, hombre. It already was. I killed him, yes, but for mercy. I never wanted to kill him! You know me. I'm not the type to kill an innocent man for a few pesos!'

He composed himself, continued in a more analytical tone. 'I believe Pelegrini ordered the squeeze. There was a matter with the writer and Pelegrini's wife. But I was told to squeeze him, not kill him. It was Vasquez who started shooting, then Domingo. I think someone else wanted him dead. And now,' he cleared his throat, 'it falls to me to solve the crime.'

The criminal stared at him with a mixture of pity and amazement. He felt comfortable with the old Fortunato, the arranger, the tranquil bureaucrat. This other Fortunato made him nervous. '*Estás loco, Comiso.*'

'*Mirá*, Cacho,' the policeman said hurriedly. 'You used to be for the Revolution, those years ago. Even the worst of the subversives had their idealism. A search for some . . .' the word felt strange and hypocritical to him, 'justice.' He shrugged. 'Maybe I'm looking for the same thing.'

'What could you know about the Revolution!' Cacho returned harshly. 'It was a thing of the spirit! You were dedicated to killing all that!'

Fortunato gazed down his drink, his shoulders bowed around his gray head. 'It's not so *thus*, Cacho.'

Cacho looked at the crumpled man in front of him. He had seen a thousand little plays tried out by petty criminals and petty cops, and if this were a lie it would be such an obvious ridiculous lie that the Comisario wouldn't even bother telling it. Something had happened to the Comisario. His wife's death or the murder had tripped some strange switch that was changing him, cell by cell, giving him a conscience. Or maybe not. Maybe it was just the cheap remorse of those who know they are about to fall.

'Forget it, Miguel.' He stood up again, but he couldn't make himself walk away. 'Where do you see Berenski in this?'

Fortunato was heartened by the reprieve. 'I'm still not sure where he enters.' He thought of telling about RapidMail and Pelegrini, but it was too vague in his own mind and it might spook Cacho. 'But I know that Berenski had started to investigate the Waterbury case when they killed him. If Vasquez knows who really killed Waterbury, maybe it will tell us who put down Berenski.'

Cacho seemed drawn into the possibility for a few seconds then shook his head. 'You talk about it as if it wasn't you! You're selling something! This is a trap!'

Fortunato heard him out and didn't bother with denials. 'You don't believe me, Cacho. With reason. I'm an *hijo de puta* and if there is justice in Argentina I'll end up rotting in Devoto for that crime and many others. Maybe it will turn out that way, but those are things that will be arranged later. In this case, I'm simply trying to do what is just.'

He stopped talking. Cacho was considering it and Fortunato could sense him handling the contours of his own history and whatever fierce idealism had once sent him on operations so unlikely that only the most visionary hopes for the future could induce a person to begin.

'Three green sticks,' he said at last. 'And you pay me in advance.'

CHAPTER 26

Athena had never been a liar, she'd always clung to the Truth as some sort of holy text which automatically sanctified one's cause. The Truth had failed her miserably here. It upheld no righteous banner, attracted no allies other than Berenski and Carmen Amado de los Santos, who were unable to help her now. All she had left were lies, and the facts of the murder as revealed in the faulty *expediente*. Her mentor was Comisario Fortunato.

She picked up the small packet of business cards and looked at them. It amazed her how the tiny print and pasteboard of a business card could wipe out in one stroke her entire identity. How easily one erased and remade oneself. Now she was Helen Kuhn, a Vice-President of Development at American Telepictures. She handed out the card as she made the rounds of the tango schools. She was looking for a dancer named Paulé who had been suggested for a role in a movie they were shooting. Who had recommended Paulé? Why, the maestra of the classes at the Confitería Ideal, or of the Dance Club El Arrabal, or the Escuela de Tango Carlos Gardel. She acquired a list of names and facts as she went, dropping them casually into her inquiries. Edmundo, the booking agent at Carlito's, had spoken highly of Paulé, and Norma, of the Teatro Colón, had attested to her thick French accent.

To her surprise, the lying came easily and not unpleasantly. The faces she spoke to always brightened credulously at her introduction, eager to slip into the world she created for them. For someone like her, passing through Buenos Aires without history or future, it didn't really matter who she pretended to be. She became a memory as soon as they turned their backs, a story they might tell their husbands that night and remember as the vague blonde woman with the disappearing face. She became like the lurid characters of Fabian's movie script, or the violent personages delineated by

Enrique Boguso in his first, false confession: a vapor in a world made of vapor.

Nevertheless, after three days something real began to emerge from all the half-truths. Paulé had moved some months ago, a dance teacher said, and had given instructions to keep her new address strictly private. Something of a too-insistent ex-boyfriend, although she wondered if it might be problems with immigration. But for the chance at a film role! Why not come here to the ballroom at ten o'clock the following night, when she would surely come to teach the beginners!

Athena called the Comisario as soon as she reached her hotel.

'I found her!'

'Where?'

His eagerness made her cagey. 'At a ballroom in Palermo. She'll be there at ten tomorrow night. Why don't you come and get me at nine at my hotel and we'll go over there together.'

'Which ballroom is it?'

'Just come and get me!'

She heard a brief, hurt silence. '*Bien*,' he said. 'At nine.'

For Fortunato, the string was getting tighter. Thirty thousand American dollars had persuaded Cacho to pick up Vasquez and bring him to his house for questioning, but the following day he had almost backed out. 'It's too hot, hombre. It's a nest of vipers.'

The reason had been written in the afternoon newspaper: Chief Bianco's name appeared for the first time alongside that of Carlo Pelegrini. It wasn't a large mention, merely that Pelegrini's security man, Abel Santamarina, had called Bianco's cell phone twice in the days prior to Berenski's murder. A lawyer might have called a detail like that circumstantial but Fortunato knew that the circumstances could only be damning and it dropped a stone at the bottom of his stomach. The journalists and investigators were working their way down the chain, from Pelegrini to Santamarina to Bianco, and within a day or two they would connect Santamarina to Boguso's fabricated story about Waterbury, and then, *chico*, the race would be on. And this would be a race with a lot of losers.

'It's not for so much, Cacho! A few questions and I turn him loose to find his own destiny.'

'That's the point, Miguel. I don't want his destiny to become my destiny.'

Fortunato snorted. 'You're immortal, Cacho. You had a whole

army trying to assassinate you and they failed. But I'll give you another two green sticks.'

'Five?'

'Five.'

The phone went quiet as Cacho considered the suspiciously high price of fifty thousand dollars for a simple conversation with a petty *puntero*. His voice became cold as he dictated his terms: 'You play me, and I'll kill you.'

Fortunato thought about the threat as he drove to meet the Chief for a little talk. All the old relationships were shifting, relationships whose mutual agreements about how the world *was* had formed the foundation of his career. The Chief had summoned him to his residence, and though Leon hadn't said so, Fortunato assumed it was because he didn't want to be seen meeting in public.

The five-bedroom house lay enclosed by a high concrete wall with sharp wrought iron points crisscrossed at the top. Embedded metal plaques from the Chief's private security company implied dire consequences for whatever *gil* was stupid enough to try and break in. Bianco liked to explain that he'd gotten the money to buy the big house, and another at the beach, through various business opportunities that he'd been fortunate enough to grasp over the years. His company provided security for homes and businesses and rock concerts, and he couldn't help it if friends had included him in lucrative real-estate ventures. Fortunato had watched his economic status rise over the years, neither resenting nor wanting to imitate it, but when Marcela saw the house go up ten years ago she had begun subtly putting distance between themselves and the Biancos. Pleasant enough when they met on Fridays at the 17 Stone Angels to listen to tango, she'd found ways to refuse invitations to the house itself, so that Fortunato hadn't been there in five years.

This afternoon the Chief himself let him in at the heavy iron gate, from which Fortunato inferred that no one else was home. Bianco led him into the dark, cool house, filled with carved gilded furniture and various paintings of Spanish street scenes. When he brought him a cola on ice he served it with a little too much solicitation. Fortunato had never seen Bianco look this nervous before; the smile came a little too rapidly to his face and seemed to go slightly rotten before he could finish uttering the pleasantries. Fortunato noticed a copy of the morning newspaper on the coffee table.

'Miguel,' he began at last, 'the situation is getting complicated.'

Fortunato didn't bother answering.

'Re-complicated, *amor*. I've heard that *La Gallega* is extending her investigation to include the *Caso* Waterbury. They're federalizing everything. They want you off the case and they want all the files.'

Fortunato refused to react, and Bianco hurried to minimize the bad news. 'It's all spectacle! If they suspected you, they would have sequestered everything with an order of the judge. They just want to show the Press how hard they are trying.'

They both knew the last part was a lie. The footsteps were getting closer and their reverberations were shuddering through the Chief's twitchy eyes. He managed to recover some of his old command presence as he laid out the course of action. 'They're going to requisition the files in the next day or two. I want you to revise absolutely everything: the *expediente*, your personal archives.' He thumped his fingertips on the table. 'Every *declaración* and every *diligencia* must be in perfect order. Likewise, revise your own files so that there is no record of any activities which could embarrass the Institution. For the doubts, take them to your home until all this cools down again.'

The Comisario knew what he meant. Ten years of *arreglos* had to be purged before Faviola Hocht's investigators started holding them up to the light. He rocked his head forward slowly. 'Those of the *Caso* Waterbury I can clean out in an hour, but the rest would take weeks. If they want to re-open and explore every case –'

'It's not for so much! It's a precaution.' Bianco shrugged disdainfully. 'Two weeks and they'll be busy with the next scandal. But promise me you'll take care of that cursed gringo as soon as you leave here.'

'Fine.' Fortunato thought of lighting a cigarette but he didn't see an ashtray at hand and didn't want to ask for one. He swallowed to steady his voice. 'I saw that Onda was cut.'

Bianco put his hand up to show that he knew where Fortunato was going with it. He spoke in a quiet, serious voice. 'You enter on the other theme, Miguel. I'll tell you directly: Vasquez also needs to be put down. People like him and Onda aren't reliable. They make deals when they get squeezed.' He put some gravel in his voice. 'They're not hombres!'

'And?'

'Domingo needs someone to help him. Since you're the one responsible you're going to have to do it.'

It took Fortunato a moment to absorb it. He looked at Bianco carefully, wondering what he knew. 'I'm starting to think I wasn't responsible,' he said calmly.

The denial annoyed the Chief, but he seemed inclined to humor his inferior. 'Of course not! The idiot was responsible for his own stupidities. But it was you who let it get out of control.'

'What I'm saying is that maybe it was supposed to get out of control. Maybe Vasquez killed the gringo for reasons of his own. It was rare how Vasquez started shooting. There was no real reason for it.'

'He's a violent criminal with a head stuffed full of *merca* and you have to look for a reason?' Anger was hardening the Chief's voice. 'Don't go inventing something to find a way out of this, Miguel! You have to take care of Vasquez. You and Domingo. Get over your weakness and finish what you started.'

Bianco was glaring at him with disgust. Fortunato thought of revealing the bits he'd learned about Pablo Moya and the mysterious Renssaelaer, but suddenly he didn't really care to. He'd found it on his own, in his private investigation, and that information didn't belong to the Chief or anyone else at the Institution. Let the Chief go on sweating for a while. Moreover, he wasn't so sure Leon was telling him everything either.

As to Vasquez; if someone had to die, Vasquez made an excellent candidate. A drug addict, bully, thief and *puntero*, the 'somethings' he was guilty of were anything but vague. Of course, he'd make them find someone else to do the job, but better to play along with the Chief for the moment. Refusing might have other consequences. 'When do you want to do it?'

'Tonight. Domingo is setting it up.' He handed him a small phone. 'Here's a clean cellular. Domingo will call you later to arrange the program.'

Fortunato took the cellular and slipped it into his pocket. He thought about his own interview with Vasquez that he'd scheduled for that night, and reflected that his fifty thousand dollars might be buying Vasquez another day of life. The silence started ticking away and Bianco stiffly offered him another cola as a way of reminding him it was time to leave. 'It will all come out well,' he encouraged as he led him to the iron bars. 'You'll see.'

*

Fortunato drove back to the comisaria. The weight of *La Gallega's* investigation was beginning to flatten him. Beyond the fear, it was the humiliation of the whole situation that stung him most intensely. The entire comisaria had become aware of the tension surrounding the Waterbury case, and as the news of his removal trickled out the respect he had earned with his decades of cautious management would begin to erode. Federal officers would come in to take possession of the files, someone in Hocht's office would trumpet it to the journalists and his name would appear in an article the next morning, in small print or large, depending on that particular day's toll of catastrophe: *Federal Police Remove Comisario From Case.* Everyone would see it: his subordinates, his colleagues, his neighbors, Athena.

Even Marcela, somewhere, would see it.

CHAPTER 27

He began to clean out his files, as he'd promised the Chief. The sins of the Waterbury *expediente* involved lack of ambition rather than much fraud, so he had little challenge with that. Aside from the ballistics tests he had substituted to match 'Boguso's' Astra, they were relatively clean. The ledgers in which he accounted for the various institutional maneuvers and the formula for dividing their proceeds could be packed into his briefcase. The rest he could only clear out by setting fire to the office. Scores of cases had died without a prosecution or displayed other irregularities, and it wouldn't take a grandiose investigation to start picking them apart. As he leafed through them he also came across some of his best cases. Now he recalled them: the Bordero case, where he'd found the gang rapists; the Pretini case, with its fatal robbery; the *Caso* Gomez; the *Caso* Novoa. So many many cases that had ended with the gratitude of the victims or their families, their handshakes, and their knowledge that on some battered imperfect level, there was justice in the world. Why must they all be erased by the *Caso* Waterbury?

He called in his sub-comisario and told him he was going home early, then returned to his house with the files. Winter had sent its outriders into the city that day, giving the walls a frigid, tomb-like feeling. He looked at the pictures of Marcela as he came in, glanced reflexively through the half-open door at the hospital bed in her deathroom. He filled the kettle and prepared the *mate*. Berenski kept coming to mind, along with Waterbury. That desperate appeal he'd made over the seat at him: *I have a wife and daughter.* And all the time, Waterbury hadn't been a blackmailer at all, just a man who had believed his own ruinous stories and was struggling to make them real with one last play. Like him, Miguel Fortunato.

The Comisario poured the hot water over the herb and pulled at the straw, watching the pale green foam sink into the leaves. He'd put a lemon in it again, and sugar, the way Marcela liked it, and the *mate* had the foreign taste of when she had been alive and sitting across from him. He remembered her as she was before she'd gotten sick, with her strong fleshy arms and those wise eyes.

'It's a mess, *Negra*. I tried to do something and it went for the worst.' The sound of his own voice had a comforting effect, like the prayer of a man without religion. At last he could say out loud all the things whose concealment had calcified his life. He could never reveal this to the real Marcela, but to this shadow Marcela he could confess everything. 'Thirty-seven years I've gone along with the Institution. No, not always to your measure, but at least within the bounds of the normal. I enforced the law, in our fashion. I arrested many criminals. Remember the child molester that I trapped? They wrote it up in *El Clarín* and gave me a medal. Who gave more to the police family fund than I? Even this last, with the writer: that was an accident. They tricked me into it, *Negra*. That was Domingo and Vasquez. I didn't want it to turn out that way.'

The fantasy Marcela took on a look of tender absolution. 'It's fine, *amor*. Life brings these situations sometimes and one arranges it as one can. You did what you could for the writer. It was the other two, that Leon assigned you. It doesn't erase those years of good work. How many children were saved when you captured that murderer?'

His chin had sunk into his hand and the white plaster walls gave off a cold silence. The water in the kettle had gone tepid, and the herbs in the *mate* were washed clean. Without any thought about it, he felt himself being drawn into the bedroom to sit on their marital bed, facing the wardrobe.

He opened up the left half of the chest and Marcela's talcum powder scent came billowing over him. He filled his eyes with her flower-print dresses and her Evita hats with their net veils, and inhaled deeply. For an instant he felt close to her again, could be transported to her side, to something alive and transcendent, but with each successive breath the smell became fainter and fainter, and finally he was looking only at a closet full of old dresses and shoes, the last remnant of what had been worthwhile in his life.

The doorbell rang. It was the *sodero*, dropping off six new siphons of seltzer water. The Comisario paid him absently and was about to close the door when something on the street caught his eye.

Most people wouldn't have noticed it, but Fortunato, with his years of experience in the Division of Investigations, caught it almost immediately and was *piola* enough to pretend he hadn't seen anything at all. A half a block away a blue Peugeot sat parked next to the curb, holding a man with sunglasses. Fortunato's impression of it lasted only a second, imprecise, then he went inside again and glanced out his bedroom window to the other street. Nothing. He picked up a bag of garbage and brought it to the little elevated cage outside his house, taking the opportunity to glance the other way to see how many there were. Only the Peugeot, which meant it was just surveillance, not a grab. It could be federal police: they drove Peugeot. But would they be stupid enough to take a standard-issue car on an *operativo*? It could be Pelegrini's men, tracking him.

He glanced at his watch and calculated the time. Seven o'clock now, nine o'clock at the Sheraton for Athena, ten o'clock at the ballroom to interview the French woman, and near midnight an expected summons from Cacho for his fifty thousand dollar interview. At some point he had to call Domingo to see what plans he had for killing Vasquez. That was the night he'd planned. What plans the man in the car had he couldn't know.

Fortunato went to the wardrobe and quickly opened the compartment where the neat rows of green money looked back at him. He took out three bundles and stuffed them into his pockets for any necessities that came up. Thirty thousand dollars. Along with that, a thousand in pesos and a subway token from his dresser. The rest of the money he quickly loaded into his briefcase with the vague notion that he might never come back.

Fortunato took his Browning from its holster and switched off the safety, chambering the first round and laying it on the seat of his car. He unlocked the metal doors of the carport and swung them open, then started the engine. If they were going to move on him, it would be right now, as he was backing out to the street and securing the carport behind him. He swung his vision in an arc that included the Peugeot, stuck the nine millimeter in his belt, and edged his Fiat into the roadway. The surveillance car didn't move. Fortunato closed the doors and then turned straight for it, glancing at it as he drove past. One man in a brown sports jacket, age about thirty-five, black hair cut short, sunglasses. He pretended to be reading a newspaper as Fortunato passed. As Fortunato glanced in his rear-view mirror he saw a white Toyota pickup coming around the corner from his house with two occupants. It must have been out of sight, waiting for the Peugeot to radio. Fortunato went another block then checked his mirror again. The Toyota lagged him by a block, and the Peugeot was making a U-turn. *Mierda!*

He stayed calm, considering how to lose them. A half-kilometer away lay a block of abandoned factories with alleys in back of them, but if he lost them there, it would be obvious. Better to make an idiot face, be a *gil* on an evening drive to the pizzeria.

He ran through the scenarios that included the car behind him. Maybe the Federales; they might know enough now to call him a suspect. Maybe they'd examined the *expediente*, talked to the clerk at the San Antonio, been tipped by Fabian. Maybe Athena had told them something, or the FBI. Pelegrini the other possibility: one of those efficient men in suits arming a *capacho*, as he'd armed one for Waterbury. And in that case, could Bianco know about it?

He drove all the way to Palermo and brought his car into the parking garage of the elegant new *shopping* that had opened the previous year and was already taking business from the traditional stores on the street. The Toyota was two cars behind him in the entrance line, the Peugeot out of sight. His tires squealed as he drove up the ramp as fast as he could. He found a space near the entrance, then grabbed the briefcase of cash and hurried into the *shopping*. It was one of those *shoppings* that had opened up in the past few years, all with the same stores and the same smell of climate control and floor polish, Northamerican style. This was a new Argentina, foreign to him, glossy and without a trace of tango or history, a collection of brand names. He walked quickly along the indoor street with its fountains and potted shrubbery. He wanted to take off his jacket, but he couldn't with his black pistol strapped in its shoulder holster. He came to what he was looking for, a point where the mall had exits to either side. He paused for a moment behind a swath of greenery to glance behind him. No one. He ducked out the exit and made for the *subte* station across the street, then took the train three stops out before getting off. From there, he hailed a taxi. Easy to stop one: with his briefcase and his suit jacket he might be a travel agent or an insurance salesman, a man who sat at a desk all day, making arrangements. A man nearing the end of an undistinguished career. 'To Lomas de Zamora, maestro,' and then he could sit back and rest for a moment, craning his head once in a while to look behind him. The initial victory dissipated the fear that had been trying to move in from the edges of his consciousness. He was Fortunato the clever, the master of reality. Too clever to fall.

He directed the *taxista* to let him off in front of a restaurant, then walked two blocks to a mechanical shop he knew. The proprietor specialized in repairing and selling stolen autos and Fortunato had done business with him when he'd been a sub-comisario in the area. He looked over the cars. 'Give me a clean one, Mario.' He pulled fifteen thousand dollars from his jacket and picked up a blue Ford Taurus with falsified papers. The vendor's nervous twitch made him give an involuntary wink. 'For you, Comisario, I'll guarantee the motor for six months.' Fortunato didn't answer. He wouldn't be needing it that long. He took several more bundles of money out of the briefcase and stuffed them into his jacket, then dialed Cacho's number.

'It's Fortunato. How's it going with the matter we spoke of?'

'We'll go fishing at the Cyclone. Be ready after midnight.'

'Ready,' Fortunato said agreeably, and hung up. He looked at his watch. Eight fifteen. His official cell phone rang. Bianco. In the background he could hear the faint strains of a tango.

'Miguel. Where are you?'

In the fraction of a second before he answered Fortunato tried to weigh the exact intent behind the Chief's voice. 'I'm in Lomas de San Isidro,' he lied. 'I'm going to visit my cousin for the birthday of his daughter.'

'I'm going to give you a number. Are you ready?'

Fortunato wrestled his notebook from his pocket. The Chief hadn't pressed him for details, as he would if he were trying to get him back under surveillance. So it might be the Federales alone watching him, or Pelegrini alone. '*Listo.*'

The Chief dictated the number. Fortunato felt reassured by his voice. 'Call that number on the phone I gave you.'

'*Bien.*' He pulled out the clean cell phone. Domingo answered.

'The Chief said to call you.'

'Sí, Comisario.' Fortunato cringed at the slightly mocking tone that always hung in Domingo's thick voice when he addressed him by rank. 'We have a little job to do.'

Fortunato stalled. 'I read about Onda.'

Domingo allowed an ironic tone to color his regret. 'Yes, killed robbing a kiosk. They break their mothers' hearts.'

The Comisario pictured Domingo's fleshy cheeks and fat lips. 'I'm not putting myself in this.'

'You're already in it, Comiso. Don't grow a conscience now. Vasquez is a piece of shit that nobody's going to miss.'

'That point, I have to concede.' Even so, he had no desire to kill him. To talk to him, yes. But not to be dragged into another homicide. A delicate pass here. If he agreed to kill him, it would be difficult to turn back. If he refused, though, the numbers might shift to the other side of the equation. 'It's not going to be so easy. It's sure he knows Onda fell. He's not going to go marching into an alley with his hands on his head.'

Domingo laughed. 'You're too sentimental, Comiso. Who do you think helped set Onda up? I still owe him five *lucas* for that little work. Tonight I pay him.'

Fortunato swallowed. 'What plan do you have?'

'I'm still arranging it. It depends on his schedule. The important thing is that you be ready between one and two tonight. I'll call you on your cellular. You call me back and we'll finalize it.'

'It's very soon, Domingo. One should control him for a few days, to find the right moment, the right place.'

'There's no time to whine, Fortunato! It already *is*. I'll call you between one and two. *Está?*'

Domingo's dismissive tone angered the Comisario. '*Está*,' he said coolly. 'We'll see each other.'

But, happily, he knew he wouldn't see Domingo that night. Cacho would grab Vasquez for their little chat, Domingo would be unable to find him, and the whole *operativo* would evaporate. After that, who knew? Maybe things would solve themselves.

He drove to Palermo and parked beside a dim little pizzeria some five blocks from the embassy, taking a few more bundles of bills from the satchel. His own phone might be tapped, so he flashed his badge and borrowed the phone in the tiny back office to call Athena.

'It's I, Fortunato.'

'Are you downstairs?'

'No. I'm at a pizzeria some five blocks from your hotel. Listen. There's a little change in plans.' He described the location, then continued in as casual a voice as possible. 'What you should do is find the service elevator. Take it to the basement then leave the building by the service entrance. Avoid the lobby.'

She didn't answer immediately but when she did he could hear the nervousness in her voice. 'What's happening, Miguel?'

'Don't worry yourself, nothing's happening! I'll explain it when you arrive. There's no danger of anything. It's for the doubts . . .'

She agreed to it reluctantly and he ordered a coffee and sat down to wait for her.

Boca was beating Almirante Brown on a television screen whose distressed tube showed the world in supersaturated colors. The field was the same brilliant lime green as Fabian's jacket. Smeary jerseys in blood red or a celestial blue arced and sizzled across the electric turf while the paper-colored light of the fluorescent tube rained down on his shoulders. The descriptions of Robert Waterbury kept coming back to him. A decent man; he could tell that from their short acquaintance. In the car he'd had a certain calm that innocent people can sometimes maintain in the face of extremities. That sympathetic little look he had thrown to Fortunato, as if recognizing that they were two good men thrown into a bad situation. '*Mirá*, Waterbury. The matter is this: I didn't know the whole story. I thought it would turn out fine.'

But you were the one who picked me up. You organized it. If it wasn't for you –

'*Someone* was going to pick you up. At least I had good intentions. I tried to control the situation –'

Who are you trying to deceive? You spent your whole life putting yourself in that situation.

Fortunato felt his blood pounding through his temples and glanced up at the tiny scrambling figures on their hyper-real palette. The referee was blowing his whistle and motioning frantically with his arms.

Marcela broke in at the back of his head, the young and alluring Marcela. She was in one of her exasperated moods when she got down to the reality. 'What did you expect? You pretended to be the virtuous police, and all the while you were sucking money out of the people like every other corrupt one. Moreover, you couldn't even father a baby!'

Fortunato recalled without wanting to the vision of her near the end, shrunken in her bed, her beautiful Inca nose filed into a narrow hook. Their whole life together had passed between those two points, and his whole career as a man and a policeman, and what remained now? A botched squeeze and a pile of lies. Orders to go with a piece of shit to kill another piece of shit. He had given up his family for the backslaps of liars and criminals in the hallways of provincial comisarias, for the glorious comradeship of the Institution, and now the Institution was spitting him out.

Fortunato put his forehead in his palm as the television erupted into a burst of tinny noise. The frantic wail of the commentator: 'Go-o-o-o-o-o-o-o-o-o-o-o-o-o-o-o-o-o-o-o-o-o-o-o-o-o-o-o-o-ol-l-l-l-l!' The Comisario looked up. Boca had just scored another goal. Boca: the mouth that devoured everything. They were unstoppable this year.

CHAPTER 28

Athena found him ten minutes later in the back of the dingy restaurant. She could see from the speed with which he came to his feet that his imperturbable calm had worn thin, but his sad-eyed, weary presence still reassured her.

'You look very pretty,' he told her.

She'd chosen a navy suit and white blouse, wanting to look convincingly professional when they met the Frenchwoman. 'I want to know more about who might be following me.'

'That's nothing,' he said as he steered her out of the pizzeria. 'It's a precaution. We want to keep our interview confidential, so we take these small precautions. Look! I'm all prepared for tonight.' He took something from his pocket and pinned it to his lapel. Leaning closer in a streetlight, she could see it was a dove with an olive branch in its mouth: not typical adornment for the Buenos Aires police.

Fortunato made a grand flourish. 'I present you to Dr Miguel Castelli, lawyer. Specialist in Human Rights. Assessor for Amnesty International.'

She looked at the newly minted human rights lawyer. 'Miguel . . . We'll leave this part out of the report, okay?' He opened the door of the blue Ford, and she looked at it quizzically before getting in. 'Whose car is this?

'It's borrowed. Mine has lost its brakes.'

The ballroom was in the basement of the Armenian Mutual Benefit Society, some fifty meters long with a bar at one end and seating for two hundred or more around the polished dance floor. At the moment Argentine rock music was bouncing through the speakers but at ten o'clock, the bartender said, they would change to tango and all the beginners could get free lessons. 'Will the Frenchwoman be teaching tonight?' Athena asked him. He returned a sour look. 'With her, who knows?'

She took a small table while the Comisario excused himself, and two young men a few seats away smiled at her and struck up a conversation. Did she know how to dance the tango? Where was she from? She glanced past them around the room while she answered their questions. In the midst of it she saw a face that gave her a clammy sensation along her ribs.

Fabian was leaning against the wall in a nondescript tweed sports jacket, looking at her. When their eyes met he pushed his face into a grin and lifted his arms as if to say, 'Of course!' He made his way toward her through the crowd.

'Fabian! I thought you hated tango!'

'I'm giving it another opportunity. It's my culture, no? And moreover, there's a certain social movement here that I like.'

She didn't believe the lie, but she put on her idiot face. 'It's the women!'

He shrugged. 'You already know me, Athena. But you see; perhaps it was destiny that you and I should tango together. I am here. You are here –'

'Actually, I'm here with Comisario Fortunato. He said I shouldn't leave Buenos Aires without learning a few steps.'

'Even better! We can all sit and drink a bottle of champagne together! I will join you!'

She gave her best imitation of enthusiasm and he wedged himself between the tightly packed tables and pulled a chair up. The two young men at the next table looked disappointed. 'You're dressed very quietly, Fabian. I would have expected more.'

'I was in a quiet mood, Athena. Sometimes a man is more contemplative. But you!' He ran his eyes along her body. 'Very . . .' He squared his shoulders. '*Thus.* Super competent! Professional! But still with that touch of sensuality that is yours alone.' His words seemed slightly mechanical and he kept glancing over her shoulder toward the entrance as he spoke. 'Ah, here is the Comisario! This is perfection!'

Fortunato approached. 'Good evening, Fabian.'

'Comiso! What a pleasure. I insist that you let me invite you to a bottle of champagne!'

'I didn't know you were an aficionado of tango.'

'The truth is I'm more for rock and roll. I'm not a *tanguero* like you, Comisario, or like Comisario Bianco. He sings, no?'

'He sings,' Fortunato said absently.

While Fabian tried to attract a waitress Athena exchanged glances with Fortunato. They understood each other: Fabian had come to find the Frenchwoman. If they wanted to talk to her alone their best chance now would be to wait outside on the street and intercept her there, and to do that, they would have to shake their unwelcome host. The champagne came and she tried to feign the proper gratitude as Fabian poured out three glasses. She waited a few minutes and then put a distressed look on her face.

'Oh! Miguel.' She squirmed a bit, adopted that reluctant anguish perfected on a dozen bad dates. 'I'm sorry, I have to go back to the hotel right away.' The two men looked at her with concern. She shrugged. 'It's a feminine thing. I wasn't prepared . . . I'm sorry, Fabian. Let me give you money for the champagne.'

Beneath his graciousness he seemed slightly alarmed. 'No! Don't even mention it!'

'Better that we go quickly,' she told the Comisario, standing up.

Fabian also rose to his feet. 'I'll accompany you! I'll walk you to your car.'

'But the champagne –'

'It's nothing!'

'Really, Fabian: we can go alone!'

'No, no!'

She was desperate to get rid of him. The Frenchwoman would be arriving any minute and if they couldn't shake him, they would lose their best chance. She searched furiously for an excuse as they began to thread their way through the tightly packed tables, but Fabian stuck to her like a leech, only inches behind and with no intention of letting go. The music stopped, the crowd of dancers came flooding their way back to their seats, and a knot of boisterous young men accidentally jostled her backwards a half-pace. She felt Fabian brush inadvertently against her behind, and after the flicker of indignation the idea came to her. It was so right in so many ways that she didn't question it. Without deliberation, she turned and slapped him across the face so hard that her hand tingled.

'Stop grabbing me!'

Fabian was rocked backwards by the shock of the blow, struggling to comprehend the unexpected attack. 'It was an accident!'

'That's a lie! You've been after me since the day I arrived! You think you can touch me like an animal in a room full of people? What's your problem? Why don't you go find a prostitute and pay for it!'

'You might learn something from a prostitute.'

'Beast! Don't talk to me like that!' She moved to slap him again, but he caught it in mid-air and held it there. For a moment their eyes were locked together in an angry stalemate, and just as he began to break into a smug little laugh she came up from below and slapped him with her other hand, catching him on the jawline with a crisp snap that could be heard by all the nearby spectators.

He looked at her with disbelief. '*Puta!*' he said. His playboy superiority was gone and for a moment she thought he might hit her back.

Fortunato appeared suddenly between them. 'Fabian –' the Comisario said calmly.

'Leave her alone, *tarado*,' another man shouted excitedly. 'Or I'll explode you!' It was one of the two men she had been flirting with ten minutes earlier.

'Keep swelling, *boludo*, and you'll spend the next three months in the *calabozo*.'

'And you'll spend the next three months in the hospital!' The man swung his fist around Fortunato's shoulder and clipped the top of Fabian's head. Fabian exploded from the knot of people and flung himself at him.

The Comisario put on his best peacemaker voice. 'It's fine, Fabian. We'll go. You stay here and enjoy yourself.'

They moved quickly through the crowd as Fabian continued the exchange with the two men. When Athena glanced back from the stairwell the three were embroiled in a knot of pushing and punching, and the bouncers were moving towards them. In a few seconds they were out in the bright quiet lobby.

'Did he really grab you?' Fortunato asked her.

She tipped her head towards her shoulder, giving a little frown. 'It was an accident.' She arched her eyebrows. 'But he was guilty of *something*.'

The Comisario laughed the deepest longest laugh she'd ever heard from him. He was still laughing when they got to the sidewalk. They both went silent when they realized that they had come face to face with Paulé.

CHAPTER 29

Her hair had grown longer than in the picture, falling now to her shoulders, and she was dressed in a black one-piece dress and a red sweater. She wore lipstick and eye shadow and carried a black athletic bag towards the ballroom of the Armenian Mutual Benefit Society. Athena's heart pounded as she recognized her, as though she were seeing a celebrity. 'Paulé!' she greeted her.

La Francesa looked at her, trying to recognize her. 'Do I know you?'

'No. My name is Athena Fowler. I'm a human rights investigator from the United States. Could I talk to you for a few minutes?'

Paulé's face suddenly closed. 'I'm sorry. I'm too busy. I have to teach a class.'

'Please. I'd like to talk to you about Robert Waterbury.'

The Frenchwoman mustered as much hauteur as she could, but the fear was starting to undermine it. 'What are you talking about? I don't even know Robert Waterbury! With your permission . . .' She pushed on the door but Athena held it.

'Don't go down there.'

'What?'

Fortunato came forward now and when Paulé saw him she began to panic, pushing on the door. 'Let me pass!'

'Señorita!' Fortunato said in his kindest voice. 'Don't go down there. They're looking for you.'

She let go of the door and then put her hands stiffly at her sides and stamped her foot on the pavement. After a few seconds she began to cry.

Closer up, she looked older than Athena had expected. Though her pale skin was virtually unwrinkled, something about her face made Athena place her in her late thirties. What was it? A hardness around

260

the eyes? The set of her mouth? She was a pretty woman, but Athena thought it a harsh sort of beauty, stiffened with cosmetics and wariness. So this was Waterbury's Patron Saint of Desperation. Athena wondered for the first time if Paulé had ever really said that, or if the whole story was Waterbury's fictionalization of his own life – or Fabian's – or some combined fiction with which the two of them had created a world that each, for his own reasons, preferred. Where was the Truth in a world like that?

They walked to a quiet café and took a seat in the corner, calmed Paulé with a pastis and a business card. She talked in a wistful voice.

'What can I tell you about Robert Waterbury? A very gentle man. He was very kind to the children who live in the streets. He wanted to write a story about the abandoned children that live around the Plaza Misereres, that they were the angels on the fountains that came to life at night. He was like that: a man always living half in his imagination. He told me he used to work in finance, but he must have been a very bad banker.'

'We heard it wasn't going well as a writer, either.'

'It went for shit. He had a million complaints about the publishing business and the injustice of it all, and he had resolved himself to write something cheap and like a formula. That's how he got involved with the wife of Carlo Pelegrini.'

'I understand he was working on something with her,' Athena said.

Paulé scoffed. 'Working! He was prostituting himself to her to try to keep his career going. She wanted him to write some sort of monument to her ego. Her life story. She offered him thirty thousand dollars for it.'

'Not two hundred thousand?'

The pale face twisted with scorn. 'Don't be an idiot! She knew how desperate he was. It would be too humane to pay him so much money. For someone like her it's much more satisfying to pay him the minimum he would accept and then keep him jumping for every penny. She used it as a hook to control him. That's the part she enjoyed. She knew he was married but she insisted on seducing him anyway. She took pleasure in corrupting him. She's a good match for her husband.'

'He slept with her?'

The Frenchwoman looked at her with scorn. 'I told him not to, but he was half-*boludo* in that respect. You don't sleep with the queen and expect that the king won't cut off your head. Robert was a toy for her. In her advanced age she thinks herself some sort of artist, but she's the coldest hardest prostitute you ever saw.'

Athena led her. 'So you think Carlo Pelegrini killed Robert?'

Paulé glanced away as she spoke. 'How would I know?'

Athena sensed she was hiding something, and knew Fortunato had picked it up, too.

The Comisario continued in a soft voice. 'Paulé, did Robert ever mention that Teresa Castex had revealed confidential information about her husband's businesses to him? Things that might make problems for Carlo Pelegrini?'

'No! Robert knew nothing about Pelegrini's business. He would have told me. We had a very close relationship.' She looked at the two investigators. 'We weren't lovers, because I know that's what you are thinking. We were friends. Does that seem so impossible? Although . . .' at this, her eyes began to loosen up and her voice went suddenly high and shaky, 'if I had known they were going to kill him I might have insisted, because it was his last days anyway!' Her pretty features warped out of shape at that moment and several tears fell silently down her cheeks. Of all the people Athena had talked to about Waterbury's murder, Paulé was the only one who had cried.

Fortunato beamed at her with an open, compassionate face, a saint's face that seemed to open the *danseuse* up like a flower. 'Paulé, has anyone else talked to you about this?'

She nodded, wiping at the tears. 'A week after Robert was killed a man broke into my apartment.'

Athena looked at the Comisario in alarm, but he continued calmly. 'What did he look like?'

'Short blond hair, well-dressed. Maybe forty-five. Milico-type. He was already inside my apartment when I came home. He wanted to know about Robert.'

Athena broke in. 'Did he identify himself? Was he a policeman?'

'He's going to force his way into my apartment and then hand me his card?'

Fortunato took over again. 'What did you tell him, Paulé?'

'I told him that I knew Robert but I hadn't seen him in at least a week and I thought he had gone back to the United States. After that I changed apartments.'

Athena and Fortunato considered her answer. Fortunato spoke first, gently. 'Señorita Dupère, I understand your situation. It's frightening. I too would be frightened. But if you don't tell us, it doesn't end here. Others also will want the answers to these questions, and they may not be so sympathetic to your situation.'

She turned to Athena. 'You'll get me killed. The United States is famous for that: they use you for their shows and then they leave you to hang.'

'I won't do that,' Athena said, though she had no idea what protection she could offer. 'If you know who killed him, I promise I'll have him extradited –'

'Are you crazy? There's not going to be a trial! When these people murder someone they are celebrated in the financial papers because they're improving the economy for casket makers!'

'What people?'

She shook her head bitterly. 'AmiBank!'

'What do you mean?'

'He saw them together.'

'Who?'

'The American who runs Pelegrini's security.'

'William Renssaelaer?'

'Yes! That was the name. Robert saw him with Pablo Moya, of the Grupo AmiBank.'

Fortunato sat upright in his chair, his dark eyes incandescent.

Paulé went on unsteadily, intimidated by her own forbidden words. 'Robert had met this William Renssaelaer before at Pelegrini's house, and since they were both Americans they had a little conversation. He knew only that Renssaelaer worked for Pelegrini in security. Some weeks later he saw Pablo by chance in the center and he followed behind him, thinking he would surprise him. Pablo was approaching a limousine with polarized windows, so Robert hurried ahead to catch him before he closed the door and disappeared. When he looked into the car, there was Renssaelaer, the American that he'd met at Pelegrini's. He didn't understand at first. And then, with the newspaper articles that had started to come out about Pelegrini's bribes at the Post Office, Robert developed a hypothesis that Renssaelaer was acting as a sort of spy, that he was really working for AmiBank, destroying Pelegrini from inside by giving his enemies information, that they passed it to the journalists like that Ricardo Berenski. And that, yes, that frightened him, because it put him in the middle. But he trusted in Pablo!' she said bitterly. 'The idiot trusted in *Pablo*!'

Paulé started crying again and Athena turned to Miguel. He had a stricken look on his face, a distant gaze into the surface of the table as if he were watching something unfold before him. She was too stunned to ask him anything but the obvious: 'Could Renssaelaer and Pablo Moya have really killed Robert Waterbury to protect their arrangement?'

Fortunato had put his hands to his temples. 'Don't talk,' he said.

'Miguel –'

'Please! Don't talk!'

She obeyed him, exchanging worried eyes with *La Francesa*, who was watching the windows and entrance nervously.

'It was Renssaelaer,' Fortunato said, almost to himself. 'It was an operation within an operation. Pelegrini wanted him squeezed for sleeping with the wife. Renssaelaer wanted him dead, knowing that after that, if necessary, he and AmiBank could put the murder on Pelegrini. Pelegrini arranged it with Santamarina, Renssaelaer kept his hands off, but he paid someone inside the squeeze to make sure Waterbury ended up dead. It was all Renssaelaer.'

'But Fabian never mentioned Renssaelaer!'

The Comisario gave a long nauseated sigh and looked silently at her for a moment before speaking. 'Because that's who Fabian is working for.'

The pieces were falling into place with a clarity that felt deceptive after so many lies. 'So you think Pablo Moya had his own friend murdered?'

'I think that probably Moya found out afterwards, but he has to go along with it. Bankers always hold their nose and protect their capital. For the good of the institution.'

She remembered the feeling of shame Moya had radiated at the interview, as if trapped in his own comfortable little hell. He'd probably get over it. People like him usually did. 'But why would Fabian tell us about Paulé if she could lead us to Renssaelaer?'

'That's an error I'm sure they intend to correct.' He looked at Paulé as he said it and the woman quivered. She'd been growing increasingly agitated as the discussion confirmed Pablo's involvement in the murder.

'Don't worry,' Athena told *La Francesa*. 'It's going to be fine.' Though her words didn't seem to comfort the woman, Athena was already swelling into a peculiar form of exultation. With this she could open the case, incite the dreaded Judge Hocht and a dozen journalists to rip people like William Renssaelaer and Pablo Moya out of the background and hold them up to the world, along with all their corrupt sponsors. 'Do you know what this means?' she asked *La Francesa*. 'With your testimony, we can start a real investigation. You can do something that –'

Fortunato interrupted, touching the dancer's arm. 'Daughter, give me your bag.'

She gave it to him and he shifted around so that he faced the wall and opened it. A purse and a pair of square-heeled black tango shoes were inside. Fortunato reached inside his sportscoat and to Athena's amazement pulled out three thick bundles of hundred-dollar bills and stuffed them into the bag. He zipped it up and put it in the shocked Paulé's lap.

'This is thirty thousand dollars. Go back to France and keep your mouth closed. If you stay here, they'll kill you. Like they killed Waterbury.'

Athena was too stunned to be angry. 'Miguel, what are you doing? This is . . .'

The Comisario kept talking to *La Francesa* in a soft voice. 'Athena can't protect you. Neither can I. They're already looking for you. If I were you I would go tonight. Don't even pack your clothes.'

The *tanguera* looked from one to the other and clutched at the bag. 'Who are you? You're not lawyers, or . . . or professors!' She stood up.

'Paulé! Wait a minute! I really am –'

'It's enough! I'm going!' She was backing away from the table.

Athena stood up. 'No! Please, Paulé. We need to punish Robert's murderers!'

La Francesa looked from one to the other of them, trembling between fear and disbelief. '*Estás loca!*' She turned and reached the door in a few strides, seeming desperate to get out into the open air.

'Paulé!' Athena cried. 'Please! For Robert!'

Waterbury's Patron Saint turned one last time towards Athena, clutching the bag that held her tango shoes and thirty thousand dollars. The face of the pornographic grimace and of cynical hope reflected a sorrow that seemed to spring from her own sense of profound failure. 'I can't!' She flickered out the door.

Athena began to go after her when she felt Fortunato's hand on her forearm.

'Let her go,' he told her. 'She's marked. They'll kill her if they have to, or even for the doubts.'

'But only she can –!'

'You have nothing to offer her, Athena. Let her go.' Athena was still pulling away and he spoke more forcefully. 'Let her go or I swear I'll make you identify her body after they put a bullet in her head!'

Now *La Francesa* was gliding across the front window of the café in the dark night. Athena turned to Fortunato and looked into his weary beaten-dog face. Whatever she needed to say was obstructed by her rage and frustration, and instead she pounded her fists against his chest. 'How could you do that! How could you do that!'

Fortunato let her hit him, impassive before her blows and the alarmed expressions of the spectators. 'Do you want her dead?'

'We need her testimony!'

'For who? Who? For the Federales? Don't joke with me! For the FBI? The FBI is controlled by your State Department, and who do you think controls your State Department? It's not your friend Carmen Amado!'

Athena looked at him, stunned. 'How do you know about Carmen Amado?'

Fortunato didn't care. He was tired of lying. 'Of course I know you went to INCORP! Of course! Do you think the police are going to hold their hands over their heads while you put your finger in their ass?'

'You've been spying on me the whole time?'

'You have been spying on *me*! With INCORP, with Berenski! Don't play the innocent!'

'This was all a farce! All of it! Your job was just to spy on me and keep me from finding the truth, because it was the police that did it, wasn't it? That's why you sent her back to France! To protect your friends!'

'I sent her back to save her life! Only that!'

'Then where did you get thirty thousand dollars? Where?'

Fortunato felt it all exploding in his head. 'I'm corrupt!' he shouted in a low intense voice. 'Corrupt! Corrupt! Do you under-stand? Do you know what that is? You, that always takes the good side? You that has never dared? I did difficult things! I did things other men are afraid to do! Of the forty-five thousand integrants of the Buenos Aires police only one in one hundred become com-isarios, and I succeeded! Do you think you could have done that?'

'Some difficult things aren't worth doing.'

'Yes. Very legalistic! I expect that from you. But I caught a man who was killing children! He had already killed three! *I* caught him! Was that worth doing? Another was a man who had violated six women! Another who had kidnapped an adolescent! I saved her life! The same as I just saved the Frenchwoman's life, that you were ready to throw away to make yourself a better résumé!'

'Don't drag me into your sewer! This has nothing to do with my résumé! You think you can justify taking bribes, and extorting money and killing people, like the police did in the Dictatorship? You –'

'I never killed anyone!' Fortunato was so carried away by the passion of his denial that in that moment he believed it. Vasquez had killed someone. Domingo had killed. 'How can you accuse me of that?'

'If you cover for assassins then you're an accomplice!' She grabbed her purse and began walking towards the door, then whipped around to face him. 'How did you explain all this to your wife, Miguel? What did you tell her when you brought home your bribes?'

'You don't know anything about my wife! She wouldn't touch the money!' Athena had reached the door and Fortunato suddenly couldn't bear to see her abandon him. 'You saw how we lived! Even when they found her cancer she wouldn't accept a trip to a specialist in the United States! That's how good she was.' Athena had stopped now, amazed at his confession. He began to falter. 'Because she thought it better to die than to accept . . .' He ran out of words then, lost in the open recognition of what he had never allowed himself to fully admit: that Marcela knew how he was and what he did, that she had tried both to absolve and to punish him with her death, and that her only way of reconciling her love for him with her condemnation was to close her eyes like the beautiful blindfolded figure above the doorway of the 17 Stone Angels.

Athena had halted near the entry, arrested by the exhausted wonder shining in his face. He spoke softly, as if surprised to hear his own words. 'I spent all my life stuffing money in a wardrobe and hiding it from my wife, playing the good one. And she knew all the time. It's incredible, no?' He had lost all caution, gave in to the compulsion to fill in the silence over which Athena gazed at him. 'I never even cared about the money.'

'Then why, Miguel? Why?'

He shook his head. He'd always answered that question internally with the rationale that it was simply how the law *was* in Argentina, that doing a little wrong enabled him to do some good. Now that justification dropped away to reveal something far simpler. 'To see if I could. And so my colleagues would think well of me.'

He had finally made it clear to her. This was the emptiness of the Joseph Carvers and the Pablo Moyas and the fine men in suits who had made the rules that ruined Argentina. Their defective dreams of grandeur were at root no different from those of the battered man before her, except that their wealth had bought them a chorus of like-minded people to validate their exploits while Miguel Fortunato had only an apprehended child-killer, a foiled kidnapping, a yellowed citation from the mayor.

Fortunato slumped back down into his chair and looked out the window. She took the seat across from him. Despite everything she knew, she couldn't bring herself to leave him.

'And now what?' she asked after a few minutes.

He answered slowly. 'You can go to the INCORP and ruin me. Call up the boys from *Pagina/12* and give them the story. They'll destroy me by the end of the week. I don't care anymore. In that case, tranquilly, I'll go home and put a bullet in my head. What does it matter?'

'But what do you want, Miguel? Really.'

A long silence went by, then he shrugged. 'Perhaps at this late stage of my life I'm taking an interest in justice.' He composed himself a bit, and she saw the old competent Comisario Fortunato return. He took out a cigarette, lit it. 'There are a few inquiries I still need to make. But I think tomorrow it will be clearer.'

'Miguel, I have to be honest about what's happened. That might make problems for you.'

He gave the fatalistic sneer of the Porteño, but underlaid by a deep melancholy. 'It already is, daughter. It already is. There will be no happy finale for Fortunato.'

He dropped her off a few blocks from the Sheraton and looked at his watch. Eleven o'clock. His cell phone rang and he picked it up. Cacho's voice came through.

'We have a package for you, Comiso.'

CHAPTER 30

It was a turnkey *capacho*, with the former urban guerilla supplying everything. He procured a woman from the furthest outskirts of the city and floated her into the Cyclone with Hugo, who would point out Vasquez in the crowd. The dance music came crashing over everything like an incessant wave that made conversation impossible at less than a shout, but the woman found ways to get his attention. An hour later they were stumbling out the door, Vasquez congratulating himself on his charm and the returns he could get on his *merca*. They walked around the corner and down one of the shady side streets. 'My apartment is this way,' the woman said, and she seemed as surprised as Vasquez himself when the three men closed in quickly and calmly from the shadows.

'Christian, *que tal?*' Cacho said, extending his hand. 'How are things going in Mataderos?' Hugo closed in from behind as Vasquez tried to sort out the sudden change of signals going through his brain. In the initial seconds, he was still trying to get rid of Cacho so he could go on to claim the girl, but as he felt things closing in he held on to Cacho's reassuring smile. Hugo chambered a round in his semi-automatic, Chispa pointed his weapon at the victim's groin. '*Tranquilo*, Christian. We don't want an accident.' '*Dios mio!*' the girl gasped, then clicked off down the street in an ungainly trot.

'They sent you to cut me, didn't they?'

'It's not for so much, Christian,' Cacho said as he removed the .32 revolver from Vasquez's belt. 'It's just to chat a little, to ask a few questions. Then you can go back to chasing the *mina*.' They had him cuffed and in the car in seconds, went gliding through the streets with the windows rolled up and a tape of the Rolling Stones punched into the cassette. The great Mick Jagger was singing 'Gimme Shelter', while the chords of the guitar strayed over Vasquez's sullen frown.

It reminded Cacho of when they'd grabbed General Lopez. That time they'd had to kill the bodyguards, had lost a man in the shootout. Vincente something: a student of biochemistry from the university. It was a good commando, but all dead by 1975, the poor stiffs. Victory or Death for Argentina. Not just a few *lucas* and a favor for the police. They'd named each commando in honor of some fallen comrade. His first one had been the Commando Antonio Fernandez, then the Commando Heroes de Trelew, the Commando José Luis Baxter. Then all these years of nameless commandos forged from delinquents with no ideas of a better world or a just society. And this one? The Commando Ricardo Berenski? No. Not really. A time arrived when the only dignity left lay in not lying to oneself.

By the time the Comisario reached his house Vasquez was already cuffed to a chair. He had slumped his lanky body as deeply into the heavy wooden chair as he could, his legs akimbo. At Fortunato's entrance Vasquez instinctively drew his knees together, then replaced his momentary expression of dread with a smug grin. 'Comisario Fortunato! Here we are!'

'Here we are, Christian. How is your foot? Recovering well?'

'Yes. I can be in perfect shape when you dump me out of the trunk of your car.'

'*Christian!* I'm sorry you have such a low opinion of me. Such things aren't necessary if you don't make them so.' Fortunato signaled to Cacho that he wanted to be alone with the prisoner and then he pulled a chair up a meter in front of Vasquez, the way he did at his police interrogations. He could see from Vasquez's brilliant eyes that the cocaine and the alcohol were still lending him a sense of immortality.

'Let me guess,' the criminal said, exposing a little crescent of yellowed teeth. 'You're trying to solve the Waterbury murder. Looking for Enrique Boguso's accomplices.'

Fortunato stood up. 'You have a lively sense of humor for a man tied to a chair.' He hit him hard across the face. The criminal flinched away from the open hand and Fortunato caught him across the ear, a blow that almost burst his ear-drum. A strange sensation for Fortunato: he'd never beaten a bound man before. That was the job of the Bad Cops. He usually came in afterward, to coax out a confession with *mate* and promises. The bureaucrat. The guardian angel. Now he was pleased to see the ear turn bright pink, thought of that old tango about the man who beat his unfaithful wife to death: *And the bifes rained down like applause at the Teatro Colón.* He could understand the man in the tango, a working stiff sick of the lies and the broken promises. A man deceived by everyone.

Vasquez grasped immediately the new game and dropped into a sullen silence.

'I'm going to ask you some questions and you're going to sing. Are we clear?'

'Just kill me,' Vasquez said. 'That's what you were sent to do.'

Fortunato recognized it as the criminal's first bargaining position. He was begging Fortunato to make an offer. 'And who would send me to do that? Who would want to cut you?'

'Don't treat me like an adolescent.'

Fortunato stood and took off his jacket, draping it across the back of the chair. Something he'd seen a hundred times, coming into a room and spying the jackets hung over the chairs. No one wanted to ruin a good suit. Vasquez recognized the symbolism also.

'What are you looking for, Comiso? You already have all the answers.'

Fortunato stepped up and backhanded him across the face. 'What "Comiso!" To you I'm Comisario Fortunato. Understood?' He took out his nine millimeter and Vasquez's eyes were sucked in by its black gravity. The criminal had a small trickle of blood welling up in his split lip.

'I understand.'

'Say it!'

'I understand, Comisario Fortunato.'

'Fine, Christian. Now we'll chat a bit.' Fortunato became the Good Cop again, his face beaming compassionately at a benign distance from human failure. Cacho had heard the sound of the blows and was standing at the doorway, watching. Fortunato could tell that he was nervous about the gun being out.

'*Mirá.* I have no interest in judging you, *muchacho.* I just need a few answers so that we can both leave here and go back to our own things. But amigo Christian' – he looked almost sorrowful as he tapped his gun on Vasquez's leg – 'if you don't help me, it's going to come out badly.'

Cacho spoke quickly. 'Tell him, *boludo.* The Comisario is talking seriously.'

'What can I know that you don't?' Vasquez tried to reason with him. 'You were there from beginning to end.' His arrogant slum-voice had lost much of its force and Fortunato was pleased to see the improvement in his attitude.

'Listen well, Christian. I know that the gringo's death wasn't an accident. I know that someone else ordered it. I want to hear your version of that history.'

'I don't know what –'

Fortunato swung the barrel of the Browning up and around and caught Vasquez across the jaw with it. A fleshy little pop came as the criminal yelped and rocked to the side. 'What's happening with you, Christian? This is how you treated the gringo! It was fun then, wasn't it? Isn't it fun now?' He back-handed him with the gun from the other side, catching him on the nose. Vasquez cried out with pain.

Cacho was yelling at him from the door. 'Enough, Miguel! We didn't agree on this!'

'He won't talk.'

'Put the gun away,' he told the Comisario. Fortunato stuck the gun in his waistband while the former guerilla fetched a tissue and dabbed at the slime under Vasquez's nose, held a glass of water to his mouth. '*El Comisario esta loco*, Vasquez,' he muttered anxiously. 'Tell him what he wants to know, or he's going to kill you.'

Fortunato liked the introduction. *Or he's going to kill you.* He wished Waterbury were around to see this, to see that his murder was being redressed. *I am writing your ending for you, Waterbury. One sentence at a time.* The night had assumed its own logic now, and Fortunato found himself drawn along its strangely joyful lineaments.

Vasquez had slumped down in his chair and was staring silently at the floor, and the Comisario put his face a few inches from the criminal's, adopting his most sympathetic tone. 'It was Domingo, wasn't it? Domingo used you for something you never intended.' The detective reached over and touched Vasquez gently on the shoulder. 'It's fine, Christian. I understand. Tell me now who it was, we can pass you by and take up the matter with the proper person. You will return to how you were before, with my gratitude and excellent relations with the Institution. Because it seems that Domingo betrayed his *compañeros* in the Force.'

Vasquez didn't reply, and Fortunato developed the theme. 'This concerns Domingo, not you. Domingo went beyond his authority. You only did what you thought you were supposed to. You were tricked. As I was. Domingo played you. That's why you're sitting here right now, and he's at home with his wife drinking red wine and watching Boca versus Almirante Brown.'

Vasquez began to break. 'The whore! I knew I shouldn't get involved with the cops.'

'Clearly. But there he is, in front of the television figuring out how he'll cut you. And you, Christian, are here with me.' He pulled the chair closer. 'So why don't you make it easy and tell what you know. Then we can be done with this mess and go home.'

'If Domingo finds out I talked, he'll kill me.'

Fortunato gave a rich chuckle. 'He intends to kill you anyway, Christian. I know, because he asked me to help. But if you're clean with me, Domingo will be taken care of long before he thinks to look for Christian Vasquez. It's simple. I confirm who is responsible, my people take care of the situation, and the whole matter disappears. We're very close to that, Christian. You only need to confirm the last pieces.'

The criminal reconstituted himself as best he could with his puffy mouth and swollen nose. He spoke with a slight lisp. 'It was all Domingo. Domingo said someone wanted the Northamerican dead. There was an extra three thousand for me if he ended up dead.'

Fortunato sensed the presence of the truth, though how whole or plain he wasn't sure. 'Go on.'

'Domingo wanted me to fire the first shots so you wouldn't know he was behind it. He said you thought it was only a squeeze.'

'Who? Who wanted him dead?' He leaned in. 'Give me a name, Christian.'

'I don't know who, but that night, before we grabbed the gringo, I heard Domingo report to someone on his cellular. He had a gringo name, that's why I remembered it. *Renssaelaer*. Something like that. Señor Renssaelaer.'

Fortunato went silent. So *La Francesa* had been right. William Renssaelaer had been spying on Pelegrini for RapidMail and Ami-Bank and he'd had Waterbury cut to protect his arrangement. And he, Fortunato, had been played, played badly, made into an accessory to an innocent man's murder. He felt his anger rising again. 'What others were in on it?'

'I know nothing more! I swear!'

'Comisario Bianco?' he shouted into his face.

'I don't know!'

'And Fabian Diaz?'

'I told you everything!'

He stepped back from the prisoner and walked in a tight aimless circle. His gaze ended up on Cacho. 'You see!' he growled. 'You see! I didn't kill him! They played me! They played me, the *hijos de puta*!' He crossed quickly to Vasquez and shouted at him. 'You played me!'

'It was Domingo –'

'What, *Domingo*! Don't put it on Domingo! You beat the gringo! You terrorized him! You shot him to start everything!'

'*Tranquilo*, Miguel,' Cacho warned. 'You already have your information. You need to get out of here and settle accounts somewhere else.'

The enraged policeman clenched his fists. 'Shut up, Cacho! He played me!'

Cacho's black eyes started to blaze. 'Get out!'

'But they played me!'

Cacho's protection made Vasquez swell up again. 'So they played you,' the criminal sneered. 'What's it matter? You're as dirty as the rest of them, you son of a bitch!'

Fortunato whipped out his gun and raised it, blanking Vasquez' features with surprise and fear. In the corner of his mind he heard Cacho shout 'Noooo!' and then the Browning exploded in his hand, and Vasquez's body lunged backward in its chair and then slumped down, an angry red stain blossoming over his heart. The fist in which Fortunato held the pistol seemed far away from him, as if it was floating out there, attached to someone else's body. The savory smell of the gun's exhaust filled the room, and he became aware that Cacho was still screaming at him. '*Hijo de puta!* Are you crazy? Are you crazy?' The words faded again as he saw Vasquez twitch a few more times. Slowly, he lowered the gun and turned his face to Cacho. The criminal had his pistol out and was holding it with both hands in front of him, pointing it at the side of Fortunato's head as he screamed a torrent of swear words. 'Drop it! Drop it!' Two of Cacho's gang were standing at the door with their weapons drawn on him. He lowered his gun slowly, dazed, and put it into his holster.

Cacho was screaming. 'Look what you did, you son of a bitch!

This is your shit! Not my shit! Now what am I supposed to do with him? You take him away!'

The bloodstain had spread down to Vasquez' waist now, reddening the tops of his blue jeans. Fortunato looked at Cacho, spoke in an even voice. 'Vasquez killed Waterbury. He had to die.'

Cacho didn't lower the gun, but he seemed to relax into a wary disbelief. '*Estás loco, hombre!* You're crazy. *Chiflado!* I should kill you for dragging me into this.' He nodded towards the door. 'Get out and take this piece of shit with you!'

They dragged the body out to the courtyard and slumped it into the trunk of Fortunato's car. Cacho kept his pistol in his hand the whole time, pointing the gun at the Comisario. He didn't relax as Fortunato climbed in and started the engine.

Fortunato put the car in gear and then glanced up at the former subversive. For a moment Cacho's anger dropped away and a softer expression came over his face.

'What are you going to do, Miguel?'

Fortunato looked straight through the windshield and then back at Cacho. 'A wrong has been committed. One has to rectify the situation.'

Cacho stared at him silently, finally speaking in a gentle voice. 'You poor *boludo*.' He leaned down towards the open window. 'Welcome to the Revolution.'

CHAPTER 31

The truth was, Hell felt curiously invigorating. He drove down the dark blighted street, with Vasquez riding along in the trunk like a piece of evidence sequestered for an investigation in which all the answers were already known. He was guilty, guilty of everything and yet innocent in some peculiar way.

He thought of Bianco in a blue suit, or his white one. Bianco at La Gloria and in his office at Central. Bianco smiling and Bianco wearing that hard expression of resolve. Bianco in 1976, beating that newborn baby to make the mother talk. Bianco, the brotherly superior who had brought him up through the ranks.

His cell phone chirped and he patted his body until he found the phone the Chief had given him.

'*Comisario!*' Domingo addressed him with his usual slick mockery. Bar music was blaring in the background.

Fortunato remembered that he and Domingo were scheduled to cut Vasquez that night, but the mortal remains of Christian Vasquez were currently riding along two meters behind him. Now Domingo would say that he couldn't locate the target and that they would have to cut him another night. Everything fine. The night would never come, the matter would fade. He would figure out how to deal with Domingo later. And the Chief? Better now to play the *boludo*.

'Where are you?' the Inspector Fausto demanded.

'I'm at a petrol station on the Accesso Norte, just outside of Lomas de San Isidro.' He was actually in Liniers, fifteen kilometers from the Accesso Norte.

'What are you doing out there?'

'I went to a friend's birthday party. What's the plan?'

'I'm at the Cyclone, near Liniers. Vasquez is waiting for me outside.'

Domingo sounded so certain that Fortunato had to reassure

himself that he'd just killed Vasquez twenty minutes ago. It took Fortunato a moment to come to grips with the realization that Domingo could only have one reason for claiming that Vasquez was with him.

The eternal reflex: an idiot face. 'Very good. Has anyone seen you with Vasquez?'

'No.'

In that, at least, the *hijo de puta* spoke the truth. He imagined the puffy face, oily and pocked, the face of the schoolyard bully grown into an adult. 'So, what plan do you have?'

'I'll pay him for Onda, and after I give him the money I'll invite him to go to a *kilombo* in San Justo. Do you know the one at the corner of Conde and Benito Perez?'

'Near the old appliance factory,' Fortunato offered. It had once been a whorehouse for factory workers of the zone, but as the factories were globalized they had adjusted by expanding into an hourly hotel for illicit lovers. The bureaucrat at the back of his head noted that they paid a thousand pesos on the tenth of each month.

'That's it.'

'It's a good choice,' Fortunato complimented him coolly. 'It's half-deserted. Tranquil.'

'Exactly. Vasquez and I have gone there before, so it's nothing unusual. I'll park around the corner in front of the loading door of the factory. I'll make sure he's had some drinks and some *merca*. You wait in the lot next to the factory. We pull up from the direction of Triumvirato. He gets out the car, you step out behind and finish him and we load him into the trunk. We can do it all in fifteen seconds. If there's someone around I pass a minute looking for my cigarettes on the floor of the car, and then you cork him.'

'And the body?'

'I have a place in Tigre, in the swamps. Do you have a clean iron?'

'Yes. When do you want me there?'

'In a half-hour, around one. I'll show up with Christian between one and one thirty. *Está?*'

Fortunato could get to the whorehouse in ten minutes. 'That's too soon,' he said, letting his voice weaken a little at the protest. 'I might hit traffic. Give me until one-fifteen.'

'Fine. Between one-thirty and two I'll bring him.'

The Comisario let a note of sincerity warm his voice. 'Thanks for arranging this, Domingo. We'll all rest better afterwards.'

Domingo hesitated for a few seconds. 'Clearly, Comiso. But you can thank the Chief.'

Fortunato held the dead plastic to his ear after Domingo hung up. So they were going to kill him. The dull recognition that he should be frightened passed before him, but that fear gave way before a sense of insult. They wanted to kill him! Him! A Comisario Mayor with thirty-seven years of service in the Institution! When had that decision been made? He could imagine the conversation between the Chief and Domingo when they'd decided to cut him. *He's spent, the old man. He was always too soft. Too weak!* That from Bianco, his 'friend.' *He's incompetent*, Domingo would answer. *A coward. Better we get rid of him before he turns pink and starts singing.* Maybe one of Pelegrini's men had been there too, in his fine suit and his military cut, still not realizing that Waterbury's accidental death had been planned from the beginning. *We should have cut him the first time he fucked up, the idiot.* Or saying nothing, just smirking. *He'll be as easy to kill as Waterbury.*

They would expect him to be stupid, to walk right into the muzzle of a gun like a retard. How rapid they'd all imagined themselves in arranging Waterbury's murder! So easy to kill an innocent. Because Waterbury, in the end, was in other things, he was in his world of destiny, of writing his books and returning home to his family. He didn't pay attention. But he, Fortunato, was now without family or hope. And they certainly had his attention. Now they would see who was more *piola*. He turned the car towards the abandoned factory.

The Comisario felt a rush of feeling he'd never known before. Maybe this was how it was supposed to turn out. Maybe he was on a new path now, or the path he'd once had a foot on but left behind to climb the ranks of the Institution. He, who'd never believed in destiny or in causes, had become the avenger. A proxy. The man who had to finish Waterbury's novel.

A contrary thought blew in. He could still escape. With the half-million in his briefcase he could drive to the border of Paraguay and have himself smuggled across, get a new passport and identity. Easy for him in Paraguay, with his policeman's nose. From there, to Brazil, someplace near the beach, with flowers on the porch. Invent a past in insurance or real estate. *El Porteño*, people would call him. A half-million could last a long time in such a place, living simply, investing well.

But no. Fortunato didn't run. Better to die in one's own law than to flee the rest of his life. Something he had always respected in Cacho and the doomed integrants of the People's Revolutionary Army. Most of them died rather than flee. This life was over. Only the exact time and place remained a mystery; a mystery whose solution he intended to find right away.

He reached Ramos Mejia. The dark facades of the upper-story buildings faced each other in the air, laden with flowers and shields. Frozen garlands of victory draped over shabby doorways, wrapped across grimy columns. The sound of the transit trains muttering along Rivadavia bumped in through the open window carrying a cargo of intense nostalgia, a sound of his childhood. A memory came to him of standing beside the tracks with his father, holding a pail of something. Every traffic light seemed a supernatural red or green, like the overly intense colors of the broken television screen. Heartbreakingly beautiful colors; the most beautiful he'd ever seen. He was a dead man now. Nothing more than a spirit, living in a city of spirits. From a great distance he observed the lovers clustered together at the street corners and the diners above their steel plates in the wide glowing windows of the restaurants. All of life was burning around him, filled with people believing intensely in their loves or their scanty hoards of knowledge. He'd always kept away from passion, from believing in anything too deeply. That was the realm of teachers and soldiers, of the crusading human rights workers and the great lovers. A world of delusion, filled with false ideas like Waterbury's destiny or Athena's mission. Life was always payable in cash, he told Marcela. Not in silly dreams. In the end, his own life had come payable just like all others.

He bore down on the situation at hand, cool again, thinking like a cop. He would reach the abandoned factory in five minutes. He had to be rapid now, more rapid than he'd ever been in his life. Domingo intended to get there first to ambush him when he arrived. His one chance: to get there before Domingo and kill him as he stepped out of the car. If anyone were with him he would kill the passenger first, through the side window, then take out Domingo before he knew which direction the attack was coming from.

A dead man now, he had to think like a dead man, without fear or excitement. In five minutes he had reached the area of the *kilombo*. He stopped his car two blocks away and walked up to the corner to have a look. The streetlight down there didn't function and the darkness looked musty. The uncertain shadows bore no sign of Domingo's car, but Domingo wouldn't be so stupid as to park right in front. Racking his memory of a place he'd driven past a hundred times over the years as a young *ayudante* and sub-inspector, back when the factory had clanged in double shifts and the trucks had roared off from the loading dock filled with products stamped *Industria Argentina*. What remained? An opening now covered over with corrugated metal, an empty lot that had once held sheet steel and enamel paint. In his mind it merged with the weedy space they'd left Waterbury in: another flat weedy rectangle.

Fortunato took out his Browning and snapped off the safety, chambering the first round with a dry mechanical click. It occurred to him he should have gotten a clean gun, but there hadn't been time for that. A good policeman had to improvise.

He began walking carefully towards the factory, keeping close to the wall on the other side of the street. The leaves had fallen from the plane trees and he could hear the wide dry platters scraping beneath his feet, as loud as cannonfire. The air had the curry smell of autumn, of dust and motor oil, of metal. He expected that they might have a lookout at the next corner, and the emptiness of the street encouraged him. He kept walking, slowly, passing the side of an abandoned warehouse, an overgrown spur of track that had once served the local factories. A breeze rustled through the branches overhead and the dim charcoal light that penetrated them slithered over his shoulders in little pieces. No sign of anyone. He surveyed the shadowy limits of the factory and the lot and saw a dark space at the back. He remembered now that a narrow passage cut from the back of the lot over to the next street: his escape route. Fine; that was covered. But how to ambush them? If he succeeded in that, he wouldn't be needing an escape route.

Domingo had told him to wait in the empty lot, then to step out and cork Vasquez after he parked the car. They would assume that Fortunato would park his car on the least trafficked street, where he had. They would assume he was approaching from the south, in which case they would want to have someone against the south wall of the empty lot. They would station a lookout a block away with a radio, he would give the signal, and when Fortunato came up he would step out: tock! tock! *Adios, Comiso.*

So they would want to kill him in the lot. Here the first good fortune: an old guard shack made of corrugated tin was collapsing in the front corner near the street, where Fortunato was supposed to wait. It looked dark and diseased; no good even for the destitute madmen who had begun to pile up around the city. The silhouette of the roof slanted at a ruinous angle to the walls, one of which was tumbling slowly inward. The door formed an opaque black rectangle, as if printed on a piece of paper. He could wait there until Domingo approached, as perhaps Domingo had been planning to wait for him. The window that had once looked out on the street had been partly covered by a piece of wood, and the vertical gap at its edge gave him a narrow field of vision and room to stick the barrel of his nine millimeter. After that, there was no predicting.

He heard rats scratching around the back edges of the lot, and as he approached the tin structure he heard their metallic skitterings inside. The shack had the odor of human feces and a form of decay he didn't want to identify. He tried to let his eyes adjust but he could make out only a few slanting timbers in the darkness. Rusty corrugations flexed beneath his feet with a low booming sound as he picked his way through. He moved over to the crack and waited.

Always the devil, this waiting. This might be his last fifteen minutes, and he was spending it sitting in a tin coffin with the smell of shit in his nose and the scurrying of rats in his ears. Maybe it was a fitting end. Outside the shack the little sliver of night world looked dreamy and calm. His eyes had adjusted to the dark and he could see the black tree trunks against the translucent penumbra on the other side of the street. Something beautiful about even such a simple sight, of the dim sparkle of the pavement, the arching forms of the weeds in the dirty pink city light. A tiny fragment of the Buenos Aires that he now felt receding from him even as it had never seemed closer. He remembered this area from when he'd been a child, all grassy fields and ditches filled with singing frogs. Gone now. He'd never been a dishonest child or adolescent. Not even one of those cops who go around flashing their badges and asking for handouts. Who could foresee all the forces that pushed a life this way and that? His mother had always said that a simple sense of decency is the only guide a person needs in life, but when those around you had a different sense, one learned to see the world their way.

A figure came walking up to the lot, and he recognized Domingo's portly silhouette. He held something in his hand, but Fortunato couldn't make out what it was. The Inspector looked around, then called softly, 'Comisario! Comisario!'

Domingo waited and Fortunato held absolutely still. The soft, respectful timbre of the call brought on a strange nostalgia, and he had an unexpected urge to answer back. Maybe then everything would return to how it had been before: Domingo and Fabian the dutiful inferiors, everyone loyal to the Institution and the game. He drifted for a moment in that quiet fantasy, then Domingo dispelled it by taking a walkie-talkie out of his pocket and murmuring into it. In a minute a second man came walking up from the same direction. In the pale pink light reflected from the clouds Fortunato recognized Santamarina. They hissed through the weeds into the shadow of the factory wall less than three meters away from him. Fortunato reasoned that he could always stand there and do nothing until they gave up and went away.

'It was very considerate of him to advise us he might be late,' Santamarina said.

'The Comiso is always very punctual. A man of great confidence.'

They laughed, and the rats, emboldened by the renewed stillness in the shed, began to scurry among the metal. Both men looked towards Fortunato.

'It's rats,' Domingo said. Santamarina examined the shed a while longer, then turned away. Domingo continued, 'What if he has his gun in his hand when he shows up?'

'You'll just have to be a good actor. "Oh, Comisario! Forgive me!" Look regretful: that Vasquez wandered off, that the *operativo* is cancelled. Things like that, until you can get close to him.'

'I can tell him we had to put it off because I didn't finish the necessary paperwork!' Domingo joked. 'That's his style.'

Fortunato's stomach hardened. *Laugh*, gil. *Laugh*. Any thought of waiting quietly for them to leave disappeared. One had to confront it. Slowly, he raised his gun to the opening. He would shoot Domingo first, a quick one into the back, then get Santamarina before he had time to realize what had happened. With luck he could get out the back opening to the lot before the lookouts knew who had gone down. After that, perhaps Paraguay.

Slowly, careful not to shift his weight on the corrugated tin, he brought the gun towards the gap. Both were facing away from him. A pity. He would have enjoyed shooting Domingo in the front. Better thus. Even now, one could still blunder and get killed. A little more, threading his arm around the encumbrances of a fallen shelf and a nail. Another two seconds and Domingo would be in his sights.

The incongruous beeping sang out from his hip with the force of an air raid siren. For a couple of pulses he simply listened to it in disbelief. His cell phone!

The two men snapped around. 'In the shed!' In an instant they were moving in opposite directions, and before Fortunato could take aim they had both gotten out of the line of sight of the crack, Santamarina circling behind him and Domingo moving across in front, hidden by the wall of tin.

Fortunato lurched towards the door, desperate to get a shot off at Domingo before the Inspector could prepare himself. He still had the advantage. They couldn't see into the dark shed, and he might be some other cop, or another operative. They would have to try to see who it was before they opened fire. He scrambled over the tin, thrusting his left hand into the darkness to ward off any obstructions, but then something caught at his foot and as he tried to lurch onto his other leg a piece of tin seemed to clamp down on it at the ankle.

Slowly he fell, sickeningly, with all the time in the world to realize what a failure he was, shot to death in a tin shack that smelled like human shit. He landed unevenly on his stomach, bruising his forearm, his head and shoulders sticking out the doorway into the impossibly clear and open night air. A pair of trousers flickered at the edge of his vision and then a soft white light seemed to go off in his head along with an impact at the base of his skull.

Fortunato remembered a time he'd played in the ocean as a child. A wave had knocked him down and tumbled him over and over through the surf. Strange to have it happening again now. He felt himself being lifted and turned, unevenly carried through a frothing white noise. A dull cold ache pulled at his wrists. Vague phrases at the edge of the long tranquil gulf.

'He must weigh a hundred kilos, the pig! He's worse than the journalist!'

A high resonance in his head, like the humming of an electric current. The wave receded and left him lying on his back on a hard even surface. He kept his eyes closed, listening to the world with a sleepy contentment.

A voice he didn't recognize: 'Here's the rope.'

The lethargy receded slowly. Domingo, Santamarina. The shed. A rope.

'How is he?'

His eyelids turned into an orange curtain as a flashlight beam played across his face. 'He's still out,' Domingo said from just above his head. 'If we hurry there's no great drama.'

'Maybe we should strangle him first,' the unknown third one suggested.

Santamarina answered. 'No. Let's do it clean. I don't want problems at the forensic examination.'

'Comisario Bianco can take care of that,' Domingo offered, but no one answered.

It was becoming clear. They would hang him. For that reason he'd been told to clean out his files: they would make it look like the last desperate act of a guilty cop. Leon would be the one explaining things. His friend, Leon! *Poor Fortunato. He was never the same after his wife died! And the pressure of having his role in the Waterbury murder exposed . . . It was too much!* Fortunato heard a soft scraping high over his head and then something flopping beside him. The rope had been thrown over a beam. Domingo kneeled by his head, probably fashioning a noose. What would he do? Three adversaries, his gun gone. He could feel the cuffs on his hands. Cuffed in front, like Waterbury.

An upwelling of fear came surging out of his stomach and pumped a jolt of adrenaline into his system. He didn't want to hang! To die with a rope around his neck, in defeat, with Domingo and Santamarina smoking cigarettes and telling jokes while they waited to make sure. Fortunato the *boludo*! Fortunato the incompetent, who didn't have the balls to kill anyone properly without shitting himself about it afterwards.

'What did he say in his note?' Domingo asked aloud.

Santamarina answered. 'He confesses to the murder, the *puta*. That Waterbury tried to blackmail Don Carlo and that when Don Carlo asked the police to investigate it, he killed the gringo in the hope of gaining favor. He mentions Berenski also. After, we'll tie him to Berenski and calm the whole thing.'

'Did you mention his wife? She always thought she was too good to associate with police.'

'The dear departed wife. Of course. Now they can be together eternally.'

284

Domingo's laugh scraped out from two feet above his head, then Fortunato felt his head being lifted and the slithery weight of a rope around his neck. 'Give me more light here,' Domingo said, and the soft wall of color before his eyes flickered from dark umber to orange again. He felt Domingo tightening the noose. 'You can give my regards to your bitch of a wife.'

Fortunato struggled to control his breath. In only seconds it would be too late, and yet with the adrenaline pumping through his veins he felt acutely alive and so molten with hatred. He hated Domingo. He hated the casual Santamarina, and Bianco who had set him up for all this. To die by Domingo's hand, to be dispatched like that dog on the street three weeks before. Domingo's look of contentment that time: *I was doing him a favor.*

The image of that moment flickered back to him; the dead animal and the screaming boy, Domingo's satisfied face as he knelt to put the .25 back in his ankle holster. Always so proud of that little gun. Always with his ankle holster because he was the Man of Action, the Bad One from the television show who sneered at the victim before he killed him. Domingo and his ankle holster . . .

Fortunato's mind suddenly veered from its red haze of anger and became cool again. It was the left ankle that had the holster. The ankle just inches from his head. Domingo would be using both hands to tie the noose right now. Would the safety be on? Would a round be chambered? At least he might put a round into Domingo, force them to shoot him. No. Better to wait. Maybe they were only testing him, or some rescuer would suddenly appear. Absurdly, Fabian's voice mocked him from the back of his head: 'In the detective novel, the hero always goes for the gun.'

Santamarina said, 'Point the light up here for a minute,' and Fortunato's eyelids turned black again. His best chance. One could make all the calculations in the world, but in the end it came down to the moment. Domingo's shoe ground softly against the dirty pavement. Fortunato took a slow deep breath. If he was going to commit suicide, at least he would do it on his own terms.

He rolled, reaching blindly with his cuffed hands toward the ankle above his head. The smooth leather curves of Domingo's shoe came under his fingers, then his manacled hands closed on the ankle like two pouncing spiders, working their way quickly under the cuff to where the hard irregular lump of the holster hunched.

'*Que . . . ?*' Domingo said.

Fortunato felt the rounded angles of the automatic surging from the leather. He had twisted onto his side now, could see Domingo's kneeling legs and the black V of his crotch in the flashlight beam. The Inspector tried to stand up but Fortunato yanked at the ankle and brought him off balance. Santamarina, with urgency: 'Hit him!'

Now he heard Domingo swearing and felt him tearing at his fingers. He felt a blow at his ear, but he had the gun partly out of the holster, enough to get his finger into the trigger, to flip off the safety. The gun went off only a few inches from his head, shooting through the holster and into Domingo's leg. A scream, the sudden dark weight across his body. He had the gun now, was pointing into Domingo's crotch from below. His hand tightened and he felt the hot backblast of the gasses against his fist, then a stickiness as Domingo's screaming became a high choking wail. Domingo's legs were kicking around his head now and he fired again and the kicking stopped. The flashlight was directly in his eyes now, and he heard another gun go off and Domingo's body jumped with the impact.

'Give me light! I need my gun!' Santamarina screamed, and Fortunato grasped that Santamarina had put his gun down to manage the rope and couldn't find it.

The light! Fortunato jerked his hands free and shot in the direction of the light as another roar erupted behind him and another bullet went shuddering into Domingo's body. He fired again at the bright circle. A strange gasp went through the dark space, and the flashlight fell to the ground, pointing away from him and towards the wall. The radiant afterimage of the light kept burning white in his retina, Santamarina somewhere above him, with a gun now. Another cannon blast and he heard an impact and felt a tingling at the side of his face as little chips of concrete spattered his cheek. He stretched upward with the gun in his manacled hands and Domingo's black leather shoes sprawled on either side of his face, saw Santamarina's faint smudge edging the white circle of afterflash. Blinding light, a rush of air along his arm. Another flash, Domingo's leg flinching at his stomach, then a stab of heat in his gut. Fortunato rolled halfway beneath the dead weight and aimed upside down from the floor. Shooting through the round ghost of light that haunted his retina, he fired, fired again, heard a shout of surprise and pain above the ringing in his

286

ears, then Santamarina went tumbling off the loading dock and onto the floor behind him, writhing slowly against the oil-stained cement.

Fortunato pushed Domingo's body aside and tried to sit up, but as he did he felt the noose tightening around his neck and a wave of horror lurched through him. As he worked the noose off he felt giddy, as if the old Fortunato had departed and left a new, better version in his place. The protruding slide of the .25 reminded him that it had no more bullets, and he wiped it down quickly on Domingo's bloody jacket and left it on the floor. Ignoring the pain that minced his stomach, he came to his feet and tried to put some order to the scene that had a moment ago been nothing but sound and flashes.

A weak illumination bounced off the wall from the discarded flashlight. Santamarina was groaning softly and there were faint sounds of movement from the body near the door. Domingo lay still and dark, an evil shadow against the vague surface of the floor. *Kill me, you son of a bitch? How stupid is Fortunato now?* He kicked him in the side, then made out Santamarina's gun lying several feet away from him. He picked it up: a .357 Magnum revolver with three shots expended and three in the cylinder. Santamarina was groaning, curling into a fetal position and holding his chest. *Kill me? Cursed torturer! Now who is the owner of life and death?* Fortunato bent down and pointed the .357 at Santamarina's head. The gun exploded into Santamarina's skull, and Fortunato moved through the dim light to the doorway. The third man was rolling from side to side, groaning. A lucky shot from that distance: the small bullet of the .25 had hit him in the throat. Santamarina's colleague from La Gloria three weeks ago. Fortunato put the muzzle of the .357 next to the man's heart and pulled the trigger, taking in the ferocious report as if it were the opening blast of a symphony. He watched the body jerk and then become still. *Strangle me now, bastard!* The butt of his own Browning stuck out of the man's waistband, and Fortunato pulled it out. He picked up the flashlight and looked over three dead men with a feeling of deep satisfaction. A pool of blood was dyeing the noose they'd intended for him. All tranquil now. *A good piece of work, eh Domingo?* He found Domingo's keychain and quickly unfastened the cuffs from his hand. 'Give my regards to Vasquez.' As if in answer, Domingo moved, and Fortunato pointed the nine millimeter at his skull and ruined his head in a burst of metal and fire. He heard himself say in an amiable tone: 'I was doing you a favor, *boludo*.'

An undefined sense of urgency sprang from the fresh carnage as the analytical part of his mind made its first weak attempts to reassert control. The sound of Santamarina's radio clicking, a soft staticky voice. '*Que pasa, Abel?*' He forced himself back to the scene. A fourth man, the lookout, was wondering about the shots. He would be approaching, checking it out carefully.

Fortunato turned off the flashlight and put it in his pocket. The memory of light persisted in his old eyes as all memories persisted, floating across the screen of the present. He could run, of course. That would be most cautious. But caution felt like something exceedingly frivolous right now, so far from the essential ingredients of the world. The universe had gone out of balance some time ago, and it couldn't be brought to equilibrium with the old methods. He was Fortunato, now. He had a job to finish.

A granite-colored glow oozed through a gap between the wall and ceiling, barely enough to make out the dim shadows of the bodies against the floor. The sentry would be coming, approaching the closed door with caution and a bit of fear. He would have his gun out, would be wondering what had gone wrong and who had been hit, he might guess that the final rounds had been finishing shots. What he would never suspect would be that Fortunato would be the last one standing. Fortunato waited silently to the side of the closed door, pointing his nine millimeter at the tin in front of him. He heard the sound of footsteps in the leaves that filled the gutter, saw a flashlight playing against the cracks of the crooked doorway. The man approached closer, calling softly. 'Abel! Abel!'

The calling stopped, and Fortunato heard his footsteps mount the curb and scutter against the pavement by the door. Only a half meter of space and the thin sheet of tin separated him from Fortunato now. The slim crack of light around the door began to widen.

Fortunato fired through the wall in three evenly spaced shots, heard a cry, then stepped quickly into the doorway. The man had turned and was shooting wildly at the wall, and before he could get his bearings Fortunato fired again and the man went spiraling to the pavement. The Comisario shot him again in the chest, then sent a round into the man's head, watching him quiver there on the sidewalk like a fish that had just received the sharp hard blow of the club. *La concha de tu madre.*

288

The Comisario started laughing, listening to the dry mad sound of his mirth and feeling better than he had in his entire life. They were dead, all four of them, and he was still breathing the night air. *He!* Comisario Fortunato of the 35th Precinto. The *boludo* who was supposed to have committed suicide five minutes before to suit the plans of bigger men! He wished Waterbury could see this now, that Berenski could see it. Berenski would shit himself laughing at this. *This is better than the SuperClassic, Comi!* Fortunato considered trying to wipe off all his prints, but it already was. Fortunato was of spirit now, already departing. He was beyond the laws of the Republic. Now there was only Fortunato's law. He took the spare clip from his holster and slid it home, then chambered a round. He began to walk towards his car.

The thought came to him gently, with a certain irony rather than alarm: someone somewhere might have called the police. Illicit lovers lifting heads from rumpled pillows, a bored prostitute wandering down for the excitement. *They're shooting outside!* Sub-Comisario Pignoli would be the commander on duty. Nicolosi would probably respond first to this sector. Poor Nicolosi: the honest working stiff who'd put in fifteen years of service and never gotten beyond patrolman. For some reason, he'd be ashamed to have Nicolosi see him here. At least Nicolosi, as an honest man, would understand his reasons. *I had to do it, Amadeo. It was the only justice that remained.*

As he started towards his car the pain began to insist a bit more. It was in his stomach, but better not to look at it. A gooey friction constrained the fingers of his left hand and his clothes were painted with blood. As he neared the car he felt a faint trickle at his thighs. With it, the distant sound of a siren. A first-class crime scene, *muchachos*. Five calibers of bullets and four suspects who would never talk. One a cop. The others security operatives for Carlo Pelegrini. What a sumptuous *expediente* this one will inspire!

He got into the car and began driving from the area. He'd begun to sweat, but he felt elated and confident. He was dead now, anyway. What did it matter, the little ache in his stomach or the blood all over him? Thus the dead should look. *You see, Waterbury; at least I've evened your score a bit. More than evened it.* Only a spirit now, far above the considerations of caution or morality. That was all behind him. He was an angel. The one in the tango who plays it all to recover an insult or an act of infidelity. Maybe this had been his destiny, all those years. All those decades he had been carefully measuring and accumulating, never imagining that in the end all he'd done would be reversed in a few hours.

There remained only Leon. The Chief. His friend and mentor all these years, always ahead of him in rank, directing him in his career and at last, directing its end. Fortunato knew he should feel some anger, but it didn't come. Perhaps because he was already dead, and the dead don't feel anger. There were simply things to do and ways to do them, and the rest remained for people still in life, who had egos and hopes to protect.

At his home? Perhaps. Ringing the bell. *What say, tanguero!* Raising the gun and blowing him backwards. But no. The wife might answer. Moreover, the Chief always went out on weekends. He loved to play the *transnochero*, taking coffee and whiskey at four in the morning, singing tango at Los Angeles de Piedra . . .

Fortunato imagined the Chief in his ivory suit within the fluorescent interior of the old worn *milonga*. Osvaldo with his gold tooth and all of the regulars filtering in from the barrio. Of course. It had to be thus, as if obeying some law of symmetry not apparent before. Fortunato's law.

Fortunato turned the car towards the center. It would take him forty minutes to reach La Boca. At two-thirty in the morning the Chief would already have sung four or five songs, would have critiqued poor Gustavo, the ancient sailor, for his lack of tone.

His cellular rang. The voice was trying hard to suppress its excitement.

'Comisario Fortunato, forgive that I disturb you! It's Nicolosi! There's been a quadruple murder here in San Justo! Can you come!'

'Where is it?' the Comisario asked calmly.

'Behind the *kilombo* on Benito Perez. At a factory.'

'Can't Sub-Comisario Pignoli take it?'

'It's a massacre, Comisario! Better that you come!' A brief pause. 'One of the dead is Domingo Fausto!'

'Inspector Fausto? They killed Inspector Fausto?'

'Sí, Comisario!'

'Are there witnesses?'

'No, Comisario.'

Fortunato smiled. '*Está bien*, Nicolosi. Remain *tranquilo*. In this case, at least, justice is at hand. I'm on my way.'

290

He turned off the cell phone and continued towards the Autopista 25 de Mayo. He turned on the radio and found the all-tango station that they played at La Gloria. Goyeneche was singing 'Makeup', Piazzola's classic about an illusory world. *Lies, they're lies: your virtue, your love, your kindness* . . . Sing, Polack, sing! He turned it up. The booming dissonance of the accordion, the sour strings tearing at the heart. Fortunato felt a glorious sense of belonging. After a lifetime of lies he had finally grasped a bigger truth and was bearing down on its brilliant focal point.

The common sights of the city had never looked more beautiful. Goodbye, little mechanic shop, goodbye, seller of flowers. There was darkness and a pink sky, and the tired glorious buildings. All his life he'd spent in this suburb, this provincial town of church and fields now swallowed up by the endless sprawl of the city. The ditches where he hunted frogs, all gone. The gardens and ragged little football fields with goals made of tin cans. The humming factories, now silent. As a boy everything had seemed so permanent, and one had to live a whole life to realize how transient were the things one most deeply loved. His mother and father, his Marcela. Even the cool luscious air of this autumn night streaming through the windows to caress his cheeks. What a farcical life, hoarding little green papers and the respect of empty men! All those years with Marcela wasted. If only she could see him now. Her low playful voice – 'You're acting well, Miguel. At last you're arranging things as they should be.'

He crossed Avenida General Paz and entered Buenos Aires proper and continued down Teniente General Dellepiane towards the autopista. The buildings became larger and more ornate with stonework as he passed through the barrios of Flores and Caballito. The city shook off its provincial stupor and began to snap. The store windows were wider, the clothes more elegant. The long-gone boom of Buenos Aires began to assert itself again in columns and curlicues. The whole city was out for the evening, ablaze at two in the morning as if at two in the afternoon. People were dancing and people were trying out love poems and people were getting knifed and snorting *merca* and launching long slow pirouettes beneath the covers. Every sidewalk and every café window was illuminated now by the burning destinies of the lives that skittered along the thoroughfare and by the vivid afterglow of the legions who had walked those streets before.

Thus, Buenos Aires! Thus the furious dream! As if obeying Fortunato's law, Carlos Gardel took over the radio in his scratchy 1920s voice and began singing the operatic lament that began his most famous song. *My beloved Buenos Aires, when I see you again . . .* Fortunato intoned along with Gardel's longing and hope: *There will be no more sorrow or forgetting.*

The autopista flew away beneath him, skating majestically above the buildings and into the heart of the city. Through Constitución and San Telmo, down to La Boca, a world of smaller buildings and narrower streets. The Mouth of Buenos Aires, eagerly devouring the goods of the world, articulating Argentina's language of beef and cereals on a multitude of rusty freighters. These beaten buildings that formed its teeth, ragged and decayed. Foreign sailors and the poor dressed up for evenings out. He left his car in an alley beside the bar, was delayed when he suddenly had to bend over and vomit. The pain was getting worse now. When he looked up he could see that the angel above his head was laughing.

The Comisario walked ten paces and stopped for a moment at the window. The Chief was in the midst of a song, a white canary before the three slouching musicians of the band. Out the open door came the sound of the bandoneon. He was singing 'Tabaco', the one about the man who sits awake at midnight, seeing the figure of the woman he wronged in his cigarette smoke. An elegy to regret and the corrosive effect of guilt. Ambitious, the Chief. Even the best struggled with that one. An ironic choice for a man who never felt regret.

Fortunato stepped in the door with the nine millimeter hidden under a newspaper he'd found in the alley. He was coming in from behind the Chief, but those on the other side of the room could see him and he could tell that the carnage of his jacket was upsetting them. He wished he'd worn the navy blue today. He was feeling a bit light-headed, so he leaned up against the wall. Norberto was looking at him in horror and came rushing over.

'It's only paint, Norberto. Don't worry yourself.'

Now every eye in the room was on him and the Chief noticed that he had lost the crowd's attention. He glanced over and stopped singing with a startled pop of the eyes. The musicians dragged on a few more bars and came to a ragged dénouement, turning, like everyone else, to the Comisario.

Fortunato raised his hand. 'Continue! Continue, Leon. I didn't want to steal your audience!' He moved over to a table in front of the band, only two meters away from the Comisario General of the Buenos Aires Provincial Police. He half-sat, half-collapsed onto its edge.

'You're badly off, Miguel,' the Chief said. Perhaps to the others in the room he sounded concerned, but Fortunato could read the fear in his voice.

He waved his hand. 'It's only makeup. Like the song.' He intoned a few lines. *Mentiras! Son mentiras tu virtud* . . . The effort was too much for him and he stopped. He saw the Chief glance worriedly at the sheet of newspaper that covered his right hand.

'What happened?' he asked. 'You're covered with blood!'

'Do you mean why have your men failed to kill me? Is that what you want to know? I'll tell you. It went well at first. They knocked me out, they put me in the factory. They even tied the noose around my neck. But amigo,' he shook his head in mock condolence, 'it all went badly from there. Depending on your point of view.'

Osvaldo the pimp had good intuition and Fortunato saw him reach down for his gun. '*Tranquilo*, Osvaldo. This has nothing to do with you. Enjoy the show.' Glancing towards the owner. 'And Norberto, please do not call the police. There's no drama here. Besides, it's sure they're going to find some violation of your license and separate you from a few *mangos*. Is it not thus, Osvaldo?'

'Thus it is, Capitan!' The pimp answered with the enthusiasm of one with front row seats to a long-awaited heavyweight bout.

'No, amigos. My complaint is with this *tanguero*, who tried to have me killed tonight.' A deathly quiet came over the 17 Stone Angels. The Chief stood by the band in his ivory suit like the master of ceremonies.

'They're all dead now,' Fortunato went on. 'Domingo, Santamarina, the other two –'

The Chief interrupted him loudly. 'You're badly off, Miguel! I don't know what you're talking about!' Looking towards Norberto and raising his voice, 'Someone call an ambulance!'

'No!' Fortunato shouted, clearing the gun from the newspapers and pointing it at the Chief's white breast. 'I came here to make you confess!' The musicians put their instruments down and evaporated away to the sides.

'To what, amigo? You're confused by your injuries.'

'Don't play with me, Leon. I've already killed five tonight. You can be the sixth.'

'You've killed five?' He turned to the room. 'Did you hear that? He'll kill us. Osvaldo –!'

'You ordered me to pick up Waterbury so you could have him killed!'

'It's fantasy, Miguel!'

Fortunato pulled the trigger and a blast of smoke and flame shot through the café. The bullet missed Bianco and burrowed into the wall.

'It was only a squeeze!' Bianco shouted. 'I didn't order his death!'

'But you ordered mine! You sent them to kill me! And not even to die like a man! You wanted them to hang me like a suicide. Like some poor bastard who didn't have the strength to keep struggling.'

'*Hermano*, it's me, Leon!'

Again a blast filled the room with billows of gunsmoke that hung in the fluorescent light. Fortunato struggled to rise from the table and walked forward to within a few paces of Bianco. The denizens of the 17 Stone Angels watched without a word. Osvaldo had drawn his pistol but he held it calmly on the table, surveying the drama before him with glittering eyes. Fortunato exchanged a brief look with him, then turned back to the Chief. The Chief's face looked chalky beneath the cold lights and their reflection off the sky-blue walls.

'Tell them about the baby you tortured in 1976, Leon, to make the mother talk. About the people you kidnapped and murdered so you could sell their furniture! How you conspired to kill Ricardo Berenski because he was approaching the truth. Of how you corrupted all who came under you. Including me.'

'You're not seeing clearly, Miguel! You're confused!'

'*Al contrario, Jefe*. At last I'm seeing *cristal*.' Fortunato felt an infinite silence come over the world, the timeless space in which all events flickered and roared. 'I'm purging the Institution.' He pulled the trigger and the nine millimeter jumped in his fist. The bullet and its shroud of gasses sped from the muzzle and the lead punched the Chief in his clean white breast and knocked him over a music stand and a guitar. As he tumbled he flung one hand out to the side and one over his heart, as if rendering the finale of a tango. One of the women let out a little shriek, but the place was eerily silent as the Chief made a few gasping sounds and then rolled partially onto his side.

All were looking at the Comisario, who pushed the gun painfully into his waistband and backed towards the door. His head went fuzzy again and he had to steady himself against the wall for a moment until his senses returned. To Norberto he said calmly: '*Perdón*, amigo, that I leave you with this mess.' He reached into his jacket and took out a bundle of ten thousand dollars, threw it towards him. The throw was weak and ended up on the floor. 'Buy champagne for everyone. And use the rest to pay the necessary bribes when the police come.' A sickened little shrug, the ghost of one of his rare smiles. 'And that you can't remember my name for a while when they do.'

As he backed out the door he heard a single pair of applauding hands and Osvaldo's unmistakable voice. 'Bravo! Bravo! *That* is tango!'

When he reached the alley he looked back to see Osvaldo and the *puntero* hurrying into the night with the fresh news. The place would be empty long before the cops came. He was legend now, a story more powerful than a man. Maybe they would write a tango about this someday. The tango about the old policeman who exacted his revenge for a lifetime of corruption, who turned Good at the end and purified himself with blood.

So he was only a song now. Nothing left for this life, only to go home before the police arrived and die quietly. They would get their suicide. He was beginning to have bouts of light-headedness. His soaked pants cuffs were flapping at his heels. He groaned into the car and vomited again before beginning the long drive back to Villa Luzuriaga. He had gotten the Chief and the others, but where were Pablo Moya and Pelegrini? Where was William Renssaelaer? They were everywhere around him, in every building and in the pavement that glittered beneath his headlights. Where are you, William Renssaelaer? Where are you?

The pain was growing more intense and crowding out other thoughts. At Liniers he had to pull over and woke up after a few minutes feeling hazy and spent. It took some effort to dial Cacho's number, but he managed it through the blur and held the receiver to his ear as he got the car underway again. 'Cacho!'

Cacho began swearing at him and the Comisario cut him off. 'Leave it, leave it! There's no time. I'm calling you on a clean line. I wanted to tell you that I avenged Waterbury and Berenski.'

That quieted the criminal. 'What?'

'It was Bianco who had Berenski cut. Bianco, working for Carlo Pelegrini. So that you know: he was singing at a tango bar and I sent him a cork in the middle of "Tabaco".'

A moment of wonderment, and then Cacho's voice without any patina of toughness. 'Truly? You killed him?'

'Truly.'

'And Domingo?'

A weird labored chuckle. 'I killed Domingo and three others when they were trying to hang me.' He grinned vaguely. '*Estilo* Hollywood: in a rain of lead.'

A short silence as Cacho seemed to grapple with the idea. He sidestepped the matter. 'You sound half-dead, Miguel.'

'They got me in the stomach. I'm going home to die.'

He hadn't expected any remonstrance to go to the hospital and none came. Cacho understood what he was telling him. The line stayed quiet as the buildings slid past outside his windshield, but he knew Cacho hadn't left him.

'You did well, Miguel,' Cacho said at last. 'You did well.'

Cacho's approval affected the Comisario and he felt an unaccustomed bond with the former revolutionary. '*Mirá*, Cacho. We're not friends. But maybe we're *compañeros*, in some sense. For this I wanted you to know what I discovered and what you've forgotten. We pass our lives among garbage. Illusions impose themselves at every turn. But it's a world of spirit, *hermano*. It's a world of spirit.' He clicked off the phone to relieve Cacho of any necessity of answering.

He fumbled through the buttons again. A few seconds later Athena's groggy voice came to him.

'It's I, Fortunato.'

'Miguel! It's three in the morning!'

'You must come to my house now. I need you.'

'You sound strange.'

'I'm dying, *chica*. The end has arrived. At least I arranged everything as it should be.'

A wary silence, then her uncertain voice. 'You sound terrible, Miguel. What's wrong? Do you need a doctor?'

'No, daughter. It already is. Please come to my house right now. I need you very much and there is no other person to call. Please. I have much to tell you about the Waterbury case. I can tell you everything now.'

'Can't this wait until tomorrow?'

'No. There is no tomorrow. Will you come?'

There was a short silence on the line. 'I'll be there as soon as I can.'

An eternity for him now. As he pulled down the familiar streets near his house he thought he saw a herd of cows chewing grass in the intersection, the old candy store on the corner, where it hadn't been in thirty years. There might be someone still watching his place, whoever it was. He knew a way to enter from the far side of the block, passing through a neighboring courtyard to his own house, and he parked his car out of sight and stumbled the last block to his patio door. As an afterthought he dragged along the briefcase with four hundred thousand dollars in it.

He lay down on his bed in the dark to die unmolested. The pain was ringing in his stomach like an infernal bell, resounding through his body in molten pulsating waves. In the half light that came in the windows he could see the outlines of the room, and though a part of him recognized it as his own it all seemed incredibly distant. Thus was life: it disappeared behind you. You turn around, and there's nothing.

The floor was rocking and he tried to put one leg down to steady it – the old drinking trick. It seemed to work for a moment and the events of the night came back to him in a skiffle of violent images. He'd settled what accounts he could. Beyond his reach though, there were still the Joseph Carvers and Pablo Moyas, for whom the violent passions played out that night represented only a bit of turbulence on the way to new markets and new profits, and whose exploits in Argentina would be lauded in the financial pages by which their deeds were measured. The criminal geniuses of the age, always clean.

He was the last piece of evidence, and when he died it would all be irrelevant. Pelegrini would fall. William Renssaelaer would go to work for AmiBank, RapidMail would take over the Post Office, and make guaranteed profits from the People. The plunder would click forward as it had for the last thirty years: a continuous ring of business, politics and police always devising new forms of stealing and decorating it in new forms of propriety. Moving the ball up and down the field at the behest of the crooked referee, who always ruled for The Mouth and always against The People.

*

A knock at the door, someone calling his name. He struggled to the window and dropped a key between the bars, then collapsed backwards onto the bed again.

'Miguel!'

'Here, Marcela.'

In a moment a vague flicker filled the doorway of his bedroom and came closer until she hovered beside his bed. His bedside lamp popped on.

'Miguel! What's happened to you?'

'Marcela! They got me.'

'I'll call the hospital! Hold on!'

'No, old woman. It already *is*. Get the money. In the wardrobe. It was there all the time. I'm sorry.'

Marcela didn't move, was doing something with the telephone. 'The money! Get it now!' he said with as much force as he could muster. 'In the wardrobe.' The old woman was still fiddling with the telephone, flipping through the telephone guide. 'Get it! Get it! We'll go to that clinic in the United States for your treatment.'

She bent down into the wardrobe. 'There's nothing, Miguel!'

'Now is not the time to change your clothes! The other side! It's there! Get it out!'

She kept fumbling around. 'There's no money here!'

He forced out a hoarse whisper. 'Get it out! It's all dirty! Everything!'

She bent her face down and she was crying, and he saw that it was not Marcela. It was Athena, with her blonde hair, wiping something from his mouth with the side of the bedspread. Marcela had drifted off to the doorway, watching them. 'Athena. In my briefcase. There!' He tried to indicate the case but the effort was too much for him.

'What happened, Miguel? Who did this?'

It was Athena, and she was asking about the night. 'Don't worry yourself, daughter. We won this round. I killed them all tonight: Leon, Domingo, Santamarina, Vasquez.' He grimaced in an attempt at irony. 'Even myself. But . . . I couldn't find Renssaelaer. I couldn't finish it.'

Another wave of pain came over him and the room faded out before it. When he could see and hear again Athena was back above him. 'Forgive me, Athena. I killed Waterbury. *I* killed him.'

'Miguel –!'

'It was a mistake. I thought it was just to frighten him, but

Domingo and Vasquez . . . They . . .' He felt a blockage in his throat and then his breath getting shorter and shorter, as if his lungs were shrinking. 'They shot him with the .32. I killed him to end his misery. But the guilt is mine. I'm guilty of everything.'

'No, Miguel!'

'Ask my forgiveness from the family. And give the money to his daughter.'

Tears were falling from Athena's eyes onto his face. He was losing the ability to speak, but he had already said everything. Athena touched a cloth to his face, asking him something that it was too late to answer. Marcela had come back into the room, was standing at the foot of his bed with a secret humor. With great effort he caught his breath and managed to give what he imagined was a smile. '*India!*' he muttered at last. 'You look good in that dress.'

He said nothing else, rattled through the last contortions of the dying and then went empty. Athena reached down and closed his eyes, then sat for a moment in the silence of the room.

So it had been Miguel. She understood now the frantic struggle revealed in the *expediente* in the light of the Comisario's final confession, sensed that in his last hours he had pieced together some personal salvation through his own private apocalypse. It should have disgusted her, but somehow the evil of Miguel was pushed aside by the sight of his drooping mustache and the terminal exhaustion of his face. A little boy had turned into an old man while the world flickered past him, changing horses to motorcars, *tangueros* to rock stars, giving loved ones and then withering them before his eyes. So strange, this life. People dreamed themselves and then went tumbling after their vision, maybe never understanding what the vision really was until they no longer had the strength to escape it. She barely knew Miguel Fortunato. Why was she weeping now?

The world collapsed briefly into a tiny pool of her own sorrow, then began to expand again to new and different dimensions. Fortunato had chosen to step up rather than lie low, and by doing so had exposed the outlines of the entire crime, from the sordid murder of one inconvenient witness to the vast gray movements of RapidMail, Grupo AmiBank and Carlo Pelegrini. Now the case would have to be laboriously excavated from the ruins of the night. Facts would be obscured and documents destroyed, but there was still Judge Hocht, and the journalists, and some ragged hope for a better society that no government or tyrant could ever completely extinguish. Maybe that was one of the few noble things about the human race, about Miguel Fortunato. Now he had left everything up to her.

She heard the slight tick of sheet metal at the door and then a soft footfall in the next room. Her breath caught, and she listened as the stealthy creeping came closer. 'Who is that?'

Fabian appeared in the doorway of the bedroom. He'd exchanged his tweed jacket for a black windbreaker and he had his pistol in his hand. 'Athena. So many unexpected meetings tonight!'

He was smiling, but it didn't run very deep. The face she'd always considered so handsome now gave off a sense of cold cunning. 'You know that your friend Fortunato shot Comisario Bianco an hour ago in front of a full audience at the 17 Stone Angels.'

'No!'

'Sí, Doctora. In cold blood. Not to mention a quadruple homicide some fifteen blocks from here. Among the deceased our own Inspector Domingo Fausto! Very disagreeable: each victim was finished with a shot to the head. My guess is that the ballistics will show that at least one of them was finalized with a nine millimeter bullet from the Comisario's gun. He is also under suspicion in the murder of Robert Waterbury.' Fabian sighed, a parody of his old self. 'It's logical, I suppose. The thriller must always end with a bloodbath, where the bad ones take the bullet and the good one dies with the beautiful woman shedding tears above his bleeding body, or goes limping off into the rainy night as the colored lights of the police car –'

'Shut up, Fabian. He already told me that he killed Waterbury. He said it was all arranged beforehand between Domingo and someone else. They tricked him. He thought it was going to be for intimidation, and then the other two shot him. He finished him out of mercy.'

'And you believe him? Who would want to kill a harmless *boludo* like Waterbury?'

She remembered who Fabian worked for, and put on an idiot face. 'We never got that far.'

The answer seemed to please Fabian. 'To die without knowing the truth. That, yes, seems to me quite sad. He lived in illusion and he died in another set of illusions. That is all we can put on poor

Comisario Fortunato's tomb. He was the man who made ten thousand arrangements, and in the end he was played by an inspector and a *merquero* of the lower depths.'

Fabian moved further into the room, his gun still in hand, and noticed the scattered pile of green bundles spilling out of the briefcase. 'What do we have here? The Comiso's savings?' He bent over and pawed quickly through it, leafing through the interior of the bundles to check their denominations. 'It looks like he still has the first peso he ever stole!' He quickly sifted the bundles. 'It must be close to four hundred thousand dollars. What a pretty pension.' He gave a sigh and clicked his tongue, still kneeling by the money. 'What a shame, Doctora, that you have to see this. It gives a very poor picture of the Institución. But there it is, all that black silver. Soon the police will get here, and surely the money will go into the first pocket on the scene, or else disappear into police funds.' He looked up at her, no longer smiling. 'If I wasn't so honest I would say half for you, half for me, and we leave here immediately and let the Federales take care of this mess.'

'Sorry. That's not my way.'

'No, you're too *idealista* for something so realistic. So it must be . . .' He lifted his gun towards her, the irony stripped from his voice. 'All of it for me, and none for you.'

She refused to take him seriously. 'You're an idiot, Fabian. They'd catch you in an hour.'

'Oh?' He reached down quickly and took the Comisario's gun from inside his jacket. 'In my version of the story, the Comisario did it.' He glanced at the window, seemed to be nerving himself up as he tried out his story. 'You come upon the Comiso collecting his money to make an escape. You threaten him, and he shoots you with this gun to protect his escape.' He quickly checked the chamber to see if it was loaded. Now his voice sounded uncharacteristically tense, and he threw his hand spasmodically to the side. 'It's not so bad, that story.'

A squeal of tires nearby interrupted the moment. Fabian glanced at the money and at the window. 'The reinforcements!' It seemed to confuse him for a moment. 'I frightened you, no?' He hurriedly put Fortunato's gun back in its holster. Outside, doors slammed and a voice shouted, 'Police! Drop it, *hijo de puta*!'

Fabian lowered his own gun down to his side, shrugged, and looked out the window. 'Ah, our colleagues, the Federales. It was a joke, eh? I wanted to give you a taste of the real police life. Just for fun.' He gave her an alligator smile and returned to the window. 'I'm Police! Inspector Fabian Diaz,' he yelled, his gun pointing loosely at the ground. 'Don't shoot!'

There was a silence, then she heard a thunder and the whine of bullets bouncing through the room. Bits of chipped plaster sprinkled in her hair as she threw herself to the floor, and she saw Fabian flung backwards into a pirouette, hitting his face on the bedpost as he collapsed. He tried to reincorporate himself for a moment, pushing his torso up, then a burst of fire from right outside the window cut the last strings. Everything was quiet for a moment.

Athena wasn't sure what to do. They had executed Fabian as efficiently as any firing squad, and she didn't know if she might be the next. 'It's me!' she shouted. 'Doctora Fowler of the United States! Don't shoot!' She heard footsteps running up to the door, then suddenly three men in plainclothes stood around her in a semicircle, all of them pointing at her with shotguns or pistols. She could see the officers look at each other, as if wondering whether to pull the trigger once more, then their commander came into the room, a man of about forty-five dressed in a leather jacket.

'What are you doing here?' the Federal Comisario shouted at her.

'Señor Fortunato called and asked me to come.'

The Federal stared down at her aggressively, a man accustomed to having his questions answered. 'What about him?' he asked sharply, indicating Fabian's body. 'Did he say anything?'

'Him?' Athena came slowly to her feet and leveled her cool green eyes on those of her interrogator. 'He was talking about the Boca-River game.'

It seemed to confuse the Federal: he looked for guidance to a man that lurked in the doorway. The man had thinning hair combed over a bald spot and a navy blazer. He examined her coldly, like a carpet cleaner examining a troublesome stain. There was a long, nerve-wracking pause.

Suddenly a voice came from the next room. 'I'm Nicolosi, of the *Bonaerense*,' it announced, and an officer wearing the uniform of the Buenos Aires Provincial Police walked in. 'Inspector Nicolosi!' he said stiffly, pulling out his identification. 'Of the precinct of San Justo!' His mouth dropped open as he got sight of Fortunato's ruined body, then formed into an 'o' as he noticed Fabian. He shook his head to clear it, then looked at Athena with astonishment. 'Doctora Fowler,' he asked her gently. 'Do you need assistance?'

The Federal Comisario turned to Nicolosi and motioned towards Fabian. 'He's a bad cop, and we had reason to believe the girl was in danger. He raised his weapon at us.' To Athena, 'You saw him raise his weapon, didn't you?'

'It was difficult to see from my angle, Comisario.'

'Hernandez!' he barked at another policeman. 'She didn't see anything! Get her declaración right now!'

CHAPTER 32

The initial explanation by the Federales was the classic: a settling of accounts between a band of corrupt police had left four police and three civilians dead in what would soon become known as the Night of the 17 Stone Angels. A few days later, at a press conference with Doctora Athena Fowler, a very different story was told, one that began a new frenzy of journalistic activity around the Grupo AmiBank, Carlo Pelegrini and the previously unknown name of William Renssaelaer. Questions were raised as to why Fabian Diaz had been shot when his weapon was pointed harmlessly at the ground, and why William Renssaelaer, a foreign citizen, had accompanied a Federal task force to that final execution. Judge Faviola Hocht widened her investigation to the Grupo AmiBank and RapidMail. In the most bizarre and comic headline of the entire scandal, a top executive of the Grupo AmiBank appeared on the front page of *Pagina / 12* under the headline *Pablo Moya: Red Hot and Wet!*

Much was made of the *fantasma Francesa* referred to by Doctora Fowler, but without her testimony no intellectual author could be definitively linked to the murder of Robert Waterbury, and it appeared that the material authors had already submitted to an alternative and more exacting justice system. Athena Fowler stayed four more weeks in Buenos Aires, a guest in the home of Carmen Amado de los Santos. By the time she departed all plans to privatize the Argentine Post Office had collapsed under the eye of public scrutiny. Beyond that, without the presence of the mysterious Paulé or other hard evidence, neither Carlo Pelegrini nor William Renssaelaer could be officially accused of anything.

When Athena returned to the United States she had been away two months. In comparison her own country seemed half asleep, anaesthetized by consumer goods and narcotized by a steady stream of corporate news blended into a placenta of entertaining facts. No one had heard anything about the events in Argentina, and American newspapers displayed little interest in the complex foreign policies of RapidMail and AmiBank. A week later a small yellow slip arrived from her local post office: they were holding a piece of registered mail for a Doctor Athena Fowler.

She walked there with the slip in her pocket, cheered by the sight of the modest but orderly building, with its flag above the doorway and its plain black letters spelling out the branch and zip code. She'd grown up with this post office, remembered going there with her parents to pick up packages at Christmas. It was one of the institutions that worked reliably and without change, beyond politics or party lines. She stopped a few steps inside the entryway.

A large poster had been hung above the counter, with the Stars and Stripes pulling into their embrace two logos: RAPIDMAIL AND THE US POSTAL SERVICE: PARTNERS FOR THE 21ST CENTURY! Next to the counter stood a neat metal RapidMail box, with its logo expropriating the colors of the American flag.

'They just started rolling it out three weeks ago,' the clerk told her. 'RapidMail gets a drop-box in every post office in the country. They help us move the parcels so we can concentrate on the mail. They call that a strategic partnership.'

She looked at the cheerful, contented face. 'Strategic for whom?' she answered. 'They'll take the profits and leave the taxpayers with the crap, and ten years from now they'll replace you with someone who earns twenty percent less. Because by their calculation, you make too much money.'

The clerk went sour and looked at the yellow registered mail slip that she gave him. 'Brazil, eh?'

He disappeared and returned a minute later carrying a thick manila envelope with no return address. The bulk of it made her think of letter bombs, and she felt carefully around its edges with her fingers. As a consideration she opened it outside.

It was a different sort of letter bomb. The envelope was stuffed with photocopies of documents detailing financial transactions between Argentina and various off-shore banks. Carlo Pelegrini's name appeared all over them. On top was a letter from Paulé. Paulé – the Patron Saint of Desperation.

Estimada Doctor, she wrote in her flawed Spanish, *even here in Rio one can buy the Argentine papers*. There were things she had not told her on the Night of the 17 Stone Angels. That Robert had given her these documents two days before his death, and one more thing, maybe useful to her. Robert had not been alone on the day he had spotted William Renssaelaer and Pablo Moya together. She too had seen them, could identify William Renssaelaer from his pictures in the newspaper. She was ready to make her *declaración*.

Athena put the papers back in the envelope and clutched it tightly to her side as she began to walk. A sudden surge of emotion seemed to lift her off her feet and carry her through the streets. She was thinking of her night out with Fortunato, and his story of the sculptures that were supposed to have looked down from the Palacio de Justicia and instead had ended up surveying the errands of pimps and fading tango singers. *Thus is life*, Fortunato would have said. Even in a world where seventeen stone angels are stranded beyond reach, one more can always be found.